The
iCandidate

MIKAEL CARLSON

Warrington Publishing
New York

The iCandidate
Copyright © 2013 by Mikael Carlson

Warrington Publishing
P.O. Box 2349
New York, NY 10163

Printed in the United States of America
Second Edition (Revised)
ISBN: 978-0-9897673-0-9 (Paperback)
978-0-9897673-1-6 (E-book)

Cover design by Ranilo Cabo www.rcabo.co.nr.

Dedicated to all the great teachers of the world who work to inspire their students to become more than they are.

"The evolution of social media into a robust mechanism for social transformation is already visible. Despite many adamant critics who insist that tools like Facebook, Twitter, and YouTube are little more than faddish distractions useful only to exchange trivial information, these critics are being proven wrong time and again."
— Simon Mainwaring

"Our social tools are not an improvement to modern society, they are a challenge to it."
— Clay Shirky

PART I

THE BET

-ONE-

CHELSEA

I need to set the alarm to play music or something. I fumble for the phone on the nightstand and silence the shrieking before falling back into the plush comfort of my bed. It only takes a couple of minutes to change the shrill, wailing sound into something more soothing. Not that any of the preloaded tones can be construed that way. I should just buy something trendy online, but really, what's the point? Who has time for that? Well, most of my friends and nearly everyone I go to school with do. But how many of them are taking all honors classes and an Advanced Placement course? And they say high school is supposed to be fun.

I throw on my worn terry cloth robe and head to the bathroom. The house I live in with my father is small by comparison to the others in town, meaning we share the only bathroom. Considering I drag myself out of bed at six and he is up and around at least an hour earlier, sharing seldom poses a problem.

After a quick shower, I put my straight red hair up in a ponytail, dress, and look at myself in the full-length mirror glued to my bedroom door. And when I say glued to the door, I mean affixed with several big tubes of stuff Dad bought at the Home Depot. Nothing short of a jackhammer is going to remove it.

We moved into the house right before I started high school, just months after Mom died. Installing this mirror was the first thing he did after the moving truck pulled away. I think the purpose was to help me be as comfortable here as I could.

In Dad's mind, a teenage girl with a mirror is the equivalent of a redneck with a shotgun on the happiness scale. I'm sure he read that in some magazine, or one of those parenting books he picked up when the terrifying thought of raising a girl on his own hit him. Not as if he ever complained, or let on to his fears, but I know all the same. Frankly, from what little I have read, the books are full of crap. At least he cares enough to try, which is more than I can say for some of my friends' fathers.

Most girls my age consume themselves with their appearance, but my ritual comprises a quick check in the mirror to ensure my clothes match and my hair is at least presentable. It's not that I don't care about my appearance, just not to the point of obsession. Cassandra, my closest friend, never takes her nose out of magazines the like of *Cosmo* and *Glamour*. I prefer reading a book. She says I would be far prettier wearing makeup, dressing in trendy clothes, and spending more than five minutes on my hair. Cassie is almost certainly right, but I find the whole thought of a morning beauty routine exhausting.

Only a couple of seconds is required to traverse the hall to the kitchen, where I find my father reading the paper over a cup of coffee. Dad is nothing if not a man of strict routine. Every morning is the same thing: a shower, a small breakfast, a cup of joe, and a date with the local newspaper before starting his shift at the factory. Bill Clinton was playing the saxophone the last time he took a vacation, and I am sure Bruce Stanton taking a sick day would be a noteworthy event at the plant. After Mom, his whole existence revolves around providing a roof over my head, putting food on the table, and planning for college. God bless him. I guess maybe that is why I'm the way I am. Or so I imagine a therapist would say.

"Morning, Dad."

"Good Morning, Snuggle Bear."

Hearing that term of endearment is usually the highlight of my day. "Snuggle Bear" has been his nickname for me since before I could walk, and while most girls my age would hate the childish name coming from a parent, I find it endearing. I pour some coffee into a travel mug and move to the dining room table to cram the mountain of books and papers spread out from last night's studying into my book bag. Dad watches me over the top of his newspaper.

"Last night was a late one, huh?"

Oh, boy. I already know where this conversation is going given the matter-of-fact tone.

"Mister Bennit is throwing another of his epic quizzes, so I had to study," I respond, probably with a little too much edge to my voice. This talk is getting old, particularly on a Monday morning when I'm already in a dour mood.

"Ya know, you work too hard. I know you keep telling me that junior year is important to get into college and all that, but why don't you enjoy what little time you have left in high school?"

"I am enjoying it, Dad."

He gives me his patented look of disbelief. I have a better shot at convincing him the Red Sox signed a pact with Satan to win the World Series in 2004. Perhaps that's a bad example, because they did.

"Look, Snuggle Bear, I know what always working feels like, and I just want you to appreciate not having that responsibility while you can. Go out and do something you enjoy before you're forced to do the things you don't."

"Maybe I think forcing Mister Bennit to give me an A is enjoyment."

"You're not normal. Ya know that, right?"

I can't help but smile as I sling the overstuffed backpack on my shoulder and grab my to-go mug.

"Runs in the family, Dad," I conclude as I give him a kiss on the cheek and head for the kitchen door. "And don't say that's from Mom's side—you know that's a Stanton family trait."

Dad flashes that little smirk he has when he's amused and not amused at the same time. That's a surefire signal this chat will continue after school, following his extended shift at the factory. No, the untiring Bruce Stanton is not going to drop the subject until I relent and have "fun." I bet most teenagers are not having this conversation with their parents.

I tell my father to have a good day and be safe, and that I love him. Probably not the words most fathers hear from their teenage daughters. But hey, he said it—I'm not normal. The thought occupies me during the routine fifteen-minute drive to school, in lieu of trying to ignore the check engine light glowing ominously on my dash.

The roads are clogged with the typical morning traffic, and thus easy to mindlessly navigate. Staring out the window at a stoplight, I notice the buds growing on the trees in the center of town, indicating the promise of spring following a long Connecticut winter.

I pull into the driveway of the aptly named Millfield High School and navigate to my assigned parking space. I don't think about how my ten-year-old Toyota Camry is in the unenviable position of being parked next to a brand new BMW Z4 and like-new Range Rover on a daily basis. I don't even think about the friends I will get to see today or what idle gossip they will try to get me to engage in. I can only think about fact that my father thinks I'm not normal and the fact that I know he's right.

-TWO-
MICHAEL

You might think after three years of teaching I would find the routine a little tiring. Days come and go and the students come and go with them. Lesson plans may change slightly, but the curriculum stays pretty static thanks to the stifling bureaucracy created by the simple-minded state Department of Education. That group of half-wits thinks they actually know something about schooling. With their constant meddling, teaching can be a dull existence if you follow their stale approach.

While not as seasoned as many of my peers, I have seen enough to understand there are two types of teachers who burn out. The first are the mindless trolls who show up every day to collect a paycheck. Their students are subjected to countless videos so they don't have to face them from the front of the room and teach.

Students are told to read aloud from dull, watered-down textbooks in the futile hope simple oral pronouncement somehow allows the information to seep into the teenage mind faster. Generally, these teachers are tenured, and thus being secure in their jobs, forget that we exist to inspire and instruct young minds. They don't interact or try to improve themselves. Simply put, they don't care, and I see the indifference every day.

On the other side of the spectrum are the crusaders. Take Miss Peterton, by far the school's best math teacher. She wears math-themed clothing, and hosts a Pie Day to celebrate, well, pi. When I ask her how much she eats, she wryly responds, "3.14 pieces." I'm not a math guy, but it still cracks me up.

I don't envy science teachers at all, but Mister Blumb has teaching to an apathetic audience figured out. Precious few American students pursue the sciences these days, and he understands full well the absence of interest in what he teaches. He dedicated his life to the study of science, but doesn't expect understanding ionic and covalent bonds, valance numbers, and memorizing the periodic table of elements to be at the top of his students' list of interests. Yet through the use of practical experiments that often includes small, semi-controlled explosions and other strange results, he manages to keep class interesting. Who doesn't like explosions?

Literature can be mind-numbingly boring, but a sprinkling of English teachers likes to spice things up. I've heard one compare Greek heroic epics like the *Iliad* and the *Odyssey* to Luke Skywalker's struggles against the Darth Vader and the Empire in *Star Wars*. Others, like Miss Slater, work in stories with age-old dilemmas and relate them with more contemporary themes. Oh, Miss Slater. The thought of her contorts my mouth into a Cheshire cat smile.

All these teachers realize the fundamental truth of modern education that, in the age of Xbox, Facebook, and smartphones, you have to compete for the occupied minds of the American teenager. Today, good teachers are forty percent comedian, thirty percent circus performer, twenty percent educator, and ten percent parent. My colleagues may argue over the percentages, but I'm sure they'll agree with the sentiment.

The 7:35 bell rings and I rise from the desk in the corner of my extravagantly decorated classroom. One advantage to being a history teacher is the sheer amount of posters and artifacts available to wallpaper an otherwise bland room with. The decorating job took days, and while I doubt the students care, I did it more for me than them. With the eyes of legendary men like George Washington, Abraham Lincoln, and Martin Luther King Jr. looking down on me, I tend to give rousing lectures in an effort to gain an approval I know can never come.

The warning bell signals students to end their socializing and start heading to class. It also means the teachers in the school have to be outside their classrooms to supervise the chaos and encourage them to get moving. Generally, that's a waste of time, but you ignore this simple duty at your own peril. Our principal is known for his Draconian approach to both education and order. And by order, I mean for the teachers even more than the students.

The crowd of teenagers at the far end of the corridor parts and boys' heads turn farther than I thought was possible for a human to accomplish. They used to be somewhat subtle about these things, but when Jessica Slater is involved, subtlety is the first thing to go. To say she is a vision does not begin to do her justice.

She strides with grace and elegance down the hall, dressed smartly in a conservative, yet somehow still provocative red dress. The click of her high heels echoes off the walls, announcing every footfall as the boys speak in only hushed voices as they gawk. She walks up to me and I'm a bit short of breath myself just from watching her.

"A little light reading, honey?" I ask as she repositions the large stack of papers in the crook of her arm.

"Just need to get some of these essays graded before second period," she responds, flashing her beautiful smile. "It's the only advantage of having my planning time first thing in the morning."

"That's why I teach history and not English—far fewer essays to grade. Why didn't you just do them this weekend?" Of course, I can't help but think I know the reason.

"Oh, you mean with all the free time I had after planning a small wedding?" she asks sarcastically, emphasizing the word *small.*

"A small wedding I'm thrilled I'm not paying for." Given what her parents are going to be spending to marry off their eldest daughter, there's nothing but truth in my comment. All the same, I am still in awe it will be me standing at the altar waiting for her to come down the aisle during this *small* wedding. Yes, this vision in red, with blonde hair swooping past her shoulders in long and breezy curls, is my fiancée. I should probably pinch myself.

"Speaking of my parents, we need to be at their house by four tonight." She playfully grabs my shirt at the chest, the overhead fluorescent lighting bouncing off the glittering one-carat diamond engagement ring adorning her long, slender finger. Yeah, that rock was worth every dime. "And don't think you can slip off to the gym and still make it on time."

"Is this what I have to look forward to for the rest of my life?" God, I hope so.

"Well, at least until I decide to get rid of you," she says smiling, as she turns and starts to saunter down the hall toward her classroom.

"Any chance of that happening by four?" I call out to her before she wanders too far away to hear me over the din of the hallway.

"Nope!" she responds back over her shoulder, the pleasure in her voice evident.

"If you keep violating the dress code, Principal Howell may make getting rid of you by four a real possibility," I hear uttered from behind me. The sweet yet still commanding voice of Chalice Ramsey can never be mistaken. The head of the Social Studies department, she is my guardian angel in this building. Thank God for her. She runs more interference for me than an offensive lineman.

"Good morning, Chalice." I turn to face my immediate boss, who stands a full foot shorter than me at five feet two with her heels on. A teacher at Millfield High since the dawn of time, she is fiercely loyal to the good teachers in her department, having seen the damage lousy ones can do. Fortunately, she considers me the best, and that is no small thing in her eyes. I also realize loyalty only goes so far, as I learned the hard way during my time in the Army.

"Seriously, Michael. The sport jacket is a nice touch, but wearing jeans everyday is giving Howell fits. He's practically tattooed a target on your back, so why do you insist on pushing his buttons?"

I can't suppress the smirk creeping across my face despite the fact my biggest champion might consider such behavior insubordinate. "You know why, Chalice." She knows my long list of issues with Robinson Howell better than anyone. Although she is political and diplomatic with her own thoughts and words, there is no doubt in my mind that she agrees with every one of them.

The halls are nearly empty now as the final bell rings announcing the start of the day. The dull roar emanating from my classroom reminds me I was oblivious to them walking in. Chalice gives me a slight nod. "I fight for you, and I always will. But there will come a time when I can't protect you. Don't make it over something as stupid as this."

She walks past me, nothing further needing to be said between us. Jessica, as a seasoned veteran in the teaching trenches, gives me the same advice. Hell, numerous former commanding officers gave me the same warnings what feels like a lifetime ago. I have ignored them all my life, but I should change my ways, at least a little bit. I know I can, and probably need to before it catches up with me.

I smile. "Nah," I mumble to myself as I enter my classroom to start a brand-new day.

-THREE-
KYLIE

Eleven years. Eleven years of faithful service and now here I sit, in my pajamas at nine a.m., looking for anything worth watching on TV. I was double major in journalism and political science at Notre Dame, for crying out loud. I earned a master's degree from Columbia in Government Studies, interned at ABC News, and landed a first job as a political writer for MSNBC. Then I realized my dream by writing about politics for the "Old Gray Lady" herself, the *New York Times*. Now, after one conversation with my editor, I've gone from the top of the world to being crushed by it.

I can't stop the tears from pouring down my cheeks and falling on to the clothes I haven't bothered changing out of for the last three days. I spent the weekend on the same worn couch I am curled up on now. With no reason to dress or shower, the West Village apartment I can really no longer afford to call home is beginning to reek of body odor and the unfamiliar stench of failure.

My cell phone rings for what has to be the umpteenth million time since I was fired on Friday. I let the damn thing ring until it gives up getting my attention and forwards the caller to voice mail. Of course, they can't even leave a message. The mailbox filled up sometime Saturday afternoon.

I know everyone is concerned about me, but I just can't bring myself to answer their calls. Part of it is shame and another part is humiliation, I guess. Part is ... I don't know. Maybe the feeling I brought this on myself, which, I suppose, I did. But right now, I can't think straight, let alone talk straight. A hundred thoughts are vying for time in my head, while simultaneously fighting an avalanche of emotion. I'm stuck in the endless cycle of trying to reconcile what happened with what I thought would happen.

There is no point in trying to muffle the sobs in a pillow anymore. I just let it all out. I cry out of frustration with my editor, over being fired, and with the political elite that put me in this position to begin with.

I guess that's the crux of the issue. After a decade of covering the arrogance and egos in politics, I just couldn't deal with it anymore. There is too much corruption and cronyism among the people who claim to love America and do everything they can to destroy it. These veteran politicians look at their seats as a birthright and not an honor. Men and women who hold office only to satiate themselves, and their benefactors, at the expense of the citizens who put them there in the futile hope that their own interests will be represented. Liberal or conservative, Republican or Democrat; who holds the reins of power in America doesn't matter because the paradigm never seems to change.

I tried though. A pair of whistleblowers came to me and implicated several high-profile politicians in Congress in all sorts of underhanded dealings with the private sector and other special interest groups. That was the subject of the last investigative article I will ever work on as an employee of the *New York Times*. The consequences would've been worthwhile if it had gone to print and not fallen under the crushing axe of my jack-booted thug of an editor.

But, like most in the modern media, he has an agenda to push and listening to me constantly decrying the system he holds so dear didn't advance it. Bastard. In politics, reasonable people should be allowed to disagree. It is the nature of how our republic was set up by the Framers. Hell, they couldn't agree on much of anything back when they wrote the Constitution. They debated, swayed opinion, and ultimately compromised. And now?

The phone rings again, and the image of my mom flashes on the screen. She's the last person I need a lecture from. Sure, the conversation would start off with the usual, "Are you okay, Kylie?" and, "I am worried sick about you." Before long, she would devolve into a monologue about how I threw a promising career away. After all, she had to make sacrifices to be successful in her career as a journalist, so why couldn't I have just left my idealism behind in college and done the same?

I stop crying. I refuse to shed tears over not having the approval of my mother. She does not deserve that. In my mind, she has compromised every principle she claims to hold dear. Journalistic integrity, the accurate reporting of facts, and speaking truth to power were among the time-honored dogmas sacrificed at the altar of her career ambitions. In essence, she is a part of the very problem I espoused in the article that will never be printed. Worse still, she passed those traits on to my little sister. But I can't worry about my mother or sister now. I must focus on what I am going to do.

I know I will rebound, because with unpaid bills, rent, and such, there is no other choice. I will have to find work, someway, somehow. That can wait though. After a lifetime of getting up off the mat after a fall, I want to stay down right now. I want to feel sorry for myself after all the times I refused to do so. My world has been shattered, so I will take the time to mourn its loss before picking up the pieces. Hopefully, I will someday get inspired to be as passionate as I was on Friday morning before they fired me.

No stopping the tsunami of emotion welling up inside me this time. The phone rings again, and I ignore it as I go back to crying.

-FOUR-
BLAKE

These people need to get the hell out of my way. "Excuse me. Excuse me. Sorry. Excuse me." I hear myself saying the words as I struggle up the escalator at the Capitol South station on the Orange Line of the Washington, D.C. Metro. What I really mean is, "Move your fat asses out of my way." Under normal circumstances, I would say precisely that. However, being an aide of one of the country's most prominent politicians, I'm forced to exercise a little prudence. Although in the same situation, no doubt he wouldn't.

I have one major problem this Monday morning—I'm running way behind schedule. I check my watch more than the White Rabbit from *Alice in Wonderland* on the Metro ride into the heart of the city. I am supposed to be sitting at my desk by seven a.m. The congressman feels it is important to maintain the illusion we are up early working hard for the people of the Connecticut Sixth District. I feel it's more important to actually be working hard for them instead of worrying about keeping up appearances. Maybe that is what the congressman meant, or at least that's what I hope he did.

Even though spring has not exactly hit the Beltway yet, I notice the cherry blossoms are out in force. I even feel myself starting to perspire through my suit on this warm morning. These shoes are not made for running, but if there is any chance to make it to the Rayburn House Office Building in time to beat the boss, I have to hustle, sweat and sore feet be damned.

The rush of getting from the Metro to the office proves fruitless, as I end up waiting to be granted access to the building. The threat of terror attacks and rowdy constituents itching to settle a score with their elected leaders makes entry into any area guarded by Capitol Police an exercise in patience. Patience I do not own right now.

Having passed through security, I race up the stairs and down the hall to the office. I know I am screwed upon arrival. At twenty-five years old, I'm the most junior, and by extension, most expendable member of the congressman's staff. Sporting the laughable title of Staff Assistant, I get paid the least to perform the most work. On paper I am nothing more than a gofer for Roger Bean, the congressman's chief of staff and top political advisor. So you would think the other thirteen members of the staff wouldn't see me as much of a threat, but you'd be wrong.

They find me a threat to their own jobs because I'm driven, ambitious, and way smarter than them. Like Alex Trebek on *Jeopardy*—I know the questions and the answers. With the exception of the chief of staff, there isn't a job in this organization I couldn't do—and do a great deal better. I know everything that happens in both our district and D.C. offices. I see things and make the connections to how they can benefit us with far more frequency than the others on staff. Most importantly, my loyalty has garnered favor with Roger. He trusts me implicitly, and that, of course, makes everyone jealous.

So as I stroll into work over two hours late, no shortage of colleagues take notice. Not helping matters is the need to pass everybody to reach my desk, which is tucked in the corner of the congressman's outer office. Of our fourteen full-time staff members, eight work in the Rayburn Building. Seven of them glare at me as I walk over and scramble to power up my desktop computer.

"You picked a helluva day to be late, Blake." I look up to see the press secretary standing in front of me, dressed in a stylish jacket and skirt. Her long, teased blonde hair shimmers, even under the harsh fluorescent light of the office. Somehow, she manages to package smarts, confidence, and sex appeal in an athletic, 5'7" frame. Of course, I'm still way smarter, but just being kind since we are seeing each other "socially."

"Not like it was planned," I respond, suppressing the smile on my lips. "How bad's the situation?"

Madison hazards a glance over her shoulder before leaning in and whispering, "Deena has been sharpening her talons for an hour now. I hope you have a plan to keep her from sinking them into you."

"I'm working on one."

"Work fast. The congressman will be here any minute," Madison says as she turns to walk away.

"Hey," I say, slipping around my desk and moving my mouth close to her ear. I feel every pair of eyes in the office on us. "Did Marcus finish his two little projects?"

Madison stares at me, an incredulous look creeping across her beautiful face. "How did you ...? You know what, never mind," she dismisses. "I don't want to know. But I'm sure you'll find them in the blue file on Deena's desk." Madison winks and strolls back to her desk with the runway walk that throws the best of the D.C. press corps off their game.

I see Deena moving toward the door out of the corner of my eye. At almost the same instant, I hear the booming voice of the venerable Winston Beaumont III, eight-term Democratic member of the United States House of Representatives, coming down the hall. I recognize there is a window of opportunity, albeit a small one. I stride over to Deena's desk and eye the blue file folder resting on the top of a larger stack of paperwork.

I snatch it and move quickly past Deena who is consumed with straightening her suit jacket and preening herself in anticipation. She reminds me of a Prada-clad velociraptor. No amount of personal grooming could ever help her, but it did help me. I slip past her before she can notice and greet Congressman Beaumont when he enters the office.

"Good morning, Congressman," I say in the best bright, enthusiastic tone I can muster.

"Is it?" he grumbles, posed more like a statement than the rhetorical question it is. "You want something from me, Blake, because I want to at least take my coat off before being accosted by my staff."

"Of course, sir, but I do have something of interest for you—new polling data and news about your opposition in November." In the center of the room, the blood drains from Deena's already pasty, pale face as she turns back to her desk. Bewilderment searching for the now absent blue file morphs into rage as she realizes I just stole her thunder. And I did, in more ways than one, since she was the one who told me what Marcus was working on in the first place. Oops. "I was going to wait until Roger got here, but thought you might find this of immediate interest."

"Okay, let's get on with it. I have a vote on the floor in a few minutes." The congressman impatiently gestures me to follow him as he walks past a stunned Deena. She tries to recover.

"Congressman, I need to—"

"Not now, Deena," Congressman Beaumont snaps as he crosses into his inner office. I follow, only to get snagged by the arm. She has talons after all.

"You think you're slick, Mister Peoni, but that was a very bad move on your part."

"Hmm. It looks like checkmate to me. Now if you don't mind." I pry her spindly fingers off my arm and hurry to catch the congressman.

Entering the inner office feels a bit like walking into Versailles. It is finely decorated, with antiques and works of art hanging from the walls in ornate frames. The feel of wealth and status is palpable, because Winston Beaumont III has both in spades. The décor is symbolic of invincibility after over a decade in Congress.

Fast becoming an institution in Washington, D.C., he harbors no aspirations of early retirement. Even further from his mind is losing his seat. I am about to put to rest any lingering doubts the congressman might harbor concerning the latter while saving my own ass in the process.

"Sir, our latest internal poll has you at a seventy-nine percent approval among registered voters in the district."

"Down three percent?" The congressman actually made eye contact with me when he responded, forgoing his usual inattentiveness as he peruses the *Washington Post*. "Did three percent of the people in the district suddenly lose their common sense or something?"

"Could be attributed to the bad press about our little problem with the Lexington Financial Group."

"I thought we buried that story."

"We did, sir. The reporter at the *New York Times* was dismissed before she got the full story. Unfortunately, Fox News still picked up what little there was and ran with it."

The congressman makes a grunting noise, which is his sign of displeasure, so time to shift gears before it's too late. "It really isn't going to matter much come November."

"I didn't get elected by taking even a single vote for granted. We fight for every vote when you are a member of this staff. Whatever it takes," the congressman says to me. I can feel his eyes boring into my soul in an effort to see if I belong here. He wants to know if I can hack it and will do what is necessary when the time comes. Ultimately, can I do "whatever it takes" for him to win.

"Of course, sir. But you should know that the Republicans are running Richard Johnson against you." Congressman Beaumont puts the paper down on his desk. Yeah, this is how I will move up on this staff.

"The lawyer from Hillsfield?" he asks, using an incredulous tone.

I flash a sinister grin. "Yes, sir. He ran for first selectman there last year and lost in a landslide. Most of the town would have voted for Hitler over him."

"And that's the best the GOP could put up against me?" A single, hearty laugh tacked on at the end lets me know he is pleased with the news.

"Apparently you are so popular, Winston, that nobody would dare run against you," exclaims Roger Bean as he strides through the door of the inner office and stops alongside me. "But you need to gloat later, because you have to get to the floor for a vote."

Roger Bean is Winston Beaumont's chief of staff and most trusted advisor. He is in his early forties, impeccably dressed and well groomed, and right out of central casting for a political potentate. Many people, unwashed in the daily activities in Washington, easily confuse Roger for a politician himself. Despite his over seventeen-year tenure representing the Connecticut Sixth, some of Congressman Beaumont's own constituents do too.

Roger was not surprised I relayed the news about the polls or the opposition. Although he may be curious as to why, he recognized my ambition, intelligence, and political savvy when I first started work for Winston Beaumont. It is for that reason he has used me, on occasion, to handle some, well, unsavory assignments. The most recent will keep the congressman out of hot water and myself gainfully employed.

"Refresh my memory, Roger, what vote is this again?" Congressman Beaumont asks, still focused on winning the reelection in seven months in what is sure to be a monumental landslide. I believe in my heart his goal is for the press to call the race before the polls even close.

Roger checks a calendar on his iPad. "House Resolution One Thirty-Three. It's a bill to approve additional funding for Department of Veterans Affairs to screen and treat PTSD for soldiers who served in Iraq and Afghanistan."

"That's a no vote."

I wince. Admittedly, I am caught a little off guard. I normally wouldn't care, but my father fought in the first Persian Gulf War. In the waning hours of the fighting, his unit was deployed along the route that runs from Kuwait City to Safwan, Iraq. Highway 80 became a turkey shoot for the Air Force as the decimated Iraqi Army fled up the desolate road from American forces that liberated Kuwait.

He never spoke about what happened there. He wouldn't even tell the doctors much more than where his unit had been posted while they were treating him for the mysterious Gulf War Syndrome. But the road earned the moniker "The Highway of Death" for a reason, and not one that wears well on one's conscience. As a result, I know what PTSD can do to a person, because I grew up with it.

"May I ask why, sir?" The glare coming from the congressman could melt steel, and even my trusted benefactor

Roger gives me a warning glance. "I mean, with the percentage of vets in our district—" That would be the last word I get in for this conversation.

"Don't presume to know *my* district better than I do, Blake!" the congressman says in a voice that's part 1950s high school principal and part army drill sergeant. "Last I checked, I was the elected representative, so when I want *your* opinion on anything, I'll give it to you."

Congressman Beaumont rises from his chair, folds his paper, and moves to walk out of the office before stopping next to me. "The VA is an organization fraught with waste. I campaigned on making government more efficient, so I must keep up that façade. How would it look if I allowed yet another wasteful spending bill to run up our deficit?"

It's the biggest bunch of malarkey I've ever heard, considering Winston Beaumont's extensive voting record and extracurricular activities. But this is how politics works, and a lesson I need to learn if I want to rise up the ranks at the national level.

"Besides, it's a little payback for the bill's sponsor." The congressman moves his face close to my own, to the point where I can smell his acrid odor of coffee on his breath. "But you haven't earned the right to challenge my votes, Blake. Don't ever question me again."

He slaps the newspaper against my chest and leaves the room, Roger following after an "I told you so" look. I am left alone in his shrine to himself and can feel the eyes of the rest of his staff boring into me from the outer office. Yeah, he dressed me down, as I am sure they all heard. They will think

I have fallen out of favor with him, or that somehow my standing in the internal office pecking order is in peril.

I took something more profound from this conversation. I now know a seat at the table is reserved for me when I earn it. And, trust me when I say, earn it I will because nothing and nobody else in this world matters more to me.

-FIVE-
MICHAEL

I have some great kids this year, but my B Period honors American History class is my absolute favorite. In fact, it would be hard to argue against it being the best group of students I have ever had. Any teacher will tell you that there are always good groups of students and bad ones. Some classes are simply more fun to teach than others, and this is one of them.

The twenty-five students mill around the classroom until the bell rings and then promptly take their seats. I arranged the desks in a horseshoe facing the whiteboard hung in the front of the room. Since I am an ardent believer in teaching being part performance, this setup gives me a stage on which to work.

In fact, that area is even called the stage. Every year on the first day of school, while I am espousing my teaching philosophy to my new charges, I explain the etymology of the "stage." Yes, it's partly because that's where theater performances are conducted, but it has a dual military meaning. When I was in basic training, the area between the first set of bunks and the drill sergeants' office was also called "the stage." Perpetually waxed and buffed to a high-gloss shine, we lowly privates were forbidden to ever walk on those tiles. The stage was reserved for the men tasked with training us, and only them.

This being high school, and not military school, my rules are not quite so authoritarian. However, each class understands the purpose of the stage and all adopt the word. So the area in front of the whiteboard and into the space ringed by the horseshoe is my stage, and being on it is the greatest feeling in the world.

"Good Morning, all," I sound in my booming voice. "I trust everyone enjoyed their weekend, so we'll skip the pleasantries and get down to business." I walk to the center of the room as students shuffle items around their desks to get organized. The routine has been the same since day one, and they respond more favorably than you'd expect out of teenagers in their junior year.

"Essays on the Great Depression are due by fifteen hundred hours today. Homework is on the board. Please note that the reading portion is due tomorrow." Without looking back, I point to the spot on the whiteboard where the homework is posted.

I am not sure how we managed to get the Great Depression, let alone find the time to talk about the interwar period. Most of my colleagues are still struggling to get through Civil War reconstruction. As a history teacher, if you reach WWI it's been a good year. I should be able to cover the Korean War at this pace.

"The final exam is eight weeks from today, and it's cumulative. If you are not reviewing your notes and preparing now, I promise you, you will fail. What are your questions?" I look around and see there are none. "Excellent. Clear your desks. It's showtime."

I hand out the quizzes and everyone gets to work. I usually provide ten to twenty minutes to finish and, believe me, that's not a lot of time even for the easier ones. The questions are straightforward multiple choice, true or false, and a fill in the blank section my students would characterize as sadistic. More than fodder to fill a grade book with, I use quizzes as a tool to measure both learning and my effectiveness teaching. If the kids all bomb a quiz, I did something wrong and need to reinforce learning before the exam. At least, I choose to think that way.

Students take it in stride—they are not in this class because of any rumor about me being an easy teacher. My colleagues think that I am too hard on them—challenging students to rise to a high standard seems to be a foreign concept in America's public schools. Strange, since my real world experience was much different. I had standards set for me with the expectation to meet them from the day I enlisted and went to basic training.

Those standards had been enforced by ruthless sergeants every day since, from my time at Airborne School at Fort Benning, to Special Forces Selection, the Qualification Course, Language School, and even on the ground in Iraq and Afghanistan. I was charged with carrying on that tradition when I became a sergeant myself. Now a thirty-six-year-old civilian, my dedication to that principle gets exercised in a classroom instead of a battlefield. I believe reachable yet demanding standards are a good thing, despite not all teachers thinking so.

A fellow social studies teacher handed a copy of my quiz on the American Revolution to the principal because he was so upset. Since there is no love-loss between myself and Principal Howell, he smugly pronounced the short test too advanced for the high school level. He even added his own doubts about being able to pass the quiz. I didn't have the heart to tell him the average grade was an eighty-seven and not a single student failed. Okay, I actually had more than enough heart to tell him, with plenty left over to remind him a half dozen times since.

I roll my desk chair over to the middle of the stage, coffee and attendance book in hand, as students begin poring over their quizzes. Fifteen minutes later, it's apparent by the smiles on their faces that they aced this one. As I collect them, a Barbie doll-looking blonde with bright red fingernails and trendy clothes raises her hand.

"Yes, Miss Rasner?

"What'd ya do this weekend, Mister B?" Apparently Peyton thinks my social life is pretty active, because she asks the same question every Monday. It's challenging to come up with new answers.

"The same thing I do every weekend, Peyton, try to take over the world." Since the students actually chuckle, my confidence on their quiz performance is confirmed.

"How'd that work for you?" queries Amanda, a girl born to be an accountant. I am pretty sure she could do my taxes in ten minutes and get me a better refund than any tax service can manage. Ten years from now, she will enchant guys in bars, only to send them fleeing for their lives when they find out she's an auditor for the IRS or something.

"Well, I am not sitting on a throne, not carrying a scepter, and most importantly, I'm still here, right?"

"So, not so good?" Peyton asks, persistent in trying to pry some details out of me.

"Don't fret, Peyton, there are plenty of weekends left for me to try." Everyone smiles, but I am sure they are thinking they would rue the day I was ever dictator of anything. Running this class is bad enough for them. "Where did we leave off on Friday?" I add, changing the subject.

"We were talking about the European powers failing to restrain Hitler's ambitions in Europe," Chelsea is quick to explain. Many teachers will pretend they don't have favorite students. They fear the admission can be perceived as granting special treatment, even if it's not the case. I harbor no such sensitivity. I am honest with myself about having favorites, and Chelsea Stanton is one of them.

"And what did you learn?"

"That some things never change." Not hard to figure out why I like her. She's sharp.

The students nod their heads in agreement. I scan their faces for a moment, looking for my next target. I settle on Xavier, the only African-American student in the class. Millfield High is not a bastion of diversity. Tall and athletic,

Xavier likes to play the role of uncaring teenager. Truth is, this kid will not only go to college on a scholarship in any one of three sports, he'll undoubtedly be an academic All-American.

"What does she mean, Xavier?"

"Talk is cheap. And all anyone ever seems to do is run their mouths," he says.

"Then or now, X?" Yeah, I call him X. With the only possible exception being Q, it is the coolest letter to start your name with.

"Both!"

I spent all year focusing on causality, because it makes history interesting to students who would otherwise have no interest in learning. Knowing the American Revolution started in 1775 and the Union won the Civil War is important, but convincing young minds it's actually relevant for more than just an exam is the hardest part of teaching. Getting them to relate the past to the present not only keeps their interest, it exercises the critical thinking skills they will need someday.

"You all know what question is coming next. Why? Vanessa?"

It is game day for Vanessa and the team she captains, so she is dressed in her jersey. A three-sport athlete that includes field hockey and basketball, she is the school's female version of Xavier. Softball is her best sport, and if X is Millfield's king of the hard court, she ranks as queen of the diamond. Baseball is a passion of hers, and I learned early on never to get into an argument about it with her without researching ESPN first. At least she is a Yankee fan.

She finishes tying her hair in a ponytail before answering. "Because talk is easier than action," she says after a moment of reflection.

"Okay, tell me what you would have done?"

"Something to stop him." Vanessa is sincere, but she clearly doesn't have a clue what she would do. Taking a look at the rest of the class from the center of the stage, it's clear most of them don't either.

"Do something to stop him. Sounds like a plan, but remember European powers like France and England lost the better part of a generation in World War One. Their economies were still fragile and populations war-weary. The Germans had nothing left to lose after the Treaty of Versailles. Isn't stopping Hitler a little easier said than done, Brian?"

Brian exemplifies the nerd who always got bullied in school when I was growing up. You know, the one who was the least cool, never had a girlfriend, but was one of the smartest kids in class. Brian is a dorky computer geek with no sense of style, which means he will probably found the next Facebook or Microsoft, make billions of dollars, and be dating a supermodel in ten years.

"Sure, but if you can take action, you should take action," he says, tapping his pen nervously on his notebook while he speaks.

"Bold words, but doesn't everyone have the ability to take action? Not just nation-states heading down a path to inevitable war. In a broader scope, doesn't everyone have the responsibility to act when a situation arises that calls for it?"

"Not us. We're only in high school," Emilee says. She is your average teenager, although more reticent during class discussions than her peers. Like many her age, she is just trying to find her voice and develop the confidence to use it. "We can't even vote," she finishes.

"Emilee, do you think age is a prerequisite to making a difference?" The question yields the unintended consequence of driving her back into her shell. The challenge fails to deter some of my other students, and one in particular.

"It is if you want to be taken seriously," Chelsea says.

I have been pacing around the room until this point to keep everyone's focus on me. I decide to sit in my chair, right in the middle of the stage. I turn toward Chelsea and lean forward. "Chelsea, in the military there is the fine line between what's considered a reason and an excuse. I am not sure which yours is."

Chelsea leans forward in her own chair, not for a second backing down to my challenge. "We may never know," she says, smiling. Again, that's why she's a favorite of mine.

The class ends and the rest of the day's classes blur by. My academic level students are behind my honors class in the chronology of American history, so I must develop and execute several sets of lessons. Most planning happens on weekends, simply because I am exhausted at the end of a school day.

That's another way you can tell the good teachers from the bad. Bad teachers always want to engage in useless conversation at the end of the day because they didn't expend much energy teaching. Good teachers are mentally and emotionally spent. Great teachers look like they were playing chess against Garry Kasparov all day.

With quizzes in each of my five classes to grade, I have a pile to plough through. School dismisses a little after two, but teachers are not released until three o'clock. With an hour to kill before leaving, and two before the forced date with my future in-laws, I get right to work grading the quizzes. As I suspected, the honors class did really well on this one. I was about to pat myself on the back when the voice of my arch-nemesis shattered the revelry.

"The Great Depression and the lead up to World War II, huh? I am amazed, Michael, that you're the only history teacher in the entire school to get this far," I hear Principal Howell say.

I turn in my seat to find him gawking at the assignments for each class detailed out on the whiteboard. I never heard him come in. Well, slink in might be more descriptive.

Robinson Howell has been principal of the school for the last three years. He was still easing into the job when I interviewed with him, and he has regretted the decision to hire me ever since. If I am Ferris Bueller, he's my Edward Rooney. I wonder if he likes warm gummy bears.

"I wouldn't know where my colleagues are in their lessons." Not exactly accurate as I know where each one of them is. "I measure the speed of teaching by the effectiveness of the students to learn." That part is true, however.

"Yeah, right," he responds, moving toward me.

Recognizing my productivity will be zero, both during and after the lecture I know is sure to come, I put the quizzes I was grading back into a folder and begin to pack up my stuff. "Is this a social call, Robinson, or are you just going to sling derisive comments my way until I leave?" He smirks, perhaps thinking I might seriously think he was making a social call.

"I heard some concerns voiced about a few of your recent lectures. Things you discussed outside of your approved lesson plans."

"Really?" I feign surprise. "Concerns from whom?"

"I am really not at liberty to say." Of course he isn't. "But I heard you dedicated class time to the history of shopping. Is that true?" Howell folds his arms across his chest, the body-language way of saying I don't care about your explanation.

"Oh. I thought you were here to scold me for something not included in the lesson plan," I reply, barely able to contain the smile desperate to emerge on my mouth. Robinson Howell, for all his bluster and banter, is a schoolyard bully at heart. First he preys on the weak, untenured teachers with little capability or guts to fight back first.

Once that appetite is satiated, he moves on to making sure the department chairs are forced to do his bidding, thus the conversation with Chalice this morning. Finally, if he feels he has something on one of the stronger personalities in the school, he will confront them individually. Today is one of those days.

He gives me a puzzled look, trying to recollect what he read in my lesson plans. "You never mentioned—" I don't let him finish his sentence because I know he finds interruptions irritating.

"We talked about the evolution of shopping as part of the lesson on the economic boom during the Roaring Twenties. We also discussed the chronology of the skyscraper and the urbanization of America, in case you're curious."

The discussion was another end of the week causality example for my students. Fridays are always the toughest days to teach, so I like to reserve them for topics of interest. A necessity if you want to keep students engaged when they are all looking forward to the weekend.

The lesson was a simple one. You start with a product one of the students happens to be carrying, in this case a girl's purse, and talk about how she bought it. In this example, the bag was purchased at one of the countless women's accessory stores in the Danbury Mall.

We traced how she would have purchased the same item back through American history. Strip malls, online catalogues, the department store, and so on to the local village merchant who imported the item from England prior to the American Revolution. The whole exercise was exceedingly interesting for the girls, although the boys got something out of it too.

"I don't think the State of Connecticut would approve, nor do I believe parents would think much of it either," Howell says, clearly off balance.

"So you are telling me, that as principal, you feel understanding mercantilism is not an important part of American history and who we are as a society today? Because last I checked, consumerism is one of the pillars of modern American culture." Howell starts to respond, but I'm on a roll. "And while we can agree or disagree on whether the importance we place on material things is healthy for our society, understanding this in a historical context is an essential part of learning and what teaching American History is all about.

"The question you need to ask yourself, Robinson, isn't why I'm teaching this. It's why everyone else isn't." I sneak a quick look at the clock to see if I can hit the door at precisely three p.m. if I take my time getting downstairs. I normally wouldn't care leaving a minute or two early, but Chalice was right about one thing. I shouldn't be giving Howell any more excuses to come after me.

I walk past my stunned principal and wait for him to follow me out into the hallway. He puffs his chest, or at least what can loosely be called a chest, as he walks out of the room. Howell is balding, wears the goofiest glasses imaginable, and hasn't seen the inside of a gym since George Bush was in the White House. The father, not the son.

I can feel his eyes burning into me as I close the door and lock it. Howell probably practiced this confrontation in his office all afternoon, and it did not turn out the way he imagined. Losing gracefully is not his style, so cue the final words on the subject.

"Stick to the curriculum, Michael. It's developed by people who are far more educated than you. If a single parent complains about this, you'll be hearing from me again."

I could respond, but I choose to bite my tongue as Robinson Howell stomps back down the hallway. Besides, I will need to save my strength for an evening at Jess's parents anyway. With that thought, I head for the door.

-SIX-
BLAKE

As an up and coming congressional staffer, long hours are usually the first requirement. However, while performing duties for our bosses may be the order of the day, just as much business is conducted at night. The area around the Capitol is rife with establishments where young congressional staffers, lobbyists, and government types gather after the official work day is concluded. To that end, I spend an inordinate amount of time at places like the Hawk and Dove and Capitol Lounge developing contacts and trading information.

On the rare nights when no work responsibilities demand my attention, I head to the Adams Morgan section of town. The intersection of 18th Street and Columbia Road is the place to be if you're in your twenties and living in Washington. With neighborhood spots like the Toledo Lounge and Millie and Al's, nightclubs like Heaven and Hell and Habana Village, the area trumps the college crowds you find at bars in Georgetown. While Wisconsin and M Streets offer a great nightlife, the crowd is a little too young and touristy for my tastes.

For tonight's outing, I could have chosen to meet at a place around the MCI Center. As hip as they are, brew pubs like the Capitol City Brewing Company or Gordon Biersch are also favorites of Roger and Congressman Beaumont. Since all I wanted was a quiet night out with the lovely Madison Roberts, I thought a romantic Monday dinner in a small Arlington bistro would be perfect. I hold her hand across the table as another round of drinks is delivered by an all-too-eager waitress.

"How'd it go in Connecticut?" There is a dual purpose to my question. As always, I'm looking for information, but also want her to know that I missed her these last five days.

"It was fine. All the media outlets are on board. Pretty much everyone knows this election is going to be a joke," she says as she sips her Merlot. "Had any more fireworks with the Ice Queen since I've been gone?" The Ice Queen being the malevolent Deena Shilling.

"Took her a few days to talk to me after my brilliant stunt when I was late last Monday, but she got over it and returned to her typical peppy self," I reply, with not just a little sarcasm.

"You were lucky you dodged the proverbial bullet that day. What would you have done if Marcus wasn't finished with the poll and the opposition research?"

"I'm not sure, but I am supremely confident in my abilities. I would've come up with something." Plan B still would have been brilliant, if not as elegant as Plan A turned out.

Dinner comes and Madison and I continue the small talk about the staff, campaign, and what will happen following the impending victory of our liege. In her role as press secretary, she can never really turn off the propaganda. Everything is pro-Beaumont all the time, and she absolutely believes every word she utters without reservation.

My views may be a little more jaded, since the allegiance I swore to Beaumont hinges on his ability to advance me to the next level. I will play along with Madison tonight, because it advances that ambition. My unqualified support of Congressman Beaumont will get back to him through her, while serving the dual purpose of helping me explore a separate agenda after I bring her home.

We share a dessert after our meal, partly because as a beautiful woman in the public eye she is always concerned with her physical appearance. She may not want the added calories, but I just think it's romantic. So before we finish the final bites of a decadent chocolate mousse cake, I broach a subject that I need to learn more about with extreme caution.

"On a more personal note, have you spoken to your sister since ..." I let my voice trail off on purpose.

"Since she was fired from the *Times*? No. You know we have a complicated relationship, and this will only make that worse." Madison is clearly uneasy, but I am not sure why. I knew she and her sister were not close, which is surprising since the fields of journalism and public relations are not that far removed.

"You think she'll find out we were behind it?" I try to ask as matter of fact as I can.

"Let's hope not, but if she does, it won't be because I tipped her off."

"Has she found another job yet?" I ask, not really caring, but at the same time acting like I do.

"I'm sure Mom will tell me when she does. Knowing Kylie, she'll find something before too long. Look, I don't want to talk about my sister anymore. I want to talk about us." She flashes the brightest smile I have ever seen. "More specifically, Mister Peoni, where exactly we are going after dinner?"

I return her smile. Work is done for the evening, so let playtime begin. "As in, are we going dancing or for a romantic stroll in the park?" She reaches across the table and squeezes my arm.

"No, I was thinking more along the lines of your place or mine?"

-SEVEN-
KYLIE

The big problem with being married to your work is the divorce is ugly. When you devote as much energy, time, and resources to the job as I did, a sudden change like getting fired leaves behind a colossal void. My career was everything, and without one for almost a month now, I feel like I'm trying to fill the Grand Canyon with pebbles.

It took about a week to pull myself together after my termination. At least I had better luck than all the king's horses and men had with Humpty Dumpty. I finally called Mom back to face in the inevitable inquisition and sermon rolled into one. The conversation was not as bad as I feared it would be. Perhaps she heard my melancholy tone and took pity on me.

I was vague in my explanation to family and friends, except for one in particular. Bill Gibbons has been a long time acquaintance of mine and exactly who I needed to confide in. And he is the reason why I am sitting in a Starbucks on Madison Avenue right now, sipping a five-dollar café latte while collecting unemployment.

I am managing to score a little freelance work on occasion, but after being blackballed by my boss at the *New York Times*, landing something steady has been more of a challenge. The news business is a small world, despite the number of possible employers. So when an editor makes it known to his friends and colleagues that hiring a rogue journalist like me would be an incredible risk, they listen, and I remain jobless. The question is, why would he do that?

Firing me is one thing, but punishing me by sabotaging chances to find work anywhere else is quite another. I enlisted Bill's help to find out why I am persona non grata in journalism circles. I didn't notice him walk in, and am startled when he comes up behind me with a tall cup of coffee in his hand. I must be off in my own little world, since this particular Starbucks is not large.

"It's a nice day. Let's take a stroll," he almost whispers, nodding towards the door. Since I have no real job, no real life, and no other place to be, I grab my purse and coffee and follow him out the door into the pleasant mid-May Manhattan weather. We turn and begin walking toward Bryant Park, moving with the flow of office workers escaping their cubicles to enjoy one of the nicest days of the spring so far.

"So are you just keeping me in suspense or did you come up empty?" I ask.

"I assumed the story you were working on about modern politics was a puff piece," Bill says, stroking his hair and admiring a woman in heels and a short skirt breezing by. "But it was bigger, wasn't it? You had dirt on people."

"Yeah, some, but the majority was innuendo and hearsay and was not printable using any journalistic standard," I defend. Okay, so that's not the whole story. Bill doesn't need to know I had much more than simple rumors and a piece on the cusp of being ready for print. He is a friend, but nobody is registering well on my trust meter these days.

"Well, someone thought it could be."

I stop dead in the street, the stark reality finally dawning on me. "Are you saying someone got me fired?"

Bill realized a few paces later that I was no longer next to him. He turned, retrieved me, and said nothing until we made our way into the park. The small space, a stone's throw from Times Square, is packed with the lunchtime crowd on this beautiful day. Improbably, Bill finds what must be the only small green table and chairs available, and we sit down. People are moving all around us, some leaving their seats to return to the mundane tribulations of work, but most desperately searching for a place to enjoy their lunch.

"Look, Kylie, I only know what I was told. A friend of a friend said someone squeezed your editor. A player with significant clout in Washington, *and* a good enough relationship with your former paper to get you fired."

Bill has never been notorious for his focus. He possesses an uncanny ability to notice everything going on around him, which is probably why he is good at his job. But right now, in this instant, I have his undivided attention even with the leggy women in high heels walking by. Bill is a good-looking guy, tall with a square jaw and on-camera looks. I am surprised he chose print instead of television journalism.

"Who did you talk to about this article?" he asks.

"Other than my editor?" He nods. "A few coworkers and possibly a friend or two."

"One of them talked to the wrong person. Not sure if it was malicious or harmless, but you are living the result."

I don't know what to think about this. On one level, I'm stunned someone would do this to me, whether they meant it or not. Journalism can be a cutthroat occupation, especially when mixed with politics, so I shouldn't be too surprised, however. I feel a resurgence of last week's anger at my editor, but I also want a new target. I want the person responsible.

"Can you find out which slimy piece of crap did this?"

Bill exhales, and for the first time breaks eye contact with me. I am not sure why exactly, but he looks conflicted. "I could, but I won't."

"You know, don't you?" I study his face, looking for the small telltale signs you can see when a person is about to lie to you.

"You have a remarkable gift, Kylie, and if you want to waste it by running off half-cocked chasing powerful men, I can't stop you. But the end result is you are going to end up right back where you are now."

I scoff at his portrayal of me running off half-anything. My mantra has always been anything worth doing is worth doing one hundred percent. After all, you can't get a little bit pregnant. But I let him finish.

"Let me give you a piece of advice. You can find out on your own who is responsible. The pieces are there for you to put together. And if you really want to bring ... whoever ...

down, I'm sure you can find a way. Of course, you will also destroy yourself, your credibility, and your career in the process."

That's not what I wanted to hear. He is probably right, but I have bloodlust for some serious payback right now. Some of the information I obtained touched a nerve and has someone running scared enough to get me fired. Now I want to find out what information bothered whom and keep digging until I get what I need to destroy them.

"I don't care," I say, meaning it.

"Right now you don't, and I can't say I blame you. But I would wait. Do what you need to do to get yourself back in the game, and when the opportunity presents itself, get your revenge then." Bill gets up from his seat and surveys the beautiful greenery of this urban oasis before looking at me. "I need to get back to work. Good seeing you, Kylie. Think about what I said." With that, he falls in behind a throng of pretty Asian women leaving the park.

Despite my best efforts not to, I am thinking about what he said. The voice of reason chirps in my head like one of Suzanne Collins's *The Hunger Games* mockingjays. I don't really want to listen. I have always been driven to achieve a result. Rushing in has served me well, but maybe not this time. Maybe being patient is the right approach.

"Get yourself back in the game," I hear myself whisper. Yeah, but how?

-EIGHT-
CHELSEA

"So, I will ask the question again. If the twenty-four-hour news cycle existed in 1932, does this country elect FDR? Could he have survived the blogs, cable news, and social media all questioning his ability to lead because he was bound to a wheelchair? Vanessa?"

Yeah, Mister Bennit is on a roll today. The school year is waning, but he amped up this discussion as if the calendar still read February. With final exams only, like, two weeks away, the class has sort of fallen into a routine of discussing whatever Mister Bennit feels like talking about. The rest of the time he devotes to preparing us for a final sure to resemble a torture worthy of medieval Europe.

"No way," Vanessa responds. "His opponents would've used the media to humiliate him. And all that would be shared over and over on Facebook, Reddit, and Twitter. People would see him as an invalid and not presidential."

I love Vanessa. She's athletic and confident, but when she isn't wearing her jersey, looks like a J-Lo starter kit. And in this case, she's wrong. My hand shoots up to join others who are waving theirs frantically.

"Good point, Vanessa," Mister Bennit says. "Chelsea?"

"You're not giving people enough credit, V," I say. "I don't think it'd matter at all. Before Obama, they said a black man could never be president. Chris Christie was a cheeseburger away from a heart attack before his surgery, and he became governor in New Jersey, of all places. People elected Roosevelt to pull the country out of the Great Depression. Regardless of what the media said, if people thought he was the guy that can end soup lines and get Americans back to work, they'd vote for him."

My comments bring on an avalanche of rebuttals. This class can be pretty jaded, so there aren't too many people in my corner. Amanda is shaking her head feverishly. Brian, the ultimate cynic, is stopping just short of calling me naïve. The rest of the class has broken out into side arguments.

Mister Bennit is standing in the middle of his stage smirking. At over six feet tall with an athletic build, he doesn't resemble any other teacher in the school. What strikes me most are his blue eyes. They can be bright and convey warmth and understanding, or turn steel grey and melt iron. With one look, I have seen him completely terrify a misbehaving student.

Today, his eyes show amusement, and I can tell he loves starting this. Getting a group of generally apathetic teenagers to argue about history must give him a lot of satisfaction. I don't know how he does it, and other teachers in the school can't figure it out either. There is just something about him that brings out the best in his classes.

Mister Bennit holds his hands in the air to settle everyone down. The class dials down the noise level back to a tolerable decibel level.

"One at a time guys. Em?"

"All today's media really cares about is ratings. There are too many mediums to choose from. If they felt those pressures back then, FDR would've been trashed 24-7."

"You don't give the media much credit," I say. "Even they must abide by the rules of political correctness these days."

"Oh, good point, Chels," Mister Bennit chimes in.

"Yeah, but bloggers don't," Brian interjects. "There is a whole subculture on the Internet acting like journalists without any standards."

"Who has time to read blogs?" Peyton asks.

"Blogs get shared on Facebook, Peyton," Brian fires back. "For the more news savvy, there's also Reddit, Digg, and Tumblr. You know what all those sites share in common? The highest trending articles are always the most controversial."

"Excellent points all around. I'm sure you all have more to say on this, so we'll continue the discussion on Monday."

Vince raises his hand. I have never been able to figure him out. He dresses like he's in a grunge band, and all his friends have absolutely no interest in school. There are much easier teachers than Mister B, so I wonder why he is even here.

"Oh, I feel a nightmare coming on. Go ahead, Vince."

"I think I speak for the class. Since we're all going to ace the final, let's say you just give us an A now and we'll play video games on exam day instead?"

The class snickers. Vince theatrically mimics working a game controller. I laugh too, but only because the thought of us all getting over an eighty on this exam is just comical.

"Vince, I swear you're a case study on the effects of marijuana on the teenage mind," Mister Bennit replies, probably only half-joking.

"What if we did all get an A?" I have no idea why I am indulging this, but I guess I am still in an argumentative mood.

"Really, Chelsea? This is the most intelligent and gifted honors American History class I have ever taught, and I still wouldn't need all ten fingers to count the number of A grades you guys got on your midterms. Now you all think you'll smoke the final? Nice wish."

"But what if we did? What do we get?" Amanda asks, keenly interested in the conversation.

"A grade," Mister Bennit replies with his usual sarcasm.

"Other than a grade?"

"A really good grade." We all look at our teacher impatiently. Peyton even begins tapping her finely manicured fingernails on her desk. Most teachers don't like being challenged. Mister B is not one of them. "I don't do bribes, hand out candy, or dole out rewards of any kind. You all know that."

"So you, like, don't think we can do it?" Peyton asks, not willing to back down. You would think she is all style and no substance by looking at her. She will be Homecoming Queen and the Prom Queen next year, but under a pretty wrapping of designer clothes is a tough, smart girl when she lets it show.

"Peyton, I have the utmost confidence in the capabilities of this class. In that spirit, no, I don't think you have a chance."

"Fine. How about a bet then?" Vanessa just threw down the gauntlet.

"What, are we at the track now? No, I don't bet with students."

"Chicken." Oops. That sort of slipped from my mouth.

"Chels, you may be the only student I have who can get away with calling me that."

Vince starts flapping his arms and Vanessa and a few others make clucking noises, resulting in the desired effect.

"Fine, I'll play your game. What are the stakes?" As much as he was protesting, I think Mister Bennit kind of wants to do this. Or at least hear us out. It has to be something good though."

"You can buy us new video game consoles," Vince offers. I roll my eyes. Mister Bennit said good, not ridiculous.

"You swear off espresso for a month," Amanda tries. Right, you would have better luck asking the women on the *Real Housewives of Beverly Hills* to stop getting plastic surgery.

"Um, no."

"A week?" asks Xavier.

Mister Bennit just starts shaking his head and keeps shaking it.

"A day?" offers Vanessa.

"Five minutes?" Brian asks.

"Thirty seconds?" Emilee meekly adds.

Vince breaks the string. "Oh, right, and I'm the addict!" Everyone begins laughing, but not me. I am serious about making this bet, I'm just not sure why.

"Bell's about to ring. If that's the best you can—"

"You run for Congress." The class hushes as I cut him off. I now have everyone's attention, which is surprising since I really didn't think it was that good of an idea. I don't even know where the thought came from, but I go with it. "If we all get an A on the final exam, you run for Congress in the fall."

Mister Bennit is one of those teachers who rarely expresses his own opinions. When discussions about politics come up in the course of teaching history, he goes all devil's advocate on us. I can never figure out what views are his. He is so informed about issues, he can convincingly argue for either side. We have seen him switch positions in the middle of a class debate, and it's wildly entertaining.

The rest of the room breaks into enthusiastic agreement with my idea. Mister Bennit is über-military and has no tolerance for politics or pandering. He is a leader, not a politician, so it'd be an awfully interesting term in office if he won.

He stands in the middle of his stage and folds his arms across his chest. "You all clearly lost your minds. Are you that desperate to get me out of here?"

Vanessa pounces. "Mister B, all year we've listened to you lecture about making a difference in the world."

"You said those who have the ability to act have the responsibility to. Those were your words, right?" Brian is practically a human tape recorder. No doubt those words were said at some point during the year.

"Mister B, we just want to see if you walk the walk as good as you talk the talk," Xavier says.

"Be careful, Xavier," Mister Bennit warns. "I walked the walk and sacrificed more than most Americans ever will. And I can show you the scars from multiple tours in the Middle East to prove it."

"Everyone knows you'd be great," Vanessa almost whispers.

"Great at politics?" he says with a laugh. "Just so we're clear. You want me to run for office knowing the only thing I despise more than lawyers are lawyers who become politicians?"

"Nobody expects you to be any good at politics, Mister Bennit," I chime in. "It's not about politics. It's about leadership, and service, and commitment to community. It's about the things nobody sees in Washington anymore." Mister B isn't going to be swayed by calling him out or trying to guilt him into doing something he doesn't want to do. But he does respond to direct appeals to his sense of duty and to country.

"You have the honor, integrity, courage, and selflessness we should demand from our leaders. It is the same qualities the American people complain about politicians lacking. Why not be the candidate they claim to want and see what happens?"

The entire class is floored. They are riveted by my little speech, and that's saying something for my ADHD generation. Our attention span can only be measured in tenths of seconds. Everyone turns their focus back to our teacher who, for perhaps the first time since this class began in September, stands speechless.

When he finally opens his mouth, the words were not exactly what I was expecting. "Clearly, helping you all improve your debate skills this year was a bad idea. But since there is no chance in hell of you guys pulling this off anyway, I'll take your bet."

"So you'll do it?" Emilee says. Of course, she is also drowned out by about a dozen others who ask a variation of the same question.

"Yes, if you all think you are good enough to score an A on the final, I'll do it."

"Ha! We are going to smoke this final just to watch Mister B get humiliated on national television!" Vince exclaims, earning him a playful slap on the back of the head from Vanessa.

"Funny, Vince. By the way, how do you all plan on enforcing this bet? You are out of here in a couple of weeks."

"Most of us signed up for Contemporary Issues with you next year," Peyton adds in a matter the fact tone.

"I must be losing my touch. Didn't you guys get enough abuse?"

"Yeah, but we're sadists," Vince responds. He's partially right. The word on the street is that he is much easier on his seniors in that class than his American History students. I am eager to find out whether the rumor is true.

The bell rings to dismiss the class. We pack up our remaining belongings and erupt into a cacophony of conversation as we collectively head toward the door. I am smiling, pleased at not only getting him to agree to the bet, but at the prospect of actually forcing him to pay up.

As we start out into the hall, I hear Mister Bennit call out to us. "Hey, let's keep this bet between us. Nobody tells Miss Slater. I don't want to end up on the couch tonight!"

-NINE-

MICHAEL

I never make bets with my students. I am not against it in principle, just not of the opinion bribes should be used as a form of motivation. Some teachers swear by these techniques—using bets and bribes to encourage learning. It's just a tactic I choose not to employ. It is not something Jessica believes in either. Word of this wager will no doubt spread like a California forest fire through the school. I can only hope nobody whispered the news in her ear already.

I park outside my condo, right next to Jessica's blue Nissan. I had to stay late at school to get some planning done for finals, otherwise I would have beaten her home. I retrieve my trusty old military assault pack from the backseat and head for the front door. The bag has been repurposed from carrying ammunition and the tools of war to books and other various materials of a teacher.

Entering the foyer, I drop my keys in a dish on the small table and look up to see Jessica. She looks sexy standing in the entrance to the living room wearing her workout clothes. "I put an extra blanket and pillow on the couch for you for tonight … Congressman."

She stalks off down the hall. Uh-oh. I peek into the room and, sure enough, a blanket is folded neatly on one of the cushions with a pillow perched on top. Damn, so much for the class keeping this on the down low. Now it's time to find out just how much trouble I am in.

"So, we are skipping the fight and going straight into the consequences?" I ask, and am not rewarded with a response.

I change into my own gym clothes and we pile into the car in complete silence. In fact, we are almost done with our matching forty-five minute workouts on the treadmill before I even attempt communication. When she slows to a walk and removes her iPod earbuds, I seize the opening.

"So, which one of my students threw me under the bus?"

"Does it matter?" she sharply responds, not even looking at me.

"I just need to know who to fail," I respond playfully. Nope, she is having none of that.

"You made the bet," Jessica replies coldly.

"As if they have a chance of winning."

Jessica stops her treadmill, towels off her forehead and turns to me, an icy look in her eyes.

"Correct me if I'm wrong, but haven't you told me a few dozen times never to underestimate your honors American History class? But whatever," she says, as she picks up her water bottle, turns and walks away.

The dreaded "whatever." It is the word women use to say "I'm right, you're wrong, and the sooner you realize it, the sooner we'll start talking again." It also means this conversation is over for now, forcing me to wait to find out exactly why this is bothering her so much.

That's the only thing I reflect on during our drive back to my place. I can understand her being a little miffed about the bet, but she is more than miffed. She's pissed, yet not angry enough to head south and stay at her place tonight. Yes, my fiancée has well-documented degrees of anger.

Jessica essentially moved in with me when we got engaged over winter break five short months ago. My condominium is a full hour closer to the school than her residence down near the Long Island Sound, so it made plenty of sense that she stay with me. My place being far too small to make any accommodation for her furniture, and not wanting to take a chance of her things being ruined in storage, she decided to keep her apartment. Despite my pleadings about wanting to save money, she will continue to pay the rent until we do the post-wedding furniture reconciliation.

Since she maintains this retreat, if she were upset enough, some geographical distance would be inserted between us instead of simply banishing me to the couch. A skeptic would think that's the actual reason she keeps it. I'm trying not to be that cynical.

Once home, we each take showers and then eat in relative silence. After dinner, she retires to the small office originally intended to be a guest bedroom, and I am left with complete control of the television. The eleven o'clock news is on when Jessica walks into the room dressed for bed and sits next to me. She grabs the remote and turns off the power.

"Why did you make the bet?"

"Why is it bothering you so much? What does it really matter?" Answering a question with a question is a classic in the art of deflection and usually annoys her, but works this time.

"It matters because you are doing it again," she replies, a hint of exasperation in her voice.

"Doing what?"

"You really don't see it, do you? It's a losing proposition for everyone. If they don't win the bet, they feel they let you down. If they do win, you have to humiliate yourself running in an election you could never hope to win."

Jessica has always been critical of the lofty standards I set for the kids in my classes. It has been the source of countless discussions and arguments between us since the moment we met. Once we got engaged, we reached a tenuous détente, but neither of us has changed our minds on the subject.

"Three years of teaching and I have never had even half of a class all earn an A on any exam, much less a final. You know they are incredibly hard." True statements, but also a pretty weak defense.

Jessica takes a moment to think about her words. "You are counting on them losing this bet. But you are underestimating yourself and your class. Did you put any thought at all into what happens if you lose?"

"It'll be fine, honey. Trust me."

"Never trust an old Army sergeant who says 'trust me.' You'd better hope you're right." It was more of a warning than a statement. "C'mon, time to go to bed."

"I can't, you're sitting on it," I reply playfully, sensing the worst is over.

Jessica stands up and reaches her hand out to me. "I'm not asking again. Come to bed, Congressman."

I flash a little smile, turn off the light, and follow her down the dark hallway. She is right about one thing. I haven't considered what would happen if I lose this bet. Maybe Chelsea is right and I possess all the principles the American public claim to want in a politician.

Romantic as that sounds, deep down I realize I could never win. I have nobody willing to contribute money and no connections. Even if I did, I am too direct, loath the games politicians play, and could never subject myself to the personal scrutiny the modern public figure has to endure. I'm not sure how I could deal with the media's voracious appetite for news and political enemies who will use any small detail to forge an advantage in the polls.

"It won't get that far, you know," I say, more trying to convince myself than my future wife.

Her reply makes me believe she somehow already knows how this is going to turn out. "I'll remember you said that when it gets that far."

-TEN-
KYLIE

She almost never comes into the Big Apple, at least not by herself. There are occasions when her boss has some manner of business here, and that is about the only time I see her. It's a preferable arrangement for both of us, because we can't stand each other. She has her world, I have mine, and when they collide, two 747s slamming head-on at 30,000 feet is a good metaphor to describe the result.

She is someone who has gotten used to the trappings of power and the D.C. after-hours political scene, so my first thought was to torture her at one of the many tourist traps the city has to offer. I was thinking maybe something around Times Square, where typical bills of fare are offered up to tourists at obscenely marked-up prices. She would consider any such place beneath her.

I decided on a different approach. With all the Saturday matinees in the Theater District, it will be too crowded in the restaurants to initiate this confrontation, especially in early June. Plus, I want her to feel somewhat relaxed while still letting her know that she is in my city now. New York is my turf, so I settled on a nice quiet bistro in the Village where I can say my piece. It is charming enough for her to be slightly at ease, while hip and artsy enough to remind her she is swimming in my fishbowl, and not with the rest of the sharks in the Beltway aquarium.

Now fashionably late, I watch as she saunters up and glides into the seat across from me. "Long time, no see, Kylie," she says as she places her oversized purse on the floor next to her chair. "How's unemployment treating you?"

Apparently the gloves are coming off early. "Hi, Madison. It's great, thanks for asking. How's life working for the snake charmer?" I respond in a feint of innocence as she smiles smugly.

"Same old, same old. Just doing the people's work and representing the best interests of the district, like we always do."

The waiter comes over and asks us for our drink order. "I'll have the Chardonnay," I say. "And she'll have a glass of grape Kool-Aid." The Jonestown metaphor is lost on the waiter, but not on Madison.

"And can you slip some hemlock into her drink since she is committing career suicide anyway?"

The waiter stammers, stuttering something about not having Kool-Aid and asking what hemlock is. I let him off the hook just to make him go away.

"Just bring two Chardonnays." And with that, he bolts from our table, no doubt relieved to get away from the crazy women seated here.

"Well, this is almost like old times, right, sis? The two of us trading barbs across the table."

"Almost," I reply. "Except back then, our battles were small and harmless. Not the scorched earth campaigns they are now."

"I'm not sure I know what you mean."

"Oh, Madison, the innocence routine may enchant other members of the press, but it stopped working on me in grammar school. So do us both a favor and drop it, will you?" She smarts a little at the comment, but says nothing. A supreme accomplishment for a woman who talks for a living, I might add. "Despite our differences, I never thought you'd be complicit in getting me fired from a job."

"I didn't get you fired from anything, and I resent that accusation."

"No, you didn't, but your boss did. And frankly I don't give a damn what you resent."

The waiter arrives with our wine and asks us for our order. Neither one of us is hungry by this point, so he is promptly dismissed. Once he flees out of earshot, Madison leans forward, a flash of anger in her eyes.

"He did no such thing, and the mere insinuation that he did is insulting. Congressman Beaumont is an honest and capable servant of the people who would never jeopardize his position to force the firing of a second-rate journalist making unsubstantiated claims." Second-rate journalist. That was meant to hurt.

"Well, this second-rate journalist has it on good authority, from reliable sources, that Winston Beaumont was instrumental in passing legislation favorable to the Lexington Group."

"There's nothing illegal about that, Kylie."

"No, but when he personally benefits from it to the tune of over $300,000 in financial compensation not made directly to his campaign, it's called a kickback. And that, my dear little sister, is very illegal."

I just played the best card in my hand. There were only a couple of news outlets that covered the allegation, and none of them put a monetary value on it. I did, because that was the number the two sources gave me. One more person to corroborate and I could have run the story, even in the left-leaning paper I served.

"You've been watching too much Fox News and reading too many right-wing blogs. You got fired because of all the time you spent railing against modern politics. Everybody knows that."

"Everybody knows only what they have been told. It's even what I was told by my editor. But you know what? It just didn't sit right with me. So I dug, and eventually uncovered the truth," I say as I lean forward. She looks at me, the anger in her face replaced with another familiar emotion: fear.

"Madison, you're either lying, or completely brainwashed if you think for a second that Winston Beaumont didn't get me fired because I have the story in all its gory detail. Fox and a couple of others made a few reports, but so what, right? Winston Beaumont's not scared of Fox News. But having it plastered on the front page of the *New York Times*? That's another thing altogether."

I know my sister. I can read her expressions and mannerisms. Even though we've never really been close, I spent enough time growing up with her to be able to decipher her nonverbal tells. And although she's doing her best to hide it, she just can't. Not with me.

"What happened to you, Kylie? You've become so jaded. You think the whole world is out to get you. It's too bad."

Madison retrieves her purse and stands, the chair screeching against the tile floor as she rises. Her exit won't be as graceful as her entrance. No longer is she on top of the world, taking a pity lunch with her loser big sister. I have her, and now it's time to go for her throat.

"I told you what I was working on." Madison stops a few steps from the table, but she doesn't look back at me. "I didn't give you many specifics that night we talked on the phone. You remember, the one where we talked like we did from time-to-time growing up. You were in emotional distress, so you reached out to me and I listened like a big sister should. And you know what? I felt closer to you at that moment than any other point in our lives.

"So I decided to trust you by telling you what I was working on. I may have even mentioned Beaumont's name to protect you, since being a key advisor to a crooked politician is not exactly a career enhancing move. I opened up to you, and as thanks, you turned around and used that information against me."

"Good catching up with you, sis," Madison says as she walks away from the table and heads out the door. Her quick exit prompts the waiter to bring the bill over, lest I get any ideas about not paying it. I drop thirty bucks on the table and grab my things.

It was a short conversation, but we both got what we wanted today. I confirmed Bill's theory about what transpired to get me fired. Maddy didn't actually need to make an admission. Her actions told the tale in a way only a sibling could decipher. But she learned something from me too. She knows that I figured it out, am pissed, and will eventually be coming for her and the man she works for.

-ELEVEN-
CHELSEA

As I pull into the driveway, the LED sign in the front of the school reads "Final Exam Week! Good Luck!" That's exactly what we will all need. I am early to school today, so I park my car without the added humiliation of having the Range Rover and Z4 next to me.

I chat with Stephanie and Cassandra at my locker for a few minutes and then head off to Mister Bennit's classroom. Much to my surprise, I am not the first to arrive. Several others, including Emilee, and Peyton of all people, are here getting some last minute review in.

Joining them, I notice the desks once arranged in the all-too-familiar horseshoe are now neatly lined up in rows and columns. The stage is gone, and the room is in test configuration. I swear the change is more for psychological reasons than cheating prevention ones.

As time ticks by, my anxiety increases. The last students file into the classroom, still a whole five minutes before the bell. Most of us are already seated, reviewing our notes and asking questions amongst ourselves. The public address system crackles to life from the speakers set in the ceiling tiles at the front of the room.

"Students should be at their second-period class at this time for their final examination," the voice says without preamble. "Please disregard all bells. Students will be dismissed from their exam by announcement."

Mister Bennit walks from his desk in the corner to the front of the room with a stack of papers in his hand. "The great journey you all began one hundred seventy-six days ago reaches its end today. Hope you all studied hard. Clear your desks."

We oblige, but I can tell many of my peers are pretty anxious by the way they fumble their books and notes. Amanda breaks the eerie silence. "There's more than our grade at stake today. Or did you forget?"

"As if any of you would let that happen, Amanda."

"Good, because I have spent every free moment for a month studying for this thing," Vince says. Doubtful, but I suppose miracles do happen.

Mister Bennit begins handing out packets consisting of numerous sheets of paper stapled in the corner. If tradition holds, here come the rapid-fire instructions.

"All right, you have two hours to complete this exam. There are fifty multiple choice questions, fifteen short answer, and, of course, the dreaded essay of doom. As always, the only authorized positions for your eyes are the paper in front of you and the clock.

"Maintain bottom to top lip contact at all times. In the unlikely event you finish early, turn your papers over and remain silent. Cheaters will face summary judgment and execution by firing squad. Questions?"

That took around nine seconds to get out. He's slipping.

"Did you have to make this so easy?" Vince asks playfully. As usual, he earns a chuckle from the otherwise tense class.

"We'll see if you are so confident once you actually flip your test over, Vince," Mister Bennit replies with a smile. "Okay, guys, get to it."

For the next hour and forty-five minutes, I pore over the test. To my pleasant surprise, it is not as hard as I expected it to be. The questions were certainly not easy, but if the whole class took the time to prepare, this exam was not impossible.

I finish about fifteen minutes early, so I review the multiple choice questions and ensure I marked the answer sheet correctly. Then I check the short answer to make certain I answered the whole question. I have fallen into that trap on more than one occasion. No point in checking the essay. There is no time to review, let alone rewrite it.

"Three, two, one, time's up. Writing utensils down, please. Exammageddon is over and it's time to face the humanity. Bring your essay, answer sheet, and exam up to the front."

Mister Bennit begins collecting the exams and bubble sheets and places them in separate piles on his desk. I look around and don't see the panic I have in the past. Most of us confidently turn the exam in. I think he notices too.

"Will you let us know how we did?" I ask, innocently.

"So eager to fail," he states with a wink. "I'll e-mail the class when they are graded for those who are curious."

He can keep dreaming. There are a lot of things in life I am not sure of, like why girls my age find UGG boots fashionable. But I can say with certainty that I nailed this test. Maybe not a perfect score, but I will promise I didn't miss it by much. I know I did my part.

From the looks of it, I am not the only one brimming with confidence. There are a lot of smiles in the room, and some very upbeat conversations get interrupted only when the public address system crackles to life. "The B Period final exam testing period has concluded. Students may now be dismissed for their next exam."

We all begin to file out of the classroom. We have twenty minutes to get to our last exam of the day, but most of it will be spent socializing in the hallway. I look back to see Mister B flipping quickly through the answer sheets. While I doubt he has the exact order memorized yet, I bet he knows it pretty well. That would be the only reason I can see to justify the look of concern on his face.

-TWELVE-
MICHAEL

The problem when you include yourself in the stakes of a bet is maintaining impartiality. While I highly doubt any student would ever question my integrity outright, I don't even want the perception to be there. And in an instant like this, it could be because there is no way I want to run for office.

So while it would be easy to tweak a grade to ensure that doesn't happen, I have to remember who it hurts in the long run. My guidance to students and their parents at the beginning of the school year was that you get the grade you earn. So, despite any temptation I have to reach a desired outcome, I stick by that rule. Of course, I also took a few precautions.

I cashed in a favor with the Teacher Clerk to run the answer sheets through a machine that corrects them automatically. I asked her to just put them in a folder and not share any details with me. The final exam contained fifty multiple choice questions, worth two points each for a total of one hundred points. I now have no idea how they did on them.

The fifteen short answer questions are worth four points each for a total of sixty points. Basically, the only criteria are whether they answered the question correctly using the proper facts to support it. Yes to both and they get full credit. If they are wrong, they obviously get nothing. If they guess right, but fail to adequately support their answer, they get half credit.

The essay is worth forty points, and comprises the "make it or break it" part of the test. I award four points for each of ten criteria, including: style, organization, argument, factual accuracy, thesis development, and a couple of other things. Once you add this result to those of the other sections, you get a raw score out of two hundred. They all need to score a one hundred eighty-four or better for an A. The good students historically average around a one hundred seventy, or an eighty-five percent which is a B.

Students are dismissed from school once the two exams are over, so I get right to work correcting their short answer sections. It's barely lunchtime as I plod my way through the stack, and the results are all pretty much the same. A question wrong here and a half-credit answer there, but overall they did really well. I'm impressed because these questions are not something I would ever characterize as easy. I am also a little distressed, given the circumstances, for the same reason.

I receive a text from Jess explaining she is going to do much of her grading at home instead of at school. Since that means the living room will look like it threw up Shakespeare, I decide to grade the essays at my favorite local hangout. The Perkfect Buzz is a throwback coffee house not far from the school. Much larger than you would expect, it still has a quaint, comfy feel you don't get at a modern Starbucks. The java here is excellent and the espresso even better.

Laura, the shop's owner who is almost never spotted outside the store during business hours, is surprisingly not in. Her stand-in, a pleasant older woman, makes my usual quadruple latte, and I settle in to one of the plush, comfortable chairs near the window to read the essays.

I'm a fast reader, and since I only take notes and not assign grades to the essays until I have read them all, it only takes a little over five hours to finish. It is nearly summer, but the sun has lost its struggle to stay in the sky. The long shadows of the late afternoon and early evening fade as twilight begins to settle in.

I review my notes and assign the grades based on each student's performance. The highest was a 40 and the lowest was a 32. Clearly they prepared very well for this exam because I have never had essay scores this high. I begin to calculate the scores for each student by adding the essay to the short answer. Each of my pupils is in line for an A, but there are some borderline ones. A bad showing on the multiple choice questions could easily send a few plunging into B or B minus range.

I open the folder the teacher clerk gave me and begin to add the multiple choice scores to the tally. I want to not believe what I'm seeing as I type the scores into a spreadsheet. Excel will do the math, but the result is already obvious. A year of hard work paid off in this demonstration of knowledge and historical concepts. I am not so thrilled about what that means.

By the time I calculate the scores, collect all my crap, and get to the house, it's well after nine. Normally this would draw the ire of my significant other, but Jessica is in the same boat herself. The condition of the living room serves as a testament to the plight of the modern English teacher. Piles of papers are everywhere, and although she has a finely honed system for how she grades, it looks like complete chaos to me.

Jessica is passed out on the couch, a purple pen she uses to correct essays only an inch away from bleeding into my microfiber cushion. I never use purple, despite it being the official color teachers at Millfield High are supposed to correct with. Our current administrators feel red is too harsh on the fragile psyche of the American teenager. I figure if you don't like red, don't make mistakes.

Sensing my presence, Jessica opens her eyes groggily. "Well?"

"Can we not talk about this now? Sleeping on the couch isn't good for my back," I say, answering the question without really answering it.

"So much for not underestimating them."

"They must have cheated," I retort, knowing full well they didn't.

"Yeah, sure. Or maybe you are just a far better teacher than you think you are. That, or they're far more determined than you thought they'd be," she replies as a woman does when telling a man she is always right, and he's an idiot.

"How mad at me are you right now?" I exhale.

Jessica gets up from the couch, tiptoeing around the piles of paper like they were landmines. "Let's not discuss it. The couch is lumpy and you have a bad back."

That went about as expected, and as unpleasant as it was, I get the feeling it will pale in comparison once I e-mail the grades to the class. I have now resigned myself to the fact that I truly have to go through with this. I have to run for Congress. But I am also determined not to feel that pain alone. After all, what is life if not a learning opportunity?

PART II

THE CAMPAIGN

-THIRTEEN-
BLAKE

In Washington politics, there is no such thing as a normal day. Whether you are the president of the United States or a page in the House of Representatives, there are always political moves to be made and enemies coming after you. It's a hard lifestyle to get used to, unless you are someone like me. I live for it.

I am already at my desk working on something for Roger this early Tuesday morning when Madison storms into the office. For a woman who appears to be the epitome of elegance and grace, she has a vindictive streak that exudes through her designer outfit. She slams her expensive purse on the desk before meeting my gaze.

"Rough morning?" I ask, knowing full well the problem is much deeper. While working out of the district office the last five days, I know she was planning on meeting her sister at some point.

"Family can be infuriating, that's all," she says for the benefit of those around us.

Deena peers over her dark glasses from her own desk. Since she rarely wears them, I assume they are meant to showcase some sense of style I am oblivious to rather than performing any real function. Not wanting to engage in a public confessional, Madison crosses Congressman Beaumont's outer office to my desk.

"She knows," Madison whispers to me, looking around to ensure we are not drawing any more unwanted attention from the staff. I quickly glance over at Deena, who has gone back to immersing herself in whatever task she invented to feel important.

"Are you sure? I mean, there's no way—"

"Blake, my sister may be a lot of things, but she's not an idiot. We met for lunch on Saturday and she put two and two together before we even sipped our wine."

"But she can't prove anything, so who cares?"

"You don't know Kylie," Madison deadpans.

I don't know the whole story of the rift between Maddy and her sister, but it must be epic. Their sibling rivalry transcends simple competitiveness and resembles something closer to being blood enemies. Maybe someday I'll hear the full version of that saga.

"You sound like you're scared of her," I say, almost taunting her.

"I am not scared of my sister!" Madison barks, a little too loudly. Once again, the whole office looks over at us. "We just need to keep an eye on her," she says in a much softer tone.

"Why? She can't hurt us with anything about Lexington."

"Then she'll find something else. Trust me, I know her. She won't let up."

"If you're that concerned, why didn't you call me right away?" I ask, unconvinced Kylie is a threat to anything. Madison turns away from me, annoyed with the audacity of my question. A rare Alpha Female, she hates having her decisions criticized or challenged. On this staff, only Roger or the congressman himself can get away with it.

"Madison, we don't need to worry about your sister." She scoffs, now even more annoyed that I don't appear to be taking her warning seriously. Which, of course, I'm not. "Look, we're going to win reelection in a walk, and the sky's the limit from there. Kylie may be bent on revenge, but it's nothing I can't handle."

And that's the truth. I am supremely confident I can defend against any attack Kylie Roberts launches on us. It's like the *Untouchables*. She puts one of ours in the hospital and we put one of hers in the morgue. I already proved I was capable of that, metaphorically speaking.

"You say that now."

Congressman Beaumont flies through the door in a rage. The man is rarely in a good mood in the morning, but when he is this pissed, it's going to make for a long day.

"Do you believe the balls that man has!" he exclaims to no one in particular. Roger trails behind him, shaking his head. "I've been to Wisconsin. Good people up there. Why they keep electing that blowhard is beyond me!"

"Don't let him get under your skin, sir. You know he is just posturing," Roger says, trying in vain to tame the beast.

"Well, we are going to see how effectively he postures when I cut him off at the knees," the congressman says, disappearing into his inner office, Roger in tow. The door closes, but our boisterous boss can still be heard through the thick wood.

"Trust me, Madison. There are far more powerful enemies out there to be concerned about than Kylie."

-FOURTEEN-
CHELSEA

Elated. If there was ever a word to describe how I felt over the last few days, that's it. The school year is finally over, and while I may not enjoy the beach, sports, and hanging out like most of my friends, summer is still my favorite time of year.

I like school, but this year was long and hard, and I need a break. Dad may have been on my case about studying too much and not having any fun, but the work paid off. Straight A grades, including one from the notoriously difficult Michael Bennit, would bring a smile to any teenager's face.

When we got the e-mail explaining the entire class did the impossible, I was stunned. I really didn't think we could pull it off, because let's be real, how many teachers would let that happen? Most would have shaved a few points off their least favorite student's score. I should have known better though. Mister Bennit is no ordinary teacher on any level.

It is a beautiful Saturday and the parking lot is jammed with cars at the Perkfect Buzz. From the number of Millfield High window stickers on them, I can see many of my peers are already here. Mister B called this gathering, but was pretty vague about the reason. Under normal circumstances, when someone who is no longer your teacher asks a class to show up someplace outside of school, the request is wholeheartedly ignored. But apparently I am not the only one who thinks Mister Bennit is no ordinary teacher.

I park and head inside. There are around seventeen students from my class occupying a whole corner of the café. Emilee, Brian, Peyton, Amanda, Vince, Vanessa, and Xavier are all here, armed with various sizes of caffeinated concoctions. There is not enough actual seating for everyone unless we evict the other patrons, so tables, the window sill, and even the floor have all been drafted into duty as seats. A couple of us stand, not liking the other options.

I get a coffee for myself and join my peers, enjoying the revelry of the moment when I notice Mister Bennit walk in. He appears different dressed in summer clothes than he does in school—still imposing with his military haircut and swagger, but somehow more real. It's probably taboo to even think this, but he really is a good-looking guy. Not the political type though. More like someone you'd expect to toss you out of a nightclub. Next to an army of politicians with their perfectly coiffed hair, manicured nails, and tailored suits, he would stick out like a sore thumb. This ought to be a fun campaign to watch.

He walks over to our giddy little crowd from the counter, coffee in hand. Brian hops off the table to make room for our fearless, and now beholden, leader.

"Well, you know why you're here. I hate you all," he says with a smile. At least he is being good natured about it.

"Told you we could do it," Emilee gloats.

"And you didn't believe us!" Brian sings out, reinforcing the message.

"Yes, thank you for reminding me, Brian," Mister B responds sarcastically. "In all seriousness, you should be proud of yourselves for your accomplishment. And don't fret about probably costing me my future marriage," he adds playfully.

"Was Miss Slater pissed?" I ask, more out of curiosity than actual concern. Miss Slater is well liked in school, but I have never really cared for her. She always strikes me as a little too proper and snobby. My friends say she tries to mimic Mister Bennit's teaching style, but doesn't pull it off nearly as well.

"Ever watch the movie *Alien*? She did a good impersonation of Riley."

That earns a little chuckle from Brian, whose adoration of sci-fi means he's the only one to get the reference, much less the joke. I join the class in trading blank stares of bewilderment.

"Okay, once again thank you for making me feel old."

"So, why are we all here, Mister B?" Vanessa asks. "We know you didn't bring us together to let us rub our brilliance in your face."

Mister Bennit smiles and takes a long sip on his latte and grins. That smile. I know that smile. It is unique to one purpose and one purpose only. He flashes it right before he is about to drop a bomb on us. During school, that bomb was an exam, essay, or something equally distasteful. What could it possibly mean now?

"You're right, I didn't. I thought today would be a good day to hold our first campaign staff meeting."

You could hear a pin drop. I'm stunned.

Xavier recovers first. "Say what?"

"You heard me, X."

"I'm sorry, my mind wandered. I thought you said something about a staff meeting," Vince says in a mock bewildered tone.

"Your ADHD aside, Vince, you heard me right for once," Mister B deadpans.

"You like, want us to work on your campaign?" Peyton asks, still struggling with the moment.

"No, not just work on it. I want you all to run my campaign." He emphasized *run*. He can't be serious.

"You can't be serious," Amanda dismisses. Well said. She took the words right out of my mouth.

Mister Bennit takes another sip of his latte. His face has a smile, but his eyes betray him. Oh my God, he is dead serious about this.

"Why?" I ask.

"I have my reasons."

"Are you going to share them?"

"Not right now, no," he proclaims, ending the line of questioning.

I'm angry, but I am not sure why. We should have known this was coming. This is Mister Bennit, after all. He can turn anything into a lesson.

Maybe I think that if we say no, he will use it as an excuse not to run. It would explain why I'm angry. If he tries to bail, it will shatter my opinion of him.

"What do we get out of it?" Xavier asks. At least he is considering the possibility. Looking around the café, it's obvious several of my classmates are not at all interested. They are only still here out of respect. The rest of us are curious, although no one gives the impression of being excited at the prospect.

"You will be managers and staffers for a candidate running for the United States House of Representatives. That is something you can staple to every college application you fill out this fall."

"That's not much incentive for us to give up our summer." Brian may not have much of a social life, but he has a good point.

"Or the fall of our senior year," Emilee adds.

"This wasn't part of our deal." There was an edge to my voice I didn't intend to be there. Sometimes I struggle controlling my emotions and right now, it's noticeable anger. Fortunately, the nodding heads of my peers indicate they all agree.

"When you all challenged me to this bet, you said you wanted to see if I could walk the walk. Well, now it's your turn." Mister Bennit pauses to look us all in the eyes. Then he turns his attention directly on me, and I suddenly feel … I don't know. Guilty?

"Chelsea, all you ever talk about is how you want to grow, and learn, and change the world. Here's your chance." I avert my eyes. He's right.

"Vince!" Vince's head snaps up. "You play the apathetic teenager, then whine about how nobody takes you seriously. Make a choice. Do you want to be the slacker, or find out what people really think when you are the one standing at a podium?"

Michael leans over to Peyton who is seated to his side. "Peyton, you are going to be Homecoming Queen. You are going to be Prom Queen. But tell me, isn't what you really want just the opportunity to prove to everyone that you are more than just a pretty face?

"Brian, you rail about how society doesn't understand the power of technology. Can you think of a better way to show them what you mean? Or are you just content complaining about it on Facebook?" To his credit, Brian actually maintained eye contact with Mister Bennit. It was a losing battle for most of us, me included.

"You all wanted to be challenged this past year. That was why you ended up in my class. And during the year, we spent a lot of time talking about the men and women in history who made sacrifices to accomplish great things. Do you have what it takes to follow in their footsteps? Or is your summer and senior year too valuable?" He addresses Brian and Emilee, but I know his comment was intended for the larger audience. "I guess we'll see."

Mister Bennit slides off the table and takes a few steps before turning back. None of us have moved. He looks directly at me. "I will uphold my end of the bargain regardless of your decisions." Great, now embarrassment is the new emotion sweeping over me.

"But I cannot do this by myself," he says, now appealing to the group of us. "I can't hire people to help. I live on a teacher's salary, and all of my disposable income goes into buying coffee at this place."

"Thank you!" Laura yells from behind the counter. She hears everything, even when she doesn't appear to be listening.

"I am asking you all for your help. Take some time to think about it. If you're in, meet me here, same time next Saturday. If not, no hard feelings and I will catch most of you in class in September." With that, I watch Mister Bennit put on his ultra-cool Oakley sunglasses and walk out of the shop.

Did he really just ask us to help run a campaign? I shouldn't be surprised—this is Mister Bennit, after all. While most teachers can't wait to get away from us for a couple of months over the summer, he is asking for us to work with him.

My classmates begin quietly chatting with each other. Most are on the fence about what to do. I can't say I blame them, but for better or for worse, I have already made my decision.

-FIFTEEN-
BLAKE

I can get used to the life of the well-established Washington elite. I put my fork down after my last bite of the most perfectly aged and cooked piece of cow I have ever sunk my teeth into. It's a magical Tuesday evening of steak, fine wine, and a seat at the table with a political wizard and one of the most powerful men in Washington. What could be better than that?

"Did you hear what happened during Johnson's campaign announcement?" Roger asks.

"No, what?" the congressman responds in a half-chuckle. The combination of a fine meal and the brilliant political planning that accompanied it has put him in a considerably good mood.

"The audio cut out on his microphone. He was a third of the way through before he noticed," Roger exclaims after losing his battle to suppress a devious smile.

The congressman laughs heartily. "Did we plan that or was it just dumb luck?"

"I wouldn't bother wasting my time sabotaging a campaign that isn't going anywhere, Winston."

"I didn't think the Republicans would cede victory quite so easily." Congressman Beaumont is clearly pleased with the prospect of an easy election in the fall. He has a huge monetary war chest saved up for a demanding campaign, but every election he manages to save it makes the next one more secure. Money is the lifeblood of elections, because if you can outspend the other guy, your chance of winning increases exponentially. That's the nature of contemporary American politics.

A waiter stops at the table to refill our wine glasses and departs. Roger looks at me, and then waits until the server is out of earshot before speaking in a hushed tone.

"Honestly, Winston, I am surprised they are too, given the allegations the conservative media leveled against you."

Winston points a finger at his longtime ally. "They have nothing on me. It's all your typical unsubstantiated right-wing bloviating. No respectable organization picked it up."

"Sir, that's only because of Blake's tip and getting that *Times* reporter canned before anything got printed."

"Blake, I thought you said she didn't have much?" the congressman asks, his eyes boring into me.

"She didn't, sir, but she was on the right track. Somehow she knew you took money from the Lexington Group, but didn't have enough to prove it."

Beaumont pulls the napkin off his lap and dabs the corners of his mouth. "There is nothing that exists that links me to the Lexington Group." I fight hard to not smile. That isn't entirely true.

Most people will say you can't put a price on loyalty. Hell yeah you can, it's called security, and I own the ultimate insurance policy. As long as Roger and the congressman are loyal to me, those documents will stay secure and never see the light of day.

"There is always a paper trail, Winston. Always. Even when you don't think there is." The hard look Roger gives the congressman makes him a little uncomfortable. Believe me, this is a rare moment, to say the least.

"I pay you, and him for that matter," the congressman says pointing at me, "to ensure that is not the case. If there is, in fact, some mysterious paper trail left behind, then find it and destroy it. I am counting on you, and even Blake here, to ensure nothing gets out that can harm us."

"Of course, Winston," Roger concedes.

"Yes, sir," I say at the same time.

"Good. Let Fox News and the idiot bloggers say what they want. My approval rating is higher than ever and even if it drops a few points, we should have no problem coasting into a ninth term. Just keep a lid on the important press. You have already done a good job with that, Blake." Winston tips his glass toward me in a rare compliment.

Any lingering doubt I had about destroying Madison's sister's career vanished in this instant. This is a Machiavellian world where the ends justify the means, and now I have a seat at the table. I may still hold the position of a very junior level staffer, but now I have the ear of the congressman himself. And as Roger's go-to guy, it won't be long before I am out of my corner desk and sitting at Deena's. At least, what would be Deena's old desk. I smile at the thought.

"We will, Congressman," Roger says, holding his wine glass up in a toast. "To a ninth term, and even better things to follow."

Congressman Beaumont tips his own glass and smiles broadly at Roger. "Nothing will stop us from winning in a walk."

I follow suit. Nothing will stop me either.

-SIXTEEN-
MICHAEL

I sit staring out the window in the same corner of the coffee shop I did a week ago. That day was bright and shining, but today is a better reflection of my mood—dark and dreary. And now it has even started to rain.

I arrived for the appointment with my old American History class forty-five minutes early, figuring I could pass the time behind this laptop and scribbling notes on a yellow legal pad. I have been teaching history for three years, and been interested in it for three decades. And the one thing I learned is, despite my knowledge of politics and the people elected, I don't know anything about how to campaign or run for office. And I mean nothing.

I scan the room again before looking at my watch for the hundredth time. They should have been here fifteen minutes ago. Maybe I am kidding myself. Jessica thought I was a fool to even think they would be on board with this, but like the Pied Piper of Hamelin, I played my tune and hoped they would follow. Well, not to their deaths, so maybe this metaphor doesn't really work. Regardless, it looks like I was wrong again and will face the blunt end of Jess's "I told you so" speech.

I frown and return to my notes. Fundraising, petitions, advertising, and a message are all things you need to reach voters. I guess that's why everyone who runs for national office has personal wealth, connections, comes from a prominent family, or all of those traits combined.

As a high school history teacher, I certainly am not wealthy. Any teacher will tell you they didn't choose their occupation for the money. I also have absolutely no connections that are of any use in an election. Fundraising is also pointless since nobody in their right mind would give money to a guy with no track record in politics.

The only thing I can do is craft a message nobody will hear. I need media support, but only mainstream candidates from the two political parties ever get coverage. They set up the rules, and the career politicians honed this game down to a science. If I try to play it, I'm going to get killed.

I tear off the page of the pad, crumple it and toss it on the ground at my feet. This is stupid. I close my laptop in frustration and look up just in time to see a welcome sight. Chelsea, Peyton, Xavier, Brian, Vince, Emilee, Vanessa, and Amanda all walk over and stand in front of me like a phalanx.

"Did you guys carpool or something?"

"Something like that," Vanessa says.

"We actually met before we came here. We had some stuff to talk about," Vince offers in the most serious mafia-like tone I have ever heard him use. Maybe that is stereotyping a touch, but that's what it sounded like.

"Like what?" I ask innocently.

"Like whether we are crazy for thinking about helping with this," Amanda defiantly states.

"Well? Are you crazy enough?" I lean back in the chair, bracing for what I expect to be bad news. Amanda's tone didn't inspire a whole lot of confidence that they were buying tickets for this particular trip.

"It depends on how far you plan on taking it," Emilee says. I give a slight nod, but keep listening. I am not sure how to respond because, at this point, I'm not sure myself.

"We spent a year listening to you talk about never half-assing anything. So we don't want to do all this work just for you not to give it your all and live with getting killed in November."

"I understand." Nothing more I can say to that. Giving it my all or not, getting killed in November is a near certainty.

"Mister B, how can eight of us possibly do this? Don't people running for Congress have huge staffs?" Vanessa asks.

"I mean, like, none of us know anything about campaigning." Peyton is dead on. What she doesn't know is I have no idea either. Best not to admit that yet.

"She's right," Amanda says, looking at Peyton. "We don't know anything. I, like, don't really know what you expect us to do."

"I'm all about helping, Mister B, but I just don't want to waste my summer." Xavier is an athlete and is always training or practicing. I am not surprised, nor do I blame him for worrying about this being a futile exercise. Their insecurities are to be expected because I am having the same ones. But it is time to stop stalling.

"I understand your concerns. The truth is, I have no idea either."

"Well, that's encouraging."

"I know it isn't, Brian," I say, his sarcasm obvious. "You may all be teenagers, but I'm only a history teacher. We are all working on the same learning curve and we'll figure it out together. As for wasting your summers, whether this proves to be worth it will be up to each of you."

I reach into my laptop carrier on the floor and pull out a small stack of papers. I hand each student a sheet and wait until they read them.

"Permission slips?" Chelsea asks incredulously.

"Of a sort, yes. If your parents don't sign it, you don't participate. Do not pass go, do not collect two hundred dollars."

"You can't be serious," Xavier says.

"I'm dead serious. Name an extracurricular activity you participate in that doesn't require one."

"This isn't school," Amanda states.

"No, it's worse. It's a political campaign. Your parents must be okay with you being involved in this. Not to mention this is going to take up a lot of your time that could be devoted to academics and applying to colleges."

"What's this part about maintaining a B average?" Peyton asks, pointing to the permission slip.

"Self-explanatory, Peyton. You are all honors students so I know you can handle it." Most of these kids are straight A students, or at least close to it. I didn't think that would be controversial. They continue to read through the permission slip, making various faces at parts they don't like, but saying nothing.

"These are the rules of the game, guys. You are all volunteering to do this, so if you don't like them, don't play." And that's when it hits me. "If you don't like the rules, don't play," I mumble to myself. The idea washes over me like a tsunami of pure inspiration, and I suddenly know how we can do this. The students pocket their slips and wait for me to say something more, but I'm lost in thought.

"So, now what?" one of them asks. I am not really sure who.

"Get those signed and meet me at nine a.m. tomorrow at Briar Point. Try to be on time," I say as if on autopilot.

"We're not starting now?" Chelsea asks eagerly.

"Not yet. I have to work something out first." With that, I open my laptop and start typing like a madman. They all talk amongst themselves for a minute, but I am not acutely aware of what they are saying. I look up just in time to see them heading for the door.

"Hey, guys," I call out to them, causing them to turn. "Thanks for coming." I smile, a gesture that is returned, and I get back to work. After all, if you want to change the rules, you have to understand them first.

-SEVENTEEN-
CHELSEA

It is a beautiful mid-June day. We should really be hanging out with friends, or baking on a beach. Instead, we are poring over notes at a picnic table, trying to figure out how to start a campaign. We decided as a group to get here early, so when Mister Bennit showed up we could present something resembling a plan. After all, I think that's what he's expecting. But after an hour or two, the only thing we manage to accomplish is increasing our frustration. And now I have reached my limit.

"There is no way we can make this work," I exclaim to Mister Bennit as he walks up.

"Good morning to you too, Chelsea," he replies, much too cheerily for any Monday morning. Summer vacation or not, we know he is well caffeinated from a trip to the Perkfect Buzz to be in this good a mood. "Hit a little snag in the grand plan, have you?"

"That's, like, a major understatement," Peyton opines.

"We have no money for advertising, no experience in, well, any of this, and unless you plan on quitting teaching, no time to meet voters," Brian sums up with dissatisfaction.

"We can't run a campaign like this," I state. And we can't. There is no possible way to compete against a sitting member of the House with nothing. And the fact Mister Bennit is smiling at this makes me even more frustrated and annoyed. My head is starting to hurt.

"It is far worse than you think, guys," Mister Bennit says, claiming a seat at the picnic table. "You also have to look at who we are up against. Winston Beaumont has been in politics about as long as you have been alive. From what I've read, he's ruthless, and the only person in Washington more politically savvy than him happens to be running his campaign. He has millions of dollars to spend on everything from advertising to opposition research. He has the resources to do a ton of polling and an army of people to customize his message into something every voter wants to hear."

"We really need to work on your motivation skills," Amanda deadpans as we all remain silent, struggling for something to say.

This is hopeless. Even if Mister Bennit were the world's greatest motivational speaker, nothing could change that feeling. I'm sure that's the emotion all over my face because it is over all our faces. After a moment, Vince, of all people, speaks up.

"We can't beat him."

"No, Vince, we can't. At least not at his game," Mister Bennit says with a hint of a smile.

"What do you mean?" Emilee asks.

Mister Bennit pauses, takes a sip of what is sure to be a gazillion-shot latte, and looks at each one of us. "Tell me, how do you beat Bobby Fischer at chess?" We all look at each other. Who the hell is Bobby Fischer?

"No, don't say it," Vanessa tries to warn.

"Who's Bobby Fischer?' Amanda asks at the same time, beating me to the punch.

"Cue this morning's lesson," Vince laments.

"He's a master chess player who ... Okay, you know what, it's not important. If you were to sit down and play a game with a chess master, how would you beat him?"

You can't beat him unless you are really, really lucky. Not likely though. You simply don't beat a chess master at chess.

"You don't. Unless ..." I stop mid-sentence.

"Unless?" he says, encouraging me to finish my thought.

"Unless you are playing Candyland." I smile, enjoying the rare moment when I get his point before he makes it.

"Huh?" Vince asks, dumbfounded.

"I don't get it," Peyton adds, even more frustrated now.

"I do," I say. "If you can't beat them at their game, make them play ours."

"Exactly. There are two conventional wisdoms in campaign politics. Spend a lot of money and smear your opponent by going negative early and often. Well, we can't compete in the money arena and I won't go negative. We need to change the game. Don't play chess with Winston Beaumont the chess master ..."

"Play Candyland with him," Vanessa finishes, now getting with the program. She smiles along with me, but the others are not sold.

"But that's a child's game!" Vince announces, exasperated and still unconvinced. "Why would a chess master play anything other than chess?"

"Because he has no choice," Brian says, now joining the ranks of the enlightened. "If we refuse to play his game, he has to play ours."

I'm not completely sold on that being the case, but I go with it. Most likely he would ignore us, unless we give him a reason not to. And I am having a hard time coming up with a scenario where a powerful sitting congressman would bother.

"But what's our game? Do we even know?" Xavier brings up a good point, prompting us all to look to the soon-to-be candidate for support.

"We run the first modern-era front porch campaign." Mister Bennit looks at each of our faces, all caught in expressions ranging from baffled to thoroughly confused. "Let me explain," he adds.

"*Now* here comes today's history lesson," Emilee says wryly.

"In 1896, William McKinley ran a campaign with the help of an Ohio business tycoon named Mark Hanna. While his opponent traveled 18,000 miles by railroad, McKinley gave most of his speeches right from his front porch."

"Do you ever stop teaching?" Vince asks, exasperated.

"Do you even have a front porch?" I ask rhetorically, or not.

"Didn't McKinley get assassinated?" Amanda asks, grinning.

Mister Bennit exhales deeply. "No, Vince, I don't. No Chels, I don't have a porch, but that's not the point. And yes, Amanda, he did. Let's hope we have a better result. My point is, we don't need to travel, or campaign, or make big speeches. We get the people to come to us."

We all look at each other and fall into a fit of laughter. A little later in the summer and I might think Mister Bennit had spent too much time in the sun or something. "Gee, here I was thinking this was going to be hard!" I say, exercising my sarcastic streak.

"I may be having a blonde moment, but like, how do we get people to come to listen to speeches when, on a good day, only like fifty percent even vote?" Peyton asks innocently.

She brings up a good point, and we all look up at our teacher for an answer once again. He obliges with that smile we all love to hate. "It's the twenty-first century. There is more than one way to reach out and touch someone. Right, Brian?"

"The world has the iPhone, iPad, and iTunes," Brian states with a knowing smile. "Why not give it the iCandidate?"

I watch as Peyton reaches for a yellow legal pad and jots down iCandidate. It is not a horrible idea. But not a completely unique one either.

"Okay, I get it. You want to run a campaign on the Internet, but every other candidate does the same thing," I add.

"That's true, they do. So let's take it a step further. We're going to campaign exclusively using the Internet and social media. No speeches, no fundraisers, no shaking hands, and definitely no kissing babies. This will be the country's first virtual campaign."

"The new front porch," Vanessa states.

"Exactly."

"Okay, that's unique. But how will anybody notice us if all we are running is a campaign online?" Emilee asks.

"We make it go viral," Brian offers.

-EIGHTEEN-
MICHAEL

Of course, wanting any effort to go viral takes more than just a desire to. If that were the case, every corporation, charity, student organization, and attention-seeker in America would be household names because of what people see on YouTube. While such things may work for a Marine trying to land a date with Mila Kunis, dynamite surfing, or even something called planking, the only politician anyone can remotely say it worked for was Obama in 2008. But I let the students figure out how to do it. I have a good feeling whatever they came up with would work.

"Faculty don't report back for another four days, Michael. I hope you're not working on lesson plans already," a sweet voice says from in front of me.

"Chalice!" I get up and give her a big hug. While I am not eager for the summer to be over, I do miss seeing her and my other colleagues. "And, just for the record, I don't believe for a second you hope I'm not working on lesson plans. How was your summer?"

"Short, like always. Yours?"

"Oh, flew by like a movie montage."

"Does that have something to do with following through on your ill-advised bet?" she says, grinning.

"How did you know?" I ask, mystified. Not that I should be. Chalice seems to know everything about her faculty, whether it is summer or not. I offer her the seat across from me, which she accepts.

"Facebook, I think. Or maybe it was from some website called *The iCandidate.*"

It figures that was where she picked up on it. As the resident computer guy, Brian was the mastermind behind the digital launch of the iCandidate. Facebook, Google Plus, Twitter, Reddit, Tumblr, and Pinterest accounts were created, as was a YouTube channel. He even created a website called *www.icandidate.org.*

Enlisting the help of some friends, they created one database to track volunteers and another to track donors, should we ever get any. If that wasn't enough heavy lifting, he organized every tech geek in the school to create a means to host web chats, answer e-mails, and do essentially everything else an online campaign would be expected to do. The whole effort has been run from the cozy confines of the Perkfect Buzz. Thank God I've been one of Laura's best customers for years.

"I swear, nothing ever gets past you," I tell her with a laugh.

"So you actually made it on the ballot?"

The most pressing concern following our staff's Briar Point meeting was getting on the ballot. It required 7,500 signatures and a completed application be submitted to the Connecticut

Secretary of State. The application was the easy part. The signatures, well, not so much. Chelsea got the nod as the campaign manager, so it fell on her to organize the effort and make the magic happen.

"Yep. I really wasn't sure Chelsea could pull it off, but she doesn't do anything halfway. Something she was quick to remind me of when she slapped 7,737 signatures down in less than a week." Lucky, because when we met in June, we only had two weeks to get everything in. We still wouldn't have made the deadline if some administrative error hadn't forced Connecticut to change it from the second to the fourth Tuesday in June.

"That's impressive," Chalice says sincerely. "What do you have the rest of them doing?"

"Well, Amanda was appointed the Minister of Campaign Finance." While trusting a teenager with accounting responsibilities that will land a candidate in prison if they go wrong may sound insane, well, it probably is. But Amanda is a numbers girl and can tell you the balance of any of her bank accounts to the penny.

"Yeah, that makes sense."

"She was less than thrilled when I told her donations were restricted to $100 from donors, and even more so when I placed a $10 maximum for students."

"I can't imagine this virtual campaign of yours will need much money anyway. Who else?"

"I have Emilee, Vanessa, and Xavier in charge of marketing." They are in charge of the message, which I admit contains nothing of substance. That was the source of a lot of frustration as the summer began to fade and now that our announcement date looms closer.

"Did Vince sign on?"

"Media relations," I say, eliciting a raised eyebrow from Chalice in response. I gave Vince the most ambitious responsibility of all the students. He may come across as a goofy slacker, but he's a spin artist, very articulate when he wants to be, and in my estimation, the best person to be the face of the campaign for the media.

"That's a little crazy, but crazy has always worked for you. When is your official announcement?"

"We scheduled the online press conference for tomorrow, actually." A late-August date was my choice, and I still think it was the right one. If we can build up a viral social media campaign for Congress, it has to be sustainable. Start too early and it fizzles before Election Day, even in a non-presidential election year. Too late and you don't have enough momentum to make a dent against the incumbent.

"Well, Howell ought to love that," she says with a wry smile.

"Eh, he hates me anyway. Howell's objections I can handle, but I want to know what you think, Chalice." I have always found her hard to read, and today is no exception.

"I think I admire you for following through on this. You are a man of your word, and nobody can say otherwise. I'm in awe you inspired a group of students to give up their summer to work on this with you." She hesitates, taking a moment to look down at her tea.

"But?" I ask, knowing the other shoe is about to drop.

"But," she says with a slight smile, "you're a teacher first. I don't worry about this impacting your performance in the classroom, but I will be the minority. You are also opening yourself up to a lot of grief from parents and the administration once you make this announcement. I hope you're ready for that."

All I can do is nod.

"What does Jessica think about all this?"

My face gives away my answer. While Jessica has been somewhat understanding about the time I have spent on this over the summer, she has been far from my biggest cheerleader. She never wanted me to follow through on the bet, and that hasn't changed one bit over the past two months.

"I thought so," Chalice says, rising from her chair. "I wish you the best of luck on your announcement tomorrow, Michael. You know you I will support you and have already earned my vote, but please, be careful with all this."

-NINETEEN-
CHELSEA

The whole approach we laid out this summer was a gamble, and the source of the moment's frustration. It is also the reason why we are huddled around our cars in the parking lot of the Perkfect Buzz right now. Vince was never cool with Mister B making him responsible for dealing with the press, and his meltdown once we logged off from our online announcement showed everyone his confidence hasn't grown any.

As we all stand silently in search of something to say, I decide to try to break the long silence. "Well, at least there wasn't too much media actually covering that."

"Two months of work trying to get noticed. I'd hardly call that a bright spot, Chelsea!" Vanessa fumes in frustration.

"How do we get our message out if we can't even get people to listen? We can't make this go viral if nobody has seen the website and no real press showed up at the announcement which was a train wreck anyway." Emilee is on the reserved side for a teenage girl, and even she is outspoken right now.

Train wreck may be one of the most overused statements in America. Very few people have seen one, and I'm not one of them. But it may be the best way I know to describe what happened.

"Look, guys, nobody said this would be easy," I console, feeling as campaign manager I am supposed to stay optimistic.

"Nobody said it would be this hard either," Vanessa snaps back.

"So much for making a difference. We're only kidding ourselves," Emilee laments quietly.

"Is anybody else getting the feeling we like, just completely wasted our summer?" Peyton's observation hangs over the group.

Nobody agrees with her, but at the same time, they don't disagree either. I look at Mister Bennit, hoping he will launch into one of his motivational talks, because I can't come up with anything. I know as bad as things were for the announcement, they are only bound to get better. He looks as if he is about to say something when Vince comes storming over to the rest of us.

"Damn it!" Vince shouts as he violently kicks the front fender of his Subaru. "Damn, damn, damn! Stupid!" He starts mumbling to himself, but I can't really decipher what he is saying. He slams his fists on the hood one final time before collapsing against it. At least he stops taking his frustration out on his poor car. It doesn't look capable of taking much more abuse after enduring a couple of years with Vince as the owner.

"You done with your tantrum, Vince?" Mister B asks, trying to diffuse the tirade and failing.

"I, uh ... I blew it."

"Yes, you did. But you didn't swear once, so there was at least one victory."

"Actually, Mister B, I think he did," Xavier offers. Not helpful, X, not helpful at all.

"What am I supposed to say when reporters ask where you stand on the issues when you have no stance? I got killed because you're running a virtual campaign and not taking a side on what matters!" Vince practically yells. "But yeah, thanks for reminding me I suck. I couldn't even handle the local online news site that even bothered to cover this."

"Are you blaming me for that?" Vanessa shouts, moving toward Vince. I hear Emilee and Amanda start protesting as well. They worked hard this summer, and are taking Vince's comment very personally. I might too if I were in their shoes.

"Well, if you had—" Mister Bennit doesn't give Vince a chance to finish his statement. Part of being a teacher is conflict resolution. When everyone is stressed out, tempers flare and personalities can clash. We are a pretty strong-willed group, so any more drama could turn this into a *Real Housewives of New Jersey* reunion show. It would also spell the end of the campaign if it gets too far out of hand.

"Stop! Both of you! All of you!" Mister Bennit shouts, immediately bringing silence to the group. Vince and Vanessa back down, and he commands everyone's undivided attention. I rarely hear him raise his voice, something most of my classmates find shocking, given his military background.

"All of you listen like you have never listened before. Saint Francis of Assisi once said, 'Start by doing what is necessary; then do what is possible; and suddenly you are doing the impossible.'"

"When did you find religion, Mister B?" Peyton asks with a hint of sarcasm.

"There are no atheists in foxholes, Peyton. And we are all in the same foxhole right now."

"Are we?" Vince questions. "Because I don't think we are all even on the same page. We want to take a stand and do what's necessary to win. But you won't let us run that campaign. Now we're a joke."

"Vince, if a tree falls in the woods, and nobody is there to hear it, is it really worth arguing with people whether it makes a sound or not?" Mister B says while studying our defeated faces. We ran things the way we wanted over the summer, but now I get the feeling our mentor is about to step in and set some expectations.

"Remember what we said at Briar Point?" he continues. "We have to change the game. Now, it doesn't matter whether we're pro-life or pro-choice, or for bigger or smaller government. Whatever we say, mark my words, will be spun by and used against us. Winston Beaumont could make Mother Teresa seem like an exploiter and an opportunist.

"We agreed we would have to change the game or we'd lose. That started today with what happened in there. Press conferences are their thing, not ours. Luckily we don't have to do one again."

"Are you kidding, Mister B? What happened in there was that I was terrible. Is that what you wanted?" Vince asks out of frustration. He is not listening to what Mister Bennit is saying.

"Vince, stop trying to be the White House press secretary and just be you. That is why I gave you the job. I just need you to be you."

"Maybe you shouldn't have. Maybe I'm not cut out for this job."

"Vince, I know you're doubting yourself, but I'm not. I got killed in there too. You are taking this way too personally."

"Forget it, Mister B, I'm done," Vince says as he climbs in his car and slams the door. We all watch him go before the others on the staff say good-byes of their own. Mister Bennit watches each one of them leave, saying nothing.

By the time he turns around to face me, a lone tear is running down my cheek. I'm fighting valiantly to hold my emotions in, but it's a losing battle. It's hard to stay strong when it feels like the world is crashing down around me.

"I'm sorry I let you down, Mister B," is all I can mutter.

"You haven't let me down once since the day you were just a scared freshman who wandered into my classroom. Today didn't change that, Chels."

"We planned all summer. I never guessed it would be this hard," I lament, looking down at the asphalt to avoid his eyes. "Or end this way."

I feel Mister Bennit give me a little squeeze on the shoulder. I'm surprised at the gesture because he avoids hugs, or any kind of affection with female students. I'm sure he worries how they will interpret it, or for that matter, how others will. But in this situation, I could use a hug. I will settle for a reassuring squeeze, though.

"I'm not sure it's over yet, Chelsea. Everything is hard before it's easy. There's a good chance the fire hasn't gone completely out on this campaign yet. We just need a spark to rekindle it."

-TWENTY-

KYLIE

"Hello?" I ask, groggy from the escapades of whatever dream I was just rudely awakened from.

"You near a computer? I sent you a link." I reach for my phone and see it is 6:07 in the morning. Being an early riser was a requirement of my old job, but I'm not a morning person. Since being fired months ago, waking up before eight or nine a.m. has been a rare occurrence.

"Bill? Jesus, do you know what time it is?"

"Yeah, time to rise and shine. You are going to want to read this," he says.

"Okay, at least give me the highlights while I open it," I respond, groping for the laptop I'm sure is at the foot of my bed somewhere. With no boyfriend in the picture, the small computer is the only thing I share a bed with these days. Finding it teetering precariously a mere inch from the edge of the mattress, I open the top and screen comes to life.

"Someone entered the race against Winston Beaumont as an Independent," Bill deadpans.

"You woke me up for that?" I ask, disgusted. "Some retread cast out of his party and making a run at a firmly entrenched incumbent is hardly worth calling me for this early."

"You open the link yet?"

"Page is loading now," I sigh, trying to stifle a yawn.

The browser opens to an article posted last night by an online news site in the Danbury, Connecticut, area. Not a well-written product, but easy enough to conclude the author thinks this campaign is some sort of joke. He doesn't write a single complimentary thing about the candidate or his election effort. Even caffeine-deprived, I am starting to see why Bill thought I may find this interesting though.

"He's a teacher?"

"A teacher whose *students* are running his campaign," I hear Bill point out, almost amused. "Either they don't know what they are getting into mixing it up with Beaumont, or just don't care."

"Wait! Does this say what I think it does?"

"You talking about the virtual front porch campaign? Yeah, but the writer doesn't offer much of an explanation."

I reread the article in case I missed something, which I didn't. Whoever wrote this sorry excuse for a story didn't spend a second more covering the press conference than needed. Probably a recent college grad, he adopted the "write, submit, and move onto the next, hopefully more interesting assignment" mantra. It happens all the time in journalism, especially on crappy sites like this.

"No, they don't, but I think I know where they are going with this," I say with a smile.

"What does that mean?" Bill asks.

"It means I need to track down this Vince Orsini kid and find out. Thanks for the heads-up, Bill."

"Sure. Good luck," he says before disconnecting the call.

* * *

Two hours later, I'm heading north on the Hutchinson River Parkway toward the small Connecticut town of Millfield. After losing my job, I almost got rid of this little Honda Accord to save some money. Living on the island of Manhattan, there is no real need to own a car considering the mass transit options. Parking in the city can be pricey, but as I hurl north, I'm glad I decided against that particular cost-cutting measure.

Locating Vince Orsini, or at least where he lives, was laughably easy. It only took a few minutes to get a street address, so I dedicated a little time finding out what I could about him. Not much was available, but that's expected for a teenager. The bigger surprise was the dearth of information on his teacher, Michael Bennit.

Only two media outlets, if you can call them that, picked up on his campaign announcement. The rest of my findings showcased his various activities in the school and community. From what I discovered, he is both active and well liked. There was a clipping from an article that announced something he did in the Army, but the caption was light on details and made no mention of his position or unit.

I also checked out a couple of "rate my teacher" pages where students get to either praise or lambast them for the world to see. I'm no expert, but a ninety-seven percent positive rating has to be phenomenally good. I thought I would see comments about how easy and chummy he is, but was shocked to read the exact opposite. The phrases most students used to describe him included things like "tough, but fair" and "incredibly hard."

My last bit of investigating involved a quick background check which yielded nothing of interest. I showered and dressed, thinking I could not understand why this guy would run for a national office. I only scratched the surface during my fifteen minutes of research, but there was zilch that led me to believe he was a political creature. He doesn't have the connections, pedigree, a particular cause or ax to grind, and neither the money nor the free time to run for the U.S. House of Representatives. Town council I could see, but what is driving this crusade is a mystery.

It's just before lunch when I pull into the obscenely small parking lot belonging to the Millfield Public Library and look for an unoccupied spot. I find one, which surprises me because there are only a dozen stalls serving a building this big. Either people park on another street or this place is flat out empty while the residents of the town enjoy the last vestiges of the summer heat.

Turns out to be the latter, because the spacious library is relatively still, with only two people at the bank of computer terminals and a couple of others reading. A mother stands at the book checkout with her young son and daughter, as a librarian scans out a pile of children's books. I survey the main room and find no one in their teenage years anywhere to be found.

I stopped by the Orsini residence when I got to town and Vince's mom, intent on keeping her garden from wilting under the late-August sun, told me I would find him here. To say I found that highly unlikely is an exercise in understatement. More likely, he told his mom he was coming here to avoid a litany of questions from the parental units, as teenagers are prone to do every so often.

I am about to give up the search when I notice a young man seated in a plush chair in the far corner near the magazine racks. He is buried in a paperback novel, feet propped up on a matching chair across from him. Bingo.

"Hello," I say as I stop next to him.

"Hey." That's all I get from him after a quick once-over with his eyes. I must be showing all thirty years of my age these days. He turns back to his book, so I stick my hand out in the way we obnoxious journalists do when we're not done with a conversation.

"I'm Kylie Roberts."

"Vince," he states, shaking my outstretched hand halfheartedly. "Look, I hate to be rude, but I'm not really in the mood to talk." And with that, he goes back to reading his fiction thriller, or at least pretending to.

"I thought it would be hard for you to find time for pleasure reading, you know, while helping run a congressional campaign."

Vince's head snaps around in surprise so fast I half expect it to break right off his neck and roll across the floor. At least I have his attention now, and am not going to share it with whatever teenage fantasy novel he's reading.

"I'm not exactly involved in the campaign ... Who did you say you were again?"

"Kylie Roberts. I'm a freelance political columnist who used to work for the *New York Times*." Yeah, I still name-drop from time to time. "I'd like to learn a little more about your candidate and his staff if you have a moment. That is, unless you're not involved anymore."

"No, I can help you," he says, perking up a bit.

"Great! And I'd like to meet Michael Bennit as well."

"Sorry, that you can't do." Vince frowns. "At least, not yet."

"I don't understand, why not?" I'm genuinely perplexed. I would expect to be welcomed with open arms considering his campaign has no traction with the media.

"Miss Roberts, he's the iCandidate. I'm sure he'll grant you an interview, but not in person," Vince says to me, smiling now. "But that's why they invented videoconferencing." I get it. If you are going to run a virtual campaign, you might as well go all the way with it.

For the next two hours, I squeeze Vince like an orange for all the background information I can. He was remarkably forthcoming for someone who is the public face of a campaign, providing as much detail as he could on himself, the other students on the staff, and Michael Bennit. He probably gave me too much information. After bleeding Vince dry of information, we got the iCandidate himself on video chat and it was nothing like I expected.

On the drive home, everything I had learned over the last few hours swirls inside my head. The students seem amazing, and their teacher even more so. He's handsome, intelligent, articulate, manly, a decorated soldier, and dare I say, a good candidate. I may not agree with his not wanting to address issues, but I do understand why, at least in the short-term.

Where he lacks in solid positions he makes up for in patriotism and dedication to the spirit of what America really is. It is the message that will best distinguish him in every way from a scumbag like Winston Beaumont. The honorable newcomer with no money and a small staff of teenagers battles against the ultimate corrupt incumbent who commands a massive staff and war chest of political riches. It's the ultimate underdog story. Scratch that, it's the ultimate American story, one I know I can sell.

Freelancing has allowed me the time to touch base with dozens of my contacts, and in a few days, I can hand them all a feel good story. Midterm elections are not renowned for high drama, and mainstream media will be scampering for stories to keep viewers tuned in and papers selling. Hell, with a well-worded threat or two to my former editor, maybe even by my old employer. Yes, I can make this happen.

"Watch out, Winston Beaumont, you are about to meet the iCandidate," I say to myself, laughing. I hope my sister is well rested, because when I pull the lid off this, she will need all the energy she can muster. I have enough material for a series of stories, each one stoking the fire until it grows into a raging inferno. Yes, I can make this happen. For the first time in months, I feel a genuine smile creep across my lips.

-TWENTY-ONE-
MICHAEL

The Friday before school starts is reserved for faculty preparation. It is the time allotted to have meetings with our departments, get classrooms organized, and otherwise prepare for the start of another school year. Since the campaign disbanded, for lack of a better word, following the disastrous press event last week, I had the time to get my lesson plans ready. With those done, the only unfinished business left is setting up the classroom.

Preparation activities means casual dress is allowed for the faculty, evidenced by the normally formal Chalice Ramsey wearing blue jeans. Of course, whereas she is dressed in a more business-looking top, I am wearing a simple T-shirt. At least I won't get scolded until tomorrow when I wear roughly the same thing.

I write the words "Welcome Back!" in big, bold letters with a dry-erase marker on the whiteboard in the front of the room. I have already arranged the seats in my custom horseshoe formation, and the "stage"' is literally set for another year. I was thinking about grabbing Jess and skipping out when the short, middle-aged man-child I love to hate shuffles into the room and closes the door behind him.

"Principal Howell, are you paying a visit to criticize my curriculum already? School doesn't start until tomorrow."

"A little birdie told me you were running for Congress or something. Not that I found anything on it in the newspapers," Howell says with more than a hint of sarcasm.

"Yeah, we kept that secret pretty well," I respond, organizing the lesson plans on my desk and hoping he would just go away. No such luck.

"Was there a point where you thought that it might be a good idea?"

"Good idea to what, run for office?"

"To ask my permission." Whoa. Now the little hairs on my neck stand at attention. Either the building just got hit by lightning or my spider senses are telling me this goofy lout just waltzed into my classroom to pick a fight.

I nonchalantly grab the Magic 8-Ball from the corner of the desk and shake it vigorously. "Should I have asked Principal Howell?" I smirk and show him the result. "My sources say no. I'm not sixteen, Robinson. Your permission isn't required."

"It's Principal Howell to you, not Robinson. I'm your boss, and anything that affects this school, or the students in it, is my responsibility."

"There's a laundry list of things affecting this school you won't bother getting out of your chair for. Why's this any different?"

"Because it is."

I have an incredibly low threshold for stupidity as a result of too many years serving Uncle Sam in the Army. One thing about Special Forces, we have a hard time tolerating the antics of regular line units. No doubt my face has betrayed this emotion as Howell's eyes narrow at me in response. I shake the toy a second time.

"Reply hazy, try again."

"Don't mess with me, Michael. You've involved your students in a *political* campaign. That is not an appropriate teacher-student relationship. So, I will only tell you this once. You're going to drop out of this race and you're going to do it by tomorrow."

I was going to inform Robinson that the campaign is basically over anyway, but now I'm seeing red. I hate ultimatums, and the fact it is coming from him makes it even worse. If Chalice had asked me, I probably would have agreed it was the best course of action. Now, I just want to be obstinate and rude. I shake the Magic 8-Ball once again, look at the window, and shrug theatrically.

"My reply is no."

Principal Howell glares at me with rage in the eyes behind those bespeckled brown glasses. I've met goats in Iraq I was more scared of, so I just stare back at him blankly.

"Your insubordination is noted."

"Wouldn't be the first time."

"That's because you can't follow orders. Pretty remarkable for a Green Beret, actually. No wonder you aren't one anymore."

I feel the heat as my face flushes with anger. My free hand balls into a fist and, for a fleeting moment, I have the thought of dispatching this jack wagon of a principal on a one-way trip to the hospital. Everyone has buttons that can be pushed, and he just pressed mine. Seeing my reaction, and mistaking it for me being on the ropes, he moves in to finish me off. Or at least prod me to do something I'll regret.

"I make the rules in this school, Michael. You do what I tell you to. I dictate what to teach and how, so they can pass their standardized tests and—" There's my opening, and I cut him off.

"You don't want to educate, you want to control. That's the difference between you and me. You think memorizing a bunch of math formulas and useless facts for a test is education. Standardized testing doesn't measure jack, and any decent teacher will tell you that. Real education comes from experience and applying book knowledge to solve real-world problems."

"I don't agree."

"Of course you don't. You know what our problem is? You don't like me because I teach students to think critically instead of simply comply. To learn to use knowledge instead of just acquire it. Practical skills they can apply once they graduate from here."

"Are you saying math isn't practical?"

"Solving mathematical equations is practical because it teaches the methodology of working through a complex problem. Forcing students to memorize the first twenty-five digits in pi is ridiculous, but you don't understand that because you are content to accept whatever the state tells us to do."

Howell dismisses my comments with a wave of his hand. "You don't understand the politics involved. That's why you'll never be a department chair, principal, or any other leader in education."

"I understand the politics just fine. You hold your hat out to the state like a beggar, and when you take their money, they own you. As for being a leader in education, I think what happens in the classroom is what's important. Being a bureaucrat in the front office will never equal the difference I can make standing right here."

We return defiant stares for a few moments before Howell stalks off toward the door. We are at an impasse, and I am impressed with the restraint I showed in not decking him. Chalk one up for anger management skills.

"You're an idealist, Michael," he says without looking at me. "Central Office is going to get involved in this mess. Having students run a political campaign for you will put your chances for tenure at risk." He turns a little overdramatically to look at me. "Do yourself a favor and ask yourself if sacrificing your career is really worth it."

Principal Howell finally walks out just as Jessica enters. "Do I dare ask what that was about?"

"The harbinger of career-ending death paid me a short visit," I say, as effortlessly as I can, knowing the truth is written all over my face.

"The campaign?" she asks in her "I knew it" manner.

I nod. "Yeah, what's left of it."

"Are there going to be problems?"

I look at my stunning fiancée and shake the Magic 8-Ball one last time. The caption in the window causes me to smirk. While I doubt a ten-dollar toy can channel my fate, it has been dead on so far. I hold it up to her so she can read what is in the window.

"Without a doubt."

-TWENTY-TWO-
BLAKE

It should be a crime to call anyone before five a.m. I reach for my cell and check the caller ID. I punch three wrong buttons before I find the right one to answer.

"Seriously, Madison?" I grumble into the phone, still half asleep.

"Get up, get dressed, and get to the office."

"It's 4:30 in the morning. What could possibly be so import—"

"Check the news. There's another player in the race," I hear her say almost with a growl.

"So?" I reply, groggily. I don't hate mornings, but this is beyond ridiculous. My ambitions may be limitless, but getting up early has never been one of them. I never bought in to the whole "early to bed, early to rise" thing because so much work is done late at night over a good blended scotch. In my line of work, I get more accomplished at a tavern at ten p.m. than at a desk at seven in the morning.

"This is important, Blake! You think I would wake you up this early on a Monday if it were just some washed-up nobody? Check the damn news!" Madison practically shouts, causing me to hold the phone away from my ear. I grumble as I sit up in bed and turn on the light. It's way too early for this.

"Okay, okay. What news site?" I ask, assuming she is referring to something specific.

"The Hartford Courant, Danbury News-Times, Waterbury Republican. Any of them," she responds dismissively.

I scan the article posted online in the *Courant*, not believing what I'm reading.

"This is on all the major Connecticut news sites? How is that possible?"

"Kylie," she says, the anger in her voice palpable. "I'll see you in a few," and ends the call. I check some more of the news pages for Connecticut's broadcast affiliates for the major networks, and there are articles there too. That means it could see television news coverage tonight. I even browse a couple of big-name political sites like Politico and Real Clear Politics on my iPad. The article is not featured on them, at least yet. I curse under my breath and launch myself out of bed with a purpose.

Less than an hour and a half later, I am striding into the congressman's outer office. I toss my backpack down next to my corner desk and immediately head to his inner sanctum. The door is open and he is reading from the *News-Times* while Roger and Madison listen.

"Who the hell is Michael Bennit?" Congressman Beaumont angrily asks nobody in particular.

I spent the time on the Metro reading the article and doing some research. Every local paper picked up identical stories, and now even the Associated Press wire has it. The byline read the same for every article—Kylie Roberts. Damn her.

"He's a high school history teacher—" I begin to say before being silenced by the congressman.

"I don't give a shit who he is, Blake. I want to know why I am only hearing about this now when it appears in the goddamn *News-Times* and every other newspaper in the district!" the congressman states, his voice rising in volume to a near shout. "This guy announced over a week ago, so why is it suddenly news now?" He stares at each of us in anticipation of an answer no one wants to offer.

Chance favors the bold, but I'm not about to put myself in Winston Beaumont's crosshairs. Sure, Kylie Roberts may be a monster I helped create, but she's still Madison's sister. Let her take the fall. Roger, not one needing to worry about the congressman's ire being directed at him, must feel the same way. We both look at her.

With no other choice, Madison comes clean. "My sister made it a story."

The congressman's face morphs through a range of emotions, starting with confusion and ending with fury. He says nothing, but takes a closer study at the byline of the paper he's holding to confirm what we already know to be true. Despite his rather indignant reaction, he chooses not to direct his rage at us. After all, we were all complicit in the sentencing, yet Winston Beaumont himself carried out the execution order. His call to her editor, a longtime friend and drinking buddy, is what cost Kylie her job.

He turns to gaze out his office window onto the busy Capitol area below. The great political gamesman has gone to work. "Roger?"

"Most likely this is a short-term story. The teacher-student angle and campaigning only on social media are both unique, which will get it media exposure," Roger explains, "but the story doesn't have legs. It can never carry through to November and poses no threat to us."

Under normal circumstances, I would agree with his analysis, but this is driven by a woman scorned with a serious ax to grind, and the means to grind it. Kylie could earn this regional and even national coverage. I don't want to disagree with Roger, and I also can't afford to end up on the wrong side of this. I am the expendable one in the group, sitting at the intersection of two dangerous paths, one of which Deena will be happy to shove me down when she arrives.

"Madison, you know your sister better than all of us. What do you think?" I ask, coming up with a quick plan in my head.

Madison's face flushes from being put on the spot. The congressman continues to look out the window, so he doesn't see it. Roger gives me a smirk, knowing full well I just threw the girl I'm dating under the bus. I am sure he's thinking he sees a lot of himself in me. That was how he got to the top.

"She'll never relent. If the story fades, it won't be for a lack of her trying to keep it alive," Madison says, looking at me with daggers in her eyes. Time for some expert analysis only I can provide.

"Sir, it's September and I'm guessing Madison's sister somehow thinks she can keep this in the news until Election

Day by providing the mass media exposure that will let this Bennit guy ride a social media wave right into the election."

"He brings up a good point, Winston," Roger says. The congressman's head bobs up and down slightly, but he still does not turn.

"I agree, sir," Madison blurts out as she begins to realize I am stealing her thunder. "I think we should start The Machine." The comment ends any threat Madison Roberts posed to my increased involvement in this race. Roger closes his eyes in anticipation of what's about to happen.

The congressman, a moment ago the picture of serenity as he quietly admired the nation's capital out the window, immediately morphs into a man in desperate need of anger management classes.

"Have you lost your mind, Madison? You think this Bennit character is really enough of a problem where you feel compelled to make that recommendation?" he yells, crossing the office and pulling up within inches of her face. "No political upstart warrants that, I don't care how cute, or special, or unique his story is!" he continues, his voice loud and dripping with sarcasm. "Understood?"

Madison is taken aback by the aggressiveness and cowers like a cat in a thunderstorm. "Yes, sir," she responds meekly.

"Good. Get out. I will have Deena instruct you with how we respond when she gets here." Madison does not look at either me or Roger as she turns and leaves quickly.

I hate to say it, but she isn't wrong. If I were in the congressman's position, I would've heard her out about starting The Machine. An expensive proposition he was hoping to avoid this election season for sure, but better to spend the money and win than risk losing through inaction.

Over the past eight terms, Representative Winston Beaumont has managed to acquire an incredible amount of political capital and financial support. His monetary war chest for campaigns contains tens of millions of dollars. The greatest asset of The Machine is a huge network of people, from mayors and elected town officials to media contacts and business owners. They are all people who owe IOUs for past favors that he can call on to support him in a tough race. When put together, the effort acts as a giant machine, thus the name.

By picking Richard Johnson, the Republicans essentially handed Winston Beaumont a ninth term. Now all those cash reserves and favors can be saved until a tougher challenge ensues. Madison thinks that this will get far worse, and she is probably correct. It was not the savvy way to broach the subject with the boss, a man who is a political animal to his core.

I feel bad for her for a moment. Madison won't get fired, but she won't be included in the inner circle of this campaign for a while either. I made an enemy out of her today, but such is life. She can be replaced both as a friend and a lover. When opportunity knocks, you answer. With Madison now cowered and dismissed, Deena's conspicuous absence, and with Roger's support, I just earned a seat at the table. Now it's time to make the most of it.

"Sir?"

"What is it, Blake?" the congressman asks, impatient and angry. Roger gives me a stern look of warning to tread with caution.

"It was premature and imprudent for Madison to suggest starting The Machine, but there are some sensible, less costly alternatives. We should consider getting some oppo and enhanced polling to track what effect, if any, this yahoo is having." I am on the mark as the wrath in the congressman's eyes flickers out.

"Oppo" is short for opposition research, the seedy underbelly of American politics. Its activities range from the benign search of public records for embarrassing information to the far more despicable tailing of the opposing candidate to catch something awkward. Candidates distance themselves from this activity, but in politics, most campaigns go negative at some point before the polls open. This research helps a campaign fight back once it does.

Enhanced polling is just that. While we do the occasional internal poll to track where we stand with the voters in our district, our enhanced polling is far more rigorous and detailed. The near-constant effort allows us to track trends and determine the effect both sides are having on voters. This is what money buys, and we have lots of it.

The congressman picks up his copy of the *Hartford Courant*. The local press will find the whole digital campaign thing intriguing, but there is sure to be some contentious op-ed pieces decrying student involvement. Most will be sparked by us if we can't coax the genie back into the lamp. Unfortunately, I fear we're going to see more journalists and reporters gushing over this guy, using words like "pioneer" and "innovator."

The venerable Winston Beaumont has seen enough. He shows us the paper and points to it. "This guy is not a saint! Everyone has skeletons in the closet, and Roger, Blake, so help me God, find his!"

Let the games begin.

-TWENTY-THREE-
CHELSEA

I always used to like the first day of school. While I was never eager for summer vacation to end, there was always an excitement around new classes, seeing friends, and getting a year closer to graduating. I thought day one of my senior year would be much of the same. I was wrong.

It's been a week since our disastrous announcement at the Buzz. After that, the campaign pretty much ended. Vince stormed off, and everyone else effectively called it quits along with him. I tried to rally them back to the cause, but didn't get a lot of interest. It was a long summer, and I guess the result wasn't as exciting as everyone thought it would be.

So with nothing to do over the past week, I just hung around the house. Dad said I was moping and should go hang out with my friends. Basically, the same conversation we have been having forever now. He meant well, but I wasn't really up for either hanging out or getting nagged about it.

Classes will be a little challenging this year, but Contemporary Issues with Mister Bennit was the only one I was really looking forward to. Brian, Peyton, Vince, and the rest of the gang will all be in the afternoon class with me.

Between working on the campaign and how much fun we had in American History, I thought it would be great. Now I am dreading it. Each tick of the clock brings me closer to the inevitable, like a prisoner walking to the gallows.

While most kids labor to find out where their BFFs are on the first day of school, I spent the morning avoiding my two closest friends. I know they are upset with me because I did nothing with them this summer, and I don't want to try to justify why. Considering how things turned out, even I think it was wasted time. I can ignore their calls, texts, and Facebook messages, but the school is only so big. Not seeing them so far has only been matter of luck. Waiting in this obscene cafeteria line to pay for my salad, my luck runs out.

"Long time, no see, Chels," Cassie says from behind me, a frosty edge to her voice. She looks tanned, no doubt the product of frolicking on the Jersey Shore half the summer. Her family takes regular trips to Seaside Heights, and since about the fifth grade, I always went with them two or three times during the break.

"Yeah, I'm sorry, Cassie, it was a busy summer." I don't know what else to say. The excuse is pathetic, and she knows it. I never even picked up the phone to call her. Now the guilt is setting in.

"Sure. I can see how you'd be too busy for your friends." I deserved that, but the words still cut a little deep. Stephanie joins us and is even more pissed off than Cassandra.

"I told you guys what I was doing. I would have asked you if you wanted to help, but didn't think you'd be interested," I plead meekly.

Stephanie makes a face like she just got handed something off the rack at Target, or some other store she considers beneath her. "Why would we? And like, waste our summer like you did? No thanks."

"How is that campaign going, anyway?" Cassandra says in disgust. She already knows the answer—nowhere. I want to try to defend my decision and justify why I ditched my friends the summer before our last year of high school.

"Well, I, uh, it uh ..." I am getting too emotional to speak. Maybe I made a huge mistake. Why did I do it? I can't remember anymore.

"Don't sweat it," Cassie says, not even giving me the courtesy to try to explain. "A bunch of us are going to the movies this weekend. We won't bother asking if you're interested, because we know you're not." Ouch. She storms off.

"Sorry, Chels. Maybe when you're like, ready to be a real friend again, you give us a call," Steph says before giving me a little shrug and joining Cassie in another line to pay for their food. The tears welling up in my eyes begin to slip down my cheeks when I feel another set of eyes on me. Miss Slater is watching intently as I lose my emotional battle. I am only a few people from the register now, but I have lost my appetite.

I put the salad back and exit out of the lunchroom the way I came in. Today just plain sucks and the worst is yet to come.

* * *

Two hours later, the moment of truth arrives. Apparently, I am not the only one anxious about being in this class. Everyone is here, but nobody wants to be, with the possible exception of Vince. He appears completely unfazed by what happened a week ago. We exchange some muted hellos and take our seats in the all-too-familiar horseshoe. We were all extremely close for two months, but now it's like we're strangers, or maybe even ex-lovers. It's that kind of awkwardness.

The bell rings and Mister Bennit strides in with a newspaper tucked under his arm. "Welcome to Contemporary Issues," he says in the flamboyant manner we are all so used to. "This class is an examination of the events, people, and subjects that affect today's society, and what better place to begin than with the morning paper." Apparently he is skipping attendance and the usual class orientation you get on the first day of school.

Holding up a page from the *Hartford Courant*, he continues. "Let's start with this one, as it has a bearing on some of your lives. 'Meet the iCandidate. Students Run Social Media Congressional Campaign for Teacher,'" he reads.

"Wait, what?" I gasp. The others in the class look equally stunned, except for Vince. I think he's been holding out on us, which certainly explains his jovial attitude before class. We start clamoring for details in a cacophony of voices before Mister B calms us down.

"Somebody had a pleasant chat with a reporter a few days ago," he says with a smile. The students on the staff all look at each other and settle on Vince. Even the students not involved in any part of our summer campaign undertakings seem to get into the moment.

"She ambushed me when I was hiding at the library. I didn't know what to do so I answered her questions. Then she video chatted with Mister B."

"Please tell me you didn't say something stupid, Vince," Brian warns.

"And that it didn't end up in the paper," Xavier adds.

"Oh, nothing stupid, but what made the paper will probably get picked up in other media. Another teacher showed me the article this morning. I'm surprised you haven't heard about it yet. You guys living under a rock these days, or what?" Mister Bennit asks rhetorically.

He snaps the newspaper several times for effect before he reads. "Page Six, this morning's *Hartford Courant*: 'This will be a different campaign, with a different message and a new way to reach voters,' said Vincent Orsini, the campaign's teenage public relations director. 'We will use every form of social media and electronic medium available to engage the public instead of preaching to them through their televisions.'"

I'm stunned. I mean completely stunned. That sounded almost professional. Mister B smiles at all of us and continues. "'It's a new century and the growth of the information age demands we adapt to the changing ways the world communicates. The politics of old no longer serves the American public. With fresh ideas and a distinctive method of reaching voters, we are going to build a better candidate. We want to introduce the voters of the Sixth District to the iCandidate.'"

We all break out into enthusiastic applause. The dim view I had of this day was erased with the simple reading of a few lines in a newspaper. If the last week can be described as an emotional roller coaster, I just climbed from its deepest valley to its highest peak.

"The article goes on. I even get a quote or two, which I hate to admit, aren't as good as Vince's." Suddenly his face takes on a more serious look. "Of course, you quit, Vince, so I'm not sure what to do about this."

"Actually, Mister B, news of my campaign death may have been greatly exaggerated."

Mister Bennit smiles, but it is somewhat reserved. "We'll see. As of now, there is no campaign. For you guys on the staff, if you want to change that, meet me after school today right here." He tosses the paper on my desk and winks. "Read this and think about it before you make up your minds. You have five minutes while I take attendance and then class begins.

With most of the class straining to read the paper spread out on my desk, I decide to read the whole article aloud. This Kylie Roberts woman did an incredible job. I'm amazed at every word she wrote. Brian checks his phone to find the story is posted on the social media sites Digg, Reddit, and StumbleUpon. The whole state of Connecticut is reading this story. The buzz it generates could even get us exposure in the New York papers. This one reporter did what we failed to do last week with a single article. I don't know where we go from here. I am in, but despite the enthusiasm everyone shows, I'm just not sure who is in with me.

-TWENTY-FOUR-
MICHAEL

"Okay, let's cut to the chase. I need to know whether you guys are in or out, and I need to know today." I sit on a desk, copying the students in the room. I'm not sure why teenagers prefer sitting atop their desks rather than at them, but I remember doing the same thing so many years ago.

The whole gang showed up: Xavier, Brian, Amanda, Chelsea, Peyton, Emilee, Vince, and Vanessa. They are all pretty surprised by the force of the request, especially considering the high they got reading about us in the newspaper. But this is important, and no time to mince words.

"You have all already given up a lot for this. You gave up a whole summer getting signatures and preparing for an unconventional political campaign you had no idea how to run. You did far more than I should have expected from you."

"Mister B—" Chelsea starts to talk, but I hold up my hand to stop her. It's not a power thing so much as a need to finish this thought.

"Please let me finish, Chelsea. You think you screwed up somehow during the announcement. So what? We all screw up in life, but you learn from it and drive on. God knows, I've had to. Here's the problem, though," I tell them before pausing.

"You guys quit. Things didn't go your way and you decided pushing forward was too hard, so you gave up." Most of them break eye contact with me and stare at the ground. I know they agree because none in this usually argumentative group protest. I let that sink in for a moment since they are feeling pangs of guilt over the decision, before taking a deep breath and continuing.

"This campaign is going to get harder. We're on the grid, to use Brian's parlance. Beaumont will fight like a badger to keep his seat, and now he knows who we are. The element of surprise is lost. So the next question is a simple one. Can you handle adversity, or are you all going to quit again when things get tough?"

I get up from the desk I'm sitting on. I hate to lecture them like this, but it needs to be done. If I decide to go any further down this path, I can't afford to have them bail on me again. No point in storming Fort Beaumont alone.

"I'm not going to make your decisions for you regarding the campaign, and I better not hear you put any pressure on each other. This is an individual choice, and you won't hurt my feelings if you decide it's not for you. This is your senior year of high school, so I understand if you don't want to make the commitment this is certain to be. If you're in, I *need* you in until the end." I do need them, because there is no way I can do this without their help.

"Talk as a group or reflect on it yourselves. However you make your decision, I need you to tell Chelsea tonight since she's the campaign manager. Chels, send me a text with the results and we'll take it from there."

I grab the assault pack from the floor beside my desk. As it's only the first day of the school year, there isn't too much in it. That will change fast once the assignments I issue start getting returned and need grading.

"Good luck, guys, and either way, I'll catch you tomorrow." I leave the room and walk down the hall, hearing nothing coming from the classroom. No conversation, arguing, or speechmaking as they think about what the right decision is for themselves. And that is exactly what I need them to do.

* * *

With the school day over and afternoon workout completed, I showered, relaxed, and got ready for the last of my first day of school rituals. After finally meeting the requirements of becoming a teacher in the State of Connecticut, and subsequently landing a teaching position at Millfield, I went out to celebrate surviving the first day of my new job. I continued the custom the following two years, this time with a beautiful blonde English teacher who also worked in the building. Now as my future wife, this quiet outing to our favorite restaurant is a favorite tradition.

Jessica and I clicked from the moment we met. Like all couples, we've had disagreements that ranged from minor spats to the Rumble in the Jungle, but always managed to rectify things quickly. Things are different now, maybe because this is the first real rough patch we have faced during our romance. Lately, there has been an icy chill to the air when we are together, and it has nothing to do with the approaching New England autumn.

Halfway through dinner, I hear the distinctive chime of a text notification from the inside pocket of my jacket. I reach in for it, pausing.

"You wanna put some money on this?" I say, straining to be playful.

"Nope. Just read the message," Jessica responds from across the small table, her voice a mix of curiosity and annoyance.

I glance down and read the note aloud, barely containing my smile. "We're in. Energy and persistence conquer all things - Ben Franklin."

I put the phone away and am rewarded by Jessica's face contorted in disapproval. "How is it your kids remember lines you quoted five months ago and mine can't remember what I said five minutes ago?" she asks rhetorically before turning her attention back to her linguini.

The campaign is back on, and while I feel like celebrating, it's abundantly clear my fiancée had hoped for a different outcome. After a moment of awkward silence stretched into an eternity, I decide to broach the subject. Like a thunderstorm on the Great Plains, you can see this fight coming from miles away. Joy.

"You're awful quiet," I say, stating the obvious.

"I saw Chelsea in the cafeteria with her friends. They came down on her pretty hard for ditching them this summer. She was pretty upset."

I place my fork in the bowl of pasta and fold my hands. No point in stopping her until she makes her point.

"Now I'm sure Vanessa will stop playing field hockey this fall and Emilee will quit the yearbook. Xavier is not practicing as much as he needs to for basketball. Brian's more socially disconnected now than ever." She pauses to read my reaction, which is basically nothing. "The list goes on if you're interested."

"I'm sure this has been hard on their social lives."

"It's more than that and you know it!" she shouts, exasperated. "You're doing it again, Michael!"

"Doing what? Trying to make a difference?"

"No, you've been doing that all your life. It's why you went into Special Forces and why you chose teaching when you got discharged. This is more than that, so just admit it."

"Admit what, Jess? I have no idea where you're going with this, so just get to the point," I say, becoming more agitated.

"It's not about making a difference with you anymore. You have an ax to grind because of your last deployment."

"Leave Afghanistan out of this," I say before stabbing at a piece of my penne.

"Why should I? It has everything to do with this! You have this obsession to fix the world because of what happened there, and that's fine. But now you've dragged a bunch of eighteen-year-old kids into your crusade, and I'm willing to bet they have no idea why," she says, leaning forward. I say nothing, which is all the response she needs. "You have no idea what you are doing, or how it's affecting them," she concludes.

I have had enough. She may be right and may be wrong, but I am not thinking about this logically anymore. She made this debate personal by bringing up Afghanistan. Howell may push my buttons, but Jessica pressed the big red one I keep locked in a glass box.

"That's your default mindset, Jess. Let's protect them from everything so nobody gets hurt. And you wonder why this generation struggles adapting to the real world."

"Don't start! Michael, you are the most brilliant, dedicated teacher I have ever seen. The interest you take in your students is inspiring. You run your classroom like military school—"

Our waiter approaches with dessert menus, clearly having no idea what he is walking into. Without missing a beat, Jessica eyes his approach. "Not now, please come back in a few minutes." He stops mid-stride, spins on his heels, and heads to another table. Smart man, because I wish I could do the same right about now.

"Somehow you get away with it. In fact, the kids love you for it. But now you are taking things too far by including them in this ridiculous campaign. They are giving up too much—"

"Isn't that the point?" I interrupt.

"Look, you have the best of intentions, but have you considered how far is too far?"

"I'll know when I get there."

"Will you? Because if you're wrong, someone could end up permanently hurt by the time you pull back on the reins. Campaigns are dirty, nasty things today. Are you ready for the consequences?"

I reach my hands across the table and take Jessica's. Out of all our fights as a couple, this may be the most contentious. Usually, we talk things over and find common ground, but there is none here. She wants me to abandon this campaign and I'm too stubborn to do it. Holding her hands, I realize there is no warmth in her touch. There's a rift between us, and I can't help but think it's growing.

"I won't let that happen," I say, somewhat unconvincingly.

"Scary thing is, when the time comes, you may not have a say."

* * *

That was the last thing she had to say on the matter. It was late for a school night, so we paid the bill and headed home in silence. No doubt that we both had a lot on our minds.

I'm not marrying Jessica because we are a perfect fit and never disagree. She is entitled to her opinions, and while I value them, part of me also feels she should be supporting me more than she is. Her feelings are clear on this, which causes me to wonder something I have never had cause to think about. When the going gets tough, will she be there for me, or is this just a fair weather relationship?

I lie in bed with the television on, flipping through a few channels before settling on the local news. I refer to these broadcasts as the "murder and arson report" since that seems to be all they show us these days. Tonight, however, the third story was something I never expected.

"There are hundreds of campaigns this midterm election year, but one in particular is getting national attention. Bill Kalagher is live from Millfield with more," the anchor says as the scene shifts over to his field reporter.

Jessica, hearing the name of our town, emerges from the bathroom with a toothbrush hanging from her mouth. I sit up against the headboard when I realize the report is coming live from the parking lot of the Perkfect Buzz. The shop is closed, so I wonder just how long the reporter has been in town.

"As first reported in this morning's *Hartford Courant*, what is unique about this is not independent candidate Michael Bennit running for this district's congressional seat. It is his staff, made up entirely of high school students, bringing his message to the voters over social media. We caught up with campaign manager Chelsea Stanton earlier today."

This may be the first time I have ever felt elation and impending doom simultaneously. I could not be more proud of Chelsea and how she handled herself. The television media picked up the *Courant* article and ran with it, and just as I thought, the press is taking more interest in the students running the campaign than me as the candidate. I also know this is only the beginning, because as the interest in the students grows, so will the amount of media covering it.

"I guess we're going to find out if you know how far is too far after all," she says sarcastically as she returns to the bathroom. Yeah, I guess we will.

-TWENTY-FIVE-
KYLIE

"He calls himself the iCandidate and is using the Internet, Twitter, and Facebook to take the political world by storm," I hear the first reporter say as I walk behind the cameraman. As the numerous media trucks set up shop outside the Perkfect Buzz to be ready in time for the evening local broadcasts, I made sure I introduced myself to each reporter. In most cases, I even shared some information with them.

"It's a new-age campaign relying on social media to spread its message and reach the voters. There are no annoying political commercials or robocalls. Not even any fundraisers or rallies," an enthusiastic female reporter named Susan tells the camera. She is getting swept up in this, and not because she is reporting on it. I found out she started following Michael Bennit on Twitter because she likes him.

"The Bennit campaign started as a social media fad, but is quickly going viral. What was dismissed as a gimmick now has mainstream attention," opines a reporter from Channel 3, "and voters of the Sixth District are taking notice, as is the rest of the state."

Yes, they are, creating another set of problems. It's been a week and a half since my first article about Michael Bennit ran in the *Hartford Courant,* and so far, the plan is working flawlessly. Two more articles were released since the first, each picked up by all the local and now an increasing number of national newspapers. Frankly, I'm surprised only because I had to call in a lot of favors just to get the first article published locally. Each subsequent one gave the public a new piece of the puzzle on this campaign, and they want more of it. The local news reporting live from here shows that I have gotten people interested. I will know I made it big when CNN and FOX show up.

Beaumont must be getting a little scared, but before I push this any further, I need to understand what the campaign's plan is. The couple of Skype sessions I shared with Michael have been enlightening, but I need to meet the man for real to see if he is a serious candidate. Unfortunately for him, the voters will need to be shown too if he expects to win. I am not sure he does.

* * *

An hour later, I watch the activity outside the now bustling coffee shop from my car as both Chelsea and Vince head in. They are remarkably poised under the circumstances. I drift back to reading the e-mails on my phone when a sharp rap at the window causes me to jump out of my seat. Before I can say a word, the passenger door swings open and the iCandidate himself slides into the seat next to me.

"Stalking is illegal in all fifty states, Miss Roberts," he says with a smile.

"I'm not stalking, I'm chasing a story," I manage to stutter, sounding like a complete idiot. Michael Bennit is even better looking in person. I'm actually a little breathless. "And I prefer you call me Kylie," I say, with a smile he probably gets from every teenage girl with a crush that swoons over him. Recognizing the look or not, he smiles in return.

"What brings you up this way? You know you can call anytime."

"I wanted to meet you in person."

"Kinda poking holes in this whole iCandidate thing, aren't you?" he asks with a laugh.

"Maybe, but you climbed into my car, remember?" I pose playfully. Did I just bat my eyelashes at him? What the hell is wrong with me? I'm flirting with him.

"Touché," he says. "What did you want to talk about?"

As I start to regain my senses, I realize we are in a parked car at the back of the coffee shop lot with nobody around. Cameramen and reporters are making their way to their trucks from the entrance, having shot their b-roll and filled up on caffeine. That leads me to my next thought.

"Don't you want to go talk to the press before they leave?"

"Nope. That's why I'm here with you. I'm hiding from them."

"You're strange, you know that? You must be the first candidate in history to ever shy away from the cameras when they show up." And I mean that. I have never, and I do mean never, met a candidate or sitting politician who purposely avoids the press. In case there was any doubt in my mind the man in front of me is a different kind of candidate, it is now put to rest.

"You don't need me to confirm that for you. Just ask my kids."

"Okay." The direct approach always works best for me. Some journalists try to play gotcha with people. I like to hit them hard and see what the response is. "You're the candidate and they're the staff, right? Why are you putting them front and center in the campaign?"

"I didn't realize I was," he says, continuing to look out my windshield at the dispersing reporters. A classic example of deflecting the question.

"You are, you know you are, and I'm wondering why."

"Are we off the record?" he asks.

"Do we need to be?" is my quick response.

"That depends. Are you asking because you're curious or because you just want to write another story?" Apparently he likes the direct approach too. Not a trait you see in most candidates, or politicians for that matter.

"I'm already in bed with you."

He flashes me one of those looks that a guy gives to a woman when she says something unintentionally sexual. Normally, I shrug it off, but I find myself blushing.

"Figuratively, not literally. I want to know exactly where you see this going. Letting teenagers run with this is a bold move."

"But it's working."

"It is for now. What happens when parents start getting involved and begin pressuring the district to put an end to this?"

"That won't happen."

He's in denial. Beaumont got me fired from my job because he was afraid of what I might print. Not too many politicians in the country wield the clout, or the guts, to do that. Of course, Michael doesn't know anything about my past, and I'm not sure I am ready to tell him.

"You're running against Winston Beaumont. If this thing becomes a threat, trust me, it will happen."

"You sound like you speak from experience," he says, making me wonder if he does know. Time to shift gears.

"I did some research on you. Turns out you were a Noncommissioned Officer in the Army, attended Airborne School, Special Forces, HALO school, whatever that is, and did multiple tours in Iraq and Afghanistan. You're highly decorated, including a Purple Heart, a pair of Bronze Stars for valor, and a Distinguished Service Cross you earned during your last tour."

"They give those away these days," he says dryly.

"They give away the second highest award for valor in the military? I don't think so."

He finally looks over me with his piercing blue eyes and I melt. He's not angry, although I am pretty sure I would never want to see him actually mad. His expression is more one of, impatience, maybe?

I lean in, closing the space between us to something almost uncomfortable. That tactic usually causes people to back away defensively. He doesn't flinch. And he smells really good. "You are a war hero and qualified to run for Congress based on that alone."

"John Kerry won three Purple Hearts in Vietnam and still fell short in the race for the presidency. McCain spent years as a POW in Hanoi and lost to Obama. Combat service does not qualify you for anything, and certainly doesn't guarantee victory these days."

"Presidential contests are different than legislative races. There are over one hundred veterans in Congress right now, and more than fifteen of them were deployed to the Middle East."

"That's not why they were elected. Nobody cares about where you serve." Man, is this guy ever stubborn. For someone who has no particular platform, he sure is secure in his opinions. Speaking of which …

"Is that why you don't talk about issues? Because you think nobody cares about them either?" His smirk signals I struck a chord, but he still doesn't move away. Fearless and sexy. "You are going to need to address them sooner or later. You know that, right?"

"Let me ask you a question, Kylie. Why are *you* doing this?" That causes me to move away. Crap.

"What do you mean?" I ask, trying to stall for time.

"You know exactly what I mean. I appreciate the near-militant interest in this campaign, I really do. Your articles are the only reason we have any awareness whatsoever, but that doesn't explain why you wrote them in the first place."

"Now tell me, why should I answer your question if you didn't answer mine?" Michael Bennit is an honorable guy and I am really not sure how he would respond to my motives. Maybe he would understand them. Maybe he wouldn't. But I have no interest in finding out right this moment so I dodge the question. "You don't trust me, do you?"

"Trust is earned, not issued," Michael pronounces without pause. "So why don't we get to work earning each other's first before we share secrets. Figuratively, not literally," he says, winking at me. The last of the reporters huddled around the entrance to the coffee shop have moved off. He nods toward the shop and opens the door. "C'mon, let's go meet the gang."

-TWENTY-SIX-
MICHAEL

Walking into the Perkfect Buzz with Kylie prompted more than a few incredulous stares from the dozens of students occupying nearly every corner of the shop. For those used to me walking in with Jessica, seeing me enter with this beautiful "other woman" is a week's worth of rumor fuel in a high school. I wonder what they would think if they had seen me sitting next to her in a parked car three minutes ago.

Lucky for me, Vince recognizes Kylie immediately, and I am spared the Gestapo-style interrogation from my teenage workforce. Whether he took over the escort duties because of his role in the campaign or because he has a major crush on the stunning, brown-haired journalist shall remain a mystery. Wagering a guess, I would say the latter.

I realize this is becoming quite the burgeoning operation as Chelsea and Vince show Kylie around the room. In the far corner to the right of the counter, there is some sort of planning session involving students I both know and have never met. On the left side, fifteen teens are huddled into the corner of the seating area. Eight of them toil over open laptops while the others scribble notes and look on.

I walk over, my presence barely registering with them as they pore over various tweets, Facebook messages, and e-mails. One appears to be working on a blog post for Tumblr, and another is posting an image to Instagram.

"Alice Kravitz wants to know how you think you are qualified to be in Congress," Amanda reads from an e-mail without looking up.

"Tell her I have an IQ over twenty which actually makes me overqualified."

"This woman thinks you're a Mormon!" Xavier says, reading from our Twitter account. I lean over and read the tweet for myself, letting out a little chuckle.

"She spelled it wrong, X. She means moron."

"Oh, she's one to talk," Xavier muses, shaking his head.

"Everyone can't be a fan," I tell him.

"Bill Connolly wants to know why you haven't taken a stand on abortion," Vanessa reads from a Facebook post. "Should I respond with something like 'because he can't get pregnant'?"

"Ha, ha. Funny," I say, amused. Kylie was right during our short conversation in her car. If I don't address these types of issues sooner or later, some people are going to begin to ask why.

"Would it be accurate to say your feelings on global warming mean more days at the beach?" Emilee asks.

"Who wound you guys up tonight?" I deflect.

"If we ain't going to discuss issues, there's not much more to say," Vince points out from the other side of the room.

'Still a little bitter about that are we, Vince?" I fire back. "I know this feels like we're dodging questions because, well, we are, but there is a method to my madness. Trust me."

They do trust me, but I also get the feeling the annoying little voices in the back of their heads won't be silenced for long. I consider myself a man of principle, but I have no interest in taking a stand in this election. I just am not sure how long it will be before our not talking about the issues becomes *the* issue. More of a mystery is how they will react to me if it does.

"This one is from Mark Rabkin," Peyton says, looking down at a new tweet. "If you hate politicians, why would you want to be one?"

"Hating politicians makes me the perfect representative for the people in the district who generally hate politicians."

Amanda smacks her laptop a couple of times in frustration before realizing everyone stopped what they are doing and are looking at her. "Sorry," she says, blushing.

"Mister B, hash tag iCandidate is officially trending on Twitter!" Brian exclaims, raising both his arms in the air signaling a touchdown. The students in the room let out a loud whoop and exchange high fives with each other. "I have no idea how we are going to keep up with all this!"

"Better do some more recruiting, guys. You all have homework to do, including mine. You can't spend all night at this." Can't is a word of defeat, and they would turn this into an all-nighter if Laura didn't need to close up.

Kylie has joined me with Chelsea at her side. "Not bad for an iCandidate," Kylie says grinning. "I can't wait to see how you bring it to the next level." I am not certain if she means cramming eighty people in here instead of forty or something else entirely.

"Uh, Mister B? This woman posted on Facebook saying you're hunky and wants you to come home to her," Emilee reads. I exchange a quick glance with Kylie.

"Don't look at me, I didn't write it," Kylie offers, her eyes conveying that she wishes she did. Chelsea is looking at the two of us, perhaps wondering whether something may be going on. If she does, I'm sure she will bring it up before too long. For now, I just deal with the issue at hand.

"Thank her for the compliment," I say to Emilee. "Then delete any traces of the post before Miss Slater logs on and sees it."

Emilee laughs. "Uh, Miss Slater wrote it. She says at the end that you're very late for dinner."

-TWENTY-SEVEN-
BLAKE

"He is redefining how to run a modern day campaign," the pundit emphatically states from her chair under the glaring lights of their television studio. Many of these roundtable discussions are full of know-it-all gas bags who just like to listen to themselves talk.

This is one of the more respectable shows on cable news, and being left-leaning, the panel is more sympathetic to the liberal politicians in the country. The fact that we are watching a recording of last night's broadcast discussing our opponent's campaign is not a good sign. Michael Bennit has jumped from being a local novelty to a national one.

"How is he redefining anything? This isn't new. Candidates have been using the Internet for years, and social media was heavily used in the last campaign season," one of the male pundits counters.

Winston Beaumont watching this in the office at 7:30 a.m. is the type of bad omen the Mayans carved into rocks. The last time he was here this early was when Kylie first made a story out of this unknown. Since then, we watched as the gimmick campaign Roger expected to flame out after a few days grew into a three-alarm blaze. It turns out Madison was correct a couple of weeks ago. We screwed up by not starting The Machine. Now, Winston Beaumont fiddles while Rome burns.

"Not to this extent. It's one thing to use social media and the Internet as tools to reach voters, but I've never heard of a candidate using them for the whole campaign," a third pundit offers in response. "Or, should I say, used by a group of teenagers to run a campaign."

"Is this good for American politics?" the moderator of the show asks.

"Of course not!" exclaims the first pundit. "It's one more example of the human element being removed from politics. What happened to the good old days of shaking a candidate's hand and looking him right in the eyes?"

"They're long gone. The meet and greet died with television, and now we're seeing a change in how mainstream media gets used. This is the society in which we live, for better or worse. It's the age of social media and mobile communications."

"The Bennit campaign is leveraging social media to their advantage by creating a story around it. The end result is they are reaching voters in Connecticut not ordinarily involved in the political process and getting them excited about it," I hear the pundit conclude before Roger punches the mute button on the remote.

Congressman Beaumont stared at the television with a blank expression now becoming contorted in anger, and there is no doubt that Roger and I will be the recipients of the wrath. The congressman returns to his window, fuming but not lashing out with the intensity I expected.

"So much for the story dying after a few days," the congressman mumbles. "Still think this is going to go away?" he asks, turning to Roger.

"The media keeps getting fed stories to report," Roger says, embarrassed his political crystal ball is on the fritz. "I still don't think the attention is sustainable and will die out on its own."

"And if it doesn't we'll be faced with a bigger problem a month from now."

"That's a possibility," Roger concedes. "We are looking into ways to break the momentum.

"Okay, what's your plan?" The congressman is showing no interest in sharing media time with a guy who is beneath him, and I don't blame him. I want Bennit stopped too.

"Blake?" Roger is handing this off to me. I understand the ramifications of the next couple of minutes. If the congressman doesn't like this plan of action, I'll need to pawn it off as someone else's and conjure up another one quick. It's a tough game to play, and not for the weak of heart. Fortunately, I have made the necessary arrangements should it come to that.

"I spoke with our oppo guys. Michael Bennit is a Boy Scout. Unmarried, no children, distinguished military career, pays his taxes—"

"You're telling me they found nothing?" Congressman Beaumont asks, unconvinced. "I find that hard to believe."

"Nothing of any use to us, unfortunately," I respond. "Unless we want to do a character assault on him over a speeding ticket a couple of years ago."

"Roger, if Blake doesn't have anything of use, why is he here?" the congressman asks, pointing at me menacingly. "You think we should start The Machine or something too?"

Time to throw some staff under the bus. "No, sir. That was Madison and Deena's idea, and I don't think it's necessary." I actually have no clue if Deena was involved or not, but the congressman doesn't know that. Even if Roger does, he's the chief of staff and won't say anything unless necessary.

"Damn right it's not, which is why she isn't in here. So why are you?"

"Hear him out, Winston. I think he has a better plan."

"Well?"

This is the moment of truth, and I would be lying if I said I didn't live for this. The pressure of the situation is exhilarating, and I'm savoring every minute of it. I ran the idea by Roger first to ensure I was coloring within the lines. He was noncommittal, meaning he will agree with whatever Congressman Beaumont decides. Thus I have a Plan B, but I don't think I will need it. This is the best option, so I am going to present it with all the confidence I can muster.

"You beat him the same way you would beat Usain Bolt in the 50-meter dash."

"I don't have time for your rhetorical games, Blake," the congressman says dismissively with the famous wave of his hand. "So you'd better get to the point quick. How would I beat him?"

"You don't let him run against you," I say, a grin crawling across my lips, clearly implying a more literal meaning to the metaphor.

"And how do you propose we do that?"

"Public pressure," Roger says, picking up the argument.

"What am I missing? Apparently, John Q. Public loves this guy."

"Yes, sir, some of them do," I offer, adding a dramatic pause for effect. "But what do you think the parents are saying? Don't you owe it to the good people of Millfield to make sure the school board sanctions the use of these young impressionable minds in a political contest? I mean, teachers are important to the education of our country's youth. How can he possibly be devoted to instruction if he is dedicating so much energy running against you?"

The congressman ponders my argument for a second, his eyes narrowing to mere slits. For a moment I begin to think he is going to reject the brilliant idea. The look he's giving me is not impatience or annoyance. It's more of … admiration?

"Roger? Who do we know on the Millfield School Board?" the congressman asks, a devious grin replacing the scowl.

"Oh, I think we can muster a couple of loyal foot soldiers to bring up the discussion and hold a vote," Roger says with a smile. Of course we can. Influencing a small town school board is easier than stealing change from a blind cripple.

"Blake, there may be a future for you on this staff after all," the congressman promises.

Yes, yes there is.

"Go get him."

-TWENTY-EIGHT-
MICHAEL

School is out for the long Labor Day weekend, and the faculty is leaving in droves as the clock strikes three. I typically use the south set of doors to the building for two reasons. The first is the geographical relevance to where I park my car. It's the closest exit. The second, more meaningful reason, is I avoid the main office and eternal hiding place of the jackass now standing in my path.

"Did you lose your red Swingline stapler again, Milton?" I muse as I come to a stop in front of him. He either ignores the *Office Space* reference or never watched the movie. Some people just don't appreciate fine cinema.

I briefly think of walking past him, but figure I'm on thin ice as it is. I should stop antagonizing my tormentor; after all, I have a target on my back, or so Chalice keeps reminding me.

"Tell me something, Michael," he says, waving a newspaper at me, "was having your students on the cover of the *New York Post* part of your plan?"

I snatch the paper out of his hand and check out the front page. In a big color picture, like only the *Post* can do, is a group shot of them manning laptops at the Perkfect Buzz. In two short weeks, our unknown campaign now has the attention of a big New York City newspaper. I can't help but wonder how long before we start getting national exposure.

I look back up from his copy of the *Post* to catch the principal's look of disapproval. Robinson Howell has always been an attention-seeker. I am beginning to wonder if the interest the students and I are receiving for the campaign is starting to drive him a little nuts. I hope so.

"This is a pretty good picture of them," I tell him in a smug tone.

"I'm glad you're amused. I don't find this funny. You are damaging their self-esteem and disrupting their lives," Howell spats, grabbing the newspaper back from me.

"I'm sure being on the cover of a major newspaper in one of the country's largest cities isn't costing them cool points."

"This isn't about them!" Howell nearly shouts at me. Okay, now I'm actually confused.

"Didn't you just say I was damaging their self-esteem?"

"Yes, but—"

"So this is about them?" I ask, nearly causing Howell to explode.

"No."

"Robinson, you really need to make up your mind. Just pick a side of the story and go with it so we can finish this little chat." He smarts at me calling him by his first name again. What was I saying about not agitating my tormentor?

"You think you're oh so smart, don't you? Well, we'll see who gets the last laugh. The school board is meeting Tuesday night to discuss the impact your ridiculous campaign is having on the students in the school." He holds up the paper again. "Not a hard case for them to figure out. I already put in my two cents."

"Two cents, eh? Did they make change?" Again, I'm pushing my luck.

"Parents in the district are upset, Michael. Their opinions will be heard and this stunt of yours will end," Principal Howell states before walking away.

I heard rumors about some parents in town grumbling, which is not unexpected given the circumstances. Now it begins to occur to me there is a real possibility that Winston Beaumont is stirring the pot. If he holds as much sway over the elected officials in the district as Kylie says, this could be a big problem.

I pull out my cell as I reach the set of double doors that leads to the parking lot. It takes a moment to convince myself, but I decide to break a cardinal rule I've held sacred since my time in the military. I am about to trust a journalist. I dial the number from my received call log and get the voice mail as I walk out of the building.

"Kylie, it's Michael," I say, following her voice mail greeting. "Not sure where you are at the moment, but if you are going to be in the area, let me know. We may have a little problem up here."

* * *

I find coming to Briar Point therapeutic in a way. I always liked being outside since childhood, and even my years training and fighting in jungles and deserts across the globe didn't sour that. While I wait for the other party to attend this preposterous meeting we set up, I let my thoughts wander back to Robinson and his taunts about the school board. As much as I resent the man, he may have unintentionally done me a favor.

I allowed myself to fall victim to a catastrophic intelligence failure. If not for my antagonist, the board discussing my candidacy would have remained undiscovered until I walked into their decision face first. Since governing the schools is their responsibility, the elected members could easily force me to make a choice between keeping my job and running for office. It's not a choice I even want to be presented, much less be obliged to decide under duress. And by duress, I mean knowing how Jessica would come down on the issue. I just hope Kylie gets back to me and is willing to help.

I am thinking about what Kylie can pull from her playbook when a blue Chevy Impala pulls into the parking lot and finds a spot. The door swings open and out climbs a massive man in a wrinkled suit. Obesity is a growing problem in this country, but I generally give overweight people the benefit of the doubt. Genetics plays a huge roll in body type, so I try not to pass immediate judgment.

I will in this case. The head of the Republican Party for Litchfield County looks like the living embodiment of the Stay Puft Marshmallow Man. Plus, after some of the things he has already been quoted saying in the press, I just plain don't like him.

"Miles Everman, I presume? Can I get you anything? Oxygen? Blood pressure pills? Bengay?"

"I didn't set this meeting up to discuss my exercise regimen, Mister Bennit," he says, practically hyperventilating. The eighty feet from the car to the bench is probably the most rigorous activity he's seen in years. Okay, to be fair, it is a slight uphill grade. Well, ten feet of it is.

"I didn't realize you had one that doesn't include lifting Twinkies. Take a seat before you pass out, and call me Michael."

He plops down on the bench, his girth spreading. He shifts several times trying to get comfortable, and I swear I hear the bench groaning. Or maybe I am just imagining it is. Nope, it's groaning.

"You wanted to meet, Miles. What can I do for you?"

"I'll keep this short. We need you to drop out of the race," he deadpans.

"Well, you were right about it being quick. No. Have a nice day," I say, starting to get up while realizing that I'm not lucky enough to end this meeting so quickly.

"You claim to want Beaumont to lose his seat, but are costing the only real alternative a chance at winning in November. Can't you see that?"

"You know what I see, Miles? I see a Republican candidate with absolutely no chance of beating Winston Beaumont. Whether or not I'm in the race is irrelevant."

"I disagree. I've known Richard Johnson for years. He's the best man for the job," Miles says, wiping his brow with a handkerchief. I wonder if he realizes we live in New England.

You would think we were on the equator, looking at the way he's sweating.

"Johnson is an ambulance-chasing, disgrace of a lawyer with as much chance of landing a seat in Congress as my tone-deaf ass has winning a Grammy. Most of the Republicans I know won't even vote for him."

"Do you want to see Beaumont elected to a ninth term? Do you want him to advance his liberal agenda—"

"If political parties would spend more time listening to the people and less time advancing agendas, Congress might actually get their approval rating into double digits."

Being a history teacher and long-time admirer of George Washington, I'm a little jaded when it comes to political parties. Diffusing power was a big deal in post-revolutionary America, following their experiences with King George III and Parliament. He was keenly aware other governments viewed the party system as destructive because their primary concern is accumulating more power and doing whatever it takes to retain it. Washington was also afraid political parties that rise in the United States would seek revenge on opponents and destroy the nation's fragile unity. Looking at modern politics, his thoughts appear prophetic.

"That's how the system works, and if you think you can change that, you're naïve."

"I don't know if I can change it," I answer honestly. "But I think I'd like to try. That's why I am doing this."

"I heard you were doing this because you lost a bet. Look, you have had a great run, Michael, but now is the time for you to drop this charade and endorse Dick Johnson."

Not sure where he got that nugget of information from, but I've heard enough. The arrogance of this man is appalling. No wonder Republicans never win in this district. I stand up and look down at him in disgust.

"Miles, this 'charade' is ahead of your candidate in the latest Marist poll by double digits. If that isn't enough reason to tell you 'no,' try this. My students would never let me forget that I dropped out and endorsed a man whose first and last names are synonymous with penis."

I stay just long enough to watch the blood drain out of his face. Is he shocked because of what I said or because he realizes I'm right? Either way, it's irrelevant and I start off toward my car.

"This conversation isn't over, Michael," I hear him call out as he struggles off the bench.

"It is, unless by some medical miracle you beat me to my car," I shout in response without looking back.

-TWENTY-NINE-
KYLIE

In some ways, Michael is an extremely competent strategist. He knew it was only a matter of time before both political parties came after him, and was patient enough to wait until their strategy became evident before making a move to counter. On the other hand, running a campaign is all about timing, and he may have waited too long.

The problem is the sheer number of fronts his opponents could attack on. Since Michael's resources are limited and political allies nonexistent, there is little margin for error to chase red herrings. Figuring out what approach another candidate will use to beat you is tricky, but I can't help but think he should have seen this tactic coming.

Over the prior week, a series of op-ed articles were published in local newspapers by parents expressing concern over a teacher using students in a political campaign. Some were probably legitimate—if I were a parent, I'd be concerned too.

However, so many in such a short period of time reeked of sleazy politics. After a little digging, I found the root cause of our headache. My only surprise was where it's coming from.

Winston Beaumont was not launching the "March of the Parents" assault on Michael Bennit; Richard Johnson was. That man is so dense light bends around him, so the thought his ploy is gaining traction is downright scary.

The Republicans are weak in this area of the country and can do little more than focus on stirring discontent in the Sixth District. While they may cause some heartburn for Michael, Beaumont wields the clout to successfully influence members of the school board. That makes him far more dangerous in the short-term. If Dick Johnson is scared and desperate enough to attack Bennit using sympathetic parents in the press, it's a certainty Beaumont has already made his move using other means.

I went to work after Michael's frantic voice mail and the quick conversation that followed. Investigative journalism is what I was born to do, and it didn't take long to figure out Beaumont had three of the seven members of the Millfield School Board in his back pocket. Needing a majority to end things for Michael, they would need to convince one other member to join them. Swaying a vote was not an insurmountable challenge under the circumstances, so I changed the situation to something more in our favor.

Elected officials in small towns are not used to extensive media coverage outside of the local newspaper. School board members get even less love from the media. So when a reporter calls asking for a response to allegations made by an anonymous source, they clam up. It doesn't matter if claiming Winston Beaumont may be promising favors in return for a favorable decision about a certain teacher running against him is true, it just has to sound legitimate enough to print. Everyone likes a good scandal.

Planting the seed of political misconduct was Act One. To hide my rather ethically questionable attempt to do my own manipulation, I added a little color in the form of an article featuring the allegations, coupled with an appeal from a student running the campaign. By the end of the brazen piece, I practically dared Millfield's school board members to vote against Michael.

The story went out late on Saturday evening over the AP wire and was picked up by almost every major news outlet in the country. Political skullduggery means scandals, and scandals mean ratings. Cable news broadcasts seized on the opportunity to keep their weekend audiences tuned in. Sunday morning political shows on ABC and NBC devoted a segment to the brewing storm. Every major metropolitan and local paper had the write-up, including, much to my surprise, the Sunday edition of the *New York Times*.

Beaumont and Johnson did me a big favor. Their fear of Michael Bennit gave me a fresh angle to expand the coverage of his campaign. In terms of a political interest story, the plight of the iCandidate was now a national issue, and all eyes were training on the Millfield School Board.

* * *

"How many news shows did you do today, Kylie?" Chelsea asks me from the overstuffed chair in the corner of the Perkfect Buzz.

"I saw her on six," Laura calls out from behind the counter. She may be schlepping coffee all day, but that woman does not miss a beat. She was only off by one. Now that I am recognized as the deep background reporter for the Bennit camp, every media outlet in the country wanted to talk to me about my story before the big meeting tonight.

I sit in the corner of this charmingly eclectic coffee house with Michael and his inner circle. He has been tweeting almost nonstop since we got here, and only put down his iPhone to pick up his iPad. His students are equally preoccupied on their own devices. I'm pretty certain they're not playing Candy Crush or Angry Birds.

Everyone knows the campaign is at a crossroads. All that is left to do tonight is continue the social media assault as if nothing else is happening. The school board will have finished their deliberations and rendered their decision by now, so trying to further influence opinions is pointless. We are beholden to the waiting game.

"Hold on, this is my favorite part," Michael says before reading my masterpiece off one of the news sites he connected to on the iPad. "'Our campaign has faced many obstacles already,' explained Orsini, 'but our school board has the power to end the whole thing. It strikes me as counterintuitive how elected officials can, in good conscience, be against the practice of democracy and the social and political activism of teenagers.'"

"Counterintuitive?" Amanda mocks from opposite Vince, causing him to shrug.

"You had to have put lipstick on that pig," Chelsea says to me with a huge smile.

"His words, swear to God," I reply truthfully.

"Oh wait, it gets better," Michael says as he scans down the article until finding the sentence he is looking for. "'The same people this town entrusted to promote these ideals are about to take action to silence our voices and retard our learning.'"

"If anybody knows anything about being retarded, it's Vince," Brian jokes, providing a much needed tension-breaker at a time where tension is the highest. Vanessa even gives him a high five. The only one in the room that seems to be relaxed is Michael. Given the fact he has the most to lose, I have no idea why. Must be a military thing, I guess.

"Well done, Vince. You made me the school board's public enemy number one, but it's what we needed. And, of course, a special thanks to Kylie who never seems to have a problem getting anything published these days." He offers up a short round of applause and everyone joins in. I bow my head with some theatrics, but I mean it. I haven't felt appreciated in a long time, and Michael's words were sincere.

"What will you do if the board ends up voting against you?" Peyton asks.

"Fortunately, it won't come to that," a tall, leggy, blonde woman says as she breezes up to our little corner. She almost sounded disappointed. "You're on thin ice, but still in the game."

Michael rises and gives her a quick peck on the lips, which is barely returned. A guy like that only gets a peck? What the hell is wrong with her? I mean, maybe she had a long day or is stressed out, but I expected more support from the future Mrs. Bennit.

The students are exchanging celebratory high fives and fist bumps like one of them returned to the dugout after crushing a grand slam.

"And you must be Kaylee Roberts," Jessica says coolly.

"It's Kylie, actually. Pleased to meet you, Jessica," I respond, offering my hand to shake. After taking a moment to decide whether she wanted to, she begrudgingly accepts the gesture with the limpest handshake I have ever experienced. Really?

"I'm heading home. Try not to be too late tonight," she says to Michael before whirring on her heels and sulking out the door. No good-bye kiss or anything. Things between them must be worse than Michael lets on because the chill is causing the windows to frost over.

I can see what attracted him to her though. In terms of physical beauty, she has few equals outside of fashion magazines and *Sports Illustrated Swimsuit Editions*. I mean, I feel downright ugly next to her. Damn, is she ever a bitch though. Or maybe I don't like her for other, more personal reasons.

"I'm heading home, too. I have some homework to do, so I'll see you tomorrow," Vince says after packing his things.

"Bye, Vince. Great job these last couple of days," Michael calls out as Vince shuffles toward the door.

The rest of the students file out in small groups, and I am left with Michael, who, amazingly, is holding yet another refill of his espresso. How he can consume that much caffeine and still sleep is beyond me, and I consider myself a die-hard coffee drinker.

"Can I ask you a non-campaign related question?"

"So long as it doesn't end up on the front page of tomorrow's *Wall Street Journal*," he responds, only half-kidding.

"Deal." I can't come up with a clever way to approach this so I go with the direct approach. "Did I read her wrong, or was your fiancée not thrilled with the board's decision?"

Michael grimaces and pinches the bridge of his nose his index finger and thumb, pushing outward and tracing along his sinuses. He exhales deeply, and I begin to think I'm not going to get an answer. He looks at me with eyes I can only characterize as wounded. It isn't a look Michael appears comfortable wearing.

"I think she looked at this vote tonight as her 'get out of jail free' card. She's not happy with this campaign, and was probably hoping the board would end it before she had to say something."

"And when will she say something?"

Michael turns off his iPad and picks up his coffee, swirling the dark liquid around the cup. I think I overstepped a boundary in our relationship.

"I'm sorry. I understand if you don't want to talk about it with me."

"I really don't, but not because of anything to do with you. I don't know, is the honest answer." I keep forgetting he is a typical soldier, all go, no quit, and not the best at keeping in touch with his emotions. The way Jessica is acting must bother him, but he probably has no idea what to do about it.

"I don't think I have thanked you for everything you've done for this campaign. The school board would have ended this if it weren't for your article."

"I'm just a simple reporter doing my part. You dodged a bullet, but only the first shot."

"Yeah, I know, he'll really be coming after me now."

"If he can find an opening he will, and if he can't, he'll make one." I know Michael realizes the cold, hard truth, but it isn't any easier hearing someone say it. So far, the Bennit campaign has been a fun ride that could change into a nightmare at a moment's notice.

"The problem is, he won't find anything on me. His next move is a wild card. Not sure how the kids will react to what may be coming next."

"They worship you," I say. "They'll stick with you through a lot."

"I'm not sure about the worship part, but you can't question their dedication. I'm very proud of them. Watching them makes everything worth it."

I suddenly feel a little like Wile E. Coyote must when he realizes he ran off the end of the cliff and hangs there before plummeting to earth. When you are used to dealing with the egos representing us in Washington, any act of selflessness is truly shocking. So the stunning conclusion I just drew about the motive behind this race has me identifying with Looney Tunes characters.

"That's what this is about, isn't it?" I ask as I lean closer to him. "It's why you won't mention your military service or take a firm stand on issues. This campaign isn't about you, it's about them." He didn't need to say anything, because for the first time since I met him, his face gave it away.

"I will never question your investigative skills," he says, somewhat weakly trying to recover. He gave that ground up way too easily, so there must be more.

"That's not the whole story though, is it?" I press.

"Enough of it. So what happens now?"

I know I am quickly losing objectivity. I shudder at the thought that I am turning into my sister, the voice of a campaign instead of the dispassionate reporter covering it. Part of me is disappointed to discover he may not be as serious about taking on Beaumont as I thought. The other part is captivated at the thought a teacher would go so far for a lesson.

"Okay, I'll make you a deal. If you're not going to issue trust, you have to give me the chance to earn it. If you really want to make this about them, then let's make it about them. I have an idea for getting you the exposure you want. Just let me give you one warning—be careful what you wish for."

-THIRTY-
CHELSEA

Kylie ran her "Profiles" series of articles about the staff the week following the school board's decision to let Mister Bennit continue the campaign. When I read them, I was like, oh my God. I never thought the stories would get picked up by the big news companies, so it was shocking to see my name splashed on the pages of every newspaper and mentioned in every telecast in the country.

Brian, Xavier, Amanda, Peyton, Vince, Vanessa, and even Emilee got similar attention in the three-part series. The media obsesses over ratings, and since the public interest in our spartan campaign went through the roof leading up to the school board's decision, so did their appetite for stories about us. The "Profiles" pieces gave them exactly what they were looking for, and made us household names in the process.

At first, the attention was pretty cool. Kids in school who never knew my name started saying hi to me in the hallway. I became instantly recognizable in town, and started to feel like an A-List celebrity without the designer clothes, makeup, and completely flawless skin. I even got asked out on a date or two, much to Dad's dismay.

Now we are getting a firsthand lesson in the downside of popularity, too. Media interest translates into a serious lack of privacy, and working out of the Perkfect Buzz, we are practically on display like zoo animals.

"Okay, you got your shots. Now be dolls and move out please," Laura chides from outside our roped off area, shooing away three men taking pictures of us. That woman has the patience of a saint for dealing with all this.

Photographers and other members of the press follow us everywhere like paparazzi. You see things like that on TV, but never expect it to happen to you. When it does, the novelty of the experience wears off fast. I look horrible on TV when I get filmed coming and going. After the first day or two, I began questioning the sanity of every reality television star willing to let a camera follow them around.

Being chased around by photographers is just the tip of the iceberg. Reporters, cable news networks, and daytime programs like *Katie* and *The View* started ringing our phones off the hook and asking for interviews not long after the "Profiles" articles. Mister Bennit has been contacted by everyone from *The Daily Show with Jon Stewart* and *The Colbert Report*, to *60 Minutes* and *Meet the Press*. Vince even got a call from *The Tonight Show*, or so he swears. I think he's full of crap.

As the pressure for interviews increased, we made the decision as a group not to do any, over Vince and Peyton's protests. We aren't supposed to be the face of the campaign, Mister Bennit is. We did do a few feature interviews for some specialty magazines, but they were for fun and not at all political.

Turning down the repeated requests for special interviews has driven the media bonkers. We feared ignoring the offers would hurt the campaign, but it is having the opposite effect. The search for the latest scoop on the Bennit campaign has turned our little town into a media circus.

A few days ago, Laura finally had enough and made the media trucks assemble on a first-come, first-serve basis in the ten spots at the far back of the parking lot. The number of complaints from her paying customers about lack of parking prompted her to take action, but it hasn't slowed the coverage down one bit.

Mobs of reporters and photographers are everywhere around town, and the stories about us dominate the news. It is like the Jon Benet Ramsey murder, Natalie Holloway disappearance, and O.J. Simpson trial all wrapped into one, or so Dad tells me. It's completely nuts.

Life in the fishbowl resulting from the media craze has brought us closer together as a staff. Outside of Vince and Peyton, none of us want the attention. With so much to do for the campaign and grades to keep up, we rely on each other for support to keep afloat. Used to the spotlight as good athletes, Vanessa and Xavier have tolerated the constant intrusions better than the more reclusive Amanda and Emilee. Amanda shed her CPA look with Peyton's help, and we all found out she is far prettier than we ever thought. Emilee is so shy I thought she might quit the campaign. The hoopla bothered poor Brian the most, being the most introverted of our small group.

As we have become more of a media fascination, really funny things have started to happen. We have come to call it the "One Direction Effect" after the boy band that won a realty television competition and became a near-instant success. Even the people who didn't particularly like their music began to get caught up in the mania for the sole reason that everyone else was. This feels like the same.

Volunteers from the school started showing up in droves a couple of weeks ago to make signs and help recruit others. At Millfield High, being a part of the campaign was the new hip thing to do. After a long summer of doing all the grunt work, it was awesome to have an army of people to help. Best of all, it didn't end with our little town.

Word spread to surrounding towns in the area like wildfire. We've used our newfound manpower to organize efforts across the district, and the results are amazing. Signs are going up everywhere, not just in Millfield. And I don't mean the mass-produced kind you see pounded into the grass at every major traffic intersection.

No, these signs are handmade with supplies from Home Depot. Tarpaulins spray painted with "Michael Bennit for Congress" are getting hung off front porches. Cardboard placards are materializing in front yards with our "www.icandidate.org" web address on it. And despite the thrill of seeing the progress of our campaign on the way to school, it was nothing compared to what was happening in social media.

"How are we making out, Bri?" I ask, putting my hand on his shoulder.

"This is amazing. I've never seen anything like it before. Look at these numbers!" Brian exclaims, unable to stifle his over-caffeinated excitement.

Kylie put out our web address, Facebook page, and Twitter account details on each of the "Profiles" articles. Every day, literally thousands of businesses and people try to make their page go viral. We actually did it. Our Facebook page likes broke the one million mark last week. As of yesterday, @MichaelBennit had almost three times that number of Twitter followers. Not exactly Justin Bieber numbers, but not bad for a teacher-politician. And the #icandidate has been trending for two straight weeks now.

"Great work, Brian. How are we doing on content?"

"We can always use more, but I'm pretty sure Xavier and Vanessa have people working on that," Brian adds, dividing his attention between me and the screen.

"Okay, let me know if you need anything."

Of course, we haven't stopped at just Facebook and Twitter. We rank high on the sharing sites like Reddit, Digg, and StumbleUpon, and enjoy tremendous popularity on Pinterest and Instagram. Our YouTube channel is getting a lot of uploads from fans and volunteers. Students check into our volunteer meetings on FourSquare, and the new badge they offer for being a "Bennitite" has become a must have for every student in school. The list goes on from there.

We have leveraged everything we can to reach people, including e-mail and web chats. Essentially, any and every electronic medium available to get our message is being used to full effect. Looking out into the parking lot at the army of media, it seems to be working. I am now managing a campaign effort that has become the epicenter of the political world. But through it all, there is still something missing.

Mister Bennit talks about grand ideas, but he still isn't addressing controversial issues. He quotes the Framers' words at the Constitutional Convention and relates them to today's reality, but I have yet to hear him take a stand on abortion, gun control, gay marriage, or any of the other hot button issues of the day.

Not that any of that has mattered much. Despite the Beaumont and Johnson campaigns whining about it, nobody really seems to care here at the height of Bennit fever. I only wonder how long that will last.

-THIRTY-ONE-
KYLIE

"Nice to see you haven't given up all your prodigal habits considering you're unemployed," the voice behind me chirps.

"I have been spending a lot of time in a coffee shop lately," I say to Bill as he slides into the seat next to me at the long counter by the window. "Now I'm addicted. How did you know I was here?"

On a normal day, I wouldn't think twice about running into Bill at this lower Manhattan Starbucks. But since I have been spending so much time in Connecticut, I'm a little curious how he knew I was even in the city, let alone here.

"I have my sources."

"What are you, in the CIA or something?" I ask with a little laugh, but am almost serious. Anything is possible these days.

"No, just a lowly journalist whose life you've made miserable. Thanks to your antics up north, I'm now forced to write article after article about some small town named Millfield and anything and everything about its most famous teacher."

"You expect me to apologize for that?" I ask, laughing.

"No. I'm just amazed you were able to take an unknown candidate and turn him into a household name in only a month," Bill says, taking his eyes off the blonde at the other side off the shop just long enough to convey sincerity.

He is right. It's only the beginning of October and anyone in the district who hasn't heard of Michael Bennit is either out on an African safari or living under a rock. He even has the national name recognition a first-time candidate for *president* could only drool over.

"All the free media Bennit is getting is driving the Beaumont campaign bat shit crazy," Bill says, breaking eye contact again to ogle the girl at the register paying for her herbal tea concoction.

"I bet. I noticed their commercials started hitting the airwaves in force about a week after the 'Profile' articles."

"They started their political campaign machine once they realized the Bennit story wasn't going to go away on its own."

I had figured that out on my own. We dominated the evening news every night, and they had to respond. Now we highlight the evening news, and in between stories about us are commercials about him. The first barrage of paid ads stressed his leadership and service in Congress and the things he had done for the district. They must have spent a fortune, because they were on every station at every conceivable hour.

About a week ago, the second set of commercials started getting nastier, complaining about Bennit's lack of experience, and so on. He used his loyal political action committees to fill the airwaves with the same political crap people label as "mudslinging" and then try to ignore each election season. The thought of it makes by blood pressure shoot up.

"Beaumont's a coward. He is keeping himself distanced by going negative by proxy," I conclude in disgust. "Enlisting high-profile mayors to come out in force against Michael by ruthlessly questioning everything from his military service to his teaching ability is shameful."

"What do you expect? They have no voting record to distort," Bill says, eliciting a smile from me. "Don't sweat it. The airwaves may have balanced out, but you are still the center of attention."

"I don't work for Michael Bennit, Bill."

"You think that's what your sister is telling Beaumont?"

"I wouldn't know. I haven't talked to her since June," I snap, getting annoyed at the mere mention of Madison.

"Well, maybe he should consider putting you on the payroll for everything you are doing for him. How are you staying afloat financially? You've been out of work for what, six months now?"

Normally, I would tell anyone who had the audacity to question my impartiality and ask me about my financial affairs in the same breath to go piss up a rope. But since Bill got me involved in this escapade in the first place, I give him the benefit of the doubt.

"I made some freelance money on the deep background articles I have written about the campaign. The rest is coming from my rapidly dwindling savings account. Now, are you just a concerned friend, or are you pre-qualifying me for a loan?"

"Just making conversation," he replies, a sly grin creeping across his lips.

I lean into him, forcing him to pry his eyes off whatever female has his attention at the moment. "I am staying in a cheap hotel, and have been upgraded to a platinum frequent customer card at Subway for eating there so much. I'm getting by. Now, that's my story. What's yours? What are *you* working on?"

Bill smiles, always amused at his ability to get me worked up. "Nothing you don't already know about."

"Humor me."

"Richard Johnson and the Republicans."

"Yeah, what about them?"

"Except for some signs up around the district, and the occasional sound bite or appearance, his campaign has been almost nonexistent. Apparently they don't have much in terms of financing and aren't getting help from the party."

"You're right, I know. Bennit might have more in his campaign account than they do."

"I am curious as to why the Republicans are mailing this in. Beaumont looks vulnerable now because of Michael Bennit. Johnson's campaign manager Miles Everman saying something snarky in the press is the sum of their contribution to the media bazaar going on up there."

"Not much of a story there, Bill," I say, climbing off my stool and putting on my light jacket. "Johnson's a twit and Everman's a moron. The GOP named their candidate in April when Beaumont was a shoo-in. Now they're stuck with him."

I pat Bill on the shoulder and head for the door, fully aware that he is staring at my ass.

"Kylie?"

"Yeah," I say, turning around. This better not be about my ass.

"It's only a matter of time before Beaumont goes after Bennit. Deep down, you know that. Whether you work for his campaign or not, be sure you don't end up in his crosshairs when he does."

-THIRTY-TWO-
CHELSEA

The amount of time the campaign has been soaking up is getting more noticeable, so I'm not surprised to pull into my driveway to find the living room light still on. It's just after 11:00 p.m., and usually Dad is in bed by now. Since he is not a fan of *Saturday Night Live*, it can only mean he is waiting up for me.

I kind of feel like I missed curfew and am busted, only I don't have one. Until recently, being out late was never a concern Dad had to deal with. Considering I have a cop car following me, and an eruption of camera flashes to illuminate the sidewalk to the side door, I rule out attempting a stealthy entrance.

It must be quite the strobe effect from the perspective of Dad's recliner in the living room, even with the curtains drawn. Do these photographers think I am going to flip them the middle finger or something? What could be so interesting about walking from my car to the house? I swear to God, I will never understand how celebs put up with this on a daily basis.

Dad is practically deaf from years of working at the factory, so I can hear every word from the local news from the kitchen as I drop my things. Not surprisingly, the coverage is about the race for the Sixth District. As much as the constant media attention is great for the campaign, I can't believe they have nothing better to do than report live about us in the dead of night.

"It's a circus atmosphere in the Connecticut Sixth District as the iCandidate hits his stride," the reporter says, apparently from somewhere in town. "The latest Quinnipiac poll of likely voters has Michael Bennit at forty percent, within five points of incumbent Winston Beaumont. Republican hopeful Richard Johnson is lagging way behind at just seven percent. Eighteen percent of those polled say they are undecided with a little over a month remaining until Election Day."

Dad mutes the television as I sit in the worn chair across our small living room from him. I'm beat and would like nothing more than to dodge the grilling I'm expecting to get, but he has been so patient through this. I owe him better than most teens give their parents.

"You're looking pretty worn out, Snuggle Bear," Dad says, eyeing the bags under my eyes. "Everything okay?"

"Yeah, I'm just a little tired is all," I respond honestly.

"Do you have homework to finish tonight?"

I finished most of my assignments during study hall, but an English essay needs my attention. He doesn't need to know that though.

"Finished it before I left school."

Dad leans forward in his overstuffed recliner, measuring his words before speaking.

"Honey, I have tried to be supportive through all this. I hope you know that."

I nod. He actually has been, but I know what's coming next. My father isn't into social media, nor does he like any of the reality TV shows I watch. No doubt he's not thrilled his only daughter is being treated like I'm on one.

"But I am really worried about you. This is getting ridiculous," he says, pointing toward the window where the curtains are pulled to shield us from the legion of press camped on the street. "All the phone calls, the police escort … It's a lot for anyone to deal with."

"I am dealing with it fine," I reply curtly.

"I'm not so sure you are. I think I have given you too much freedom to pursue this campaign. Maybe it's time to dial it back some and start refocusing on school," he says in the most parental voice I have ever heard him use.

"Dial it back? We've come this far and accomplished so much! I'm not giving up now!"

"Chels, I—"

"No, Dad! Last year you said I was spending too much time studying. You wanted me to do something fun. Now I am having fun, and you want me to start studying harder? Which is it?" At some point during my rant, I stood up defiantly. A mistake only equaled by me cutting him off mid-sentence.

"Sit down, Chelsea," he says sternly, with a look that could melt ice. I comply immediately, more out of respect than fear. "I'm giving you the opportunity to talk to me as an adult, but the moment you start acting like a spoiled teenager is the moment I'll start treating you like one. I'll hear you out, but if you want to act up, I'll make the decision for you.

"A lot of people in the town think we are bad parents for letting you and your friends get involved in Bennit's campaign," he says, continuing. I am trying to hide the disgust on my face and failing miserably. I do know enough to shut up and let him finish, though.

"Now, I don't give a damn what other people think, but I do care about you. So when I see you looking like you're strung out on heroin, I begin to think they're right. So tell me, why should I let you continue this?"

"Because it's important to me."

"More important than applying to colleges?"

"Dad, have you seen the stack of stuff in the kitchen colleges have been sending?" I know he has, because the "Leaning Tower of College Literature" accumulating on a chair has toppled over at least twice. Since the campaign, I have gotten everything from handwritten notes from admissions offices, to signed letters from university presidents to go with with the usual propaganda materials colleges send to prospective students.

"Yes, I've seen them, but have you acted on any of them?"

"Still plenty of time for that. Look, Dad, I know what I am doing. I'm not a child anymore. I'm eighteen, and I know how much I can handle."

"Chelsea, you may think you know everything at eighteen, but you don't know anything. You'll realize that when you're my age. But you're also my daughter, I love you dearly, and until you're out of this house, I get a say in how much you can handle."

"So you're going to make me quit? I thought you taught me to never quit?" I say with a little too much attitude. Does he not understand what this means to me? Why it's important? I don't know why he can't seem to understand. All I know is I won't quit. I won't let him make me.

"No, I'm not going to make you quit. Whether you know it or not, I am proud of what you are accomplishing and will support you as best I know how. But I will tell you this. The moment I think this is no longer in your best interest, we are going to have a serious conversation about how involved you should be in this campaign. I don't care if the idiots outside think you're Madonna by then."

-THIRTY-THREE-
BLAKE

"Who would have thought that a social media campaign for a history teacher, run by teenagers, would become the talk of the country?" I hear Roger say as he sits down next to me.

My love affair with the District of Columbia started with my eighth grade field trip here. Something about the National Mall at sunset draws me to it whenever I can break free from the confines of the Rayburn Building. Adorned with museums and monuments marking our greatest achievements as a nation, it's purely American.

From my regular spot on the steps on the west side of the Capitol Building, the sun is setting behind the Lincoln Memorial and casting the entire National Mall in a glow of oranges, reds, and pinks. The bath of color is a rare moment of peace and tranquility in a city normally anything but. Unfortunately, the time to enjoy it is over because Roger is all business.

"The press is calling our campaign 'befuddled' and 'stuck in neutral' if I remember today's headlines correctly," I say with no small amount of disdain.

"A multi-million-dollar ad buy is hardly stuck in neutral," Roger says. "But it's not having the desired effect. We've flooded the airwaves in Connecticut with countless messages and none of them are getting through to the voters."

"And all of Bennit's time on TV is free," I add, noting the obvious.

"We started The Machine weeks ago. It should have turned things around by now, but we're a month away from the election and are still hemorrhaging votes. All the hopes of avoiding a hard campaign season are gone now. When this session ends, Winston is going to have to go to Connecticut and fight for his political life. You've read the polls."

"Quinnipiac has us up by three. We're down by one in both Rasmussen and Gallup. Marist has us in a dead heat." Yes, I memorized ones published today, and the results were not good news.

"Deena says our internal polls have the race within the margin of error. Madison is up there working her ass off, but it isn't making any difference. You can imagine Winston is fuming."

Congressman Beaumont is an old-school politician. He won't embrace social media or the more modern ways people use to communicate. He wouldn't be able to send a text message if his life depended on it. The fact that a novice is tied with us using those very methods must be infuriating to him.

"We're fighting an unconventional war using conventional means."

"I've read the *Art of War*, Blake."

"Yes, sir, I know. So you also realize The Machine is not going to work in this race." And it won't. Sun Tzu would love this guy. The Machine is designed to bludgeon an opponent in a straight-up, nasty fight. It worked against the Republicans every time, so Bennit simply changed campaign tactics. Now relying on this strategy is about as effective as charging a tank with a bayonet.

"Are you suggesting we try to play the game at his level?" he asks. "Because that'll never work, and Winston would never approve it anyway."

"Maybe we should just keep beating on Bennit for not taking a stand on a single issue." It was a desperate response, but I don't know what else to say. We can go negative, but there really isn't any dirt on him juicy enough to cool down this craze surrounding his campaign.

"The voters aren't listening to that message. It's like Beatlemania up in Connecticut. Everyone has lost their minds. The kids running his campaign are being treated like they're pop stars. Bennit could say he was the reincarnation of Stalin and nobody would give a damn."

"Everyone has an Achilles' heel," I point out.

"He does," Roger says looking at me. "What did our oppo team learn about his staff?"

"His staff?" I ask, confused. "You mean his students?"

"Yeah, Blake, I mean his students. What did they find?"

"A couple of things on some of them," I respond, halfheartedly. "Pretty inconsequential stuff, really. If I thought it was anything important we could use to discredit Bennit, I would have told you. You planning on going after the kids?"

"No, Blake, I'm not going after them," Roger states while getting up from our seat on the steps and brushing himself off. He regards me for a moment. "I'm sending you up to Connecticut to go after them for me."

-THIRTY-FOUR-
MICHAEL

I woke up in a foul mood this morning. To be expected after another verbal mixed martial arts bout with Jessica last night. To say this campaign is straining our relationship is an exercise in understatement. Not surprisingly, the wedding planning ground to a halt right after the school board decision. Whether the campaign is causing her second thoughts is anyone's guess, because she isn't talking about it.

Running late, I take an even more circuitous route around the Main Office than usual. My new path takes me down a hallway in the back of the school where students are pouring into the building from their buses. That is not out of the ordinary, but the mass of reporters and cameras outside the doors is. They have been cordoned off away from the building by police for weeks now, but their normal exile to the other side of the street is not in effect this morning.

The activity suddenly picks up as the media congeals into a huddled mass of humanity fifty feet from the entrance. At the center of the mob, Vince struggles to make his way to the door. It takes him a full minute to push through the crowd, open the doors, and squeeze in. Only once inside the second set of doors is he visibly secure in the thought that the horde of press will not dare try to follow. He sees me and smiles, and after a quick salute, heads off down the hall to his locker.

Safely inside the building, he is having roughly the same experience with his peers. Students gather around him like he is a movie star, and meeting up with Amanda and Vanessa down the corridor only causes the pack of admirers to grow larger. The popularity of my staff in this school has reached epic proportions.

Only then do I detect Principal Howell standing nearby with his arms folded across his chest, looking exceedingly unhappy. There's another curiosity, because our fearless leader never mingles in the halls before classes start. He always looks displeased about something, though I like to attribute it to chronic constipation. This is different.

"You didn't take my advice," Howell says in an arrogant tone from down the hallway. "Look at this mess! Kids can't even get in the building, and you're to blame! You have lost complete control of this and the school board is going to hear about it!"

I know a setup when I see one. In Afghanistan, we all developed a sort of sixth sense as to where the bad guys would plant improvised explosive devices to ambush us. Right now, I just caught my principal planting one of his own, metaphorically speaking. Howell has become more belligerent toward me and the campaign with each passing day. He has a point to make, and he's going to use this fabricated incident as the impetus to make it.

There is no doubt in my mind he asked the Millfield Police to stay off school grounds in an effort to orchestrate this little fiasco. The problem is I can't exactly accuse him without any proof. Well, *can't* is a word of defeat. I probably *shouldn't* make the accusation. Yeah, Chalice has definitely gotten inside my head.

"Control is an illusion, Robinson. If there's a problem with students getting in and out of the building, handle it. After all, anything that affects this school, or the students in it, is *your* responsibility, remember?" I catch his face turn beet red as I walk past him.

"Bennit!" he exclaims, commanding the attention of every student in the hallway. I give him a quick wave of my hand, refusing to turn back. I'm just not in the mood.

* * *

My classroom, in many respects, is a refuge. Even when the campaign's inner circle shows up during F Period, the focus is on their education and not our race for Congress. It may be a contemporary issues class, and we may be the dominant contemporary issue, but I need the freedom to escape for a while. My opponents create the illusion I am working on the campaign during school hours. Nothing could be further from the truth. I know people are watching, and wouldn't even be shocked to find my lessons are being recorded.

So I bide time in the morning before classes start doing what all teachers do and prepare the day's lessons. The retreat is welcome considering the crazy roller-coaster ride this fall. The telltale click of high heels announcing the grand entrance of the love of my life shatters my solace. Two months ago, it made my heart flutter. Now it just fills me with dread.

Jessica stalks over and tosses a magazine on my desk without preamble. The graphically busy copy of *Teen Week Magazine* features a picture of Peyton and a headline that reads: Makeup Tips for the Politically Active Teen.

"Are you saying I need to change my shade of eye shadow?" I ask her sarcastically. Unfazed, she drops another magazine in front of me. This happens to be one of Brian on the cover of *Wired Magazine*. Okay, that's cool. The caption next to his photo reads: The Master of Viral Campaigning.

Eliciting no reaction, she plops the rest of the small stack on my desk. I spread them out and glance at the covers quickly. *Teen Vogue, Seventeen, People, Entertainment Weekly,* and something called *Glitter* all include prominent photos of them on the front page.

"If you have a one of Vince on the cover of GQ, I'm going to be insanely jealous." Arms folded across her chest and a stern look on her face means she is not in the mood for games or clever comments. Lucky me, she's come to pick up where we left off last night. Joy.

"I'm glad you think this is so funny, but it's not a laughing matter. Remember that conversation we had about going too far? This has gone way too far. Even you could not have expected this," she chides, jamming her index finger at the magazines on my desk.

"You're seriously pissed off this morning because they are on the cover of a couple of magazines?"

"A couple of magazines? No, I'm pissed because *your* stupid campaign got them on the cover of almost every magazine!" Did I just hear her right?

"Stupid campaign?" I ask with no attempt to hide my irritation. "That's what you think this is, a stupid campaign?"

"What do you expect me to think?"

"I don't know, maybe I was expecting a little more support from *my* fiancée." I'm getting agitated. My run-in with Howell made a bad morning worse, so this isn't a good morning to bring this up. The best thing to do is table this discussion for later.

"And I would expect *my* fiancé to respect *my* opinion and include me on decisions affecting our lives before making them!"

"Why? There's no room for discussion with you. You just expect me to see things your way. You don't want to be included in the decisions—you want to unilaterally make them!" So much for tabling the discussion for a later time. No U-turns allowed on this particular part of the path now after that comment.

"Maybe I should, because you've been wrong every step of the way!"

"What do you mean?" I ask indignantly.

"Let's see, you were wrong about winning the bet, wrong about them joining the campaign, wrong about its effect on them, and wrong about how well you'd do. Should I continue?" she asks, with as much attitude as she can muster.

"Oh, please do. You're on fire, so don't stop on my account."

Every guy who has ever been married, engaged, or in a serious long-term relationship knows there is a point in every argument where you can go too far. It's an imaginary line you cross at your own peril. Most men do, either out of stubbornness, indifference, or ignorance. Like the Korean "Bridge of No Return," once you cross, you're stuck on the other side forever.

I'm sure the same thing applies to women, but I can't speak to that. All I know is, with a divorce rate of over fifty percent in the United States, this line gets crossed a lot. It's the point where it becomes more difficult to go back to the way things were than to forge ahead going separate ways. In terms of fights, we have had worse. Something about this one is different and tells me, somewhere along the way, I crossed that line.

Jessica stands in front of me with both rage and hurt in her eyes. She may have a valid concern in all this, but she picked the wrong way, and wrong time, to confront me with it. Now things have been said that cannot be unsaid. Knowing that, it's time to check the level of damage.

"Jess, let's not talk about this now," I say in what is bound to be a futile attempt at ratcheting down the tension. I take a calming breath. "We can work through this, we always do."

Her eyes begin to fill with tears. "Maybe, just maybe, you are wrong about that too," she says before turning and walking out of the room.

I guess I got my answer.

-THIRTY-FIVE-
KYLIE

CNN cut in with the story around one o'clock this afternoon. Obviously the leak was timed to get maximum exposure on the local stations this evening. The news is being carried nationally by every outlet, but it's the voters of the Sixth District Beaumont needs to target. To maximize effect, the information was provided directly to one of the news stations up in Hartford, knowing it would get plenty of play. Connecticut is not known for making national headlines in politics, so they are going to run with every single thing they get, and this is no exception.

I pull my car into the driveway at Millfield High School and find a space in visitor parking. With the students gone for the day, the police are not quite as militant about keeping press off the grounds, although it still takes some effort to talk my way into the building. Knowing Michael's relationship with the principal, I decide to skip visiting the Main Office and search for his classroom on my own.

I have spent a ton of time in Millfield since this all started, so I was able to develop a network of people who keep me well informed about the happenings in the life of the iCandidate. I know about his continuing problems with his dweeby, power-thirsty principal and the issues with his fiancée. I even have insight into the strain on his relationship with his students' parents. This news will make that dynamic much worse.

So when I finally find him seated at his desk in the classroom, he does not appear as defeated as one might think. It is also abundantly clear today is not going to have a positive footnote in his memoirs. Without saying a word, I take a seat on top of a student desk and wait for him to talk.

"I take it you've heard?"

"It's a small school. When the transgressions of three of your students are being reported on an endless loop on cable news, word travels pretty fast."

"You didn't think Beaumont would sit on the sidelines forever, did you? I mean, it was only a matter of time before they came after you."

"Damn it, Kylie, they're not coming after me, they're going after my kids! Peyton, Brian, and Vince aren't running for office, I am."

I look at the spread of popular magazines on Michael's desk. Each one features one of his student staff members. I had seen a couple in passing, but I didn't realize that they were in so many. He watches me flip to the article on Brian in *Wired*.

"Jessica said this was spinning out of control when she handed me those," Michael finally continues after a couple of moments. "I can only imagine what she thinks now that

Vince, Peyton, and Brian are being embarrassed on national television. I guess maybe she was right."

"You wanted this exposure," I point out, showing him the cover of the magazine. "You put them in the spotlight."

"You could've talked me out of it."

"I don't work for you or your staff," I say sharply, remembering Bill's comment from a few days ago. "I'm only a journalist. I'm more than a little partial towards you, but ultimately you set the direction and I help where I can."

"If you were only a journalist, you never would have been let into the building."

He makes a fair point, but I'm not thrilled he recognizes my lack of objectivity. I am still struggling with it myself.

"Well, I went off in a direction that led to my students getting stalked by paparazzi and the media. They need police escorts to school in the morning to avoid getting harassed by members of the press. They've alienated their friends, given up their summer and fall, and now their teenage mistakes are being broadcast onto every television in America."

Michael stops and grimaces. I give him a sympathetic look, because I think I understand what's bothering him. "You're afraid what you are trying to teach them is getting lost in the mania."

"I wasn't counting on my kids being elevated to rock star status, and I never thought Beaumont would stoop so low as to go after them."

"That's what happens when they become the focus." Michael gives me a look of chagrin. It's a bitter pill to swallow, but I'm not one to obscure the truth. "You said this was a journey for them. What is happening is part of the trip, intended or not. Politics is a dirty business. Maybe that's a lesson you both need to learn."

"Yeah, I guess."

"You know, what is getting reported is petty stuff," I say in a futile attempt to put a silver lining on this. "I mean, alcohol, marijuana, cheating, and illegal downloads? C'mon, every teenager in America is doing that stuff."

"Yeah, well, these particular teenagers happen to be working on a congressional campaign staff. And their parents don't feel like it's petty stuff right now."

"Have you talked to them?"

"I called each of them at work as soon as school let out. Vince has a tough home life. His dad split when he was a boy and his mom is too overwhelmed to care much so long as he isn't in prison. It's why he is influenced by his friends, so it's not hard to understand why he got busted for alcohol and marijuana possession. He runs with a pretty rough crowd.

"Peyton's parents are your typical white, upper-middle class, two and a half kid, white-picket fencers. They work hard to be the perfect family from the outside. They were pissed any information about their daughter that could shatter that perception was made public. I'm sure they thought her getting caught cheating was long forgotten."

"I can imagine. And Brian?"

Michael cracks a smile. "I think his parents figure he will get busted hacking the DoD or something, someday. Of all the things Brian is capable of, downloading music without paying for it was pretty low on their list of concerns. They were upset about hearing their son's name on CNN though."

"You've had a tough day," I point out, as if he didn't know that. Stupid.

"You don't know the half of it. Tell me something, Kylie. With four weeks until Election Day, does it get better or worse from here?"

"What did Vince tell me your favorite line is? It's a matter of perspective?" That got him to smile a little broader, and even let out a chuckle.

"So, what now?"

Since the day we met, I have been amazed about how quick Michael makes decisions. He takes information, processes it, and settles on a course of action in mere seconds. It's quite amazing to watch, especially now.

"First, I need to fight off the wolves. Then I need to pick up the spirits of the troops in the trenches."

"How are you planning on doing that? It's not like you're Mister Sunshine yourself right now."

"Ever heard of General McAuliffe?" he asks, pointing to a print tacked to the wall in the back of the room. Apparently he doesn't know how poorly I did in social studies in high school, and that's probably a good thing. I glance back to see a black and white poster of a man in an old army uniform and helmet.

"Is this the start of a history lesson?"

"Look around you. It's what I do," he responds, cracking the first smile of the afternoon. "General McAuliffe was the acting commanding general of the 101st Airborne Division when they got trapped in Bastogne during the Battle of the Bulge. His boss was attending a staff conference in the U.S. at the time, so all eyes were on McAuliffe when the division found itself surrounded by the German armor. When his aide presented him with the surrender demand, he tossed the crumpled paper in the trash with the words 'Aw, nuts.'"

"I'm sure you have a point to this."

"I do. His staff couldn't figure out how to respond to the German demand until a colonel suggested using the general's exact words. That simple reply became a rallying cry for the Screaming Eagles during the war and part of U.S. military lore ever since."

"Nuts," I say, still completely lost to his point. Watching the History Channel is almost a prerequisite for having a conversation with this man.

"The commander of the 327th Glider Infantry had to explain to the Germans that the message basically meant 'go to hell.' The moral of the story, since I'm sure you're about to ask, is McAuliffe was in Bastogne with his men. They were stuck in the same shitty situation, and shared the same 'we're screwed' thoughts. He wasn't going to let the Germans think that, though."

"And you're going to apply that how?" I ask, still not clear on how this applies.

"My kids made mistakes they think will hurt the campaign," he continues. "Time for them to know they aren't the only ones who have done things they're not proud of. In the process, we send our own message to Winton Beaumont that means go to hell."

I suddenly get his point, and the reason why he's opening up. I think I'm about to find out what makes Michael Bennit tick. The determination in his eyes that makes me believe he is engaged for the first time in this campaign. They went after his kids, so now this whole thing became personal.

Since the day I met Vince and talked to Michael, I have questioned my objectivity. Yes, I want to get even with Winston Beaumont in the worst possible way. No, I refuse to let myself turn into my sister to do it. Despite this, I am getting more drawn into this campaign. There is something about this man that pulls people into his sphere of influence. Now I know where Chelsea and the gang get their motivation from.

Michael's students didn't have any better success fighting this attraction, creating one motley group of friends. While they started off as classmates, they formed relationships as a staff that became real friendships. A pair of jocks, a nerd, a derelict, a beauty queen, an introvert, a hippie, and I am not even sure what category to put Chelsea in. A modern version of the *Breakfast Club*, or at least something I would expect to see as the movie of the week on the Family Channel.

Now both they and their renegade teacher finally got a bitter taste of the modern election process I knew was coming. There were days when the personal lives of politicians stayed private. Whether it was FDR in his wheelchair or JFK's womanizing, there were limits as to what was printed and played on television. In the age of the twenty-four-hour media cycle, those limits are long gone.

I guess all that remains to be answered is where the Bennit campaign, a media wonder that has captivated the nation for weeks now, goes from here. Will his students persevere through this latest challenge? Will it matter if the school administrators and town's school board decide to put an end to this?

-THIRTY-SIX-
MICHAEL

A pang of guilt jars my stomach as I pull into the parking lot of the nondescript brick building. Kylie has already done more for this campaign than I ever should expect, and this is just another instance where she might be compelled to jump into the fray. She didn't hesitate to help with the school board, but there is probably nothing she could do spare me this perp walk.

That is how I rationalize not telling her about the phone call I received just minutes before she walked into my classroom. Given the breaking news about Vince, Brian, and Peyton, this summons was no real surprise.

Unfortunately, the media is here too. Whether they heard of my arrival in advance, or were camped out looking for comment from the school system is anyone's guess. Cameramen and reporters come sprinting across the lawn at me, shouting questions the whole way. They must have been getting some long shots of the building when I arrived. Lucky for me there's more than enough distance between us for me to slip into the four-story tower of terror unmolested.

I give them a quick friendly wave before ducking in the front door. The walk to the lion's den is a short one, and I am greeted by a receptionist in the outer office. She covers the phone with her hand as I enter and stand in front of her desk.

"She's waiting for you, Mister Bennit. Please go on in."

"Thanks," I say, walking past her and coming to grips with how much my reputation precedes me these days. I have never met the receptionist before in my life.

I get waved into the office before I even reach the door. "Come in, Michael, and please have a seat," Charlene Freeman says from the executive chair behind her gigantic oak desk. As I enter the room, I begin to understand the gravity of the meeting. Standing along the wall are the town's attorney, the teacher's union representative, my department head, Chalice, and the director of personnel for the Millfield Public School District. Seated in the other stylish, upholstered chair in front of her desk is my arch nemesis, Robinson Howell.

"Thank you for coming on such short notice," Charlene says in preamble.

"Looking around the room, I don't think I had much of a choice, ma'am." She smiles politely, but also knows I am one hundred percent correct. You don't turn down the superintendent when she calls you into her office.

"Let's begin this, shall we? Irwin, why don't you start?"

"Mister Bennit, I'm certain you know why you were called here, so I will skip the preamble. Were you aware of these transgressions by the students in question prior to allowing them to participate in your campaign?"

Lawyers. They can make hitting on a girl in a bar sound like a deposition. With his yellow legal pad in his hand and the accusatory look on his face, I figure this actually is one, sans the video camera.

"Yes, I did."

"And you were okay with that?"

"I was, and I still am."

"That is a serious error in judgment on your part," the lawyer says in a condescending tone.

"Not his first," Robinson mumbles from the chair next to me. Smug bastard. I try to fight it, but can feel my face flush with anger. When I get mad, sarcasm follows.

"Did you know the information would be released to the press?"

"No, I didn't. I left my Magic 8-Ball in the classroom."

"Michael," Charlene intercedes, "there is no reason to be glib."

I glance over at Chalice who is looking at me with hardened eyes. The message I shouldn't antagonize the superintendent is transmitting clear. Returning my look to Charlene, I give her a nod out of respect.

"Did you ever discuss with your students and their parents the possibility information like this might be made public?"

"No, I did not."

"I see." He jots down some more notes, and I am beginning to wonder if they are real or just a part of the theater he is putting on.

"Is there anything else?" Charlene asks impatiently, trying to move this along. Apparently she doesn't want to be here anymore than I do.

"Mister Bennit has put us at severe risk. This requires more investigation, but I believe he exercised poor judgment and incompetence in this matter. The safest thing to do to protect ourselves would be place him on administrative leave immediately and reprimand him officially for his actions."

Being a soldier, I want to start kicking someone's ass. If we were at Fort Campbell right now, this needle-neck lawyer would be stuffed in a foot locker and Howell on an ambulance trip to the post's medical center. Violence may not be the answer, but it does feel damn good when exercised once in a while.

The problem is I'm running for Congress. As I explained to my kids when I took the bet, the only thing I hate more than lawyers are the ones who become politicians. They may deserve it, and as entertaining as it would be for most Americans, kicking people's asses on Capitol Hill is frowned upon.

So what would Chalice do? She can't exactly act as counsel in this company, so I am left to figure it out on my own. She can be a firecracker and ruthless defender of her faculty, but she also successfully navigated the treacherous waters of public education for thirty years. She'd change the paradigm and play their game better than they are. It's a skill I will need to master if I win this race, so I might as well start now.

"I concur. Given this incident and the other disruptions he is causing in the school, I believe—"

"How did the Beaumont camp find out about Vince's record?" I ask, cutting off Robinson mid-sentence.

"What?" the stuffed shirt the town calls their attorney asks.

"You heard me. Vince was a minor when he was arrested. He was tried as a juvenile for underage drinking and possession and his was record sealed. How did Beaumont find out about those proceedings?"

"I don't know. I suppose the court—"

"Does the police department maintain a copy of the arrest record?"

Chalice's face changes from one of concern to barely perceptible amusement. That's all the approval I need from my guardian. The attorney's face is contorted into a completely different emotion.

"Of course."

"Then instead of grilling me, wouldn't it be in the town's best interest to ensure the leak didn't come out of our own police department? I mean, releasing information about a minor is very serious these days."

"Michael, that's not at issue here," Howell says, recognizing the meeting was getting away from my lynch mob.

"Okay, Robinson, let's move on to the next issue. Outside of me, Peyton, and her parents, there were four people who knew what she did to get suspended. Her teacher, guidance counselor, vice principal, and ..." I count on my fingers for added theatrical effect. "Can you tell me the fourth?"

What I would pay for a picture of the look on Howell's face right now.

"Robinson?" I needle.

"Me."

"That's correct, a gold star for you. So tell me, which one of those four disclosed confidential student records to a politician for the sole purpose of using them to humiliate a teenage girl?"

Howell looks to Charlene with eyes pleading for her to save him. She only begrudgingly obliges. "That's a very serious accusation, Michael."

"Yes, ma'am, but so far I have been accused of incompetence and poor judgment for failing to anticipate the unsavory tactics of an unscrupulous incumbent. I guess I'm wondering why, if protecting the town from legal action is the real goal here, why there is no investigation into who leaked the information to begin with?"

"This meeting is about you, Michael!" Howell shouts. I ignore him.

"Because if someone ever whispers into Brian's, Peyton's, or Vince's parents' ears that they may have cause to sue the town, well, I would shudder to think how much that might cost to settle." I even wiggle my shoulders for added effect.

The point of the implied threat is not lost on my audience. Silence can be golden, but in this case, it's deafening. I wonder who will recover first.

"Are you saying you would advise their parents to sue?" the director of personnel asks incredulously. We have a winner.

"Of course not. Unfortunately, this campaign has created opportunists looking to exploit situations for their own benefit and to advance their personal agenda. Isn't that right, Robinson?"

If he gets any hotter with anger, the frames of his glasses might melt right off his face. Even Charlene, who has remained quiet through all this, is mildly amused. She would never admit it, but she doesn't like the weasel either. "I'm just trying to protect the school district and the town."

"Well, we appreciate that, Michael. And we're also happy to hear you would never engage in an activity that would seriously jeopardize your chances for tenure." I am not even sure what this woman's name is, but the threat drips off her tongue, and also explains why she's here. If you want to use tenure as leverage, the personnel director for the district would be the one to deliver the message.

"I certainly would never dream about doing anything that would hamper my chances at tenure," I reply with a smile. I recognize that getting tenure after all this is pretty much out of the question. I'd be kidding myself to think otherwise.

"We are getting off the subject. Michael, these students' parents want you fired. Can you give me a good reason why we shouldn't remove you from your position?" Howell asks smugly in a desperate attempt to salvage this meeting.

"Sure. Not one of them said I should be fired when I talked to them a couple of hours ago."

"Uh, I ..."

"In fact, the only comment about me that could even be construed as negative came from Brian's mom who blamed me for not telling him to download the Beatle's White Album for her."

Charlene smiles and leans back in her chair. Everyone seems to be at a loss for words before she breaks the silence. "Could you all excuse us for a moment? I would like to talk alone with Mister Bennit. If you are comfortable with that, of course," she adds, nodding at me. Why wouldn't I be? I'm not the kind of guy who hides behind a useless union rep, or even my benevolent department chair.

"Certainly, ma'am."

The others evacuate the room, including Howell who didn't seem eager to get off his ass and leave. Once the door closes to her office, Charlene gets out of her chair and sits on the corner of her desk.

"That was interesting," she observes. "Nearly everyone in this room wanted your head on a platter."

"So I noticed. Oh well, less Christmas cards to send out this year."

"You're an enigma, Michael. A rare breed of educator who manages to thrive in a system he otherwise hates. I suppose if you were to ever win this thing, life in Washington wouldn't be much different."

She looks at me for a reaction. She's right on both counts, but I'm not feeling compelled to tell her that. I give her a little nod to the side in acknowledgement and nothing more.

She gracefully slides off the desk and begins repositioning a potted plant on the credenza along the wall. "Your preemptive move against the school board was politically savvy, but unwise. They feel manipulated, and harbor a lot of resentment toward you because of it. Now they take it out on me."

"I apologize for causing you any heartburn, ma'am," I say, half meaning it. The other half wants to scream "that's what you get paid for."

"The board I can handle," she dismisses with a quick wave of her hand. "The parents are another thing entirely. I field dozens of complaints a week, and no, not all of them are organized by your political enemies." She read my mind. I bet the percentage is pretty high though.

"Ma'am, you didn't want to talk to me alone just to tell me that."

"Of course not. Did you know Chalice and I started teaching right around the same time?"

"No, I didn't," I respond, unable to hide my surprise.

"We go way back, and have been friends for a long time. I trust her judgment and value her opinions. She told me that your didactic approach to teaching history makes you well respected by students and parents. You're a brilliant teacher. Nothing I have seen gives me reason to doubt that."

"It's good to know Chalice speaks so well of me."

Charlene moves back around the gargantuan oak monstrosity and sits in her chair, taking the time to carefully fold her hands in front of her. The signal is unmistakable—it is back to business. In some respects, she reminds me of a colonel I knew in Afghanistan.

"As superintendent, I am not afforded the luxury of making decisions based on personal observations. Many good people here asked me to make your life miserable so you will leave on your own," she deadpans, "but I don't want to do that. In my professional opinion, the way press portrays the school district is an advantage to us. I sincerely hope recent events have not upset that paradigm. If that turns out to be the case, or another revelation paints this district in a bad light, I won't be willing to protect you anymore. Do you understand?"

"Yes, ma'am, I do."

Most Americans will say they don't like politics, never realizing that it exists all around us—church, volunteer organizations, families, and especially at our places of work. Charlene's message is a simple one. So long as I can be perceived in a positive light, she won't take action against me. This is all politics for her.

"Then there's nothing further to discuss here," she says, standing and outstretching her hand. I take it and we shake across her desk. As I am about to release, she tightens her grip. "I wish you well, Michael. Please remember what I told you. There are far too few teachers like you, and I'd hate to have to be the person who fires you."

-THIRTY-SEVEN-
CHESLEA

The air is brisk, although not bitterly cold this early in October. The sun is hanging low in the sky, but there is still a good hour or more of daylight left. I suppose that's why he wanted to meet at Briar Point instead of the coffee shop. Every inch of Laura's little haunt is covered by a phalanx of reporters and cameramen all waiting to get the official reaction from the Bennit campaign to the news about Vince, Brian, and Peyton. Considering he has not yet done a single interview over anything other than Skype, no wonder he is avoiding the place.

We piled into Peyton's SUV, breaking all sorts of Connecticut state laws for vehicle capacity in the process. Peyton agreed to let Vince drive, because face it, when trying to lose a horde of media following your every move, the resident derelict should be in charge. He ditched our tail on the first attempt and sped over to the park for our meeting.

Cramped in the back of the overstuffed car, I struggled with how to present this to Mister Bennit. We settled on the course of action, but convincing him we're right is not going to be easy. He is going to protest and fight me on this, but I don't see any other way out.

Peyton and Vince agreed that this was best, although neither is happy about not working with us anymore. Downloading music illegally was more of an accusation than something they had proof of in the article, and we need Brian too much to let him go anyway. The damage we will cause by keeping him around is acceptable.

As we untangle ourselves and climb out of Peyton's chariot, I still have no idea what I'm going to say to Mister Bennit. As we have all learned in class, no argument with him is easy. I'm trying to think up some clever way to propose this, but I got nothing. Walking through the parking lot, I only settle on the direct approach at the last possible moment.

"We decided it's in your best interests that Vince and Peyton leave the campaign," I say, without introduction to Mister Bennit and Kylie who are sitting atop a picnic table between the parking lot and the river.

"In my best interests, huh?" Mister Bennit asks. The tone he uses reminds me of what happens in class when someone makes a point he disagrees with. I get the feeling he's in teacher mode, so I wonder if Kylie got subjected to a lesson at some point today.

"Whether we like it or not, they're a liability," I plead.

"Their mistakes become the story," Amanda says, picking up the argument.

"We're okay with the decision, Mister B. Your campaign is too important to be sabotaged by our stupid mistakes," Vince concludes despondently.

Mister Bennit looks over at Peyton who nods agreement. She hasn't said much since the story broke, whether out of regret or embarrassment I'm not sure. Mister B looks like he is pondering the thought. Could he actually agree with us for a change?

"Okay, I understand your positions. As for Vince's and Peyton's resignations, I don't accept them. You're not going anywhere." Nope, guess not.

"You have to!" Vince and Peyton exclaim at the same time.

"It's the only option," Xavier adds.

"We came to an agreement Mister B. It's settled," I offer to the cause.

"Did you hear them, Kylie? My staff thinks they settled this without me. What do you say to that?"

"Nuts," Kylie says, smiling. Uh-oh, she got the Bastogne talk. We didn't cover World War II in class, but Mister B loves the story, and found some reason to tell us about the plight of the men defending the city.

"My thoughts exactly. Grab a seat, guys," Mister Bennit says, ceding his spot on the table so we can all be seated. He stands and Kylie moves off to the side. "You think you are the only ones here to ever make a mistake? Well, let me tell you how a real-world, high-stakes mistake sounds.

"During my last tour in Afghanistan, I was part of a three-man team on a recon mission in a village down near Kandahar. The Taliban were reasserting themselves in the region, killing everyone they thought assisted the U.S. and our allies there. Our unit was tasked with finding out where the head honcho was holed up so he could be taken out.

"We were observing a small hamlet from a hide site when a group of armed men showed up and started randomly pulling whole families from their homes. I regularly spent time with the village elders, and they gave us information every now and then. Their cooperation made them prime targets for retribution. An idiot could figure out what would happen next."

Mister Bennit is not here. The light in his eyes is gone, replaced by a darkness I never want to experience. This story is taking him back to Afghanistan, and he's reliving the nightmare.

"I radioed in and was denied permission to intervene. I pleaded with command, but the mission was more important, or so they said. We watched as the men made whole families kneel in the street. I couldn't stand the idea of watching them die, so I tossed my binoculars and grabbed my rifle. My two peers grabbed me and stopped me from leaving our position.

"I remember one of them shouting, 'We have orders not to do this, Mike. Do you understand me? We have orders!' I understood the orders, but I didn't care. I was about to open up on them from where I was, knowing if I squeezed the trigger on my carbine it was probably all over for us. There were fifty armed men against only three of us, with no available air support. So you know what I did?"

I am so captivated, I am unable to speak. I think we are all in the same boat until the shyest among us is finally able to mutter something. "You found a way to save them?" Emilee asks.

"I eased the grip on the rifle, took my finger off the trigger, and watched as they killed the women and children right in front of the men. Their screams of anguish were only silenced when they put a bullet in each, one by one. Then they left them in the street as a warning to others. All sixty-three of them."

We are stunned into silence. No small feat for a group of talkative teenagers. I glance over to Amanda and see the tears welled up in her eyes. You would think Mister Bennit shared war stories with us all the time. Outside of some funny stuff about basic training, he never talks about it. We all knew he was a Green Beret, and assumed he was in Iraq or Afghanistan, but he never once mentioned it. We didn't ask, either.

So to listen to him share this with us is huge. Funny thing is, we all have heard the rumors other students spread. He got a Medal of Honor, or was Captain America, or belonged to G.I. Joe fighting off the evil forces of Cobra. Okay, maybe not those particular rumors, but ones equally laughable. Knowing the truth, or at least some of it, makes Mister Bennit much more real.

Kylie is the first to break the silence. "You feel responsible for letting them die. You think you should have been punished, and instead, they gave you a medal."

"What medal did you get?"

"It's not important, Vince. Too long a story to explain, and much of it is classified anyway. What's important is I could have saved them. All of them. Lord knows I should have."

"No. You were under orders. There wasn't anything you could have done," Vanessa argues.

"I could have disobeyed orders."

"You would have gotten in trouble though."

"Yeah, X, I would have. The military calls it a court-martial."

"Would the mission have been a success if you had gone into the village?" I ask, wondering what other demons are haunting him from his time in the Army. "Yes. At least I think it would have."

"Why are you telling us this?" Amanda finally asks, after another silence that seemed to last a lifetime.

"Edmund Burke once said, 'All that is required for evil to prevail is for good men to do nothing.' I did nothing, and that was my mistake. One I relive every day.

"So I learned from it. I swore I would never sit on the sidelines and not do the right thing just because someone says to, or because it's safer, or less convenient. We make choices in life. Some of them pan out the way you want, others don't. You'll learn failures define you more than successes do because of how you cope with them. They tell you the most about your character. Which leads us back to today.

"Vince, I don't condone underage drinking or drug use, but do you think you're the only teenager to have ever gotten busted for chugging a six-pack or rolling a joint? The more important question is, did you learn a lesson from it? I mean, other than doing better at not getting caught?"

"Yes," Vince responds, his voice perking up.

"And you know I hate cheating with a burning passion, Peyton, but it happens all the time in school. You got caught and paid the price. Have you cheated since?"

"No."

"Brian, assuming their allegation is even true, if they really want to go after you for downloading illegal music, then we'd better all hope they don't check my iPod."

Being a common sense teacher is one thing I always loved about Mister Bennit. He will never condone illegal or unethical behavior like drinking, drugs, and cheating, but he's a realist. He's more concerned about the welfare of his students than living under the delusion that nothing is going on. He tries to warn about the consequences of bad behavior and help us to avoid making dumb mistakes. When he fails, the most important thing to him is we learn from our error and never repeat it.

"You made mistakes. Big friggin' deal, everyone does. You paid the price and learned the lesson. I stand by you, and that's precisely what I told Superintendent Freeman in her office a couple of hours ago."

Kylie raises her eyebrows in surprise. I guess she didn't know about that any more than we did. He went to the mat fighting for Vince, Peyton, and Brian. How many teachers are willing to do that these days? As much as I like the other teachers in school, I can't think of one.

"Guys, if this is all Beaumont can come up with, he's proving himself to be a bigger joke than people thought. Every voter watching the news will remember the stupid stuff they did in high school, so I'm not worried about the effect on the campaign. The big mistake here is thinking for a second I am letting that blowhard drive you off my staff because you made mistakes. Understood?"

We all nod in agreement.

"Okay, Mister B, so do you have a plan?" Amanda asks innocently.

"I have a feeling we wouldn't be here otherwise," Vanessa observes. I couldn't agree more.

"You guys had your fun in the spotlight, now it's my turn. Winston Beaumont wants a brawl, so we're going to take the fight to him."

"We're going negative?" Vince asks, almost excited at the prospect.

"No, sorry to disappoint you, but mudslinging isn't my style. We're going to start telling the district why they should be voting for me. Two weeks from now at the debate, they're going to see it for themselves."

"Seriously? C'mon, that's not going to happen. Neither side wants us anywhere near that auditorium," Xavier says.

"Then we need to convince them otherwise," Emilee states, with as much conviction I ever heard come from her.

"How exactly do we do that? We asked to get in and they laughed at us."

"I asked a month ago when we first announced, Brian. I wouldn't have taken me seriously either, but things have changed a lot since then," I argue, now understanding the course of action Mister Bennit wants to take. "Besides, we didn't really care at the time."

"That's because he's the iCandidate, Chels. We lose the image the moment he sets foot on stage." Brian makes a good point, one that I don't have an answer to. I look toward our fearless leader, but he is content to let us figure it out.

"I don't agree, Bri," Vanessa argues. "Television is every bit as digital as the Internet. I don't think that's the problem. Someone tell me how the debate does anything to fix our current problem?"

"Vanessa, can you think of anything more news worthy than the first-ever public appearance of the country's most intriguing candidate? Talk about must-see TV," Amanda says.

"Okay, now I see where you're going with this," Xavier pronounces, the lightbulb clicking on in his head. "What will the man who never talks about issues finally say when questioned on them?"

"You got it. The media will go nuts speculating," Emilee says with a twinkle in her eye.

"And forget about our mistakes in the process," Peyton adds, now feeling like part of the team again.

"But how do we fight our way in?"

"We don't, Amanda, we get Beaumont to do it for us."

"Okay, I'll admit it. I'm lost again. Anyone with me?" Peyton offers, getting agreement amongst most of my peers.

Mister Bennit knows exactly where I am going with this, giving me a nod of approval. It's kind of fun being on the same wavelength as him. I only wish it happened more often.

"He's the one keeping us out, Chelsea," Vanessa points out.

"He is right now, but with that ginormous ego, do you think for one second he'll let people think he's scared of us?"

"Not a chance," Kylie says, a big smile on her face.

"So let's give him a chance to prove it."

"But Chels, people don't think he's scared of us," Vanessa states.

"Not yet. Kylie, if I leak something to the press, can you make sure they pick it up?" I ask mischievously.

"Gladly."

-THIRTY-EIGHT-
BLAKE

"I think their position is crystal clear. As was reported widely this week, they don't want to be in the debate," the pundit says from his side of the table.

The only thing worse than enduring these evening political shows Roger insists on recording is watching them on live television. Our late night gaggle means I'm working in the office far later than I want to. Not unheard of for a campaign season, but considering this was supposed to be an easy one, it's a little hard to swallow.

Being back in the congressman's district should feel awesome. I love politics, so I love election years by extension. There is just something enchanting about convincing people to go to the polls and vote the way you want them to. But I was born to be a player in D.C. and was looking to staying in the nation's capital while Beaumont marched into another term. That was how it felt six months ago when we were laughing at Dick Johnson and the Republicans.

Then Michael Bennit came along with his ragtag posse of overachievers and turned everything upside down. His laughable social media blitz went from an annoyance to a serious threat thanks to Kylie Roberts. Despite the name calling in the office, no one is laughing at Bennit and his staff anymore.

"Of course they don't want to debate, there's no need. Bennit is trouncing the Republican candidate and moves closer to Winston Beaumont in every poll," another analyst on television responds.

Congressman Beaumont grumbles something under his breath. I didn't hear exactly what, but it probably wasn't flattering.

The first pundit dismisses him with a gesture. "He needs to be in the debate to be taken seriously. He realizes the importance of sharing the stage with the other candidates. Don't you think for a second that this might just be reverse psychology?"

"Reverse psychology? Are you serious? Why bother? He's practically winning the race while spending no money and not talking about any issues. We can sit here and scratch our heads over why all day, but the strategy is working. His grand ideas about the political process are capturing people's attention, so why take the chance of flopping under the lights a week before the election at a debate you don't need to be in?"

"Which is exactly why Beaumont should be pushing to include him in the debate," the only female on the panel says from the end of the table. "Winston Beaumont runs ads on TV nonstop, saying there's no substance to Michael Bennit. Yet they don't want him on that stage. His words are hollow if he excludes him. With all the resistance coming from both the

Republicans and Democrats, you can only wonder if they are scared to debate the iCandidate."

It took a nanosecond to realize the line was planted. It has Madison's sister's fingerprints all over it. I don't know how Kylie put this idea in the collective heads of the press corps, but she did. We have seriously underestimated the amount of people she knows, and the damage she can do.

"Scared? I'll show them who should be scared!" Winston shouts out with exactly the kind of unhelpful emotional response we feared.

"Sir, I—"

"Roger, get on the phone with the debate organizers and insist Bennit be included. Do whatever it takes to get him on the stage!"

"Calm down, Winston, and let's think this through," Roger says, trying to get some objectivity inserted into the conversation. Congressman Beaumont looks less than pleased, but simply folds his arms across his chest and waits. "Blake, what happened to the story about the kids?"

"It had an impact, but lacked staying power. We stopped the bleeding, but didn't win anyone back to our side. It simply didn't take up enough news cycles."

"Why not, Blake?"

"They got their response out and it made sense. They said they don't condone the behavior, but implored people to think back to their teenage years and tell them they didn't do something worse. The accusations didn't exactly have the juice the Swift Boaters had against Kerry. The mainstream media moved off the topic pretty quick."

The whole idea of going after the students was dumb. I thought so the moment Roger asked me to do it, and should have said something at the time. We were better off drumming up some more parental discontent in the district than going on the offensive against high school kids. Any strategy I came up with would have worked better than this one did.

"That doesn't explain why CNN is calling me 'scared' every half hour," Winston barks.

"They probably began planting the debate conversation right after the press ran with the stuff about his staff. It didn't go anywhere while they covered that story, but after they lost interest in the kids, it was the next topic on deck."

"How?" the congressman demands. I look over to Madison who glares back at me. We haven't spoken more than a few sentences to each other since the day she got run out of the office. I suppose we won't be anytime soon.

"You should ask Madison."

"My sister had nothing to do with this!" she exclaims. "She didn't even write an article about the debate!"

"Her fingerprints are all over this, Madison," I say calmly. "I know you don't want to hear this, but she didn't have to print anything. She just had to make sure everyone else did."

"Well, if you think Kylie and Bennit are behind this, then we are playing right into their hands." Madison is right, not that I'm going to agree with her. Congressman Beaumont has made up his mind. He is frustrated and wants to exact his pound of flesh on someone. Better Bennit than I.

"So be it. I am done playing games with this guy."

"Sir, we kept him out of the debate because it legitimizes him. That's still true," Madison implores out of desperation.

"The situation has changed, in case you didn't notice, Madison," I say with a hint of contrived contempt. "We're tied in the polls. He *is* legitimate now."

"Blake is right," the congressman decides. "Whether they are trying to trick us or not is irrelevant. He wants to debate, let's have at it. I will crush this upstart once and for all."

"Sir, we should really—"

"The matter is decided. Blake, make the call and get a third podium added to the stage. Do it now," Roger commands.

"Yes, sir," I tell him before heading out of the office. As I close the door, the congressman begins tearing apart Madison. The only thing he hates more than campaigning is losing, and now he's doing both. Since Madison has been up here running the show, she's the scapegoat du jour.

You really have to hand it to Bennit. We're getting hoodwinked, a fact Madison was both smart enough to realize and courageous enough to speak up about. Or dumb enough, depending on your perspective. Either way, they got what they wanted.

I also got what I wanted. Using unsavory tactics to take down political opponents doesn't cause me to lose sleep, but attacking teenagers just because they are media darlings feels … I don't know … not right. We never should have been put in this position, but at least we are now focusing on taking him down. That's what the campaign for an eight-term incumbent in Congress should be doing.

"Well played, Bennit, well played," I mumble to myself.

-THIRTY-NINE-
KYLIE

The life of a journalist often means healthy meals are sacrificed for the expediency fast food offers. When you're unemployed, it's also a cost-effective way to fill your stomach. I try to avoid burger joints, but there are also only so many Subway sandwiches a person can eat. Dying for a different menu to select from, I decided to stop at a quaint deli in the center of Millfield not far from the high school.

My order placed, I sip a Diet Coke at the end of the long, glass case full of deli meats. The television in the corner is tuned in to ESPN, and not one of the nation's cable news networks. It may be the only TV in Millfield that isn't. I hear the bells on the door ring, but don't bother turning around to see who walked in, at least until I hear her voice.

"Can I get a veggie wrap to go, please?" Jessica Slater asks the clerk behind the desk sweetly.

Dressed in a sharp navy blue outfit and heels, she looks like she stepped right out of an issue of *Fashion Week*. Wearing jeans and a sweatshirt, I look like I just left a football tailgate party. Of all the days.

"Hi. Kaylee, right?" she asks as she walks over to me.

"Kylie," I respond. As if she didn't know that.

"Oh, that's right. Sorry. How's the life of an unemployed journalist these days?" she says with a fake smile that makes me want to knock her ultra-white teeth out.

"Not as exciting teaching English, I'm sure," I reply, trying to walk a fine line. Under normal circumstances, I would tell this tart where to go. Unfortunately, she is Michael's fiancée, and I need to be as polite as I can. There is already enough stress in their relationship, and I don't want to be perceived as adding to it.

"It's not so exciting," she says with a laugh. "The hardest part is keeping kids focused on academics instead of their extracurricular activities. Some of them think trivial pursuits are more important than school is. You've seen that firsthand I think, haven't you?" Apparently, Jessica Slater is not a big believer in the value of life experiences.

"From what I understand, Michael's staff is managing just fine. Chelsea showed me her progress report and I thought it was pretty good."

"I'm sure it was. He didn't bother sharing that information with me," she responds, clearly agitated at that information. "But you spend *a lot* of time with him, so of course you would know more about it than I would."

"I am privileged to spend as much time as I do with him and the *staff*," I reply, using a little verbal ju-jitsu. I don't appreciate the implication she is making, and I exercise some serious willpower not to say so.

"I'm sure they feel the same. Your work for the campaign has been invaluable to Michael. It looks like he will be getting into the debate because of your idea to appeal to Beaumont's ego."

"The idea was Chelsea's, actually," I say truthfully. "I just gave her some guidance on how to execute it."

"Of course, that's what I meant." Yeah, sure it was.

People like Jessica Slater are the reason I despised high school. I was a bookworm, with few friends and even fewer boyfriends. She is the equivalent of the beautiful, smart, captain of the cheerleading team that every girl wanted to be and every boy wanted to date. Or at least sleep with.

I hope she is only being this shallow because she feels somehow threatened by me. I have had a crush on Michael since the moment he climbed in my parked car to hide from the media, but if this is the type of girl he goes for …

"You know, I don't know much about journalism, but I didn't think doing favors like that was in the scope of covering a campaign. You must be finding it so difficult to be objective being so close to them." Oh my God! How does he deal with this woman?

"I manage," is all I can say, fighting to repress my anger. I glance over to the man behind the counter who is pretending not to pay attention. He is trying to be polite, but like most men, the specter witnessing a catfight is irresistible. Despite my reservations of having it out with the diva in front of me, he is getting close to getting his wish.

"Well, I know this campaign is hard on everyone. Parents are upset, the school administration is angry, and I've even heard there is a rift between Chelsea and her dad. That's too bad, they were so close."

"And they still are. People who care about each other find common ground when they disagree on things," I say, smugly. There, she deserved that. I finally wiped the fake smile off her face. Nice to see little miss innuendo didn't miss it coming back at her.

"Here's your Reuben," the clerk behind the counter says before she can respond. I thank him, more for the interruption than the sandwich.

"Oh, a Reuben. That sounds good! I'd love to order that, but I don't want all the calories. I like to eat healthy and watch my figure," she says, giving me a quick once-over with her eyes. Okay, now I hate this bitch.

I was gifted with a fast metabolism, one of the few things I inherited from my mother that I appreciate. While I don't have Jessica's sexy hourglass figure, I still have my slender build and athletic tone, even after a couple of months without a good workout.

"Some of us have to work hard to look good," I say, soliciting another fake smile from Jessica. "Some of us just do."

The smile disappears from her face as fast as it appeared. Mine, however, lights up the room. "Nice chatting with you, Jess. See ya around."

I drop a twenty on the counter next to the register and tell the man to keep the change. Not the smartest move for the budget conscience, but I was desperate to get out of the deli.

"Thanks. Please come back again!" he says with a wink. I can only speculate whether it's because he wants to encourage repeat business or a repeat show like the one he just got.

As much fun as that was, I think I'll avoid any further contact with the future Mrs. Bennit. I hate having my appearance criticized, but I hate having my integrity as a journalist questioned even more. If there was any good that came from this chat, it's me realizing the need to keep some distance from Michael and the staff, at least publically.

I am rooting for him, but to maintain effectiveness, people can't think I am working for him. I don't know if Jessica's comment was based on what she's noticed or what he has told her. Either way, the snide bitch may have done me a favor without realizing it.

-FORTY-
BLAKE

I am not content to watch the sunset from my familiar perch on the west steps of the Capitol. Today, just a couple of days before the debate, I need to walk.

The National Mall is just shy of two miles long, offering some of the most beautiful vistas our capital has to offer. My thoughts aren't dwelling on the beauty of the museums and monuments as I pass them though.

The two weeks following the decision to let Bennit in the debate shook out pretty much like I thought it would. The story about Bennit's students drinking, cheating, and stealing had disappeared off the front page almost before the ink dried. Considering the media frenzy surrounding his campaign, accusing them of running a dog fighting ring or trafficking heroin would have yielded similar results. Many people put these kids on a pedestal, and they don't want to hear about mistakes they made.

For a former soldier and high school teacher, Bennit is a politically savvy guy. He's smart enough to know voters start paying more attention to campaigns the closer you get to the election, so he shifted the attention away from the staff and onto himself. I'm not sure if it was by design or just an attempt to shield his students from the unwanted scrutiny we initiated. Either way, it has turned out to be a brilliant strategy.

One reason Bennit is a major threat is because the Republican in the race is a complete idiot. How I wish this was a traditional two-party race. Dick Johnson can't find a coherent campaign strategy with two hands and a flashlight. Beaumont would have given him a nervous breakdown by now if we had focused all our energy on him.

Miles Everman instructed his candidate to harp on the attention the media was giving to the students for days after the Bennit camp had changed their strategy. Problem was, the media had already moved on to speculating about what he would say during the debate, making Johnson look like a bigger idiot. I didn't think that feat was even possible.

Fueled by teasers his staff was tweeting and posting on Facebook and Google Plus, the Super Bowl sees less analysis than this debate has. Every taste Bennit's teenage workforce gave the press left reporters begging for more and provided pundits endless material to analyze on their political shows. Pure genius.

The students are social media ninjas. They understand exactly what needs to be done to get the desired results. Their posts and tweets focus on big ideas while avoiding divisive issues. A politician bloviating about what makes America unique, and what it means to live in a free country sounds contrite, but the kids working for Bennit are sincere. It makes Johnson look petty, and worse, ill-informed.

We fared little better. I tried to convince the congressman to start attacking Michael Bennit for not addressing the issues facing our nation, but I was ignored. Instead, Madison convinced him to go barnstorming through the district for a week with a message about the money we secured for each town. Despite my warnings, Roger thought the idea of this populist appeal sounded good. It turned out to be a disaster.

Our own message foundered. The congressman wanted to portray himself as the Sixth District's personal Robin Hood. Money talks in this country, but a politician dwelling on the pork barrel funding he bleeds from Washington is easy to spin as a negative. Michael Bennit never tweeted about that himself and stuck to the high road. His student's weren't shy about it though. Vince Orsini, the kid fast becoming the mouthpiece of their campaign, likened our leveraging cash for votes as "a parent threatening to take away a child's allowance."

Chelsea Stanton went a step further in a Tumblr blog post, writing how the congressman was treating voters "like they were something he could pick up on the shelves of Wal-Mart." I wanted to reply with a message explaining Winston Beaumont would never be caught dead in a discount store, but decided that would hurt more than help. It's true though.

Worst of all, everything they tweeted and said on Facebook went viral. Many of their quotes were incorporated into Internet memes and shared all over Facebook. If we spent every dollar our campaign had, we could still have not reached the number of people Bennit had the last couple of weeks.

Things got so brutal, Roger actually floated the idea past me to hire hackers to take down Bennit's Twitter, Facebook, and other social media accounts. It was not a practical solution to the problem, and I finally convinced him the ensuing public relations disaster if we ever got caught wasn't worth the short-term benefit. Think Nixon signing off on the Watergate break-in. It's not something you want to be caught doing a couple of weeks before voters go to the polls.

As the week began, we looked like pawns in some game of partisan squabbling while Bennit came across as a founding father, without the powdered wig and tricorne hat. Bennit proved ideas are more powerful and persuasive than cheap political platforms. So despite all the appearances and millions spent on television commercials, Beaumont was rewarded by polls that had the race tighter than Steven Tyler's pants.

The March of the Rookies had a few tiny missteps, but watching them run this campaign is a little like observing a neurosurgeon with a scalpel. Every move is precise and exceedingly effective. I have no idea how much Bennit is guiding them, but I get the impression that he's letting the students do much of it on their own.

If that is the case, I really need to meet Chelsea Stanton. She may be the enemy in this race, but at eighteen years old, she has an eight-term professional politician tied in knots and one of the most respected political operatives in the country searching for answers. No small feat as anyone who knows Winston Beaumont and Roger Bean can attest.

So, for the last few days, we have devoted all our time to debate preparation. Why an eight-term congressman and lifelong politician would need that much time to prepare is beyond me. Maybe he needed it to review his own voting record, which is admittedly all over the place.

As I pass in front of the Lincoln Memorial, I begin getting angry. Bennit has taken the opportunity to monopolize the media cycles while both our campaign and Johnson's are in hiding. It's embarrassing that a sixteen-year congressional veteran feels compelled to study, while a history teacher acts like he already knows all the answers. Pretty amazing considering the expectations the media set for him to deliver actual positions is so high.

Am I working for the wrong person? I have never before questioned my loyalty to Roger and the congressman. Six months ago, I would have burned down Congress itself if they asked me to. However, watching Bennit and his students, I wonder if my loyalties are misplaced. Has my ambition blinded me to the fact that I am really working for a cheap salesman and not the distinguished lawmaker I thought I was?

"Can I help you, son?" I hear a voice in front of me ask. Coming out of my trance, I realize I am standing in front of one of the veteran's memorabilia booths positioned between the Lincoln Memorial and the Vietnam Veteran's Memorial.

"You look like you have the weight of the world on your shoulders," the grizzled, rather rotund man observes.

"Uh, yeah, I sorta do."

"You ever serve?"

"Uh, no, sir, my dad did. First Gulf War." A pang of guilt hits me right in the chest. Dad always wanted me to follow his path, convinced the military was the best way to learn about the values every man needs in life—honor, integrity, and selfless service. "When were you in Vietnam?"

"Hell, son, don't be calling me sir. Never did meet an officer worth a damn. Call me John," he says, removing the "Vietnam Veteran" baseball cap adorned with pins from his head and brushing his long, mostly gray hair back. He puts the hat back on and strokes his beard before continuing. "Sixty-eight to seventy. I did two tours."

"You were there for Tet," I say, a measure of respect in my voice. The Tet Offensive was the turning point of the war, a simultaneous attack by the Viet Cong and North Vietnamese Army during their lunar new year celebration. They lost miserably on the battlefield, but scored a major victory on the American home front. Ho Chi Minh understood politics, too.

"Yeah, but I was injured for most of it. Got caught in an explosion in Saigon on the third day and woke up in the hospital five days later. You visiting D.C.?"

"Nah," I say with a slight laugh. "I work up on the Hill," I add, gesturing to the imposing marble structure on the far side of the National Mall that houses Congress. The magnificent building is now bathed in artificial light as darkness conquers the final light of the day.

"Sorry to hear that. The only thing the bastards do in that building for me is raise my taxes and cut my V.A. benefits," John grumbles in disgust.

"Yeah. My boss always votes against the Veteran's Administration." I only realized what I said after the words left my mouth. John's face contorts into a mix of disbelief and anger.

"And you still work for him! What the hell's the matter with you, son? The guy sounds like a real scumbag. What does your dad think about that?"

The words cut deeper than any wound he could inflict by stabbing me with a knife. I have always been Beaumont's loyal foot soldier—doing whatever he deemed necessary for me to do. I wanted to be the go-to guy on the staff and make a name for myself in Washington. Only once have I ever questioned his motives on a vote, and ironically, it was about medical funding for veterans. I only remember because I was ridiculed in front of the other staff because of it.

Beaumont wants me at the table because I have no conscience. He doesn't value my opinion. He just needs someone willing to do the unsavory things necessary for him to stay in power. He wants a soldier unhampered by integrity, honor, and a moral compass to execute his orders without prejudice.

What would my father think about that? What would he think of who I have become and what I have been willing to do to get here? Would he be proud that my ambitions, drive, and savvy have propelled me to achieve so much at such a young age in this town? Or would the man who served his nation with honor think of me as a cheap sell-out?

"My father died two years ago. Gulf War Syndrome," I tell John, his hard face instantly softening.

"I'm sorry to hear that, son," he replies, taking a moment to close his eyes and say a quick prayer for a departed vet.

"John, can I ask you a question? What do you think of Michael Bennit?" I figure pretty much everybody in the country has at least heard of him at this point.

"The teacher running for Congress up north?" he asks, getting a nod from me. "Don't know much about him. But he's a Green Beret and they don't just give those things out. He's gonna bring integrity and leadership to this town if he wins though. From everything I've read in the papers, I think he's gonna fight for his district the same way he fights for those kids on his staff. Is your boss anything like that?" John asks, his eyes narrowing as if to take measure of my response.

A few months ago, I would argue that Winston Beaumont was all of that and more. Whether I argued because it was true or I was programmed is another matter, one that I'm only now questioning.

"Thanks for your time, John," I say as I turn to walk away and start my trip back up the Capitol.

"Hey, son? What unit did your father serve with in the Gulf?"

"Second Armored Division out of Germany. Tiger Brigade."

John nods, then rummages through the collection of pins in the display cases behind him, pulling out and tossing me a familiar triangle-shaped pin.

"Thanks," I say, admiring the red, yellow, and blue pin with "Hell on Wheels" printed below it. "How much do I–"

"On the house. My way of telling your father I appreciate his service to our country. Maybe it will help you find your own direction when the time comes."

PART III

THE ELECTION

-FORTY-ONE-
MICHAEL

Red, white, and blue bunting adorns the walls of the new ultra-modern Visual and Performing Arts Center at Western Connecticut State University. The debate is being hosted in the three-hundred-fifty seat concert hall instead of the theater which holds an equivalent capacity. It really is a beautiful venue.

Cameras are set up to cover every imaginable angle of the three podiums on the stage. The backdrop is a blue hue with a subdued American flag billowing across it. It is classy, and not distracting enough to command focus away from the men on the dais. A moderator's table is set up near the center, and people can be seen milling around it making their last-minute preparations for what has been promised to be quite a show.

An hour before the start of the debate, reporters are already filing live reports with their stations in the space overlooking the stage and seats from the rear of the hall. Some of my students set up camp backstage, securing a good vantage point for the show. Many others including Emilee, Vanessa, Xavier, and Brian are at the coffee shop, ready to conduct a live "iBlitzkreig" over Twitter and Facebook.

I can't help but stand in the middle of the large room and soak up the atmosphere. I breathe deep, trying to settle nerves and calm the flock of butterflies in my stomach. I'm not the wreck I thought I would be, but I also understand the gravity of the situation.

"Still clinging to hope that you can win, Michael?" I hear a voice from behind me say, ruining my moment of reflection.

"Still clinging to the hope that the all-you-can-eat buffet is open after this debate, Miles?"

I swear my students have a pack mentality, coming to my side and giving the large man a once-over as only teenagers can do. I'm more than capable of fighting my own battles, but it's also nice having a posse of sorts.

"You're Miles Everman?" Chelsea asks.

"Yes. Were you expecting someone else?"

"You're just not what we pictured," Peyton explains.

"Yeah. Peyton, can you call the organizers of the Macy's Thanksgiving Day Parade and tell them we found their lost balloon?" Chelsea says in her sweetest voice. Ouch. I thought I hit him below the belt when we first met at Briar Point.

The students snicker and Miles Everman sneers at them before continuing. "You have no prayer in this debate, Bennit. Beaumont will be gunning for you, making you come across small and weak."

"Thus making him out to be a bully, me a pushover, and leaving your guy the Prince Valiant of the race, blah, blah, blah. Is that what you told Dick Johnson? Smile a lot and hope for the best?"

"It's called a tactic."

"Actually, that would be the definition of a strategy. Tactics are how you execute the plan."

"So a strategy would be like not ever talking about the issues? Good luck with your 'tactics' in that tonight," Everman says, shaking his head slowly and waddling away toward his candidate.

Richard Johnson is not exactly what I pictured. I have seen a headshot of him once, but he is more impressive in person. With his good looks, perfectly coiffed hair and Hollywood smile, a fresh face like his should command more attention in this race. The façade is not the problem with Johnson. What happens when he opens his mouth is.

I roll my eyes to let Chelsea and Peyton know I am unfazed by the chat with Miles. They grin and we walk backstage to join Vince and Amanda. They scouted out the perfect spot to watch both the stage and televisions tuned in to the various media outlets covering the event.

"This is the most intensely watched congressional campaign I have seen in my thirty years of political reporting," one reporter from CBS comments. "Tonight these candidates square off not only in front of the people they want to represent, but an entire country caught up in the drama. The stakes are high. One mistake could spell disaster for the campaigns in the election only one short week away."

After burning a half hour with the debate producers reviewing rules and cues for our entrance, I return to where Vince and the girls are camped out backstage. The concert hall is packed, most people already in their seats anticipating the beginning of the political theatrics. Another producer is addressing the audience, explaining the proper decorum they will be expected to adhere to.

A tap on the shoulder breaks my attention. I turn to see my fiancée standing in front of me with an expression prospective patients wear in a dentist's waiting room. She kisses me lightly on the lips, a gesture executed more out of habit than love. Calling our relationship tense is like saying gangrene is a mild medical condition.

"Hi, sweetie. Glad you could come."

"Wouldn't miss it," she says, lying. Not one for the limelight, she would rather be anyplace than here.

Only then did I spot a guy in the Beaumont camp thirty feet away eyeing Chelsea like she is an item on a dessert tray. He is standing with Winston and a few others on the other side of the backstage area. I don't know what they are discussing, but you would need a machete to cut through the tension.

"Blake! Get your head in the game!" I hear Beaumont bark. "This is no time for daydreaming. Do you have my index cards?"

"Right here, Congressman."

He must be so much fun to work for. Pol Pot has a sunnier disposition, and he ran the Khmer Rouge. Robinson Howell is a pleasure to deal with by comparison.

The lighting from the stage area flashes and the house lights dim, the signals for us to take our respective positions in the wings. I give my students quick high fives and turn toward my future wife. Well, theoretically she'll be the future Mrs. Bennit.

"Wish me luck."

"Knock 'em dead," she deadpans coolly.

I get into position, trying to force the decline of our engagement out of my mind. I cannot afford to be focused on that right now. As the moderator begins to speak, Winston joins me in the left wing. I drew the center podium, so we get to enter from the same side of the stage. "Welcome to Western Connecticut State University, sight of the live debate between candidates for Congress from the ..."

"Tonight you're going to find out just how out of my league you are," I hear Winston say over the booming voice of the moderator. "Like a boa constrictor, I will squeeze the life out of you and your farcical campaign."

"You know, Congressman, people have been telling me for months you're a snake. Until now I thought they were just speaking metaphorically."

"I am going to enjoy destroying you," Winston decries, finishing the brief exchange.

"This debate is scheduled to last ninety minutes, so without further ado, let's bring out our candidates," the moderator says, completing his introduction.

We get prompted by the production staff and all step out from the wings onto the brightly lit stage to thunderous applause. I can only think how exhilarating it must be to be a rock star. We walk to our respective podiums, mine in the center, Winston stage left and Richard stage right.

"The rules for tonight's debate are simple. Each candidate is entitled to a two-minute opening statement. Following those statements, the debate is a free format where the candidates can question each other on the issues. As moderator, I will only keep the debate moving forward as necessary. Following that, each candidate will be given two minutes for their closing statements. So, let's begin. Congressman Beaumont, you drew the opportunity to speak first while backstage and may make your opening statement."

"Thank you, and allow me be the first to welcome Michael Bennit to the stage for his *first* public appearance in this race," Beaumont says, eliciting a few snickers from the crowd. I knew a comment of this nature was coming, so all I do is broaden my smile to the audience and give a playful little shrug.

"Many of you already know me, since I have been representing this district for almost sixteen years," Beaumont continues, looking directly into the camera. "I bring millions of federal dollars to this district, resulting in the creation of hundreds of jobs. I have decades of experience in politics, and belong to a family who has faithfully served the people of Connecticut for generations.

"But I have a question for you all to ponder tonight as Michael Bennit makes his opening statement. How do you think he's qualified to run for this office? I mean, can we take a campaign run by a bunch of kids seriously? His antics in this race are a mockery to the process of choosing responsible elected representatives. I believe my constituents would be best served if he, and his group of Boy Scouts, just go back home and sell cookies."

There is a smattering of applause from the audience. Winston surveys the crowd, coming to the realization that his line did not go over well. I'm sure his staff convinced him the joke would be a hit. Amanda, the ranking feminist of my little cadre of student staffers, must be going berserk backstage over the Boy Scout line. Someone forgot to inform Beaumont one inconvenient truth. Most students in my inner circle are, in fact, girls.

"Mister Bennit, you may make your two-minute statement," the moderator prompts. It's showtime.

"I'm a history teacher, not a math teacher, but I believe that was two questions, Congressman," I retort, rewarded with chuckles from the audience.

"Congressman, you have impressive credentials as a politician. I don't think anyone watching tonight is questioning that. But more interesting is what those sixteen years in D.C. and decades in politics taught you to value. I'm sure if we ran a fact check on your opening statement, we would find that you indeed have brought millions of dollars into the district. Money used to subsidize important things, I imagine. So, instead of telling us about all the beneficial programs that enrich lives you help fund, it must be confusing to our audience why you chose to focus only on the dollar amount. The answer is simple. It's not the people's interests you have in mind, it's your own."

Beaumont grimaces slightly in disgust at the comment, shaking his head as if he wants to start an argument in the middle of my opening statement. As much as I would love to hear how he'd defend himself, these two minutes of time are precious, and I'm not about to give him the chance to interrupt.

"Loyalty, sense of duty, integrity, selfless service, and the unwavering dedication to an ideal. Those are the traits people should value in a representative. It's what any member of Congress should embody after a sixteen-year career, but instead, you only choose to measure your worth in dollars you can extract from the coffers in Washington.

"As you have said again and again ... and again," I say, counting on my fingers as I speak and eliciting a snicker from the audience, "I have no experience in politics. In fact, being a former Green Beret, I will probably make a lousy politician using the standards you measure yourself by.

"What I will make is an outstanding representative. From the end of the twentieth century to today, the prevailing feeling in the country is our elected officials no longer serve the interests of the American people. Citizens in our district want more than money from Washington. They want to feel like they are actually represented and have a voice in the direction of our nation. Someone who is more interested in listening to the people than engaging in trivial partisan bickering. I stand before you tonight as that man."

The audience applauses with enthusiasm, and before they finish, I need to get one final comment in for Amanda before the moderator turns the floor over to Johnson. "As for the kids, I believe involvement with our youth is important in today's society, if for no other reason that you would know that it's the Girl Scouts who sell cookies, not the Boy Scouts."

The initial enthusiastic applause from the hall turns thunderous. Winston rocks back on his heels as if stunned by a punch.

-FORTY-TWO-
KYLIE

Roger Bean rubs his forehead in frustration. The first two opening statements were disasters for his boss. Beaumont fell flat with his jab and Michael was a hit with the audience. Having Beaumont's own line used against him was like icing someone else's cake. Roger's reaction was restrained, unless getting taken to school was part of Beaumont's debate strategy. If I were him, I would be breaking things.

I was careful to stay clear of Michael and his staff before he took to the stage, choosing to move backstage only after the event started. This is a restricted area for most press, but those of us doing deep background on the campaigns were granted special access.

I spend a couple of moments greeting some colleagues covering the other candidates as Richard Johnson stammers through his opening statement. Did he just say something about his mother? If he is the best the Republicans can offer, I'm sure the voters of the district are as concerned as I am.

Bored with what he is saying, or trying to say, I head over to the monitor the kids are glued to. *Call of Duty* couldn't command the attention they are giving the screen. I'm not sure if they are caught up in the moment or amazed their mentor owned one of the country's most prominent politicians right out of the gates on national television.

"Our first topic this evening will be about fiscal responsibility. We will begin with Representative Beaumont."

Beaumont sputters through the first thirty seconds of his response to a question on government spending. When the deficit and national debt balloons during your time in office, it behooves the incumbent to move off the topic quickly.

"Michael Bennit can't understand the complexities of governmental budgeting because he's not qualified to be in Congress! My family has been in Connecticut politics for decades! People have entrusted us in leadership roles for a reason, Mister Bennit. We deliver. Can you say that?"

Michael looks out over the audience and then to the camera with his arm outstretched, as if presenting the world to Winston Beaumont. This is the second moment of truth. Opening statements are important to help overcome nerves, but this is his first time addressing a question on stage and on camera with sixty million people watching at home.

"Did anyone else notice that the country is running trillion-dollar deficits, racked up trillions and trillions in national debt, and Congressman Beaumont finished his answer by attacking me?" Michael asks with a smile, invoking a chorus of laughs. For a serious guy, he knows how to work a crowd. "Congressman, with all due respect, running up the debt is what you manage to deliver. I read about your family's legacy in politics. They worked hard to earn their leadership positions in this state and ought to be commended. The problem is you regard your seat as a birthright."

"I most certainly do not! I have more qualifications than you ever will to sit in this office."

"So you have said. Since we are never going to move forward tonight until we address this, let's review qualifications from a Constitutional perspective."

"And here comes today's history lesson," Vince, Peyton, Amanda, and Chelsea exclaim at the same time. I haven't known Michael long, but even I knew that was coming.

"Article One, Section Two of the United States Constitution requires that The House of Representatives shall be composed of members who have reached an age of twenty-five years, been a United States citizen for seven years, and inhabit the state from which chosen," he says, looking directly at Winston.

"I think you mean Article II, Mister Bennit," Johnson croaks, clearly feeling left out of the discussion.

"What?"

"The Legislature. It's Article II of the Constitution. The Executive Branch is most powerful, so it's number one."

Vince and Peyton start laughing out loud at the comment while Chelsea shakes her head in utter disbelief. Remarkably few Americans will immediately pick up on the gaffe, but they are about to get educated. The fact that Michael's students recognized it so quickly shows how bright these kids are.

"Mister Johnson," Michael says with a barely suppressed smile. "The Framers at the Constitutional Convention feared the legislature more than the executive. Based on their experience with the British Parliament before the Revolution, they thought it was most powerful, and most prone to corruption. Thus they spent considerable time during the summer of 1787 debating how to restrain the new assembly and it became Article I."

Richard Johnson compounds his mistake by shaking his head no.

"I'll tell you what, I would be happy to wait while you check in your copy of the Constitution."

All Johnson manages to do is look at Michael sheepishly before turning and flashing a forced smile to the camera.

"Here, borrow mine," Michael says, pulling a book from the inside his suit jacket as he walks over to Johnson's lectern. He stands there, holding out the pocket-sized copy and waiting for the all-style, no-substance Republican to make the decision whether to accept it.

Michael is not about to walk away, and Beaumont isn't clamoring to rescue him, so Johnson accepts the book while the audience go nuts with laughter. To make matters an order of magnitude worse, he actually begins flipping pages on camera, in front of the audience, voters in his district, and the millions of Americans watching. In this moment, one destined to become a part of American political lore, and a viral sensation on YouTube for years to come, historians will decree the campaign of Richard Johnson for Congress officially died.

Johnson literally looks as if he wants to crawl under his lectern and cry, and to Michael's credit, he isn't rubbing it in further. Not that he needs to, but he easily can take this showmanship too far and be labeled a bully. Even the moderator is at a loss for what to do when Michael walks back to his podium.

"Do I not meet any one of those qualifications, Congressman?" he asks, refocusing on Winston Beaumont to the relief of Johnson.

Winston stands stunned at his own lectern, although I can't be certain if it is because he just watched his Republican opponent get decimated or he's now scared for himself. He fidgets nervously, probably just now realizing that he has underestimated Michael Bennit.

Beaumont clears his throat before replying, "I'm simply saying you have no experience in governing."

"The Framers never intended the House of Representatives to be full of career legislators. The Senate was originally selected by state legislatures and the president is elected by the Electoral College," Michael adds for Richard Johnson's benefit. "Members of the House were the only original popularly elected officials in the national government for a reason. They wanted an average person, elected by the people, sent to legislate for the people."

Applause ripples through the audience, causing Winston to look around nervously.

"So I will ask you again. Are there any qualifications I don't meet?"

"Constitutionally, no," Beaumont mumbles, defeated.

"Excellent. So let's move on to phase two of your debate strategy and start talking about how I never address the issues, because that's what voters really want to hear tonight." And with a single line, the audience erupts and Beaumont's plan to frame his chief opponent as an undeserving novice is finished.

Michael never seemed to want to be a candidate when I first met him. He was content to let his students bask in the limelight while he sat back and watched from a distance. The tactic was one I never really understood, even as they gained ground using it.

When Beaumont went after them, the nature of the race changed. It may be a cliché, but the attacks on Vince, Peyton, and Brian awoke the sleeping giant. The loyalty Michael's students have toward him is clearly reciprocated, because he's not just out to win this debate, he wants to humiliate Beaumont and Johnson doing it.

-FORTY-THREE-
CHELSEA

The world is finding out the same thing about Mister Bennit as we did on the first day of class, and it's entertaining to watch. If you are going to get into a debate with him, you need to have your facts straight and be quick on your feet. After the whole Constitution debacle, Richard Johnson clearly didn't and Beaumont isn't fairing much better.

The funny thing is, a half an hour into the debate and he still hasn't taken a strong stand on any issue. His opponents' attempts to box him in on foreign intervention and gay marriage still didn't force him into a firm position. Each time, he brings the discussion back to American ideals and the importance of honest, forthright debates as a society. The public was treated to weeks of hype and speculation on what he would say, and I am surprised the audience loves his answers.

I know where he stands on many things even though he is careful not to discuss his personal views in a classroom environment. I wonder why he doesn't share his opinions with the world at this point. We all thought that was the reason we pushed to be here. What is he trying to prove?

The next issue is announced by the moderator and I cringe. It's a question about gun control, and a sensitive subject in this area since the tragedy at Sandy Hook Elementary in Newtown happened only a fifteen-minute drive from here. Mister Bennit jokes his idea of strict gun control means proper stance, grip, sight alignment, and breath control. I'm sure the line won't play well in light of more recent tragedies, so I hope he doesn't use it.

"Let me guess, Mister Bennit. Your philosophy is 'kill 'em all and let God sort 'em out'?" Congressman Beaumont asks, after a long-winded soliloquy.

"No, that's a tenant of total war. Can you tell me when the last one was, Congressman?"

"The last one?"

"Yes, the last total war the United States fought. Can you tell me what it was?"

The camera focuses on the flustered and visibly shaken Winston Beaumont. I can even see the small drops of sweat forming on his forehead. How did previous generations ever cope without high-definition television?

The congressman stares at his podium, stalling as he searches for a way to dodge the question. Obviously, his debate preparations didn't include this, and Mister B won't let the reputed political genius squirm out easily. On this stage, Mister B is the chess master and Winston Beaumont is the one playing Candyland.

"Congressman, every one of my high school students would have their hands up by now. Can you answer my question? It's a simple one," Mister Bennit prods, almost daring him to reply.

"Well, if you are this good of a teacher, maybe you should consider going back to it." Oh, he left that door open.

"Right now, my students aren't in need of the lesson more than the incumbent representative from Connecticut's Sixth District. So what do you say?" Mister B asks. Yup, he walked right through the door to the amusement of the audience.

"Vietnam."

"Oh, Congressman," our mentor scolds in mock disappointment, "you would not have lasted long in my history class." From backstage, I still can hear everyone snicker as he continues. "Vietnam was a limited war focusing more on containment and relying on the hearts and minds approach popularized by the British in Malay. World War Two was the last total war."

"You should just drop out of this election and play *Jeopardy*, Mister Bennit," Johnson says, throwing a lifeline to his embattled political foe. I have no idea why. I guess he is trying to become relevant in the debate again.

"So now I am too smart to be in Congress, Mister Johnson?" our teacher chides, sending Dick to slink back into the hole he dug himself earlier. This is seriously the most entertaining thing I've seen on TV in years. I wonder what the rest of America is thinking right now.

"Are you going to answer my original question, or just narrate for the History Channel all night?" Beaumont decries harshly.

"I will be happy to answer your question, Congressman, if you answer this one first. Everyone is endowed by their creator with certain inalienable rights, among them life, liberty, and pursuit of happiness, correct?"

Beaumont pauses in a moment of uncertainty. I am sure he doesn't want to fall into a similar trap that ended his Republican nemesis's relevance, so he takes a moment to think about it. Oops.

"A copy of the Declaration of Independence is in the book I gave Mister Johnson. When he's done reading the Constitution, maybe you can borrow—"

"Yes, that's correct!" Beaumont practically shouts.

"So, as long as I kill someone with a hammer, and not a Sig Sauer 9 millimeter handgun, it's okay?"

"Of course not, that's a ridiculous thing to say."

"I agree. So gun control is not the real issue we are talking about, crime control is. When you, a family member, or friend is a victim of a violent crime, does anyone care whether the weapon was a gun, knife, or even a rock?" Mister Bennit says to the camera. "Yes, we ought to have sensible measures governing use and ownership of firearms in America. Washington's approach only puts a Band-Aid on the larger issue. Violence is violence, and until we get serious about discussing how to deal with brutality in our culture, the murders, assaults, and rapes plaguing our society are going to continue unabated."

* * *

I was pretty optimistic coming into the debate, but now I'm downright giddy. Mister Bennit is absolutely killing it tonight. Peyton, a girl who only used to only get excited about boy bands and sales at the mall, is as caught up in the moment as I am. My other classmates are equally entranced with the beating Beaumont and Johnson are getting on stage.

The only exception is Miss Slater. I am not going to pretend to understand what is happening between her and Mister B, but she has not even cracked a smile the entire time he's been out on stage. I thought they were the perfect couple from the instant the rumor mill reported they were dating. Apparently, even perfect couples go through rough patches in their relationships.

The debate is winding down, so everyone backstage is getting a little antsy. The pudgy Miles guy who runs Johnson's campaign turned out to be all bark and no bite, his bluster replaced with a burning desire to find the bottom of a bottle of Jack Daniel's.

The people with Beaumont don't look much better. The handsome, older man is practically pulling his well-styled hair out. The pretty one who looks like a constipated version of Kylie is pacing back and forth, creating a rut in floor. The only one who is calm is the cute younger guy, probably because the creepizoid is more interested in undressing me with his eyes than the happenings on stage.

Male attention is not something I ever crave and rarely receive. Foregoing the daily makeup and hair rituals helps out with that, but tonight is a different story. Since this was our first public appearance for the campaign, Peyton pleaded to let her "spruce me up." It wasn't a *Princess Diaries* level makeover, but even I was amazed what proper makeup application can do for my appearance. She also added some loose, sweeping curls into my straight red hair, and as a result, I look about five years older than I am. My father wasn't happy, but compliments have been flowing in all evening.

Beaumont is stuttering through another response to a question on stage. He sounds like a complete idiot, even though Kylie keeps telling us he is one of the most articulate voices in Congress. Being caught up in the moment, I never realized the creepy, cute guy had walked over until he was standing next to me. Peyton must think he's hot too, because she giggles a little before elbowing me gently in the side.

"Your guy is doing well," I hear him say, catching him looking out of the corner of his eye at me.

"He is doing better than well. He's kicking your guy's ass." My harsh, frigid response should serve as a good deterrent to any flirting he wants to do with me.

"Yes, he is. I'm Blake Peoni," he introduces, offering me his hand. He's either into harsh and frigid, or at the very least, undeterred by it.

"Chelsea Stanton," I state, quickly returning his handshake. "This is Peyton and that's Amanda." They give the quick "hi gesture" most teenage girls master in high school when they are talking to a hot guy.

"Can we talk in private?" he whispers to me, ignoring both my peers. I want to say no because I don't trust him. If we learned one thing during this campaign, it's Winston

Beaumont and his staff are capable of anything. I am curious, and my delay in responding must have been mistaken for consent.

Blake grasps me lightly by the arm, guiding me to a spot near some double doors out of view from the stage and most of the backstage area. Peyton and Vanessa change position so they can see me, although out of earshot. I don't expect to be attacked or anything with this many people around. Regardless, girls can't be too careful these days, especially with any scum that works in Washington.

"What do you want, Mister Peoni?" I say to him as he checks behind the doors and looks back to the stage nervously.

"The name's Blake," he replies, in a near whisper. "I have a question for you. Is Bennit a good man? I mean, is he doing this for his own benefit or—"

"I am his campaign manager, *Mister Peoni*. You knew the answer to that question before you even asked it."

"Yeah, I probably did."

"So what's your angle? Why'd you really pull me over here?"

"No angle. At least, not this time," he says with a smirk I almost mistake as sincere. "Let me explain why I asked. When we did the homework on your guy, I got a hold of his military record. Do you know what's in it?" Okay, this guy is pissing me off. Does he think he will turn me on Mister B because of something he did in the army? Is that his plan?

"Let me tell you a little story, Mister Peoni. When I was a freshman, my dad was stuck working long shifts at the factory. One day, I missed the bus and just had to wander the halls aimlessly until he could pick me up. The school was new to me, and so big, and I was scared to death. I was shy, and found it hard to make friends. None of them would have been there anyway.

"Mister Bennit saw me wandering down the hall in tears and invited me into his classroom to do my homework while his students were getting extra help. I've known him, or been a student of his, ever since. In all that time, he never once told even a single story about his time in the military." Okay, that's not entirely true considering his revelation at Briar Point, but this guy doesn't need to know that. If this lackey is going to drop a bomb on me, I am not going encourage him by pretending I know anything about Mister Bennit's time in the Special Forces.

"He's not the type to brag about his service, I get it. But the file on Bennit doesn't lie. He's a highly decorated veteran and his Distinguished Service Cross was a whisper away from being a Medal of Honor. This is politics and Americans love a hero. Why does he keep his military resume quiet?"

A Distinguished Service Cross? I've only heard of it because Dad was a Marine. Is that the medal Kylie was referring to? Damn, that's not what I was expecting. I wonder what this jerk is up to. I look him directly in the eye to let him know I'm not intimidated, which of course, I am.

"You asked if he was a good man. I think you just answered your own question."

Blake blinks a couple of times, but his eyes search my face like a poker player figuring out if the guy who went all in at a hold 'em table is bluffing. Or maybe I am reading him wrong because he exhales deeply.

"What? Don't believe me?"

"No, I do," he says before looking back toward Peyton and Amanda, who are doing a terrible job at trying be disinterested in our chat. "Here's some inside baseball for you. Winston Beaumont plans to use this next term as a launch pad for a Senate bid, and has his eye on being the majority leader in that house someday. He's not going to let himself get beaten by someone he considers an upstart."

I feel my face flush with anger. It could be the word "upstart," which we are, or the fact that this smug staffer thinks he's so smooth. Either way, I'm getting emotional.

"If you think for a second threatening us is going to intimidate—"

He holds his hands up in surrender and then places a finger over his lips. I realize I'm shouting louder than I wanted and glance around to see if anyone noticed.

"I'm not threatening you. Please don't get angry."

"I'm a redhead. I'll get mad whenever I damn well please!" Does he not know our reputation?

"Okay, okay. Look, I'm not playing games with you. I don't expect you to believe that—"

"Good, because I don't," I blurt out truthfully.

"Miss Stanton, if Winston Beaumont knew I was talking to you tonight I'd be job hunting tomorrow. You guys are running a hell of a campaign. I never thought the race would come down to this. Three months ago, Beaumont was a shoo-in. Now ..."

Blake lets his voice trail off just before a thunderous applause erupts from the audience out in the concert hall. I should be out there watching it instead of wasting my time talking to this guy. We both strain to hear what's happening on stage.

"Now hold on! Just one minute, Mister Bennit!" I hear Beaumont stammer.

"Congressman, I am simply saying it would take a Blue Ribbon House commission six months of study to figure out the rules to musical chairs. Not every problem requires a new law to fix it."

Blake shakes his head, almost in approval of the flogging his boss is getting. "Now the equation has changed, and I just wanted to warn you to watch your back, Chelsea," he says, nodding over toward the stage where the debate is still raging. "And his."

Is his warning sincere? Why would he level with me? He squeezes my shoulder gently and walks toward the stage past Peyton and Amanda, who try to check him out as discretely as they can. They look back at me with inquisitive faces, but I really don't know what to say to them.

After tonight's debate, Congressman Beaumont will be on the ropes. I may only be a high school student, but even a third grader recognizes a beating on the playground when he sees it. So if a storm's coming our way, what benefit would he have in telling us? I can't think of one. Blake Peoni can't be trusted, right?

No use trying to convince myself. I will talk it over with the group and see what they say. Maybe Kylie can offer some insight on the matter later on. Peyton and Amanda have been joined by Vince, and I meet them at our original backstage vantage point. The closing statements have to be coming soon, and I don't want to miss this.

"What was that about?" Peyton whispers.

"We were just discussing which woman was going to get the final rose on *The Bachelor*," I reply with a hint of a wry smile as I go back to watching the screen we are all huddled around.

-FORTY-FOUR-
MICHAEL

"And furthermore, Michael Bennit told you nothing tonight about how he regards the issues facing America today," Dick Johnson says, hoping the viewers at home tuned in late and missed the first eighty-five minutes of the debate. "All he has been willing to do is talk about ideas, and ladies and gentlemen, ideas aren't important to how you govern. Thank you, and I hope for your vote on the ballot next Tuesday."

The audience gives a polite, albeit weak applause. Johnson ad-libbed his final words, but after tonight's performance, he had nothing to lose by doing so. A modern version of the Gettysburg Address would not be compelling enough to recover from his earlier gaffe, and Dick is no Abraham Lincoln.

Beaumont had scripted, or at least mostly scripted, his closing statements and it showed. He sounded like a salesman offering up snake oil to treat whatever ails the American public. He keeps going back to the same well, not realizing it no longer holds water. We don't need to convince the voters that the Beaumont campaign is old and tired when the man himself is so capable of doing it for us.

"Mister Bennit, you may make your closing statement," the moderator deadpans.

I don't need to stick the landing on this. I developed a good message long before I came onto stage and could simply stay on script. Eh, what fun would that be? If I can't think on my feet when the pressure is on, I have no business being here.

"America is more than just a nation, it's an idea. A radical idea that began years before the American Revolution and grew to become the gold standard of democracy around the globe. A glimmering hope of what a free society can accomplish in a world dominated by a millennia worth of tyrants, monarchs, and despots. Our republic is reaching a crossroads though. The idea of America only works if we *trust* the people elected to represent us.

"We are losing faith in our elected officials. Politicians have never been regarded as scrupulous, but the rise of the information age has shown us our representatives are no longer instruments of the people, but of themselves and the special interests that finance them. We have allowed it to happen, so maybe that's what we deserve to get."

You could hear a pin drop in the concert hall.

"I stand before you as a simple teacher, an Army veteran, and a candidate that is beholden to no one. I have no political action committee polluting the airwaves on my behalf, nor am I in the pocket of big oil, big tobacco, or big business. Mayors and councilmen from around the district do not come out to support me because of favors I have done for them in the past.

"Despite my lack of political connections and experience, I am not naïve enough to think I can sweep into Washington and change the face of politics there. I can only offer to change it here.

"What you see is what you get. I have no hidden agenda, nor any special interests to placate. Like I did in the military, I simply want to serve the people of my district and this nation in the manner the Framers imagined. Not as a career politician or wealthy elitist, but as the people's voice in the house created for them.

"So I am not going to make promises up here I have no intention of keeping, or pledge my support to bills not yet written to win your vote. I only promise to represent you the way you were intended to be represented. After all, that's what the people of the Connecticut Sixth District really deserve. Thank you for spending your time listening to us this evening."

The slow audience applause grows into a deafening roar and standing ovation as the moderator turns to the camera to close out the debate. I'm on an adrenaline high, exhausted, and exhilarated all at the same time. This has been an amazing experience, but I'm also thrilled my ninety minutes under the lights is over.

I move with the other candidates to the middle of the stage and we all shake hands. Winston Beaumont is sweating like he just finished a half-marathon. I'm guessing more than the heat of the lights is causing that reaction. Dick Johnson may appear physically healthy to the camera, but his voice has the downtrodden tone of a defeated man. This was his coup de grâce. He understands his race is over.

Sneaking a quick peek off stage, I make out Chelsea, Amanda, Peyton, and Vince all gathered together just off stage in barely stifled enthusiasm. Jessica is standing behind them wearing a look of complete indifference. She could at least try to look happy for me, even if she isn't.

I walk over to the edge of the stage and shake hands with the moderator. Beaumont comes up on my right and follows suit. Johnson has already fled the scene, happy to put this debacle behind him, I'm sure.

"You think your sarcastic wit and empty rhetoric gained anything tonight?" Beaumont says under his breath from beside me. He's waving to the audience like he just finished his third curtain call to an enthusiastic crowd at a rock concert. "You are clearly not cut out for this, Bennit. You sounded like a fool." Yeah, says the eight-term incumbent so popular he is waving to empty seats.

"Talking about America is hardly 'empty rhetoric,' Congressman," I say, giving a wave to a throng of people in front trying to get my attention. "Nor is being true to what was produced in the summer of 1787."

"You think that matters? You're naïve."

The cameras covering the debate go dark and the lonely stage once occupied by just the three of us now feels like a subway station at rush hour. The house lights are turned back up, reducing the glare of lighting coming from the rear of the hall as reporters begin their on-scene analysis for their respective news organizations.

"Half the country is polling this race tonight, Winston." I turn to gaze him dead in his reddening face. "Guess we'll see just how naïve come tomorrow."

-FORTY-FIVE-
KYLIE

After watching tonight's bludgeoning, there's pep in my step as I head out of the concert hall and into the parking lot. Debates are challenging, mentally draining, and often disasters for first-timers. Squaring off against a seasoned incumbent, like Winston Beaumont, makes the task much more daunting. Winning under those circumstances, without taking a definitive stand on a single issue, registers as impossible.

Somehow, Michael did it. He won over the audience and the vast majority of the press covering the debate pronounced him the clear winner. I lost my objectivity weeks ago, but there is no wishful thinking involved when hearing reporters use words like "landslide" and "drubbing." The performance tonight is going to mean a significant bump in the polls for him. Winston Beaumont is in serious trouble, and that's like emotional bubble wrap for me.

The parking lot outside the theater has emptied considerably, but media vans are still parked there, along with a smattering of other vehicles. I approach my car only to see a silhouetted figure leaning against the driver side door. As a woman, I should be unnerved by this considering the circumstances, but I can't think of an instance where any attacker would be inclined to wear a skirt and high heels.

"Your boy put on quite a show tonight," I hear as I get closer.

"He's not *my boy*, but yeah, I think he did very well." I am beginning to wish he was my boy, or more appropriately, my man. Too bad Jessica got to him first.

"Oh, right, I forgot. You're the impartial journalist who hates having her integrity challenged."

"Only by sleazy political operatives working for a crooked, has-been congressman who is either too stubborn or stupid to know when it's time to get out of the game." Those words felt good to say. "What do you want, Madison?"

"Such harsh words, Kylie. Can't I say a quick hello to my big sister? I mean, we haven't talked since back in New York when you were accusing me of trashing your career."

"Yes, it's been a pleasant few months, hasn't it?" I say with as much pleasantness as my voice will allow me to conjure. "Given the results of the debate tonight, I thought you'd be off finding a big, soft pillow to cry in." Or smother yourself in, you arrogant bitch.

"You think this is over?" she asks menacingly. "I'm just getting started. I'm going to beat you, Kylie, I swear to God I am!"

"This isn't about us, Madison. We're not the candidates. I don't even work for Bennit." She is taking this more personally than I thought she ever would.

"Don't kid yourself. You may fool others with your 'deep cover' journalistic garbage, but not me."

"You need therapy, Maddie."

She gets within inches of my face. I begin to wonder if the remaining press lingering in the parking lot are about to be treated to a cat fight. If so, I'd bet the deli clerk would wish he was here. Madison is no Jessica, but girls fighting is always entertaining, with or without Jell-O. So if she makes a move, I'm sure he'll see it anyway. Images of me gouging out her eyes would be eleven o'clock news material for sure.

"I am going to wipe the floor with you," she states in a quiet yet menacing voice. "And when I'm done, you will need an army of shrinks to put the pieces of your life back together. You wanted a war, well, now you've got one."

I pucker my lips and kiss the air between us. A little lame in terms of a response, but the coolest thing I could come up with at the moment. Disgusted, she struts off toward the visual arts building without looking back. I find myself almost disappointed she backed down.

My sister doesn't intimidate me, but she cannot be underestimated either. A desperate Winston Beaumont and a bloodthirsty Madison Roberts make a volatile and dangerous combination. Once again, she has unwittingly given me another piece of information.

They will be coming for us. Dealing with Roger Bean and Winston Beaumont is enough to keep anyone busy. Now, with Madison adamant about destroying me in the process, I just added another person to worry about.

I've done my best to help Michael Bennit every way my journalistic skills and contacts can afford. As I climb into my car, I'm lost in a singular thought. Despite my best intentions, I only made matters worse for him.

-FORTY-SIX-
BLAKE

Candidates seeking office generally make use of whatever vacant space is available for their headquarters in some geographically desirable part of the district. Ours is no exception, despite the millions of dollars in the Beaumont campaign coffers. We occupy old retail space in a strip mall like any other candidate would.

The main area is called the "war room," and features rows of long tables, folding chairs, and plenty of phones. Outside of the call center, other small meeting areas are set aside for managing various aspects of the "get out the vote" effort. As most retail spaces offer nothing in the way of offices, Roger had some temporary walls erected to allow the congressman a quiet place to confer in peace with members of the staff.

Other than the extra added spaces, Beaumont Campaign Headquarters is your typical political election command center. Well, typical for everyone except maybe Michael Bennit who has managed to become the frontrunner running his effort out of a coffee shop.

Pollsters were out in full force after the debate last night. Every major polling organization got one in the field, and we contracted our own for the district to verify the numbers. They aren't good, which is why the key players of the Beaumont for Congress staff are crammed into his small, makeshift office.

Congressman Beaumont is seething behind a desk while Roger, Madison, Deena, and I are gathered around it waiting for Marcus to arrive with the results.

The national polls already published their findings on websites and reported them on the morning news shows. The conclusions vary, but the one thing they share in common is the bottom line containing the only information of importance at the moment. Despite having an eighty percent approval rating last spring, we're now losing.

This is not a national race like a presidential election, so nobody cares what some country bumkin' in Arkansas thinks. The only important numbers belong to the poll of likely voters in the Connecticut Sixth District, and the bad news we're expecting to be delivered about them.

"Well?" Congressman Beaumont demands, as Marcus enters the minuscule office and wedges himself into the crowd around the desk.

"Uh, sir, well, uh, we've slipped," Marcus says with dread.

"No shit, Marcus. By how much?" Roger asks impatiently.

"Well, uh, the polling data ... well it has a, uh larger margin of error than we—"

"Eleven points, Congressman," I say, reading the paper in Marcus's hand. "Bennit now has an eight-point lead outside the margin of error."

Marcus stares at me incredulously. I wasn't eager to deliver the bad news, but let's just rip the Band-Aid off and get it over with. Roger rubs his forehead and the congressman just glares through my soul with piercing eyes.

"Now is not the time to grow a set of balls with me, Blake."

"Yes, sir," is what I say, "whatever" is what I mean. If they had listened to me to begin with, we wouldn't be staring defeat in the face.

"Sir, maybe we should view this as an opportunity."

"Oh, shut up, Deena!" the congressman barks. "We have spent millions on this campaign. An eleven-point deficit is the best you all can do?"

"Sir, Bennit scored big last night and—"

"I don't want excuses, Madison! I expect results!"

The room grows eerily still as the congressman grabs a copy of the *Times* off his desk and sticks it in Deena's face. The pixie startles at the aggressive gesture and, as a result, everyone, including Roger, collectively takes a step back.

"All the press is talking about is Bennit and those misfit students of his! You can't get our message out, and you failed miserably in prepping me for the debate," he rants.

"Sir, I—"

"I said shut up! You add no value to this campaign. I have no idea why I keep you around. Get out of my sight."

Deena doesn't move, her body immobilized by fear and face frozen in shock. The congressman has a temper, but on his worst day has never been this enraged.

"Did I stutter? I said get out!" he shouts, throwing the newspaper at her. This time, Deena's fight or flight instinct kicks in, and choosing the latter, wastes no time in pushing for the door and getting out of the office. In a way I feel bad for her. While I don't much like her, I thought she did a good job during debate preparation. It was just not executed well on stage. Unfortunately, there's no point in trying to tell Winston Beaumont he failed without risking earning myself a pink slip.

"Marcus, you're dismissed too. I need to talk to the others." While Deena may be shocked and wounded at her dismissal, Marcus getting out of the office reminds me of a kid racing to the swing set at recess.

"With due respect, sir, it's not Deena's or Marcus's fault," Roger says to his old friend. "You know that. Now, we have less than a week before the election."

"I'm aware of that, Roger. It's time for you all to earn your paychecks. If I am not reading about how Bennit uses hookers or is supported by the Nazi Party while drinking my coffee tomorrow morning, the only thing you'll ever do again in D.C. is visit monuments."

"We checked his background. It's clean. Why are we—"

"Didn't I warn you once before about questioning me, Blake? Stop thinking and do what I tell you. I want Bennit destroyed! Now!" he says, pounding the desk as he rises to his feet.

"A small little scandal isn't going to get it done, Congressman," Madison says. For the first time in months, I'm relieved she takes my side.

"Madison—"

"Hear me out, sir. I'm not saying we shouldn't go negative, but the story has to be something scandalous enough to dominate headlines and not easy for Bennit to counter and dismiss."

"You have something in mind?" Roger inquires.

Beaumont calms down as Madison details her plan. Roger listens intently, weighing the political ramifications as only he can do. I am sick to my stomach listening to her.

"Roger?" the congressman asks when Madison finishes.

"It could work if executed properly. At a minimum we'll bring back some independents and crossover democrats whose support for Bennit is soft at best."

"One more thing, sir," Madison continues. "I can't be the one who leaks this to the press. There can be no appearance this came from our campaign. We're late in the game. Leaving a trail linking this to us will label you petty and desperate." Which he is, but I'm not about to say that.

"Roger, you are good at this sort of thing. Do you think—"

"Blake should do it," Madison blurts out, cutting off the congressman mid-sentence.

The blood drains from my face. How could she say that? Why? Actually, I think I know why. She knows I have disagreed with some of the tactics we used during this campaign. She may have even noticed me talking to Chelsea during the debate. Either way, she knows I won't support this course of action. This is payback time for what I did to her earlier in the campaign.

"He has the contacts in the media to get coverage and the ability to make this stick through Tuesday," she implores through the evil grin on her face. "Trust me, sir, he's your man for this."

I am living the textbook definition of "set up for failure." If I go through with this, I destroy innocent lives. Bennit doesn't deserve this, and neither does Chelsea or the rest of his staff. If we discovered something that was true, that's one thing, but this?

If I don't do it, though, we lose the election. No scheme I can come up with is going to make up enough ground following our dreadful debate performance. I wouldn't have even debated this with myself three months ago, but now? Bennit and Chelsea have proven themselves to be worthy adversaries. Beaumont doesn't deserve to win. I need to tap dance my way out of this.

"This is a terrible idea, sir. I understand the premise, and earlier in the race I'd be all for it. But, sir, we are days away from the finish line and there are too many ways the ploy can go wrong before then. Perhaps if we focus on —"

"Madison, can you excuse us for a moment?" Roger asks. "We need a word in private with Blake."

Madison winks at me as she spins on her heels and leaves the small office, closing the door behind her. The congressman, who had been pacing in the small space behind the desk, now settles back in his chair. Roger sits on the corner of the aging piece of furniture and turns towards me as a clear indication he is with Beaumont, and against me, if I protest.

"All right, Blake. You've done this sort of thing before without flinching. Why are you hesitating now?" Roger asks, getting straight to the point.

He sounds almost sincere with his question. I never experience problems talking myself out of jams like this, but now I've developed some sort of mutism. The words simply aren't coming. I can't tell him the truth, so I rack my brain for some reason or excuse this won't work. Unfortunately, logic is being overruled by emotion. Still, nothing is coming. Seconds tick by and now my time has run out.

"I don't give a damn, Roger," Winston states unequivocally. "Blake, you wanted a seat at the big boy table. Look around, you've made it. This is exactly where you wanted to be. You earned the right to be here, but now you need to earn the right to stay. You will do this, understand?" All I can do is nod.

"There is no place in politics for a conscience. You can deal with the guilt over whatever little ethical dilemma you're having once we win. Until then, get this done."

"We'll discuss the details in a few minutes," Roger utters as I leave without acknowledging him, pulling the door closed behind me. It was like the congressman was reading my mind. Did my face betray me? Does it matter? He's right, this is exactly where I wanted to be.

"I can do this," I murmur to myself in the futile attempt of being convincing. I'm fooling myself, because deep down I know I really don't want to.

-FORTY-SEVEN-
CHELSEA

I may be the figurehead of a campaign to send a popular teacher to Congress, but tell that to my other teachers. While many of them support what nearly every student in the school is working toward, they certainly aren't letting our education suffer because of it.

There are five days left until the voters decide whether months of hard work pays off, and here I am, sitting at the dining room table, laboring over another science worksheet. I haven't even had time to open the book. The time I have spent on the campaign has let the homework pile up, so I need a night away from my duties at the coffee shop to catch up. After the science work, I need to finish a backlog of math problems and read half of *Romeo and Juliet* for my English class.

Dad is in his chair in the living room watching CNN. His hearing is shot after a day of work at the factory, so I can hear the TV as if I were sitting next to it. Luckily, there has been nothing of any interest to keep me from focusing on my academic responsibilities.

"This just in to the news desk," the anchorwoman announces. "The AP is reporting that candidate for Congress Michael Bennit may have engaged in inappropriate sexual relations with one of his students." So much for nothing of interest.

I pop out of my seat like a snake crawled on it and race the short distance to the living room where Dad is leaning forward in his chair. He breaks his gaze from the screen only to peer up at me with trepidation, as the woman on CNN continues.

"These allegations come mere days before the election and claim there is an ongoing sexual affair between Bennit and his campaign manager, Chelsea Stanton."

Wait, what?

My father practically jumps out of his chair with such force that I have to move a step or two away from him to avoid getting knocked over. "This latest allegation is bad news for a campaign already forced to address other earlier assertions about student conduct including cheating, pirating, underage drinking, and illegal drug use."

She continues on, but I'm too stunned to listen. Did she really announce to the world that I'm sleeping with my teacher? I'm still processing the information when I look over at my father.

"What the hell is she talking about, Chelsea?" Dad says with anger in his voice and fists clenched.

"What?" I ask innocently, half not hearing him, half still not comprehending what I just heard.

"Don't play dumb with me, missy! What happened between you two?"

"What do you mean? Nothing!"

"Don't lie to me!"

"Lie to you! Dad! How could you possibly …" I lose the handle on my emotions as tears begin streaming down my cheeks. I can't believe I'm having this conversation. How could he think any of this is true? Doesn't he trust me?

"Chelsea," he consoles as he realizes how upset I am.

"Nothing happened, Dad," I blurt out between sobs. "They're lying. Why would they do that?"

He reaches for me and I step away.

"No! You believe them over your own daughter!" I scream, the emotion of the moment blocking out any logic. "What kind of parent are you?"

"Chelsea, listen to me! I never said I believed them! But you spend a lot of time with him and he's very persuasive—"

"Dad! He's not like that!"

"Okay, okay," he assures, reaching for me again.

I push him away, even though his embrace may be the only safe place for me right now. How could my father question me like this?

"No! I want to know! Why would you believe them?"

Dad's anger morphs into something far more surprising. His instinct to protect me has given in to his fear of having hurt me. For me, reading Dad's face is like a linguist reading Spanish. Neither of us has to study it too long to figure out exactly what it means.

"You're all I have left, Snuggle Bear. I'm sorry, I overreacted. I know you're a better person than that," he chokes, fighting back his own emotions. "You're my little girl and I just don't want anything bad to happen to you."

Tears begin to well in his eyes. He pulls me into his arms and gives me a hard hug. I bury my face into his chest, trying to find some comfort there.

"How could you believe I would do that? Why would you believe them?" I sob, my wounded voice muffled by his shirt. "You know I would never do that."

"I know, I know. I'm sorry. It's okay."

The world goes on around us, but here I am safe. I can hear the anchorwoman on the news repeating the same headline that she announced moments ago for the benefit of the millions of Americans sure to be tuning in as word spreads. At this moment in time, right here, right now, it feels like me and Dad against the world.

Our embrace is disrupted by a loud rap on our front door. That's strange, since over the last few months, when the rare occasion we get a visitor arises, they call in advance to try to get cleared through our town-funded security. The police have been present in force outside our home, and only the most daring would challenge that cordon.

Dad gives me a gentle, paternal kiss on the forehead before letting me go. Our front door only has four small windows at the top, offering no chance to peer outside. We have no way to identify who is knocking. It could be Mister Bennit, or maybe one of my friends on the staff who heard the news and rushed over.

When he opens the door, Dad is greeted by a mob of photographers and the blinding flashes of their cameras. A chorus of voices shout out questions to add to the chaos. I don't think I'm a chicken, but I retreat deeper into the living room.

"Get off my front stoop!" Dad yells. "Get these people off my property now!" he bellows, probably to our police caretakers. I can hear a scuffle in the crowd as reporters jockey for position, but the incessant questions persist.

"What do you think of the allegations about your daughter?"

"Did she have an affair with Michael Bennit?"

"Have you talked to Bennit yet?"

Those were among the questions I hear as I dare to approach the door. I instantly regret it. Seeing me, the crush of media surges forward, knocking the lead reporter right into my father's face. That was the last straw. My father shoves the man gruffly, bringing his arm back. Oh no!

"Dad!" I yell too late as he lands a hard right on the young reporter's chin causing him to careen into the mob before hitting the sidewalk. Cameras click away without slowing, but the barrage of questions ceases as reporters watch their colleague get helped up from the ground. The assault gives the police time to get between us and the mass of humanity on our step, and they begin herding the media back off the lawn as reinforcements arrive with lights and sirens blazing.

"That's right! Get off my property and don't ever set foot on it again!" Dad rails from the door.

Oh, it's going to be a long day tomorrow.

-FORTY-EIGHT-
MICHAEL

A copy of the *New York Times* is slapped down on my desk. I don't bother looking up to see who did this, as I already know the answer. I pick up the folded paper where the above-the-fold headline reads: iCandidate Implicated in Affair with Student.

I scan the article for any more sordid details not included in last night's coverage. My body tenses with renewed anger reading the accusations. Last night's rage circled more around Chelsea's dad's reaction and the effect this will have on her. Then, after the tenth attempt to reach Jessica, who is still staying at her own place instead of mine, it changed into what will happen to my future marriage. At a distant third, fourth, and fifth is what other people think, the impact on my current job, and my future teaching career. Dead last is consequence to the campaign.

"Whoever made this up watches a lot of porn."

"I tried to warn you, Michael, but you wouldn't listen. Now an innocent girl has been destroyed," Principal Howell vaingloriously trumpets.

"Was that your 'I told you so'?"

"The superintendent called this morning. She asked me to inform you of your official suspension, with pay, pending an investigation by the school board. I've been instructed to walk you out of the building," Howell decrees in a triumphant tone. "That was my 'I told you so.'"

I can't blame Charlene for making the decision she did. After all, she did warn me, and under the circumstances, I would make the same judgment in her position. Neither Chalice nor Charlene can protect me from something like this.

"If I have my way, you'll never teach here again. I guess it's not up to me though. Your fate will depend on her parents, and their reaction to these ... allegations."

"Parent, as in singular. She only lives with her father. And I guess I should be fortunate it isn't up to you."

Principal Howell doesn't flinch. He's dreamed of this day since the moment I joined the staff at Millfield High. Now I'm lined up in his crosshairs and there's nothing I can do about it. It's only a suspension, but he has all the leverage he needs to make my dismissal permanent. The worst thing is, he knows it.

"Yes, you probably should be, but I doubt you will garner much sympathy from the school board either. I mean, considering your propensity for insubordination and all." I don't need a Magic 8-Ball to tell me he is dead on with that analysis.

"Your classes will report to study hall today and we'll find a long-term sub for you. Now get out of here and finish your campaign. For your sake, I hope you win, because you won't be teaching in this town again."

* * *

Howell gives me ten minutes to collect my things, promising to be back to personally show me the door. He wasn't out of my classroom for thirty seconds when Xavier and Peyton came screaming in.

"What happened?" Xavier asks in a panic as I pull the "in case of absence" folder from my desk drawer.

"I've been suspended."

"For how long?"

I don't bother responding, letting my eyes do the talking. Xavier got the message, Peyton not so much.

"How could this happen? I mean, they can't believe this is true. Why would they suspend you?" Peyton is a sweet girl, but still a little naïve as to the way the world works.

"They are protecting the district," I respond with a half-truth. The other half being I'm not exactly a fan-favorite among the administration of the school or central office.

"So Beaumont makes this crap up because you kicked his ass in the debate and everyone believes it?"

"Dirty politics 101, Xavier, the October surprise."

"Surprises are supposed to be fun," Emilee says rushing into the classroom with Vince in tow.

"Tell that to George Bush. Someone dropped the dime about getting arrested for DWI days before the 2000 election. His father, H.W. Bush, had the Weinberger indictment, and the list goes on."

"Yeah, well, this still sucks." Vince has the Italian anger in his voice you hear when watching *The Sopranos.*

"We need to start working on a statement right away," Emilee decrees. "The press is going nuts and our Twitter account has been blowing up since last night."

Vanessa and Brian come charging in with the same sense of urgency the others did. Amanda joins us about ten seconds later. Except for Chelsea, who is probably not at school today, the band is back together.

"What'd we miss?" she asks, in the hopes to come up to speed.

"Mister B's been suspended."

"They can do that?" Vanessa asks incredulously. After everything we've already been through, she should know better.

"More importantly, we need to figure out how the campaign is going to respond," Vince interjects in an effort to get everyone on task. "I think we should—"

"Isn't someone going to ask me whether or not it's true?" I interrupt. Truth is, I don't care how the campaign responds. Right now, I care about my kids and what they think.

"We know it's not true," Vanessa dismisses.

"How do you know, V?"

"Because we know you," Emilee adds.

"And we know Chelsea," Amanda says.

"You're like a second father to most of us," Vince states. In his case, the statement is truer than people could imagine. "Just as we try not to disappoint you, you would never disappoint us."

I am not the warm, fuzzy, emotional type. However, Vince's comment hits me like a sledgehammer. He's right, of course, but the fact they recognize that is nothing short of amazing. It's also another reason why these kids are so special.

"And we know Miss Slater. She'd kill you slowly just to enjoy watching you die." Unfortunately, they don't know the whole story about what is going on between us right now. Some things even prized students don't need to be trusted with.

"Well, the accusation is out there, regardless. The damage is done, and I'm guilty in the court of public opinion, even if we say otherwise."

"Without a shred of proof?" Brian asks.

"Anonymous sources are a reporter's defense against accountability and a politician's favorite weapon. Remember, life is a matter of perspective. From the voters' point of view, they've seen New York's governor resign for hiring prostitutes and a congressman leave office for taking pictures of his genitals and sexting. Is this outlandish by comparison?"

"Don't they need to offer someone up to make their claims stick?" Xavier asks.

"The story only has to last a few days. By the time the press gets around to figuring out the truth, it will be Election Day and Beaumont will cruise into his ninth term."

My staff shakes their heads in utter disgust. I understand how they feel. I never thought they would sink this low. It's one thing to come after me for being inexperienced. Even exposing some of my students' transgressions, although slimy, were at least grounded in fact. Lying about something like this is just … deplorable.

"We have to do something to stop this," Amanda proclaims. "What's Kylie doing?"

"She's doing some digging to figure out where this came from, but I haven't heard from her yet this morning. You guys will need to work out what to say on behalf of the campaign. I have some things I need to take care of first."

"Miss Slater?" Amanda asks, understanding the topic is both sensitive and personal.

"Among other things, yes."

"But we have no idea what to do."

"You're all smart and will figure it out. I have all the faith in the world in you," I state truthfully.

"This is too big for us, Mister B," Brian laments.

"All right, this may be one of the last lessons I am ever able to give you, so listen up." Undivided attention is an oxymoron with teenagers today, but I get theirs now. I take a deep breath and exhale slowly, the reality of this actually being their last lesson beginning to sink in.

"You are all going to be faced with hard decisions in life, and we don't do a good job of preparing you for making them. Those decisions will play a big part in the men and women you'll become.

"Choices about careers, love, where to live … they will help define your existence. Ethical and moral dilemmas will steer you down the path you choose in life and help uncover your character. When you punch out of this world, you will have a legacy of good choices and bad ones, but how you respond to both is what people around you will remember.

"The most important thing you can learn in high school is how to process the information available, analyze it, and make the best decision you can. The rest falls into place, and you live with those consequences.

"I made a choice to involve you in this. I made that decision because I knew you could handle it. The campaign is important, but right now other, more critical things need my attention."

Howell shows up with a security guard and walks into the classroom. The students stare at him with contempt, but he ignores them and gestures toward the door melodramatically. Man, is he ever enjoying this moment.

"Really, Robinson? Security?"

"Just in case you resist," Howell says, flashing a toothy smile.

I turn to the gray-haired guard. "Ralph, if I chose to resist, is there anything you could do?"

I like Ralph. A crusty, old Korean War veteran and long-retired gym teacher, he must have been built like a tank in his youth. Now in his eighties, and struggling with his health, Ralph works in the building because he enjoys being around kids. We have a great rapport, the product of swapping stories and mutual respect former soldiers from different generations have for each other. I'm sure he's only here because the priggish Howell forced him to come.

"Yes, sir, there are exactly two things I could do. Piss my pants and scream like a little girl."

The self-contented smile disappears off Howell's face. Yep, I like Ralph.

* * *

The media was on the scent from the moment I walked out the doors of the building. The flurry of activity was unmistakable across the street. I don't have much to thank Robinson Howell for, but his unrelenting push to keep media off school grounds finally paid dividends for me.

All bets were off once I pulled out of the parking lot, though. A half dozen reporters surrounded my car at the traffic light to pull onto the main road. Thank God the red didn't last long.

The journey across town was more like leading an army convoy than a solitary drive. At least two dozen news vans, satellite trucks, and other vehicles followed me all the way to my destination.

The scene at the house was not much different. Thanks to last night's debacle, enough Millfield police were on hand to keep the media corralled on the street and off the property. By the time I park and climb out of my car, a legion of reporters are shouting questions, their cameramen capturing every move I make for posterity.

I follow the sidewalk to the front door and ring the bell, aware that this simple act will lead every news broadcast in the country. I almost wonder if someone is tweeting about it in real-time when the door opens revealing the hulking figure of Bruce Stanton.

"I was wondering if you'd show up," he says, stepping back and waving me in. I cross the threshold and enter the living room of the small yet tidy house. The door slams closed behind me as I notice the curtains drawn on the picture window, leaving the room darker than the gray day outside. Privacy has been a scarce commodity for Chelsea and her dad since the campaign started. I begin to turn back to face him.

"Mister Stanton, I—"

I feel the punch land squarely on my jaw and I stagger a few steps backward.

Bruce launches himself into me and we careen through the living room. I lose my balance and he slams me into the couch, our momentum causing us to bounce off and crash into an end table. The cheap faux-porcelain lamp perched atop the small piece of furniture flies through the air and crashes to the ground the same time we do.

I manage to roll away from him and get to my feet before he can use his size to pin me to the ground. Bruce is a large man, but agile for his build. He jumps to his feet, kicking the remains of the table out of the way. Marines are skilled in hand-to-hand fighting, but he served a long time ago, and like most amateur fighters, is relying on landing a haymaker to end this donnybrook.

The Krav Maga training I got in Special Forces kicks in and I'm ready for his second punch before he even lets it fly. I dodge his fist, step into him, hook his right arm with my left, and apply pressure with my right hand on the back of his neck. Using his momentum against him, he goes to the ground quickly.

With control of his arm, I can end this engagement with one of a dozen moves. Many of them will require a trip to the emergency room and several months in a cast. I then realize where I am, and what I'm doing.

Fighting my training and indoctrination, I release him and take a few steps away from where he lays on the ground. I'm not scared of Bruce Stanton; I simply did not come here to fight him.

He gets up, lumbers over to me, and grabs a fistful of my shirt, his other arm cocked back and ready to unleash what is bound to be a painful hit.

"Dad!" Chelsea screams from the hallway entrance to the living room. "Dad! Let him go!"

Bruce takes a quick glance over his shoulder to see the horror and fear on his only child's face. She is puffy-eyed from crying over an emotional trauma, now exacerbated by the sight of her father and favorite teacher brawling in the living room.

"I don't give a damn whether you were a Green Beret or not," he growls, looking me directly in the eye. "You're lucky I'm not ripping your arms off."

"So what's stopping you?"

"I said let him go, Dad!" Chelsea pleads, now close enough to reach out and place a hand on her father's shoulder. "Please," she whispers, touching his forearm with her other hand and coaxing him to release me. He decocks the arm poised to do significant damage to my face and unclamps the fist he made around the material of my shirt.

"I asked my daughter if anything happened between you two. She swears nothing did and I believe her. She wouldn't lie to me about something like that."

I rub my jaw to make sure it is still attached. The unmistakable tang of fresh blood hits my tongue, but considering the time spent surrounded by alpha males at army posts, I've been in far worse condition than this. I did think the days of brawling were behind me when I started teaching, though.

"So what was that all about?"

"You're not a father, are you?" I immediately get his point and give a slight nod. The fight isn't about the allegation of sleeping with his daughter, but the helpless feeling of trying to protect her from the world I introduced by starting this in the first place.

No parent wants to see their kid in pain—emotional, physical, or otherwise. Events spun out of control, leading to comments broadcasted publically to hurt Chelsea. Bruce needed to lash out at somebody. I made a convenient target.

"You're both bleeding. I'll get some ice and bandages."

Bruce surveys the damage to his arm, which has a gash running down it inflicted from a shard of the shattered lamp. I touch my fingers to my gums to determine how bad my mouth is bleeding.

"She worships you, ya know. I think you understand that," he says after she disappears down the hall. "I also think you are man enough never to take advantage of anyone, much less a young woman."

I nod. Bruce gestures me to sit down on the couch and I take a seat. He sits in an overstuffed recliner, careful not to get blood on the upholstery.

"My wife died when Chelsea was a child. Her mom was Irish and could really piss me off, but man, I loved that woman. After she passed, I tried to be the best father I could be, ya know, but a girl needs her mother. I could never get Chels to come out of her shell when she hit high school. Never get her excited about anything.

"That changed when she took your class. She actually looked forward to doing her homework and writing essays."

"Nobody looks forward to homework, Dad. It was just easier to tolerate than most," Chelsea corrects, emerging from the kitchen and handing me a bag of ice and a washcloth. I dab the blood away and hold the ice to my jaw to reduce any swelling. Glad I'm the iCandidate or I might be trouble for the campaign's makeup department.

"Well, it was something I never did myself," Bruce confesses as Chelsea cleans his cut with a piece of gauze soaked in peroxide. The laceration's not deep, but must sting like hell. Bruce is a tough old Marine, because he didn't pretend not to notice—I don't think he actually did.

"Ya know, she would come home and quote the things you said in class like it was gospel."

"Okay, now you're just embarrassing me."

"Good teachers instruct, great teachers mentor, but you go further. You inspire your students to do more and be more than they thought they ever could. Ya know, only rare people have that kind of impact. That's why I let her work on this campaign of yours."

A long pause between us begins to turn into an awkward moment. I want to interject something, but nothing comes to mind. In this conversation, I am intent to let him be on transmit and me on receive.

"Ya know, people will find it easy to believe you did it. It's the way things are these days."

"Yeah, unfortunately."

"I'm sure whoever did this was counting on you not getting the benefit of the doubt. So, I guess all I want is ..."

Bruce's voice trails off and I know what he's going to ask even before he does. It is the same thing I've been thinking since the story broke last night.

"You want to know who 'whoever' is so you can wrap your hands around his throat."

-FORTY-NINE-
CHELSEA

"I would hate to be forced to settle for beating the crap out of you, ya know?" my dad tells Mister B.

"I'm not worried. For a former Marine, I was surprised to learn you hit like a girl."

They both laugh, the tension between them apparently fully subsided. It's surreal considering they were about to kill each other five minutes ago, but now we have moved into the male bonding portion of today's program.

"So, do you know who made this trash up yet?"

"No. I mean, who benefits is clear though."

"Beaumont."

Mister Bennit nods.

"So what are we going to do about it?" I ask, curious as to what the next step is.

Mister Bennit leans back on the couch, setting the now melting bag of ice I gave him on our only remaining intact end table. "I can't prove anything, nor confirm them as the source directly. This could easily have been made up by one of the dozen groups running ads on television supporting him.

Outside of a denial, which nobody is going to believe anyway, there isn't much I can do."

My father thinks about that for a second then gets out of his chair.

"Where are you going, Dad?"

"Snuggle Bear, I need you to go in my closet and find me a new shirt. A nice one that will look good on television. Mister Bennit here may not be able to set the record straight, but those rules don't apply to me."

* * *

"Applying cover-up to my teacher is a little awkward, just so you know," I say, applying the finishing touches to his chin. Can't say I ever expected to be doing this in my lifetime.

"No more awkward than me wearing it, Chels," Mister B says with a smile. "Lucky I don't bruise easily."

"That should do it. It's not too swollen, so it shouldn't be noticeable," I say as my father emerges from the hallway, struggling to button the sleeve of the shirt covering the gash in his arm. I walk over to give him a hand. "Are you sure you want to do this, Dad? I mean, I can handle the press myself."

He kisses me on the forehead. "I know you can, Snuggle Bear, but you have the same problem he does. You're the manager and the accused, so no, this has to come from me. Now, how do I look?" Dad asks, straightening his shirt.

"You look good."

"Okay, let's roll." Dad sets off toward the front door to face the Spanish Inquisition waiting on the other side.

"Are we sure this is a good idea?" I whisper to Mister Bennit.

He shrugs. "I have no idea, but sometimes things need to be done based on principal, consequences be damned."

I walk out the door first, Mister Bennit and my dad close behind. The media camped out on the street in front of the house erupts into a flurry of activity as we start crossing the lawn toward them. The police on scene stand no chance in holding back the tsunami of humanity rushing toward us.

"You really want this life for yourself, Michael?" I hear my father say behind me.

"No, but if it's the price for beating Beaumont, at this point I will gladly pay it."

-FIFTY-
KYLIE

After spending most of the night tracking down the source of the accusations against Michael and Chelsea, the morning was spent trading notes with the brigade of media in town. Since everyone in the news business knows I am close to the Bennit campaign, I don't expect them to accept what I say at face value. But they already smelled a rat, and I just provided the direction to where they should start looking for it. Now I have no energy left to keep up the fight. The rest is up to Michael and his students.

Turning on the television before crashing onto my cheap, uncomfortable bed, I appreciate how a public relations guy must feel when the celebrity he represents ends up on TMZ. Michael didn't pick up the last time I called, and now I think I know why. From the confines of my hotel room, I'm powerless to do anything but watch the events transpiring on Bruce Stanton's front lawn.

I flip through the channels to find every station interrupted normal programming to show the mob of reporters, photographers, and cameramen gathering around the trio of Michael, Chelsea, and her father. Even the broadcast networks

CBS, NBC, ABC, and FOX interrupt their daytime television shows. In a campaign chock-full of sensationalized stories and big moments, this is the biggest. What happens in the next few minutes will determine the fate of Michael Bennit.

Chelsea's father looks a little overwhelmed by the attention, and rightfully so. Chelsea has clearly been crying, but she stands proudly with defiance in her eyes. Michael is stoic in front of the cameras, brave, considering the circumstances. Professional and unfazed, you might never realize this is the first time he ever faced a hostile press corps. His chin looks a little swollen to me, but the horde asking questions don't seem to notice. It makes me wonder exactly what happened inside that house.

"Why did you see Michael Bennit?"

"Are you angry with him?"

"Mister Bennit, is it true?"

"Is there any truth to the allegation?"

"Mister Stanton, do you believe he did it?"

"Are the police involved?"

Those are some of the questions shouted from the phalanx of reporters surrounding them. The rest of shouts blur into a cacophony of unintelligible sound. Michael, Chelsea, and her father are standing in the eye of a ferocious storm from which there is no shelter from.

"C'mon, guys! Say something!" I yell at the television. I can't figure out what they're waiting for. They are standing there like statues and not saying anything while the press torments them. Finally, Michael raises his hands to shush the reporters so he can speak. Much to my surprise, the gesture works, and the rabble quiets enough for him to talk.

"This will go a whole lot faster if you ask your questions one at a time," Michael says, a picture of calm, control, and patience. In a first for the modern media, the reporters simmer down to the point of near placidity. Forget iCandidate, he would have been a great *candidate*.

"Are you finally going to speak to us, Mister Bennit?" a reporter from the back shouts. Michael turns to Bruce and then back to the eager journalists surrounding him.

"No, I'm not. He is."

The horde erupts again and Bruce listens to the wave of shouted questions pouring in. I finally realize what's going on. Like a batter waiting for a good pitch in baseball, Bruce is looking for the perfect one to answer, and the media is beginning to get frustrated because of it.

"Mister Stanton, did Michael Bennit convince you nothing happened?" The question came from somewhere in the back of the crowd.

"No," Bruce says with conviction, to the shock of everybody around him. "He didn't convince me because I never believed it to begin with." He qualified that just in time. A split-second longer and the Beaumont campaign would have his sound bite on continuous loop.

After another brief barrage, a female from the front manages to outshout the rest. "Then why did you meet with Michael Bennit?"

"Well, my daughter, the people on television, and Winston Beaumont all keep telling me what I should think. I wanted to see for myself what kind of man he is."

"What did you learn, Mister Stanton?" the same reporter asks as a follow-up. Bruce Stanton pauses for a moment and then looks the reporter dead in the face.

"He's going to make a terrible congressman."

I bury my head in my hands. Getting trashed by your campaign manager's father on live television is a death sentence for an aspiring politician. I can't bear to watch.

"Why do you say that, Mister Stanton?"

"Because Michael Bennit is too good a man to be a politician. I may be a factory worker with an eighth grade education, but I'm a Marine, and I know something about character. This crap you're hearing about him and my daughter is nothing more than a desperate smear campaign from a crusty, old, washed-up lawmaker. If any of you thinks otherwise, then you're idiots."

My head snaps back up. Did I really just hear that, or was it wishful thinking?

"Do you know for a fact this was made up?"

"Do you know who started the story?"

"Are you blaming the Beaumont campaign?"

Amazing. In answering one question, he has not only discredited the story, but pointed the press in the direction of who to blame for it.

"I can only guess who started this rumor about my daughter. I'm sure you guys can figure it out once you get around to asking the hard questions. Unless, of course, you're all comfortable letting unnamed sources destroy my eighteen-year-old daughter's reputation."

Oh my God, he just called out the national media to guilt them into finding answers. Whether he realizes or not, his challenge will have the major news organizations climbing over each other to find the truth.

"I'll tell you one more thing. If I ever to get my hands on this unnamed source, I'm going to rip his head off and use it as an ashtray." Spoken like a true Marine.

"Was that a threat?"

"Call it whatever you want. But the bastard who made this up should consider himself warned."

Bruce, Michael, and Chelsea turn to begin to head back into the house.

"Mister Stanton, will you be voting for Michael Bennit?" a young reporter asks, managing to get all three to stop, turn, and look back. The mass of humanity lurches forward to capture his response.

"You've been brilliant, Bruce. Please don't screw it up when you're home free," I counsel, as if the television will transmit my message to him. I lean forward to the edge of my hotel room bed in eager anticipation of the response about to be beamed onto the cheap flat screen. "Please, please, please," I whisper to myself as I lace my hands together and chomp down on an index finger.

"Ya know, I've been a union man and proud Democrat since the day I left the Marine Corps. Election after election, I never saw a reason to vote against my party. I supported Beaumont each time he ran. Couldn't imagine ever voting against him. There's never been any good alternative." Oh, no. Please, don't let it end like this.

Bruce looks around at all the reporters and the cameras. Any fear or trepidation he had facing them has long since subsided. "Until now."

-FIFTY-ONE-
MICHAEL

The sound of Jessica rummaging through dresser drawers in the bedroom echoes in the hall as I enter my condo following the fracas at Chelsea's house. The telltale thuds of violent slamming serves notice that the next confrontation will not be a pleasant one. Today has already sucked.

It's three p.m., but being suspended from work and getting punched in the face by Bruce were only the undercards. With Jessica here for the first time in weeks, we arrive at the main event.

"Jessica?" I call out to her as I drop my assault pack on the floor and walk into the bedroom. The normally tidy room is in disarray. An open, half-packed suitcase sits on the bed and Jess is rummaging around in the walk-in closet. She emerges with a pile of her clothes still on their hangers.

"Well, this can't be good," I say, reprising my role as Captain Obvious.

"What did you expect?" she responds, plopping the clothes into the suitcase.

"I've tried calling you a couple of dozen times last night, and tried to find you at school this morning."

"Well, those of us not suspended still had to teach today. Besides, we're way beyond talking now, don't you think?"

"Seriously? You can't possibly believe—"

"I don't!" she snaps, an edge to her voice and boring into me with ice cold eyes.

"Okay, so why are you packing?"

"Because I'm leaving," she says, going back into the closet. Her turn to point out the obvious, I guess.

"Yeah, I got that part. Why?"

"There's no room for me *and* a political campaign in your life. You prioritized one at the expense of another."

"Jess, I was the victim of a sleazy tactic. Nothing more," I say as she returns clutching several pairs of shoes from the closet.

"Wow, you just don't get it do you?"

"Get what?" I fire back, getting increasingly annoyed.

"You really want me to spell it out? You asked for this! You decided to make the bet! You decided to go through with it! You involved your students! You set them up to be used as pawns in a political game—"

"I'm teaching them what it takes to make a difference! They're experiencing something they can't learn in a book!"

"That's a bunch of bullshit and you know it!" she screams, slamming the shoes into the suitcase. "Oh, sure, you brought them along for the ride. Decided to take away the last year they can enjoy being kids to help you settle your personal vendetta."

"What the hell are you talking about?"

"This isn't about them anymore, it's about you! You've had an ax to grind with America since you got back from the desert. This whole thing may have started as a lesson, but once you actually started participating, you decided to teach a lesson to the rest of the country too. It's why you are running your campaign like a high school class election and not talking about a single issue. You're making the race a popularity contest to prove a point."

I'm a pretty good poker player, but she learned my tells long ago. She's right, of course, but since I haven't told anybody, I can't help but think who else might have come to that conclusion too.

"What? You think I didn't know why you were doing this?" she mocks. Actually, considering we've barely talked in the last few weeks, no, I didn't.

"So you think you've got it all figured out, don't you? You don't know what you're talking about," I dismiss with a shake of my head.

"Don't play that game with me, Michael! You may have the rest of the country fooled, but I know *you*."

Jessica's flushed with anger as she closes the flap and zips her suitcase shut. She yanks the oversize bag to the floor and extends the handle.

"This thing spun out of control and you couldn't back off. I should have known you wouldn't. It's not in your DNA," she continues. "I'm sure you never thought it'd get this big, with all the attention, news reports, and people hanging on your every tweet. Who would have thought you'd ever be winning? God knows you don't need to get elected to prove your point."

"You're mad that I'm winning?"

"No! I'm mad that you ran at all! I'm mad I had to fight my way through a bunch of reporters just to get to my car and drive here! I'm mad that you didn't see where this was going and stop when you had the chance!"

"Look, I'm sorry you got hassled leaving work. But why would I stop? Why even expect me to? You were clear from the start you wouldn't support me. I hoped you would, but no, it's always about *you*. What *you* want, what *you* need. For once can you please think about somebody other than yourself?"

Now I'm angry. I dammed up all the emotions about our relationship to work on the campaign, and the dam has burst. All the feelings of not having her support, encouragement, and even love come rushing forward. I clung to the thought that we could make it through this. Now it is apparent the wedding we have been planning for months will never happen.

"One to talk," she says, shaking her head. "You want to teach your students about life? You want America to learn a lesson? Fine, but you're about to learn a lesson of your own. Let's see if you can live with the consequences of *your* actions. You've already lost your job and the respect and trust of, well, pretty much everybody. Now you've lost me. Hope it all ends up being worth it."

Jessica brushes by me on the way out the bedroom, struggling to lug the large rolling suitcase behind her. I turn and follow her down the hall, stopping short of the foyer. Her key to my place drops with a clang onto the glass plate atop the small table near the door. The message is clear. She won't need them anymore.

"I asked you to listen to me. I begged you to listen to reason. I told you this campaign was dangerous. You chose to ignore me."

"You wanted me to tow your line. It's your way or the highway, right? Always has been in our relationship. There's no room for discussion with you, only listen and obey. I get it now. You don't want a husband, you want a lap dog."

She slides her engagement ring off her ring finger and throws it at me. I catch it against my chest, and take a moment to admire how it reflects the light from the room. In colonial America, men gave women a thimble as a sign of eternal companionship. The women would remove the top in order to create a ring. Looking at the precious diamond fastened to this one, we've come a long way. Or maybe not.

"Rationalize all you want, Michael. It really doesn't matter now."

Her words hang in the air as she leaves, the suitcase trailing behind her providing the media circling outside everything they need to know about our relationship. The competing images of Bruce coming to my defense and my fiancée leaving over this scandal will provide debate fodder over the truth for the political pundits right up to election day.

As the door slams in her wake, I begin to realize the enormity of what's happening in my life. She's right, I am losing everything. In the span of a few hours, I have lost my livelihood, fiancée, and probably the election. And even if people in town haven't lost respect for me because of Bruce's comments, they'll always look at me and wonder if the story is true.

I need time to think clearly, but all the emotions of the day have left me numb. Running, exercising, or even breaking something might help ease the enormous feeling of stress, but I can't do any of them without drawing unwanted attention. I slide down the wall I was leaning on, tucking my knees into my chest, and bury my head in my hands.

-FIFTY-TWO-
KYLIE

This is not your typical New England sports bar. Being closer to New York, the walls are adorned with copious amounts of memorabilia from the Yankees, Mets, Giants, and Jets instead of the Boston teams. There are televisions everywhere, and the big screen is currently tuned into ESPN. The place is busy, but not crowded for a Friday night.

Michael is sitting in a booth tucked away from the bar, a nearly empty glass of beer in front of him. There is no media present, and I am left to wonder how he managed to ditch them. Worse, how long it will be before they find him here? What will that report sound like?

Each booth has its own little TV, and while most are tuned into one sporting event or another, he has Fox News on. I would have figured he'd seen enough for today.

"While the flap about Michael Bennit's possible affair with a student has cost him in the polls, the race may still go down to the wire," the anchorwoman says. "No doubt both candidates will be working hard tonight, and this weekend, to make their plea to the voters."

"If she only knew how wrong she was."

Michael looks up in time to see me slide into the bench seat across from him. A waitress in a black waist apron and New York Giants jersey comes over to take my order.

"Sam Adams Boston Lager," I tell her, "and bring another for him."

"Good choice," he affirms as she departs. "You know what I like."

"So, drinking yourself under the table is your idea of last minute campaigning?"

"In light of recent events, my doctor says I need to drink more. In other news, I changed my name to Doctor. Nice to meet you," he says, finishing the lame joke. "Besides, the one advantage to being a social media candidate is I can work from anywhere." He drains the last of the beer in the pint glass in front of him.

"Yeah, you're working real hard."

"How'd you find me?"

"I'm a reporter. It's my job."

The waitress returns with the beers. He downs more than half of it while I take a sip of mine.

"I heard about you and Jess. I'm sorry."

"Damn, bad news travels fast. It is what it is. She made her choice." Michael shakes his head dismissively.

"Is that what you said about getting suspended from teaching, too?" Michael only rewards me with an annoyed grin, so I'll give him another verbal poke or two. "I wouldn't have guessed you'd pick drinking as a way to run from your problems. I didn't picture you to be the quitting type either."

"I'm not. But even Atlas went down on a knee when they put the weight of the world on his shoulders."

"Fair enough. How's the staff handling all this?" I ask, more than a little curious how they're faring.

"They think they're in over their heads."

"They didn't actually believe the Beaumont attack machine's propaganda, did they?"

Michael exhales impatiently. "No, even teenagers know bullshit when they see it. Look, Kylie, I'm not in the mood for a chat right now."

"Good. Then shut up and listen."

I take a long sip of beer from the glass. I'm not sure exactly what I want to say to him. A lot of things are rattling around my mind. I'm sad, angry, and disappointed all at the same time, but I'm not sure how to articulate those feelings. Eh, screw it.

"You know what the real tragedy of this mess is? There's going to be a whole generation of students who will not get to learn from the great Michael Bennit. You went 'all in' with these particular kids at the expense of those who follow. Maybe it was worth it. I think you're a jackass."

"That's some pep talk, Kylie."

"I'm a reporter, not a cheerleader. I don't give pep talks, I get facts. Why did you really do it?"

"You know why."

"No, I want the whole story this time. Nobody goes through all this for a civics lesson to eighteen-year-olds. I want the other reason."

"We off the record?"

"Screw you. We're beyond that crap now. I can't help you anymore unless I know the whole story. Answer the question."

Michael takes a long pull of his own draught and then returns the glass to the table, swirling it in circles as he gets lost in his thoughts. I am about to lose my patience until he finally speaks.

"We like to believe all kids are equal. They're not. Chelsea, Vince, Peyton, Amanda, Brian, Emilee, Vanessa, Xavier—they are special, and I challenge anybody to say otherwise. I saw an opportunity to take an active role in their lives instead of just being a bystander. Maybe for once I was trying to actually make a difference as an alternative to sitting in my classroom and reading from a textbook. That's the whole story."

"Bullshit." I study his face intently, and it betrays him. There's more to the "why" he is doing this and I deserve to know. I've been patient through this process, but I am at the end of my rope. "Earned, not issued," is all I say in pleading my case.

"You're beginning to sound like Jess," he says with a smile before exhaling deeply. "And yes, you're right, it has been earned."

He then goes on to explain everything. Why he took the bet in the first place, decided to include his students, how he ran the campaign, everything. Suddenly the enigma that is Bennit for Congress has an answer, and the world makes perfect sense because of the answer.

Michael Bennit is either an evil genius or a reincarnated founding father. He is one of those rare breeds willing go to great lengths to prove a point because he thinks it's the right thing to do. Not in the negative way, but in the "I'm not asking you to believe me, let me show you" way important men and women of the world have throughout human history.

The founders fought a war to prove America was better off without the Crown. Lincoln went to war to mend the divide between north and south. FDR went to war with the Supreme Court over the benefits of the New Deal. Michael Bennit is going to war over the American election process itself.

Well, the comparisons may be a little extreme, but I'm excited. Bruce Stanton was right. Michael will make a terrible politician, but he would be one hell of a leader.

"Wow," is all I manage to say when he finishes. My mind is racing. It is the most selfless thing I have seen in politics. Ever. All I want to do is find ways to help. I'm just not sure what more I can do.

"You're paying an awful steep price for this. Your kids are going to pay up too. Is it worth it just to make a point?"

"That's for them to decide. Is it worth it for me? Well, I guess we'll see next week."

"If you win?"

"No. If the country gets it."

-FIFTY-THREE-
BLAKE

Thirty-six hours. That's the sum of time it took for Michael Bennit to recover from the biggest political bomb our campaign could drop and come back swinging.

The ten-point lead he enjoyed following the debate was a brief one. Once I leaked the news about the affair, he plummeted thirty points overnight to a twenty-point deficit, or so Marcus said when he reported our internal poll. Beaumont was ecstatic at the result, and I got a huge pat on the back.

"Your political future is secure," he told me. Maybe, but I sure didn't feel like celebrating. I figured the Bennit campaign had suffered a fatal blow and would go out with a whisper.

I was wrong. The man took our best knockout punch, but didn't stay on the mat long. Yesterday morning, he took to every social media site in existence, and even hosted an eight-hour web chat to answer any question a reporter could dream of asking. Bruce Stanton's interview got posted to YouTube seconds after he finished it and had generated a record number of views by then. The Bennit camp tackled the accusation head-on, and as a result, Roger watched in horror as the well-planted story burned out by the end of the day.

Then the iCandidate went on an offensive of his own last night. He twisted the issue so the question was no longer whether he slept with a student, but who *made up* the story he did. Bennit commanded the media's attention, and could have spent the time going negative and accusing us of dirty politics. Roger thought he would, and wasted a ton of time preparing to counter his accusations. Hell, it made perfect sense because they'd be right. We were dirty.

Michael Bennit doesn't use that playbook though. Instead of going negative on us as predicted, his campaign went positive. No other candidate in the country could ever pull off such a move. The focus again shifted right back to his message and the ideas about both America and the future we collectively share in this country. He even used the incident to highlight everything wrong with the modern election process. His staff still addressed the occasional scandal question when it surfaced, but they managed to move everyone in the media off the subject. It's worked brilliantly, but it will fall short.

It's a weekend, so people are going to spend a lot more time watching college and pro football than news about politics. He'll get back to within ten points or so, but it won't be a suspenseful election night. On paper, anyone reading about this race twenty years from now will see an independent candidate make a brilliant run, but still fail to unseat a popular incumbent. They won't ever learn the back story.

So no, Bennit won't be able to recover from the hit he took, but he won't go down without a fight. You have to admire the tenacity he inspires in his students. Fox News practically has his Twitter feed scrolling live at the bottom of their screen. Kylie worked the media up into a frenzy over him again, and we gave her the reason.

"I hope you're not worried about the flurry of Bennit-related activity," I hear Madison say from the office door. I have no idea how long she's been standing there.

"Sorry. No, I was just lost in my thoughts."

"He's finished, Blake. It's a Sunday night. The news can say what they want, and he can tweet, post to Facebook, and all that other crap they do, but nobody is listening or watching. He can't recover."

"Yeah, I know."

"Well, don't sound so thrilled."

I flash the best fake genuine smile I can. I should be elated we are frontrunners again. I would have taken Dick Johnson out at any point in this campaign and slept like a baby afterwards. Even taking on the iCandidate for something he did in his past would have been acceptable. Going after Bennit by using his teenage staff? That is wearing on my conscience.

"I set you up for failure, Blake, I hope you know that. I never thought you'd go through with it. You'd waffle, and complain, and ultimately fail and I'd swoop in to the rescue and do it myself. But you came through."

"Yeah, well, you should never have doubted me, Madison."

"Nope, you're right," she says. She crosses the small office and leans across the desk until her face is mere inches from mine. "This thing between us isn't over. Not for a second. You trampled me to get ahead, and I haven't forgotten. Remember, I can be every bit as ambitious as you, and someday it'll be your turn to take the knife in the back."

She winks at me before retreating out of the small office and out into the war room. The fact is, she had every reason to doubt me. I didn't want to do what I did to Michael Bennit and Chelsea. They deserve better. Making the story up of them having a sexual relationship epitomizes everything Americans hate about politicians. Scandals make for great ratings in the press, but making one up for political gain is the ultimate in slimy politics.

The Bennit campaign is dead, and I pulled the trigger. Beaumont has no business getting reelected after the race he's run. He's offered no fresh ideas or bold initiatives. His message was the same tired reliance on funneling money into the district and buying his way to another term. It's a shame.

I actually think Michael Bennit would make a better congressman. A man of principle, he would be despised by most of the members of the House. With the right guidance, he could actually shake things up and make life interesting in D.C. Too bad he will never make it there.

I lean back in the chair at the desk and stare at the ceiling. There is a lot of uncertainty with the voters of the district. Can they be influenced again? He's finished in this race, at least on paper. Unless, of course, something drastic is done to even the score and give him a fighting chance.

-FIFTY-FOUR-
CHELSEA

"The polls open in like, fourteen hours, Chels," Brian says despondently. "We're just not going to make up enough ground."

"Down eight in the Rasmussen poll," Vanessa says, peering at her laptop. "Eleven in the ABC-*Washington Post* poll, but they've never liked us."

"What does Marist have us at?" Emilee asks.

"Ten, but with a larger margin of error," Amanda says.

"We can't let them beat us over a lie," I say, slamming my hand in the table.

"Chels, if it wasn't for your dad, we wouldn't even be this close," Vanessa consoles. "We're lucky we've gotten ten points back so quick."

"Well, the mainstream media is questioning the integrity of the story, thanks to Kylie. Our numbers should be better," Vince adds, grasping for reasons why we are still low in the polls.

"It's gonna take a while for the word to spread," Xavier tells me. Maybe he's right, but I doubt it. People have chosen to stop believing in us. I have to hand it to the Beaumont camp, they timed this little nightmare perfectly.

"I don't know what to do, guys."

"We keep fighting," Vince tells me. "We don't quit."

A long silence fills the room before Amanda finally breaks it. "What do you think, Mister B?"

Mister Bennit is preoccupied with his thoughts, staring blankly out the window. We convened at the shop immediately after school to make one last plea to the public for votes, but even he can't be optimistic about what he's hearing. He doesn't even turn when he speaks.

"People are confused. They don't know what or whom to believe anymore. Everybody has a side, including the media."

"With all the accusations flying over the last week, who could blame people if they stop listening," Emilee decrees.

"I wouldn't," Vanessa agrees.

"If I wasn't working on this campaign, I would have stopped listening months ago," Vince adds.

"What can we do to make them listen?" Amanda asks in frustration.

"Nothing. It's out of our hands now."

-FIFTY-FIVE-
BLAKE

If I press this button, it's all over. My job, career in politics, and everything I've worked for to this point will go up in flames. Ones and zeros sent over an invisible network to the world will lead to real repercussions.

I sit in the war room of our campaign headquarters among the rows of phones prepped for tonight's action. Volunteers are starting to arrive for the final stages of the get out the vote effort designed to propel Winston Beaumont to victory tomorrow. Of course, recent events have considerably reduced the urgency of the work.

I stare at the message I typed on @WinstonBeaumontIII, the official Beaumont for Congress Twitter account, as my finger hovers over the tweet button. My heart tells me this is the right thing to do, but my head is screaming that it's also futile. Problem is, they're both correct.

"Big night tonight, right, Blake?" a volunteer asks me with a slap on the shoulder as he walks by. I have no idea who he is.

"The biggest," I say, eliciting a smile of glee from the puffy man as he continues to the table with the donuts and coffee for an afternoon snack.

The people around me are oblivious to the battle I am waging with myself. Confused and lost, I have become my own worst enemy. The internal drive that pushed me to do Beaumont and Roger's dirty work is the same drive pushing me to undo it.

This isn't going to help Bennit much, but maybe it helps validate the denials they already issued. Too much damage has already been done, and our campaign can spin this tweet as hacking, a rogue staffer, or a practical joke. No, a tweet alone won't get it done, and am I prepared to go all the way with this?

I look at the triangular Second Armored pin in front of me. My father's old unit, a token of remembrance and a gift from an old, broken man with more courage and honor than I will ever have. He was ready to fight and die for the men next to him, just like my father was. They were warriors who fought their battle, now it's time for me to fight mine. I affix the pin to my lapel, and once satisfied with its position, look back at the screen.

"Screw it." I press tweet and watch as the message posts to the feed for the world to see:

Bennit and media are asking who could be so deplorable as to fabricate an affair with a student. Simple. We are. I know because I did it. #Beaumontlies

-FIFTY-SIX-
KYLIE

I ignore my Twitter feed more often than I read it, and today was no different. I didn't know it happened until a colleague covering the race showed me the tweet. That and the simple message set off a firestorm of activity around me within seconds of it posting.

For the last five hours, I have been with the media in the far recesses of Laura's coffee shop parking lot trying to figure out who sent it and why. The Beaumont spin doctors immediately went into defense mode, offering a litany of excuses for the tweet that ranged from hacking, to being victims of a disgruntled campaign volunteer. While the excuses satisfied unobjective Beaumont supporters, the rest of us are on a mission to find the truth.

Media organizations rarely cooperate in the race to scoop each other, but reporters on the ground covering this campaign have created an atmosphere comparable to a fraternity. This tweet means ratings for everyone, and finding the source guarantees a huge audience going into Election Day. For that reason, I have been treated to the rare sight of reporters and journalists working together and comparing notes, two hours before the eleven o'clock news airs.

I am chatting with a young reporter from the CBS affiliate in Hartford when someone spots him walking toward us. Even under the glow of parking lot lighting, he looks sharp, decked out in a navy blue suit and a pin on his lapel. Blake Peoni makes it thirty feet from me before the mass of microphone-clad humanity blocks any further progress. No member of the Beaumont campaign would dare show up here, and I sense something special is about to happen.

Not being a television journalist, there is no need for me to be standing here. I also know that the staff inside is too focused to be watching the news. I run for Laura's door and barge through, only to be greeted by Michael standing in front of me with a worried look on his face.

"What the hell is going on out there? Why are you running?" I hear Michael ask, as I brush past him to get to the counter.

"Can you change the channel to the news, Laura?" I ask, looking back to see half the students starting at me and the other half gawking out the window at the flurry of activity where members of the press are camped out.

"Sure, dear. Any particular station?"

"Just pick one. Any of the cable news networks will carry this live. You guys are going to want to see this," I shout over my shoulder at the gang, beckoning them over to the large plasma screen hung on the wall with a sense of urgency.

Laura changes the channel to CNN and the unmistakable image of the Perkfect Buzz parking lot fills the television.

Cameramen are rushing over to Blake like bees responding to a wasp attacking their hive, reminding me a little of how Chelsea, Bruce, and Michael were ambushed on her front lawn. The camera finally focuses on Blake when he begins to speak.

"My name is Blake Peoni, and I am a key advisor to Representative Winston Beaumont and the Beaumont for Congress campaign," he says in preamble. "As you have reported, there was a tweet sent from our campaign Twitter account several hours ago accepting responsibility for manufacturing allegations of an affair between Michael Bennit and his student, Chelsea Stanton.

"Since then, the campaign has offered several plausible reasons why the tweet was sent in error, causing confusion among the media and the voters. I'm here to clear up any uncertainty."

Reporters and journalists begin shouting questions, causing Blake to pause until he can finish.

"This ought to be interesting," Vanessa mumbles aloud. "I wonder what fresh excuse they have this time."

"I can tell you with one hundred percent certainty that the message in question was *not* sent by a hacker or a disgruntled staffer," Blake continues. "I know this because I'm the one who sent it."

As a journalist, I try to hide my reaction when something surprises me. In this case, my jaw drops. Vanessa and Amanda gasp and even Michael looks like he can't believe what he's hearing. Even his Magic 8-Ball would never have predicted this.

The gaggle erupts with questions, and once again, Blake has to struggle to quiet them and continue speaking.

"Furthermore ... furthermore, the content of the tweet is also accurate. The knowledge I have of the Beaumont campaign creating this story is not secondhand. I was in the room when the decision was made to pursue this course of action because we were struggling in the polls."

Blake still isn't finished, but the reporters around them have been silent for thirty seconds longer than they usually can stay quiet. Another flood of questions ends with a reporter from the Connecticut NBC affiliate right in front of him, holding a microphone in his face, getting one in.

"Do you know who specifically in the campaign leaked the fake story of the affair?"

"Yes, I do."

"Who was it?" a chorus of people sing out simultaneously. Blake looks around at the reporters and into the cameras. Only a few seconds elapse, but it feels like a lifetime.

"Me."

-FIFTY-SEVEN-
MICHAEL

"It's Election Day in America and people from across the country are heading to the polls in this pivotal midterm election. There are a lot of tight races this year, and while the balance of power in Congress is at stake, all eyes are riveted on the Connecticut Sixth District."

Video footage rolls of me at my polling place. As usual, I didn't make any statements, but I guess seeing me out in public is enough for the media in this race. The highlight reel then shifts to the polling station where Winston casts his ballot.

"Both Michael Bennit and Winston Beaumont have been to the polls to cast their vote this morning, and now the people are lining up to do the same in towns and cities across the district."

Compared to the orgasm the media had after the Blake Peoni impromptu tell-all last night, no coverage is going to seem interesting to me until after the polls close. Bored, I change the channel to see what other stations are covering. Fox News has a roundtable discussion of sorts on, and the subject matter is, not surprisingly, about the Connecticut

Sixth. I flip over to CNN where an anchor narrates more video footage of towns in the district.

"It has been a roller-coaster week following the debate and the apparently fabricated allegations about an affair between Michael Bennit and his teenage student campaign manager. But the dramatic turn of events following the admission from a Beaumont staff member of making the incident up makes this the race to watch tonight. Winston Beaumont and Michael Bennit are in a statistical tie according to Real Clear Politics, with Republican Richard Johnson a distant third."

Police direct traffic and erect barriers to control pedestrian traffic on a city street outside one of our more urban voting districts. From the looks of it, the scene is probably somewhere in neighboring Waterbury.

"A record turnout is expected, and no one can predict the outcome of this race. What we do know is it will be a very interesting evening once the polls close here at 8:00 p.m."

I change the channel again, much to the chagrin of the pretty brunette curled up in an overstuffed chair to my left.

"It's two o'clock. Are you going to sit and watch TV all day?" Kylie asks.

"Coming from the girl comfortably ensconced in my favorite chair? I'm still suspended, remember? What's your excuse? Is this how you always do deep background reporting?"

"Only with the cute candidates. Why, are you afraid CNN will report that I'm lounging in your favorite chair?"

"They probably would. Nothing stopped them from making the end of my engagement public knowledge." And that's true. I must have watched the video of Jessica storming out a few dozen times on Fox News.

"Would you rather have me sitting on Winston Beaumont's couch instead?" Kylie asks, sporting a look of disgust.

"Why not? Beaumont doesn't do it for you?"

"Okay, now you're just making me nauseous."

We share a laugh, because I know what she means. Winston has been stuffing himself with prime rib for years, and wouldn't recognize a treadmill if I installed one in his living room. I can imagine that even in his younger years, a century or two ago, he's not someone you'd expect to see popping out of an Abercrombie and Fitch catalogue. More likely he'd be confused for wildlife in *Field and Stream* or *National Geographic*.

I sit up a little straighter on the couch, realizing this subject must be broached eventually. Procrastinating all morning, I realize it's getting too late in the day to delay any longer.

"Kylie, I have one more favor I need you to do for me, regardless of what happens tonight."

"No, I'm not writing it." Either the girl is psychic or has been waiting for me to bring this up for as long as I have been putting off asking.

"You have to."

"If you win, and I write that, it will destroy any chance you have to be reelected, or even make a difference while you're there."

"Maybe, if I win. But if you don't write it, this was all for nothing."

"You are calling being a member of the U.S. House of Representatives nothing?"

She's right. I am a history teacher, so I know exactly what she means. As a soldier, defending the people of this nation is a powerful motivator. But there is no higher honor than being elected by a group of citizens to represent their voice in government. Maybe I'm an idealist. I know Winston Beaumont thinks so, but that's how I feel.

"No, you're right, but I also told you it has never been the point. Promise me."

Kylie nods, but I can tell she wants nothing to do with writing this article. "They'll get it on their own," she states, not sounding like she really believes it.

"Not in light of the scandals and post-election jockeying for power." I lean forward, my eyes pleading with her. "You are close to this campaign. If it comes from anyone else, it'll be dismissed as partisan reporting. I need you to do this. It has to be you. Promise me."

"You're asking a lot."

"And you have already given more to this campaign than I could ever ask, but I'm doing it anyway," I say, pleading with her with my eyes. "Promise me."

"Okay."

I smile. "Say it."

"Fine, I promise."

-FIFTY-EIGHT-
CHELSEA

On Election Day, 8:00 p.m. is when the magic begins to happen in Connecticut. Polls close and the laborious task of counting and certifying results starts. For this first time in months, there is nothing more that can be done. The tweets, Facebook posts, and e-mails are all for fun now, or to thank the many volunteers who took up our cause across the district.

We probably have the money to host a fancy shindig at a ballroom or meeting place, but the Perkfect Buzz was where this ride started, and thus we decided that's where it would end. Laura agreed to close the place down tonight for the occasion, and even found someone to cater the event.

Despite this being our operations center since the beginning, except for the ever-present media, the shop never betrayed that fact until tonight. The exterior is now adorned with red, white, and blue bunting and a large sign that reads "Bennit Campaign Headquarters."

Outside the locked doors, it's bedlam. Red and blue flashing lights pierce the dimly lit street as police try to control traffic moving past. As has been the status quo for months now, there are news vans everywhere, and several reporters are filing live reports under the glare of lights. It may be a national midterm election, but the epicenter of interest is the little town of Millfield.

Crowds of locals are gathering across the street and in the center of town, not far away, in a show of solidarity and support. It's as if people sense history is being made tonight and everybody wants to be a part of it. If they can't be with us when the results come in, they want to be celebrating at close proximity.

Everyone in the Buzz is there by invitation only, a group comprised mostly of students and volunteers willing to make the trip from across the district on the big night. Many of them are posing for pictures with Michael, who despite maintaining a near exclusive social media presence, has spent the last couple of hours working the room and thanking the dozens of people now filling the quaint coffee shop to capacity.

The sounds of idle chatter fills the space, but everyone is keeping an eye focused on the large flat-screen television now tuned to one of the network news stations. Leading up until the hour the polls closed in many East Coast states, much of the discussion centered on Mister Bennit and the race against Beaumont. Now, as results pour in and other races are determined, we are only mentioned every few minutes or so.

I am standing in the back of the shop with my father when Mister Bennit finally works his way over to us. He shakes my father's hand and gives him a respectful nod.

"Whatever happens tonight, Chels, I am extremely proud of you."

"Be proud when we win, Mister B," I state with excitement and determination.

"Whatever happened to that shy girl who used to sit in my classroom and study after school?"

"Some former Green Beret teacher she had in school brought her out of her shell and taught her to kick ass."

My dad gives him a nod in respect. The Army and Marines may have their rivalry, but there is nothing except mutual respect between the two most important figures in my life.

Amanda, Emilee, and Vince try to shush people from the other side of the room. Brian turns the volume up on the television. Updates on races from across the country as graphics scroll along the bottom, but the split screen shows the anchor and a graphic of the CT-6 District.

"The race everyone in America is watching tonight is in Connecticut, where eight-term incumbent Democrat Winston Beaumont is in the fight of his life with Independent Michael Bennit," the anchor says, the excitement noticeable in his otherwise professional voice.

"Enough with the preamble; give us the numbers!" a voice from behind me calls out before being hushed.

"This contest has seen its share of accusations, counter-accusations, and wild point swings, with both candidates having double-digit leads at some point during the last month. Going into yesterday, it looked like Winston Beaumont was a lock for a ninth term with such a large lead."

A chorus of sharp boos sound out around me, mostly from the many students here who helped with the campaign. Countless volunteers fled the campaign during our darkest days, a group Mister B came to call "sunshine patriots." Many others stuck with us, and we jammed as many of them into the Perkfect Buzz tonight as the fire marshal would allow.

"However, Blake Peoni's admission of fabricating the allegation of a sexual relationship between Michael Bennit and student campaign manager Chelsea Stanton has tilted the momentum back towards the iCandidate. The only thing we need to learn now is, was it enough?"

"C'mon, get on with it. Geez!" Vince shouts in frustration.

"We will have to wait until a little later to find out. With fifty-six percent of the precincts reporting, the race between Democratic incumbent Winston Beaumont and Independent candidate Michael Bennit is a dead heat and remains too close to call," the anchorman dramatically announces.

"The last count had Bennit down over a hundred votes, but he's gained ground, now only thirty-seven votes separating the two. What we do know is Richard Johnson is a non-factor at this point, with only eight percent of the vote."

A huge cheer goes up from the crowd at the Perkfect Buzz. Apparently, everyone is excited to only be down by a couple of handfuls of votes. I, on the other hand, am angry. We shouldn't be losing at all. The story about the affair was a fraud perpetrated by the weak and the scared, yet it looks like not everyone in the district got the message.

My father must have read my mind, because he puts his arm around me. "It'll be okay, Snuggle Bear," he mouths to me with a wink. Maybe, but right now I'm not so sure.

-FIFTY-NINE-
BLAKE

"You have some nerve to show up here!" Deena screeches, her little arms flailing around her as I walk in the door to Winston Beaumont's campaign headquarters.

Does the Ice Queen think I want to be here, especially on election night? As Roger eloquently pointed out, I'm still getting paid by the congressman, and thus will report to my appointed place of duty. Hindsight being 20/20, I should have quit before I decided to bare my soul to the press.

"I was told to be here, Deena. Now make yourself useful and let Roger know," I tell her as rudely as I can manage.

"Wait here," she says, spinning off to the small office where my future was forged less than a week ago. She mumbles something under her breath as she walks away. It doesn't matter what, but I'm positive it wasn't complimentary.

I wait in the war room, in full view of the hateful eyes of every volunteer who toiled on the phones all day to get out the vote. The polls are closed now, so nothing more to do than converse, await the results of their efforts, and talk about me in quiet whispers. This sucks.

Deena opens the office door and the sound of yet another patented Winston Beaumont tirade spills out.

"This is a disaster!"

"You are still ahead sir," Roger consoles.

"By a hundred votes! I had an eighty percent approval rating six months ago!"

"Maybe we underestimated Bennit and his staff," I hear Madison say from the office. Not surprisingly, she got promoted to be the new me.

"It was your job to get me reelected! And yours, Roger! And here I am barely beating some nobody and a bunch of kids."

Winston walks out of the office, sees me and scowls. He turns and whispers something to Roger before putting on a fake smile and working the room. He plies the mindless zombies here with false gratitude, telling them he couldn't have done it without them. I have learned Winston Beaumont III is not the type of man who sincerely acknowledges the contribution of people he considers beneath him.

Roger walks over to me, the Ice Queen in tow. Madison remains in the entrance of the small office with a look of pure satisfaction on her face. Win or lose, I am going to be metaphorically tortured tonight, and she will enjoy every minute of it.

"Blake," Roger says, not bothering to offer his hand. He doesn't shake with the disloyal.

"Roger," I respond, in the same tone. I don't shake with the dishonest. Well, now I don't.

"Go find a seat out of everyone's way. You may be here a while."

Surveying the alternatives, I choose to sit in a molded plastic chair along the wall of small offices. Why am I putting myself through this? I could leave, and Lord knows I should. Just tell Beaumont where he can stick his crotchety attitude and walk out the door with my head high, but my feet don't move.

I need to have it out with my former mentor, the man who I worshipped for so long. I was brainwashed into thinking the political games he played were for the greater good. Enemies were nothing more than mere obstacles that needed to be circumvented, or in extreme cases, destroyed. The ends justified the means, and when those means meant destroying lives, it was dismissed as collateral damage. That is the Beaumont way, and until a couple of days ago, my way.

Manson, Koresh, Jones, and Beaumont. They are all different men, but each possesses the uncanny ability to get the people around them to follow blindly their chosen course. And follow I did, up until the point I just couldn't anymore.

I look down at the "Hell on Wheels" pin stuck to the lapel of my coat. I wonder what my dad would think of me now. Would he applaud my decision to try to right a wrong, or scold me for my lack of loyalty? Seeing me through his eyes, am I courageous or foolish for what I've done? Would he think I went crazy over a beautiful teenage girl or understand there was so much more to the decision? I like to think I have the answers to those questions, but he's gone, so I'll never know for sure.

What I do know is I chose this path, and now the world looks different. I regard the people in this room I once considered allies in the cause as unwitting stooges. So, I will sit here and pay the penance for my sins under the disdainful glares of those still enchanted by Beaumont's spell. I will endure the snickers from Madison and the pettiness of Deena, just so I can get my last shot in at Winston Beaumont III.

-SIXTY-
KYLIE

I am trying not to be rude, but this is not the time anyone should expect my undivided attention. Since I arrived at the Buzz, Chelsea, Brian, Peyton, and the crew have been parading countless student volunteers from other districts over to meet me. Some want to be journalists after graduating from college. Others fancy themselves as future politicians or staffers.

They are all good kids, and I answer their barrage of questions as earnestly as I can. Under any other circumstances, I would be flattered by the attention, but my focus keeps getting drawn to the TV. It's election night, and we are approaching the finish line and finding out how this adventure ends.

I peek again at the huge screen, and with seventy-four percent in, Michael has actually taken a slight lead in the race. No longer able to divide my attention, I politely excuse myself and settle on a spot closer to the screen.

There are about a dozen people watching with zombie-like interest, and they pay me no notice as I join them. The sound coming from the speakers is muffled under the cackle of the crowd in the room, so I strain to hear what is being said on screen.

"I cannot tell you how shocked I am," a female pundit offers to her two peers. "Here's a guy who ran his entire campaign on social media using high school students for staff. With nothing more than a shoestring budget, he has positioned himself to beat a well-respected incumbent."

Well respected my ass. The pundits know it too, but this makes for better ratings.

"Regardless of what happens, do you think that this campaign will change modern politics?" the moderator of the group asks.

"Absolutely. Everyone in America now figures that if this guy can do it, they can do it! You heard it here first. Running for elected office will never be the same."

Well, that may be true now, but if Michael holds me to writing my final article about him? How can I get out of doing that? Do promises have loopholes? Great, now I sound like a politician.

I sense, more than see, Chelsea come up beside me. "Have they talked about any other race tonight?"

"Barely," I mumble. "This is the greatest show on Earth so far as the media is concerned. Control of Congress could be seized by a political party made up of disgruntled circus chimps and they would still be focusing on this race."

Chelsea laughs, but I'm pretty serious about that comment. The media attention over the past two months is on a scale I could never have imagined.

"The once untouchable Winston Beaumont has had the fight of his life in this reelection campaign. Now it looks more and more like Michael Bennit may pull off the upset," says a reporter outside our lively little coffee house. "The big question in Connecticut tonight, and especially in the small business behind me, is just how much of an effect the scandal that rocked the Bennit campaign just a few days ago will have on how people vote."

"People have gone to the polls in record numbers, and many of them told us they dismissed the allegations and cast their vote for Michael Bennit," the anchor says after his on location reporter finishes. "But will it be enough to unseat the popular incumbent? What's the word from the Beaumont camp, Bob?"

Bob is inside a ballroom, a dais with American flag backdrop set up along a wall. The room is filled with Beaumont posters, balloons, and a hundred people watching the election results on the screen.

"The feeling here has been one of nervousness over the past half hour. As the latest results came in, the crowd quieted considerably as their slim lead turned into a slim deficit. Remember, Winston Beaumont was embroiled in a scandal of his own last spring involving the Lexington Financial Group. Now, people around here are wondering whether political newcomer Michael Bennit is poised to make history."

"Thanks for your report, Bob. We are now getting ready to call some races that have been decided in other parts of the country."

"We getting close?" Michael whispers into my ear.

"Very."

* * *

Another whole hour lurches by before people begin paying rapt attention to the results. As a group, the people assembled here share a sense of the final verdict being close at hand. Peyton, Brian, Amanda, Vince, Emilee, and Amanda all move up through the mass of humanity to join us up front, Xavier and Vanessa following a few moments later. Vince begins cracking jokes about the candidates in other districts, lightening the mood a bit, but only a bit. The tension in the room is thick like a morning fog.

"Ladies and gentlemen, we are getting ready to call the race in the Connecticut Sixth District."

"Everybody quiet!" Chelsea shrieks to silence the audience behind us. Peyton, Vanessa, and Brian also turn to quiet everyone down. The cacophony of nervous sound quickly turns to an eerie silence. The pundits on the television, whose voices only moments ago could barely be heard, now boom into the room.

"Here we go. Moment of truth," Amanda says anxiously.

"What has been perhaps the most intently watched congressional race in history has lived up to its billing as the contest between Independent Michael Bennit and Democrat Winston Beaumont has gone right down to the wire. We should be getting the final results any second."

Peyton covers her mouth with her hands.

Vince bounces his leg nervously.

Emilee is literally covering her eyes with her hands.

"We're sorry for the delay, folks, but we are just awaiting some final confirmations because we want to get this right."

Vanessa hides behind Brian's shoulder.

Chelsea inhales and holds her breath.

My hands are cupped in front of my mouth, and I notice I am biting down on my index finger with my teeth.

"C'mon, c'mon!" Brian mumbles to nobody in particular.

"You're killing us here!" Vince exclaims.

For a moment, just a moment, it feels like the world has stopped spinning.

-SIXTY-ONE-
MICHAEL

"In one of the most captivating elections I have ever had the privilege of reporting, the contest between Winston Beaumont and the iCandidate Michael Bennit literally has come down to the last votes counted," the anchor says, her voice dripping with excitement.

My students are bundles of nervous energy. Even the steadfast Kylie Roberts is caught up in the moment. As the anchor prattles on, all motion in the room ceases. Deep breaths are held almost universally. Months of work, and it all comes down to the next words out of her mouth. Could I really be a U.S. Congressman?

"With one hundred percent of the precincts reporting, we can now announce that the campaign of Michael Bennit, the iCandidate, has fallen short, and Democratic incumbent Winston Beaumont has successfully retained his seat in the House."

A graphic depicting Winston Beaumont flashes on the screen with a large check mark next to it. A collective gasp, followed by an audible groan of disappointment, shakes the room.

Vince drops his head.

Vanessa covers her face with her hands to hide the tears welling up in her eyes.

Nothing stops the tears from streaming down Chelsea's and Peyton's cheeks.

Brian puts an arm around Peyton and hugs her, stunned by what he just heard.

Kylie turns to me, her eyes moistened from her own tears. "I'm sorry," she mouths to me. I reach out and pull her into my arms, giving her a tight hug as I bury my face in her hair. We hold it for a long time, before I finally break the comfort of her embrace. She nods over to the students who are consoling each other.

Peyton reaches out and hugs me, followed by Vince, of all people. One by one, they each join in a group hug as cameras flash from the crowd. There is little doubt one of those pictures will end up on the front page of every newspaper in the country. I'm not sure if my rule against physical contact would apply to an emotional moment like this, but since I am suspended anyway, I don't really give a damn.

When we finally release, it is Brian who summons the courage to speak first. "So much for our Cinderella story."

"I guess the glass slipper didn't fit after all," Emilee chimes in through her tears.

I can't help but give them a little smile. "You may not realize it when it happens, but a kick in the teeth may be the best thing in the world for you."

"What go nowhere idiot said that BS?" Vince says, upset and angry. I put my hand on his shoulder.

"Walt Disney."

They all crack little smiles which fade quickly. The crowd in the shop starts moving in closer and begins to shake hands with all of us. I haven't been around campaigns before, but I can't imagine any would be more supportive than this one.

I get everyone's attention and say a few words of thanks to all those that worked so hard for us. I keep it brief, but I'm sure I could have spoken for an hour and no one would have budged. When I finish, Chelsea comes up to me.

"I was just thinking, what about the absentee ballots?"

Kylie puts her hand gently on my shoulder. "Break even at best, Chels."

"No use in putting this off any longer. I guess I have a call to make."

To my surprise, Kylie gives me a quick kiss on the cheek.

"Don't let the bastard get the best of you."

-SIXTY-TWO-
BLAKE

The herd gathered around the TV like it's a midwestern watering hole has grown quiet. From the far side of the war room, I can almost make out the voice of the anchor on CNN reading the results of races throughout the country. Winston Beaumont is not among them, deciding to watch from the comfortable solitude of his small office like the coward he is.

Why are all these people even here? Beaumont secured a ballroom in Danbury to host his victory celebration. I imagine he is hiding here in case he loses, but I have no idea why so many others aren't at least enjoying the open bar. If they hung around the campaign office because I was coming, it wasn't so they could interact with me.

I sit alone in the plastic chair without a soul within fifty feet of me, ostracized and shunned by the army I once helped command. This is their moment, not mine. I gave up that right the moment I crossed the great and powerful Beaumont.

I don't need to see the television to know what happened. The spontaneous eruption of joy by all the people in the war room speaks volumes. I changed the course of the election and was too late in stopping it. As a result, Winston won.

The congressman emerges from his office with a beaming Roger and shakes his hand. "You need to do better in the Senate race, Roger. I'll be counting on you."

"We will, sir."

Beaumont gives a wave to the enthusiastic serfs content to suspend reason and common sense and support this arrogant blowhard.

Deena walks up to him and taps him on the shoulder, and whispers something in his ear that mercifully cuts short his bloviating.

"Bennit is making his concession call," he announces proudly. "So let me take this and I'll meet you over at the ballroom to get the party started!" The zombies erupt with pleasure.

"Why don't you join us, Blake?" he says, turning to me before walking into the office. Madison, Roger, and Marcus accompany us in the small room as Deena punches the speaker button on the desk phone.

"This is Winston Beaumont."

"Good evening, Congressman. This is Michael Bennit. I wanted to congratulate you and your staff on your victory."

"Why, thank you, Michael. You gave me a bit of a scare, but as I told you after the debate, there was no way I was going to lose."

A long silence on the other end of the line is punctuated by the sounds of the celebration outside in the war room.

"But you did lose, Congressman."

"I'm a bit confused, Michael," Winston says in the most condescending voice he can muster. "This is a concession call. Surely even a novice like you watches the news. I won."

"You won the election, yes, but for a veteran politician, you're unbelievably short-sighted."

"Oh, yeah? How so?"

"Congressman, you spent over twenty-five million dollars running a negative campaign against me, and all you have to show for the cost is the narrowest margin of victory in a congressional race in history."

It amazes me. After everything Winston did to him, he still addresses him by his title, offering a measure of respect the office, if not the officeholder, deserves. If there was any lingering doubt in my mind about Michael Bennit's character, that squashed it. I am not feeling so conciliatory.

"I still won. That's the only thing of consequence," Winston concludes.

"You won this election, but what about the next one? You won't be up against a novice next time, nor will you benefit from a huge war chest to buy your way out of defeat."

"It won't matter!"

"Your staff knows differently, and if they haven't brought it up yet, they're lying to you," Michael says in the same measured tone that made him a hit at the debate.

"I can always raise more money."

"Sure you can, but you're going to have a much harder time changing people's opinions with it. You won with the lies you spread this time, but I wouldn't count on history repeating itself. The cold, hard reality is simple. Beating me has cost you your political future, you just don't know it yet."

"Look here, Bennit—"

"Congratulations, Congressman. Enjoy your last two years in politics."

The call disconnects, but Beaumont continues to stare at phone like he is waiting for a stripper to pop out of the damn thing. Deena and Madison are equally dumfounded, if not disgusted by what they perceive as Michael's lack of respect. The only other person in the room that gets it is Roger. He is staring at me, so I give him a look of amusement. Everything Michael Bennit said is absolutely true. I may be finished in politics, but so is the man I once worshipped.

Winston seizes the phone and hurls it against the wall, shattering it. "Everyone out. Except you, Blake, you stay right here." Madison and Deena hurry out, and Roger closes the door behind them after they leave.

Winston goes into his desk and pours himself a tumbler of scotch. He replaces the bottle in the drawer without offering any and takes a long sip of the amber liquid. He swirls the whiskey in the glass, watching it intently before looking up at me.

"I expected so much more from you, Blake," he says, keenly watching my body language. I don't flinch. The bastard doesn't deserve the satisfaction. "I hope you know, you were one of the rare ones. A generous mix of ambition, loyalty, and political know-how, but you threw it all away. I find myself wanting to know why, but in the end I don't really care. And do you know why, Blake?" he asks, moving around the desk and sitting on the edge in front of me. With the same hand holding his glass, he jabs a finger a mere inch from my face. "Because you don't matter. What you did no longer matters."

"Do you even believe that yourself, Winston?" I ask. "Because what's left of your phone may have a different opinion."

Winston lets out a little laugh and removes his finger from my face. I'm not sure if his amusement is fueled by my comment or use of his first name.

"You think Bennit was right?"

"I think people have seen you for what you are. You claim to be a champion of the people, but we all know you're more concerned with power and lining your own pockets. The people you surround yourself with are lemmings. I know, because I was one. I have seen what you are capable of, what you've done, and once everyone else has, Bennit will be right. You'll be finished in politics."

"You think you know where all the skeletons are buried?" Roger asks from behind me, anger in his voice. "You don't know anything, and if you did, it's not like people would listen to you. A disgraced staffer bent on revenge against his *former* employer won't play well in the respected media. I've already seen to that."

I knew it was coming, but my face still registers shock at the notion that I was no longer in the employment of Winston Beaumont, representative from the Connecticut Sixth District.

"You can't hurt me again, son," Beaumont concludes. "Not on Lexington, or Bennit, or anything else for that matter. You are finished in politics forever, Blake, so you'd best find another line of work. As of this instant, you're officially no longer a member of my staff. You're dismissed."

I glare at him for a moment and start to leave, but stop as I reach the door. I need to say something to save face. Some pearl of wisdom, or a warning that I, too, am not one to be trifled with. When I turn back, I am cut off by Roger. Once again, he's a step ahead of me.

"Don't bother, Blake. You can lash out all you want to some drunks in whatever crappy bar you find yourself drowning your sorrows at. But don't waste our time with the empty threats you're about to spew. You made your decision, now live with it."

The revelry of Beaumont's victory devolves into hushed whispers and snickering as I do the walk of shame through the war room towards the front door. Marcus almost looks sad to see me go, but it may be the comparison against the backdrop of Madison and Deena who are delirious with joy.

Roger may not know it now, but the final piece of sage advice he offered saved me from myself. I almost tipped my hand about what I am thinking about doing. After all, I hold a trump card I have been saving for a day just like this one, and I now have to wonder if it is time to play it. You can discredit me as a witness, but it's much harder to dismiss your own paper trail.

I leave the office behind and walk through the cold November night to my car. Big decisions lie ahead of me, and once again, I am unsure which path to take.

-SIXTY-THREE-
MICHAEL

"Feel like you're harboring a fugitive?" I ask after knocking on her open door. Department chairs may be a step up in Millfield High, but the measly salary increase, cramped office, and weighty burden of responsibilities hardly makes the next rung on the ladder satisfying. Chalice looks up from her computer, a warm smile creeping across her face as she gets up and moves around her desk.

"I am surprised they even let you in the building. How was the body cavity search?" she says, giving me a tight hug.

"Pleasant. Howell used gloves this time," I respond sarcastically.

"I've missed you," she laughs, shaking her head. "This place is just not the same without you."

"I'd be lying if I said I didn't miss it."

"And Jessica?"

I shake my head. I do miss her, but maybe not as much as I thought. I loved her, and asked if she would spend the rest of her life with me. Then the going got tough, and she ran instead of standing by me. In the end, I couldn't offer her the simple, uncomplicated life she wanted. She said I had to live with the consequences of my actions. Our impending marriage turned out to be one of them. In some respects, my not being here made our split easier, but not much.

"How are my kids?" I ask, changing the subject. Chalice thinks the world of Jessica, and I really don't want to listen to her pleading for our future.

"If they were peachy, I wouldn't have asked you to come. It's only been a few days, but they lost the enthusiasm and zeal you used to bring out of them."

"They're moping." It was a statement more than a question, though Chalice confirms it with a nod of her head.

"That's because you destroyed their self-confidence just like I warned you would," a voice behind me says.

"Guess that body search isn't over after all," I whisper to Chalice as the bell rings indicating time to change classes.

I turn to find Principal Howell standing in the entrance to the department workroom, a closet-like chamber you must walk through to get to Chalice's office. His rumpled brown suit, hideous tie, and oversize glasses make him something out of an early '70's episode of *Starsky and Hutch*.

"What is he doing in the building, Chalice? He's not allowed to be here."

"He is here as a guest speaker. An appropriate one for a contemporary issues class, wouldn't you say?" Chalice replies sweetly. She can really lay it on thick.

"Why didn't you clear it through me?" Howell responds, getting annoyed at the challenge to his authority.

"Because as department chair, I'm granted authority to approve all guest speakers for the teachers in my charge,"

Chalice replies, not backing down for an instant. "You made that rule, remember, Robinson?"

Howell gets red in the face, but says nothing, instead locking his eyes on me.

"I have to run to class," Chalice says, wanting to be safe in a different port when this storm brewing between Howell and me hits. "Don't be late, Michael. You know how I hate tardiness," she says with a wink before excusing herself.

"The school board is going to decide whether or not your suspension will be permanent," Howell fires out to start the fun. "Even though the charges leveled against you turned out to be false, or so it is claimed, they feel the disruption you caused may be enough to warrant your termination."

When someone thinks they have the upper hand and sets out to push your buttons, there are only three real responses. You can get angry, which is exactly what they want. You can try to reason with them, which will never have any effect. Or you can remain silent, which will frustrate them until they get angry. When dealing with Robinson Howell, the choice is easy.

"You probably know where I stand on the issue."

I just continue to stare at him blankly.

"If I get my way, I will make sure you never teach again, not in this building, not anywhere," he exclaims, getting angrier and even pointing a finger at my chest.

Good attempt at provoking me, but not going to work.

"I warned you this would happen, remember? You should have listened to me. But no, you needed to be a maverick."

I think he forgets I spent a long time on active duty. I have been chewed out by men far better than him and still used the same thousand-yard stare I am giving him now.

"Was it worth it, Michael? I mean, was it really worth it?" he asks, exasperated and at his wit's end. Now.

"Absolutely," I say, catching him by surprise. "It was a roller-coaster ride, but I wouldn't have traded the experience for anything."

"I will never understand you," he replies in utter disgust.

"I would never expect you to. Of our many differences, there is one particularly important one," I say, getting closer to him than I ever wanted to be. "You'd never challenge yourself, or take that extra step to do something important. It's way outside of your comfort zone.

"You're content being the big fish in a small pond. And no matter how big of a man you think you are right now, at the end of the day, this building will always just be a small pond. I may have gotten eaten by sharks, but least I swam in the ocean. If people followed me, it's because they wanted to, not because I made them."

Robinson scoffs at my rebuttal. I don't expect him to listen, much less understand what I'm trying to tell him. A thirsty horse wouldn't follow this guy to water, and the only thing this sorry excuse for an educator inspires in others is a gag reflex.

"It's not that you will never understand me, Robinson, it's that you can't. You only know how to play it safe and do what you're told. I challenged a small group of students, and together we inspired a nation. You challenge and inspire nothing, including yourself. So you can stand here and gloat all you want about taking my job, but always remember that I have experienced more in the past three months than you will for the rest of your miserable, pathetic life."

Howell is speechless, his mouth agape in shock. Time for the parting words I have long wanted to say.

"Now get out of my way, you arrogant, little prick," I threaten, physically brushing him aside as I move past him. That display will officially end my teaching career at Millfield High School, but damn it felt good.

* * *

"Now that the election is over, I thought I would bring in a special Friday guest speaker who wants to get your thoughts on it," I listen to Chalice say from outside the classroom, along with a groan from the class. "Hey, it's not every day students play such an active role in an election. So without any further ado …"

I have no idea how she knew I was waiting. I guess all the best teachers have a sixth sense about such things. And despite being my former boss, I can say without hesitation, she is one of the best ever.

I am not sure exactly what they were expecting, but from the collective gasp that sucked most of the oxygen out of the room, it certainly wasn't me. The room is arranged exactly as I left it, from the horseshoe of desks to the décor on the walls. I take up my familiar place on "the stage" and look at the faces staring back at me. Chelsea, Brian, Vince, and all the primary campaign staff are there. I have also seen each and every other student in the room working on the campaign in one capacity or another. That says a lot about just how many lives we touched this fall.

"Mister Bennit, before you start, I want to say something," Chelsea says, with both confidence and remorse. The shy girl who wandered into my classroom her freshman year has definitely grown up. She never would have started this conversation six months ago. "On behalf of the class, I want to say we're sorry."

"Sorry for what?"

"Sorry we failed," Xavier says despondently. I was wrong, they aren't moping at all. They're depressed, and I feel like I need a Zoloft just talking to them.

"Isn't failure relative to how you measure success?" School is back in session for me. Chalice gives me a quick knowing smile and retreats to sit at my old desk in the corner. As a veteran of several evaluations, she has never been shy about how much she enjoys watching me teach. Or in this case, be a "guest speaker."

"You didn't win. That's how we measure success," Amanda says.

I close my eyes and sigh theatrically. "This campaign was never about me winning a seat in Congress, guys."

"Wait, what?" Peyton articulates as only she can. The class trades confused glances with each other.

"You know, I didn't sleep much last night. In fact, I really haven't slept well since the election. Too much adrenaline running through my system, and probably too much caffeine."

"Big surprise there," Vince adds with a smile. That causes a little chuckle with the class, providing a much needed tension breaker.

"At first I thought it was post-election letdown," I continue. "Then I realized that I'm not sleeping because I was afraid you missed the point of all this."

"What point?" Brian asks directly.

"Look around you. History is easy to study because you know what's going to happen. The outcome has already been decided, and based on that outcome, you can speculate on which decisions should and should not have been made."

I stare up at images of the great men and women who have played such a pivotal role in the direction of our country. I never fully appreciated what many of them went through to earn their place in history. Washington, Lincoln, Susan B. Anthony, Martin Luther King Jr., FDR … the drama, strife, and uneasiness that tormented them are never captured by textbooks or scholarly works. Now I get it, even if my own experience pales by comparison.

"Life isn't like that. How things turn out is not predetermined. If you truly want to make a difference in this world, you have to make decisions under pressure and hope the outcome is what you wanted."

"The outcome we wanted is you winning," Peyton exclaims, still not getting my point.

"Your winning would have been our legacy," Chelsea adds immediately.

"Seriously, guys, when we started this back in the summer, did any of you really think we would win? No, you stood in the middle of Briar Point and wondered what we could do to not get killed."

"But that changed," Vince says from the back of the room.

"It did change, Vince. You guys changed it. You involved yourselves in the political process and managed to somehow get other teenagers to put down their video game controllers and follow. In the process, you inspired America. Making a difference happens through action and sacrifice, not just talk. You guys proved that. That was the point I needed you to understand."

The students are quiet. Many are looking down at the ground but it is apparent that they are letting my words sink in.

"Kylie blasted you in her article. She criticized everything we did in this campaign. She called using social media to pick a representative a 'joke' and our failure to talk about issues damaging to the political process. I thought she was an ally. Why would she do that?" Emilee asks with fire in her voice. She liked Kylie a lot, so I'm not surprised she was angry and hurt by what was written. Considering I had to make her promise to even write it, she didn't hold back.

"Because she's a lying bitch, that's why," Vanessa blurts out in disgust. V doesn't mince her words.

"Typical reporter. Always looking for the next story," Vince adds.

"Guys, I hate to break this to you, but Kylie wrote exactly what I wanted her to."

"What? Why?" Vanessa asks, astonished. From the looks on the faces in the room, everyone shares that sentiment.

"Do you really want to live in a world where you select your leaders based solely on what they post on Facebook and Twitter?"

"We almost won that way," Chelsea concludes.

"Precisely my point. And it's exactly what I wanted America to see. I wanted her to write that article regardless of what happened in the election to show how ridiculous the notion is."

"That's why you never talked about issues," Amanda realizes. "You didn't care about winning. You wanted to teach America a lesson using social media as your classroom."

I nod. "Something like that, yeah."

"Always the teacher," I hear Chelsea mumble.

"I don't get it," Peyton responds, the confusion written all over her face. Many others in the class are pleading for an explanation as well.

"After getting back from my last tour in Afghanistan, I made a promise to dedicate my life to making a difference in this world. It started with teaching you. It ended with trying to teach something to all Americans. Elections have become nothing more than a popularity contest in this country. Look at who we elect. Thieves and crooks who abuse their power and make a living taking our freedoms and wasting our tax dollars. Our good buddy Winston Beaumont is the perfect exemplar of that.

"We don't demand enough from those who represent us. I tried to make a mockery out of the process by not going out and meeting people. Refusing to address the issues punctuated my point. Social media is an effective way to communicate and stay informed, but we cannot afford to rely on those means as a society. Choosing those who lead us is serious business. Americans need to start taking it more seriously. I thought I could help them reach that conclusion."

"And that's why Kylie wrote the article?" Emilee asks, realizing the woman she looked up to didn't betray us after all.

"The message was lost after election day. The media didn't connect the dots. I needed Kylie to explain it to the public so they'd understand, and now it's all anyone in the news is talking about. It will create a national debate for years to come on how we measure those running for office."

"Why didn't you tell us?" Xavier asks.

"Would you have understood if I did?"

"Wait, so you planned all this?"

"Not exactly, Peyton. I never dreamed this campaign of ours would go so far. I never imagined Beaumont would feel threatened enough to go after you guys. When he did, it made it personal for me, and I wanted to win as bad as you did. But what surprised me the most is through it all, you never gave up. You made a promise to stick with it, and you did. That took incredible courage and character. You just can't teach that in school."

Experience is the ultimate learning tool. Bureaucracies use standardized tests to measure academic performance, but how can you measure what these kids learned over the past three months? How do you quantify the strength these young adults developed and relied on throughout this process? It is impossible, which is why people like Robinson Howell are so eager to dismiss its importance.

"I underestimated you, and have from the beginning. Miss Slater recognized that from the day I made the bet, and as much as I hate to admit it, she was right." That tasted funny coming out of my mouth. Sometimes being honest with yourself just plain sucks.

"For as special as you guys are, I didn't expect you to make history by almost winning. You worked so hard on this campaign, but who could ever have expected that out of a group of teenagers? So no, you didn't get me elected to Congress. You only changed the face of the American political process, at least for a little while. That's your legacy, Chelsea."

The students are motionless as they digest what I tell them. Peyton wipes a tear from her eye. Vince nods in understanding. The others are in various stages in between. I look around the room I spent the last three years in. The eyes of Washington and Lincoln stare at me, just as they've always done. I wonder what they think now. I hope they approve of what I've done these past few months.

"I am proud of you all," I tell my class, fighting to hold back my own emotion. We may never again all be in the same room. This will certainly be the last time I ever address them this way. "We've been through a lot, and learned some hard lessons along the way. You are the new voices of your generation because you've earned the right to be. So when you speak today, speak well."

"What do you mean when we speak?"

"I scheduled our campaign's first and last press conference for this afternoon at the Buzz. I made my point. Now you get to make yours and influence how America thinks about all this. Remember, he who controls the message, controls history."

"Will you be there?" Chelsea asks.

"No."

"How do you not go to your own press conference?" Vince ponders aloud.

I let a smile slip from the corner of my mouth. "Simple. It's not my press conference; it's yours."

-SIXTY-FOUR-
KYLIE

The media vans that spent the last three months across the street from the high school and the Perkfect Buzz are gone. With their conspicuous absence, the whole town sports a different vibe now. The normalcy returning to this sleepy New England enclave feels anything but.

Now I do feel a like a stalker, waiting for Michael outside his townhouse. The chill in the air leading up to the election has given way to a more frigid temperature. The breeze coming out of the north is just adding to the bite. Maybe this is a bad idea. Basking in the warmth of the heat cranking inside of my car would be preferable to leaning against it in the cold.

The thought escapes my mind when I see him come down the drive and pull into his parking spot.

"Stalking is illegal in all fifty states," he says with a smile, as he shuts his engine off and climbs out of his car. Sometimes I swear this guy reads my mind. I wonder if he realizes those are the same words he used the first time we ever met in person in the coffee shop parking lot. Talk about coming full circle.

"So they did let you on school grounds. I'm a little surprised," I say to deflect his attention away from wondering if he needs a restraining order against me.

"Give me a little credit, will ya? I still have some pull around there."

"Really?"

"No, but the security guards all voted for me."

We laugh for a moment when he comes up next to me. I can almost feel the heat radiating off him and it warms my heart. Or maybe it's just the heat being generated between us.

"You're not going to the press conference, are you?" I ask, trying to distract myself.

"Just like I told them, it's not for me. By the way, I wanted to thank you. For the article I mean. It was a fantastic read."

"Sure. Just don't ever ask me to do it again." And I'm serious about that. It's hard enough to write bad things about a candidate you like. It's worse when the candidate is a *man* you like.

"Fair enough. How about I make it up to you?" he asks with a devilish grin on his face.

"What do you have in mind?"

"Dinner in New York City?"

"Okay, you're basically unemployed now—"

Michael holds his index finger in the air. "Suspended."

"Oh, right. So if they offered you your job back right now, would you take it?"

He pauses as if he's mulling it over. He's full of crap. Michael is a brilliant teacher, but he will never instruct again in a high school. Not so long as people like Robinson Howell are running them.

"I thought so. You're unemployed and may never get a teaching job again. So tell me why you want to blow three hundred bucks on dinner in the city?"

"Call it a celebration."

"Of what?"

"How about accomplishing my goal?"

"I'll admit, you know how to make a point in style. Of course, it cost you pretty much everything."

"It's not what they take away from you that counts. It's what you do with what you have left. Hubert Humphrey."

I fold my arms across my chest playfully and tap my foot against the asphalt. This guy has a quote for every occasion.

"Fine, how about celebrating a new beginning?" Michael asks, trying a new tactic to lure me for a night out. Not that he needs to. Like Jerry McGuire, he had me at "hello."

"No win, no job, and no Jessica?"

"Sure. You know, I told her I wouldn't win."

"No, if I remember correctly, you said you told her you would get trounced," I point out to him.

"I did get trounced."

"You lost by seventy-eight votes!"

"I know. It was a landslide by any measure," he mocks.

I shake my head in disbelief. "So, what do you do for an encore? I mean, now that you're unemployed."

"Suspended," he playfully corrects again. "You mean after I take you out to dinner?"

"Of course."

"Well, ironically, there is a conference between the Palestinians and Israelis next week. How about the Nobel Peace Prize? I can hold meetings over Skype and we can tweet—"

"Oh, just shut up," I say, pulling him by his jacket closer to me. He wraps his arms around me and we share a kiss usually seen only in old Hollywood movies. Passionate, yet tender, strong, yet still soft and romantic. The kind of kiss every girl dreams a man will give her at some point in life.

"Maybe we have something to celebrate after all," I say after our lips part. "Now get in the car. I'm driving."

"If you drive, how will I get home?"

"Who says I'm ever letting you go?"

-SIXTY-FIVE-
CHELSEA

Is this part of the experience Mister Bennit was talking about? After all, there aren't many opportunities for press conferences when you run a campaign on social media. The Perkfect Buzz is now a sea of reporters and cameras, and I'm not just unnerved, I'm terrified.

I spot my dad in the back of the coffee shop. He smiles at me and nods in encouragement. I wonder what he is thinking. Six months ago, his Snuggle Bear was still a shy teenager trying to figure out her place in the world. Now she's giving a press conference that will be seen in living rooms *around* the world.

Most of the reporters, journalists, and cameramen have cups of coffee in their hand, either through guilt, love of Laura's brews, or her persuasive sales ability that combines both. A podium is set up in the corner with dozens of microphones from recognizable national and local news outlets mounted to it. Some of the mics have names and logos I've never seen or heard of. The sheer magnitude of press present a week after the election just goes to show how closely followed this race was.

Vince, Peyton, Amanda, Xavier, Brian, Emilee, and Vanessa are lined up behind the podium with me. Vince gives me a look and I nod to him. It's showtime as he steps up to the microphones and clears his throat lightly to steady his nerves. This is new to him, too.

"Thank you all for coming out today," Vince says as the reporters hush each other. The room grows quiet, filled only with the sounds of cameras clicking away. The flashes coming from our audience creates a strobe effect I would expect at a Grammy performance.

"I know it has been a week since the election, but I appreciate your patience with us. Having you all here is a first for us, and well, we had to find a podium," he continues, eliciting hearty chuckles from everybody in the room. "Before we take your questions, we would like to make a brief statement. Chelsea?"

I am really nervous as I step forward and stand in front of the podium. Cameras continue to click away as I look at the journalists before me. This should be a piece of cake considering I've faced the media under much less forgiving circumstances, but I find myself wondering whether I should be getting some sort of course credit for public speaking out of this.

"When we started this campaign, Mister Bennit wanted to show us how much easier talking about making a difference is compared to actually making one. We didn't really understand what he meant until today."

My nerves start to settle and the high pitch of my voice takes a more normal tone.

"Election night was the most disappointing moment of our lives. But today, Mister Bennit reminded us the journey, and not the destination, matters most. And, as usual, he was right, because now we understand exactly what the journey meant.

"It required us to make sacrifices we never imagined. Time spent with our family and friends, scrutiny of the press and public, and the constant judgment of others. We endured dirty looks, vicious e-mails, and slanderous lies. But through our struggles, our laughs, and our tears, Mister Bennit was there, supporting and encouraging us every step of the way. Always the teacher, he has given us the greatest gift a mentor can give his pupils. He gave us the gift of experience."

I find my father in the crowd of media and see him rubbing his eyes to fight back tears. I look away quickly because I am already emotional, and seeing Dad cry will start my own waterworks.

"He showed us our voice can make a difference in the world. What we have learned cannot be taught by books or measured by standardized tests. Experience is a valuable part of education and often the most neglected. It's a lesson we will all cherish for a lifetime."

For the first time, I notice Principal Howell standing off to the side near the counter. Who let that jerk in? His lips are pursed and he's shaking his head in disapproval. Screw him.

"Hopefully America learned something from this campaign as well. The world is changing, and the way we communicate and interact as a society is changing with it. As the tools we use to communicate become a more integral part of our lives, we must remember not to sacrifice personal contact with each other.

"Mister Bennit sacrificed a lot to teach us that lesson. It cost him dearly, both personally and professionally, but it was what he demanded of himself. If I could ask one thing from all Americans today, it's that we honor his sacrifice by demanding more from those who want to lead us. We get the politicians we deserve. Maybe it's time we realized, as a nation, that we deserve much better."

The room is eerily quiet. Reporters hold tape recorders in the air to capture my every word. I don't know if the statement we prepared is any good, or will relay the message that we want it to. Maybe in the end it doesn't really matter.

"I speak for all of us when I say we would not trade the last six months for anything. While we failed in sending our teacher and mentor to the House of Representatives, we learned the lesson he was ultimately trying to teach us. Mister Bennit, thank you for caring enough to make a difference in all our lives."

-SIXTY-SIX-
BLAKE

State parks in Connecticut close at sunset, or so the sign tells me as I pull into the drive and head up the small hill to the parking area. At this time of November, the days are pretty short and people seem to abide by the rules. All except one person in particular. Despite all the open spots, I park right next to her aging Toyota Camry.

I walk out of the parking area and past some picnic tables before picking up a wide trail that leads to an old iron bridge over the river. The night is crisp, as one would expect during late fall in New England, but a nearly full moon casts enough illumination so I don't need a flashlight to show me the way. After a minute or two of walking, I see the bridge and the lone person standing in the middle of it. She must hear me coming, but she doesn't turn, instead continuing to look up the river toward the little town she calls home.

I make my way over to her, the moonlight reflecting off her snow-white coat like a beacon warning sailors of the rocks. Perhaps I should heed that warning. I almost want to, but that defeats the whole purpose of the drive up here. She looks peaceful, almost content. Like an angel, with her red hair falling on her shoulders and her green eyes visible even in the moonlight. My God, she is beautiful.

"Hello, Chelsea," I almost whisper, not wanting to pierce the serenity of the moment.

She turns to me, and with a little smile, slaps me as hard as she can. The cracking sound of her right hand against my flesh echoes off the hills around us as my vision explodes in stars. For a petite girl, she packs a wallop, and the chill in the air only makes my stinging cheek hurt that much more. She turns back to her view, saying nothing.

"Glad we got that out of the way," I say sincerely. "I deserved it."

"You deserve to be stabbed in your black heart and tossed over this railing," Chelsea replies coldly.

"Guess I should be thankful you aren't wielding a knife."

She turns to me and coolly produces a long Ka-Bar knife from the deep pocket of her coat. Did Bennit give that to her? She holds it near my face so I can see the dark blade with a gold eagle, globe and anchor etched into it. Even in moonlight, the emblem of the United States Marine Corps is unmistakable. Message received.

I memorized the whole opposition report on her. The reports on Bennit, his fiancée, and his staff were incredibly thorough. I know exactly whose knife this is and have no doubt he taught her to use it. Fathers are protective that way.

"Dad got it when he left the Corps," she says, returning it to her pocket. "Thought it may come in handy tonight."

"Let's hope not," I almost wish instead of just say.

"What do you want, Blake?" she asks after a moment.

"To say I'm sorry."

"To say 'I'm sorry,' she scoffs. "Sorry for what?" she asks turning toward me, the pain evident in her eyes. "Sorry for dragging us all through the mud? Sorry for lying about me sleeping with my teacher? For causing a rift between me and my father? For making me a laughing stock in front of my peers and trying to ruin my life? Sorry for actually ruining Michael Bennit's? Which part, Blake, huh? Which part are you sorry for?"

Actions have consequences. Sometimes we do things without fully appreciating all the outcomes. I tried to help win a campaign. That was all. I wanted to be a player in the political arena, and Beaumont and Roger promised to make me one. But it was all lies. I was their patsy, the most expendable asset they had to do their dirty work. By the time I realized my role and the hurt and damage I was causing, it was too late. But I never meant to hurt her, her family, or her friends. Or even Michael Bennit. I want to say all this to her. I need to tell her how I feel.

"I tried to fix it," is all that manages to come out of my mouth. Fail.

"Well, la-di-da for you."

"Doesn't that count for anything?"

She sighs deeply and turns back to her view of the river. She wipes the tears starting down her cheek with her sleeve. "You just don't get it, do you?"

"Get what?" I ask quietly.

"It doesn't matter that you tried to fix it," she mumbles, still trying to stifle her emotion. "It was a nice gesture, but it doesn't matter."

"Why not?"

"Because you did it in the first place," she exclaims, whirring around to face me once more. The emotion and hurt she was feeling mere seconds ago has transformed into something else—anger. "Who does that? What kind of person is willing to destroy others without giving it a second thought? Do you have any conscience at all? Or is your moral compass so broken you just didn't care?"

Words can hurt as surely as the knife she's carrying. She didn't actually need to stab my black heart with her dad's Ka-Bar. Her words just did it for her.

I was blinded by ambition with no values or code other than my own success. I even embraced those concepts. But coming out of her mouth, it sounds all so much different. Maybe because when we first met she had this optimism that only comes with youth and innocence. Or maybe it's because I now realize that under the shell of maturity, toughness, and confidence I saw at the debate lies a fragile teenage girl, full of insecurity about the world and her place in it.

For the first time in my life, I can honestly say I hate myself. Chelsea has put a human face on the toll of all the shady and slimy things I've done for Winston Beaumont. I hate that I didn't have courage to stand up to Roger and refuse to make up the story in the first place. I hate that I took the wrong path when the right one was so easily recognizable.

"Did you see those picnic tables near the parking lot on your way to the bridge?" she asks.

"Yes," I manage to croak out like a frog, still lost in my own thoughts.

"That was where it all started. It seems so long ago." She pauses for what seems like an eternity, but was probably only a few seconds. "It was also where we met when you went after Vince, Peyton, and Brian. And it was where I went to be alone after ..." Her voice trails off, but her message was clear.

Chelsea looks at me, waiting, but there's nothing I can say. No words can undo the past. No simple apology can ease the hurt. There is only the future yet to be written. Actions speak louder than words, and I know it's time to take action. This time I know the right path, and I don't care if it take me through the depths of Hell itself, I'm going to take it.

"I agreed to meet you, Blake. You said what you had to say. Now I think you should leave." Chelsea turns away from me again.

"I'm so sorry," I manage to mumble again before turning to walk away. She never bothers to watch me go.

I walk back to my car, determined to finish this chapter in my life once and for all. Seeing Chelsea was brutal, but I have a feeling the next visit I need to make might be worse. That will be the only thought on my mind as I drive back to my place in D.C. I have to pick something up before heading back north to New York City.

-SIXTY-SEVEN-
KYLIE

I am no stranger to staying in on weeknights. In my world, there's nothing wrong with opening a bottle of Merlot and curling up on the couch to watch reruns of old sitcoms on television. Tonight is no different, except I eschewed the sitcoms in lieu of a romantic movie. That and I'm nestled in the arms of the most amazing man I have ever met.

Fate brought us together. It was a perfect storm of events that led to this wonderful moment on a dreary, rain-soaked, mid-November night. My getting fired, Beaumont being involved, his bet with the students, breaking up with his fiancée, and all the ups and downs of the campaign have led us to this.

A dinner out in the city never materialized. We shunned it for a night in, content to laugh at ourselves trying to cook and not to burn down my building in the process. We haven't left my East Village apartment since we arrived, and with all the groceries we bought before driving down from Millfield two days ago, we shouldn't have to leave for five more. As much as I would love a night out on the town with Michael, I'm unemployed and have to bear in mind the unpleasant thought that there are bills to pay. His suspension is bound to become a permanent termination, so he will be rowing in the same part of the creek I am shortly. Savings accounts only last so long.

The knock at the door startles both of us. "Expecting company?" Michael asks.

"No. It must be a neighbor," I say, reluctantly leaving his warm embrace and getting off the couch. It is the only explanation since visitors need to be buzzed in.

Actually, an image flashes through my mind where Jessica picks the lock to the building and is waiting outside my door with a shotgun. Not realistic, I know, but still. She is out there, our relationship is new, and I am insecure about both.

I am trying to convince myself that Jessica would never want him back, but if she did, it scares me to death that he might consider it. The breakup with the woman he was about to marry was only two weeks ago, and it somehow feels wrong that we are this involved so quickly. I know there was a lot of tension between them for months, so maybe it's not as extreme as it seems. Regardless, a small part of me is nervous that I'm only a rebound fling.

I open the door and almost gasp at the sight in front of me. He looks disheveled, and is soaked from the rain, but the sad, tired eyes have this spark of determination in them. Now what is he up to?

"What do you want?" I ask sharply.

"I've come to give you something," Blake says, sounding emotionally defeated, but still somehow resilient.

"You don't have anything I want," I snap, annoyed this sorry excuse for a human being interrupted my perfect evening.

"Don't be so sure."

"Let him in, Kylie. Let's at least hear what he has to say," Michael says from behind me. Ugh. I forgot how infuriating men can be, even this one.

Blake's eyes grow to the size of saucers, shocked to see the former iCandidate himself standing in my apartment. I can only imagine what must be going through his head right now.

"Michael? I mean, are you guys—"

"Kindred spirits finding comfort and companionship while on emotional sabbatical following the rigors of prostituting ourselves to the media and money-driven American political process? Yes." Okay, infuriating or not, God, I am falling for this man. Is there a more eloquent way to say we're dating?

"Oh, okay," is all Blake can manage as he crosses the threshold into my small Manhattan apartment. We adjourn to the living room, and he declines the drink I offer him. Probably a good thing since I would have most likely poured it on him.

"I'll get straight to the point. You were writing an article last spring about Winston Beaumont being wrapped up in some shady dealings with the Lexington Group. I know, because I'm the one who got you fired."

"You're a little tornado of destruction, aren't you?" I am seriously considering throwing him out the window without opening it. It's raining out, which would ruin my couch. Then there's the expense of replacing the glass. So my unemployment will save him, but oh, imagine the satisfaction of seeing this prick go splat on the street outside. Or better yet, the sight of him impaled on the wrought iron fence below the first floor window.

"She's plotting about ten ways to kill you right now, Blake, so you should probably get to the point pretty quick." Damn! How does Michael know that?

"I need her help," he says to Michael. "I want Kylie to finish that article."

"You have some nerve," I say, getting even angrier. He got me fired over it in the first place. "I can't even if I wanted to. Everyone knows I covered Michael's campaign. And now we're together so nobody would take it seriously."

"I know, you need a source."

"A source? You mean a source like you?" I give a quick sarcastic laugh and shake my head. "News flash, Beaumont fired you, so nobody would ever believe you either. An ex-staffer spilling his guts won't get it done."

"What will get it done?" he asks, without any sarcasm.

"Hard evidence even the most ardent skeptic would find compelling. Documents, e-mails, voice mails, recordings. I need incontrovertible proof."

I didn't notice it when he walked in, but Blake takes the fat accordion file that was tucked under his arm and drops it on the coffee table. In that instant, I know our world is about to change again.

"You mean this kind of proof?"

-SIXTY-EIGHT-
CHELSEA

It's hard to believe the disappointment of Election Day was exactly a month ago. Our final press conference did little to ease the shock of the whole thing. Since then, the phone calls and interviews that accompany the fallout from any media frenzy slowly dissipated until they died out all together. What I was left with was an uneasy silence in my life, and an inability to fill the void that the absence of the campaign left.

Maybe this is the new normal for me. Things are relatively quiet now, outside of the occasional snarky comment in the hall about sleeping with my teacher. Blake admitted to the lie while trying to undo the damage he chose to inflict. It has been shown on the news a thousand times, but apparently not everyone got the memo, figuratively speaking.

If this campaign taught me anything, it's you can't stuff the genie back in the bottle once it's released. While most of my peers accept what was said were lies, the sideways glances I get from them prove an element of doubt still exists and always will. Thank God I graduate in six months.

My former campaign colleagues seem to share the uneasiness of the situation, although for different reasons. I never truly liked being in the limelight, but Vince and Peyton relished it. Now they walk around like former child actors whose shows were cancelled.

Xavier and Vanessa at least had sports to fall back on. Xavier is leading the varsity basketball team in scoring, as usual, but is not attacking the game with the zeal he showed last year. His heart is just not in it like it once was. Vanessa feels the same way, or at least that's what she told us. For them, a new world with fresh opportunities was opened up and then suddenly jerked away. For three months, they weren't just jocks like everyone had defined them. Now they are.

This whole ordeal may have hit Emilee the hardest. The campaign really brought her out of her shell and gave her a confidence she never knew she had. We have become closer since early November, and she's now a better friend than Stephanie or Cassandra ever were. I still talk to my old BFFs, but the former campaign staff shares a bond no one else in school can really understand. I think I know how soldiers who serve together in combat feel.

We are all sitting in the cafeteria, staring at our untouched lunches. All except Brian and Amanda, whose first half schedules landed them a different lunch period. Since September, the rest of us have all sat together, using our meager twenty-five minute break to plan strategies, develop action items, and outline tasks for the election. I thought when it was over we would end up going our separate ways. Each of us has other friends in the room we could eat with, but through either habit or necessity, we still all opt to sit with each other under the large flat television mounted over our heads.

"It's still a little weird looking out this window and not seeing reporters creeping around," Emilee says, staring blankly outside.

"I actually miss having the police escort us into school," Vince adds with a chuckle. "Why do you think that is?"

That forces me to smile, because I heard it was entertaining watching him fight though the mass of media until the Millfield Police finally stepped in. "You were a paparazzi favorite, Vince. You miss the attention."

"But I like my privacy," he offers, almost shamefully.

"Life in a fishbowl," Xavier mumbles, not looking up. "Just like the fish, you got used to it. Now that you're back in the wild, you miss the people staring in at you."

"I'm still having a hard time hanging out with my friends," Vanessa confesses. We all look at her, but are at a loss for anything to say. It's silent agreement. We all know what she means.

"It's just different," she continues after a moment. "They are different. It's like after all this happened, they changed."

"She's right. Who would have thought I could ever relate better to my parents than my friends?" Peyton asks.

"Maybe you changed," Emilee says.

"I think we all changed," I conclude. And that explains it. It is why, more than a month after we had no business sitting together, we still do. We're participants in a teenage alcoholics' anonymous meeting where notoriety and value was our booze. We're a support group for each other, and this isn't lunch in a high school cafeteria so much as a group therapy session.

Nobody can relate to what we have been through, and that includes Mister Bennit. He may have shared many of the ups and downs that came with the experience, but the view is different for us than him. I'm sure it is different for Miss Slater, too.

When I see her in the hallway between classes, her face is devoid of both emotion and interest. Friends of mine that have her for class say she hasn't been herself since she called off the engagement. Rumors circulating around school claim she is dating again, but they are only rumors. She doesn't talk to any of Mister Bennit's former campaign staff anymore, so none of us really knows how she's doing.

"Do you think they are ever going to reinstate Mister Bennit?"

"I wouldn't hold your breath, Peyton," Emilee says. "They know he did nothing wrong but they're still dragging this out."

"He's not coming back," I whisper remorsefully. Nobody challenges me because deep down I think they know the truth as well. Mister Bennit took on the principal, the school board, and a lot of parents who thought he was out of line having students run his campaign. He won the chance to run in the race, but lost everything else in the process.

As far as the Millfield Public School District is concerned, he's a maverick. A loose cannon that broke its tether and must be kicked off the deck before it sinks the ship. How well he teaches, and what he means to his students, are secondary in their minds. Welcome to twenty-first century America. What a shame.

It's absurd that they haven't at least bothered to apologize after the truth about the accusation against us came out. I guess the school board has their reasons, but I don't understand them. All I know is I miss him in class. Ms. Ramsey is a good teacher, and she keeps class interesting, but it's not the same. The building just seems emptier with him not in it.

"You are awfully quiet for once, Vince," Xavier asks, barely looking up from his tray.

"I'm still tired from being the voice of the campaign. A human being should not be forced to exist on four hours of sleep a night."

We all smile because we know exactly how he feels. Between the campaign, school, and tons of homework, I was buried. Sacrificing sleep was the only way to keep up. "You have bags under your eyes I could put groceries in," my dad kept saying. I guess it took its toll on me.

To everyone's surprise, my grades never really suffered during the campaign. I somehow always found a way to get it all done. The only one of us who struggled was Vince, although he found a way to stay above Mister Bennit's B grade threshold. Peyton's grades dipped a little too, but nothing that wouldn't have been attributed to a case of senioritis if she wasn't involved in the campaign.

The only real positive from all my new-found free time is the attention I can devote to the "Leaning Tower of College Literature" in our kitchen. Before the campaign, I really wanted to go to Marist up in Poughkeepsie. As good a value as you can find in colleges these days, it was still out of Dad's price range.

Thanks to my role in Bennitmania, paying for school isn't a concern anymore. More than a dozen schools offered me full scholarships, including a few from the Ivy League. As appealing as Harvard and Princeton are, I am seriously considering Yale since it is much closer to Millfield. I love Marist, but you just can't turn down a free Ivy League education.

"I'm bored," Emilee says, tossing her fork back onto her tray. "Is this what the rest of the year is going to be like?"

"You mean feeling like we should be doing something more than sitting here waiting for the bell to ring?" I ask.

"Better get used to it, Em," Vince warns. "This is our new reality."

Vince is right. This is our new reality. And as much as it is hard to swallow, we might as well get used to it. That is easier said than done though, because part of me is still clinging to hope that the rest of the year doesn't feel like this.

"Yeah, unless a small miracle happens to change it."

-SIXTY-NINE-
KYLIE

This is a call three weeks in the making. I have dreamt of pressing send ever since Blake showed up at my apartment in the pouring rain. He ruined my perfect night with Michael, and then made my day each of the nineteen that followed.

The phone calls from Madison ceased about two weeks after the election. Her desire to rub her ill-gotten victory in my face succumbed to the realization that I would never pick up the phone. In truth, we had other plans that needed to be executed before I spoke with her.

Things like this take time. There are a lot of moving pieces to be accounted for. A lot of things have to happen when playing the game at this level.

I know where I need to be at the exact moment the lights dim and the curtain goes up on the next great political scandal of our era. It was a lot of work, but Michael supported me every step of the way like I imagined the man of my dreams would. With all the pieces finally in place, I press send on my phone.

"Kylie?" she says, answering on the third ring.

"Hi, Madison."

"I didn't think I would ever hear back from you. I called a few times after the election."

"You called a few dozen times, actually," I say without exaggerating. I know because I sent her straight to voice mail for most of those calls.

"Well, I was pretty excited, as you can imagine."

"Of course."

"Oh, Kylie, don't sound so glum. It's not like you didn't see this coming. I told you I would beat you." Not yet. Reel her in a little more.

"Yeah, I suppose you did."

Madison actually squeals in delight. "Well, it was very brave of you to face me in defeat like this. Even if it took you this long." Almost there, just a little longer.

"Yeah, you won, even if you had to lie and destroy people's lives to do it."

"Don't be like that, Kylie. The ends justify the means, or didn't you read Machiavelli in college?" Now.

"Sorry, I must have missed that class, Madison. But since we're speaking in clichés, have you ever heard the phrase 'he who laughs last, laughs loudest'?"

"Yeah, but so what?" she scoffs derisively.

"Well, tune into CNN and you'll find out exactly what. There's about to be some breaking news you'll be interested in."

"What?"

"Five minutes, Miss Roberts," a newsroom producer announces to me.

"Who was that?"

"All glory is fleeting, sis. And so is gloating. I'd say have a nice day, but after this, I know you won't. And I would say have a nice life, but I doubt that will be much fun either."

"What are you talking about? Who was that?" she demands.

"Just get to a TV. Good-bye, Madison."

-SEVENTY-
CHELSEA

"Turn on CNN!" Brian yells from fifty feet away.

We all look up and turn our heads when we hear a commotion on the other side of the lunch room. Brian is almost sprinting between tables on his way over to us, Amanda in tow, and several faculty members in hot pursuit. He is almost out of breath by the time he reaches us and starts pointing emphatically at the TV above us.

"Quick! Turn on CNN!" he gasps.

"Calm down, bro," Vince scolds. "Take a deep breath and tell us what's wrong."

"We'll show you!" Amanda barks, equally excited. "Change the damn channel!"

By now the teachers have come over and start reprimanding Brian for running. He mumbles something to them about leaving him alone, as Emilee reaches up to scroll through the channels on the television above us. After only a few stations, she reaches CNN. We read the headline and gasp as Emilee cranks the volume.

A pretty, dark-haired anchorwoman is seated with a breaking news graphic on the bottom of the screen. The text beside it makes my heart flutter:

Grand Jury Indicts Congressman Winston Beaumont on Conspiracy, Bribery

"As we have been reporting, eight-term Democratic Congressman Winston Beaumont and three of his staff have just been indicted on eleven federal charges of conspiracy and bribery by a federal grand jury," the anchorwoman reads off her teleprompter. "The grand jury was convened in secret by federal prosecutors after compelling new evidence was brought forth that extensively outlined the congressman's dealings with several prominent financiers.

"The indictments spell more trouble for the embattled Connecticut congressman who narrowly won the election in against Michael Bennit, the high school teacher whose students ran his campaign almost exclusively on social media."

As I watch, I slowly become aware that the normal roar of the cafeteria has become only a soft buzz. Students and faculty alike all congregate around this one television and strain to listen in. Being at the center of the campaign, I sometimes forget that almost the whole school supported the effort in one way or another.

Everyone got caught up in the frenzy and wanted to be a part of it. I thought that it was just because it was the cool thing to do. But as I notice my peers intently watching, I can't help but think maybe they were more invested in it than I thought.

"The indictments were passed down after the damaging testimony by Blake Peoni, a long-time aide to Congressman Beaumont and the man instrumental in his reelection," the CNN anchorwoman continues. In the upper corner of the screen, a picture of Blake taken during the campaign is flashed.

"It is being reported that Peoni, in exchange for clemency, also has turned over files containing hundreds of documents implicating Beaumont in illegal dealings with a prominent New York financial company, the Lexington Group. Also indicted for obstruction of justice and interfering with an investigation are Chief of Staff Roger Bean, Office Manager Deena Blightly, and Press Secretary Madison Roberts."

I turn to Brian, my curiosity having got the best of me. It looks like he has finally recovered from his sprint down here. "How did you know?" I ask him.

He shows me his phone and smiles. The screen is lit up with alerts from numerous news sources about the scandal. He must have had it on in class, breaking one of the principal's cardinal rules.

"You know that you're not supposed to have that with you," I tell him with a smirk.

"You can add it to the list of my transgressions today. Right after getting up and bolting out of English," he says as we turn our attention back to the news.

"To answer the question what this means for Congressman Beaumont, and for the man he narrowly beat in the last election, we turn to our New York studio and Kylie Roberts, who extensively covered the Bennit campaign. Good morning, Kylie."

And with that introduction, I now understand. There's a collective reaction of everyone around me at Kylie's familiar face. Only a few of us will ever know how events of this year have now come full-circle. We were told after the election about the story, how she was fired over it, and why it brought her to our campaign, bent on revenge. While the article may forever remain an unpublished Word document on her laptop, she got the final source she needed, and ultimately the last laugh.

"Do you think Mister B is watching this?" Peyton asks, speaking over the anchorwoman asking her question.

"Oh, somehow I doubt Kylie would let him miss this," I add, giving the others a knowing smile. I learned more about chemistry watching them than I ever did in junior year science class.

"With these indictments, Congressman Beaumont will be forced to resign his seat before he even takes it," Kylie says into the camera. "Unlike a Senate seat that can be filled by appointment from a governor in most states, a vacancy in the House requires a special election. Since the parties will have to hold primaries, the election probably won't be held until early spring."

"What were you saying about sleep, Vince?" Vanessa asks playfully.

"It's highly overrated. Sleep is for the weak. No human needs more than four hours of sleep a night."

"Nice spin," Xavier says, leaning over to him.

"Hey, it's what I do," Vince responds with a broad smile.

There is no means of stopping, or even suppressing, the tears welling up in my eyes from spilling out and down my cheeks. The weeks since the election have been so hard to deal with. Worse than the lies and shady politics was having to accept that we lost because of them.

But that's not why I'm crying. I knew I would do it all again if given the chance. I would sacrifice sleep, a social life, and the activities of normal teenager to once again have a purpose outside of just graduating and moving on to the next chapter of my life. But I didn't know if the others would join me. Maybe Vince and Peyton would, because they loved the attention so much. But I didn't know about the others, at least not until now. I know in my heart that if Michael Bennit runs, we are all in. And we all know he'll run.

"What does that mean for Michael Bennit?" the anchorwoman asks.

"Simply put, given his name recognition and no need to survive a primary battle, the iCandidate will be an early favorite to claim the seat."

"Will he run another campaign on social media, or will this one have more substance?"

"He is a principled man of ideas and strong convictions who made bold sacrifices to prove a point to America," Kylie exclaims. Yeah, she is totally falling in love with him. "This next campaign could be the new standard for which all others are judged."

"And what about his staff made up of high school students?"

Kylie stares directly in the camera, almost leaning forward. She may be talking to the world, but at this moment in time, I feel like she is talking directly at us. She smiles broadly.

"I hope they didn't make any big plans for the rest of their senior year."

Acknowledgements

My sincerest thanks go to you, the reader, for investing your time into reading this story. *The iCandidate* has been years in the making, starting off as a full-length motion picture screenplay and evolving into the novel you just finished. It has been a long road to travel for these characters, and I hope you enjoyed their journey and will recommend it to others.

Writing is a labor of love, and many a long night was devoted to bringing these characters to life. For that, I would like to thank Michele for all her love, support, and most importantly, patience throughout this process. I simply could not have done this without her. I also would like to thank my parents, Ronald and Nancy, and my sister, Kristina, for all the encouragement they provided me in bringing this story to the world.

Special thanks go to my editor, Caroline, her husband Gary, and to BubbleCow for the excellent job they did. Their thorough edits made this a better story. I also need to give major credit to Ranilo Cabo for his excellent image design. With scant guidance, he managed to provide a front cover that was exactly what I was looking for, but couldn't articulate.

Many people ask where the ideas for my characters come from, so I wanted to share with you a little explanation. Chelsea, Vince, Amanda, Peyton, Emilee, Xavier, Vanessa, and Brian were not inspired by any single person. However, during my time as a substitute teacher, I had the opportunity to meet and mentor some wonderful students. While the thought of teenagers working on a campaign may seem far-fetched, I know that any number of them could easily have done this had they been afforded the opportunity. I wish them all the best of luck in all their endeavors.

Michael Bennit is a compilation of nearly every military man with whom I have ever had the privilege of serving, mixed with every great teacher I ever had the opportunity to work with. He was a fun character to create, and one whose continued journey I look forward to writing about.

Jessica Slater's character cannot be attributed to any one person, but I can thank a host of ex-girlfriends for their contributions to her persona.

Although *The iCandidate* is a work of fiction, several of the characters were inspired by real-life people. Michael's department chair and mentor, Chalice, shares a name with my ninth grade English teacher, whom I hold in the highest regard. She pushed me, challenged me, and gave me the only detention I ever served in high school. After becoming a department chair herself, she recently retired after a long teaching career. I cannot thank her enough for her impact on my life.

John, the vet Blake meets and gets the pin from, is a nod to a respected colleague of mine who served two tours in Vietnam and was injured during the Tet Offensive. The inclusion of this in the book is my way of paying respect to both him, and to a generation of soldiers who never got to feel the appreciation for their service to our country military personnel enjoy today.

Bill, Kylie's friend who sends her the link about the iCandidate and meets her later in the city, is named after an old army buddy of mine and close friend for fifteen years. To Chris, another close friend and fellow comrade in arms, don't worry buddy, your time is coming in the next book.

Every other character in the novel sprang straight from my imagination, including Kylie who was so much fun to write about in this story.

I would be remiss not to point out that Chelsea's desire to go to Marist College is a homage to my alma mater. Being the Student Body President there sparked my interest in politics, and I would not trade my four years there for anything.

As a final note, to my knowledge there is no coffee shop named The Perkfect Buzz. Michael's love affair with coffee developed from my own love of espresso. If I were to ever run for office, I would want to do it out of a coffee shop too.

About the Author

Mikael Carlson has written three full-length motion picture screenplays, including *The iCandidate* which was a finalist in the Page International Screenplay Competition in 2010. Additionally, he has written the romantic drama *La Vie Dansante* and the thrilling drama *Through the Eyes of Others*.

Mikael currently serves as a noncommissioned officer in the Rhode Island Army National Guard. An eighteen-year veteran, he has been deployed twice in support of military operations. He has served in field artillery, infantry, and in support of special operations units during his career on active duty at Fort Bragg and in the Army National Guard.

A proud U.S. Army Paratrooper, he conducted over fifty airborne operations following the completion of jump school at Fort Benning in 1998. Since then, he has trained with the militaries of countless foreign nations.

Academically, Mikael earned a master of arts in American history from American Military University in 2010 and is working towards a second master's in American military history. He also graduated with a BS in international business from Marist College in 1996.

He was raised in New Milford, Connecticut, and currently lives in nearby Danbury.

The Sequel to the iCandidate:

The iCongressman

–Second Book in the Michael Bennit Series–

Coming Spring 2014

WARRINGTON
PUBLISHING

Discover other works by Mikael Carlson at:
www.mikaelcarlson.com

Since this is a novel that focuses on social media, Mikael
also can be reached on:

Facebook: authormikaelcarlson

Twitter: mikaelcarlson

Tumblr: mikaelcarlson.tumblr.com/

Pinterest: pinterest.com/carmikael/the-icandidate/

Reddit: reddit.com/user/MikaelCarlson/

Linked In: linkedin.com/pub/mikael-carlson/75/476/97b

Google +: mikaelcarlson

Instagram: authormikaelcarlson

34247867R00240

Made in the USA
Lexington, KY
30 July 2014

AMITYVILLE PUBLIC LIBRARY